Cicely's
Second
King

Cicely's Second King

A Story of
King Richard III
and
King Henry VII

Sandra Heath Wilson

buried
river
press

ISBN 978-0-7198-1261-3

Buried River Press
Clerkenwell House
Clerkenwell Green
London EC1R 0HT

Buried River Press is an imprint of Robert Hale Ltd

www.halebooks.com

2 4 6 8 10 9 7 5 3 1

Typeset in Palatino
Printed in the UK by Berforts Information Press Ltd

Chapter One

September 1485

SHE WAS IN Westminster Palace again, after the long journey south from Sheriff Hutton. It was the same room she had once shared with her older sister Bess. The palace was the same. London and the Thames were the same. But she, Lady Cicely Plantagenet of the House of York, had changed forever.

If only Richard were still here. Her king, her uncle and her lover. Her matchless Richard, father of the child she now carried so secretly. He had been the third King of England to bear the name, and now, at the age of only thirty-two, he was dead, betrayed and hacked to death in battle at Bosworth Field. Salt pricked her eyes. It had been barely a month since he was killed, but each minute since then had been as brutal as the very first. Would this insupportable grief relent?

He would always bind her to him with a love that was both earthly and divine, and she would always be glad of it. Always. To love her blood uncle like this was a sin, but she did not care. In the cause of Richard III, King of England and France, Lord of Ireland, she would outface the Almighty and Satan combined.

Time was about to tell tales on her. She was already three months with child, and soon it would be impossible to hide her condition, even though it was the fashion for gowns to be full beneath the breasts. Everyone would know that the sister of the new king's intended bride was paying the price of immorality. But they would *not* know it had been with her uncle, or how gladly and lovingly she had given herself. Nor would they know how she abhorred Richard's conqueror, soon to be crowned King Henry VII.

Despair engulfed her, and she clenched her fists until her nails drew blood. 'Why did you leave me, Richard?' she cried. '*Why?* I need you. Oh, dear God, I need you . . .'

Her voice broke, and she had to lean forward, her hands on a chair back to steady herself. Feelings she had tried so hard to suppress were suddenly unmanageable. Every sense was in agony, and the desolation of bereavement was so raw that she wept unrestrainedly. Sobs were wrenched through her whole body, and she leaned weakly forward against the chair, overcome by sheer devastation. She wanted to go with him, and willed him to come back for her . . . *beseeched* him to.

'Cicely?'

Her breath caught, for it was his voice, and it was not merely imagination. She really did hear him. But if she turned, how could he be there? Surely she was deluded, for it was impossible for him to be with her again . . . was it not?

'Look at me, Cicely.' His soft-spoken voice seemed to caress her.

She turned, and her heart almost stopped with the force of her love, for he lounged back against the wall in the way that had bewitched her from the first time of seeing him again after years apart. That had been the moment she left childhood far behind.

He was not a giant of a man, as her father, Edward IV, had been, more was he of barely medium height, slender and graceful. He would have been taller had he not suf-fered from a sideways curve of his back that caused his shoulders to be a little unequal. His long, dark chestnut hair clung about his sleeveless grey velvet coat, beneath which he wore a doublet, shirt, hose and delicately worked shoes that were pointed, but not by a great deal. They were the garments he had worn one Christmas, and even without the sovereign's circlet around his pale brow, he was unmistakably a king. There was something about him that was beyond mere handsomeness. He was time-lessly beautiful, his face fine-boned with compelling grey eyes, his lips sculpted and always ready to smile at her. And to kiss her. He surpassed other men, and was still the only true monarch, not Henry Tudor, the mean-hearted Lancastrian felon who now dared to replace him.

Richard smiled, and held out his hand. 'I have missed you, sweetheart.' His rings shone in the sunlight that streamed in through the window overlooking the Thames.

Still gripped by emotion, she took a hesitant step, gazing at him through tears. 'Richard?' she whispered.

'Come.' His hand was still extended.

Her legs would not obey.

He straightened. 'Once again your king must come to you? But not as far as from Nottingham to Sheriff Hutton this time, mm? So be it, because one way or another I must embrace you. You need me, I think.'

He came towards her, his light tread made very slightly uneven by his back. Most people would not even notice, but she did. Because she was his lover and was sensitive to everything about him. Every sweet, beloved detail.

She was transfixed. He could not be here like this, it was impossible. But he *was* here, and as his arms enclosed her again, he took her effortlessly back into his spell. He held her to his body, his lips finding hers as they had in the past. She could feel the coldness of his heavy gold livery collar, smell the costmary on his clothes and taste the mint on his breath. Share his heartbeats. Know his love.

She closed her eyes, adoring him so much that it bruised her heart. His kiss was exquisite, for he alone knew her like this. No one else understood or held her as dear as he did, and now he had returned to her. How, she did not know. Nor did she care. It mattered only that he had.

He sank his fingers into the hair at the nape of her neck, and stroked her. 'You have to be strong, Cicely,' he said gently.

'I cannot. I feel so lost and alone, and all common sense has gone. I will not be able to behave as I should. I know it so well. How *can* I be strong and logical without you?' She blinked as more tears wended down her cheeks.

'You must be resolute, Cicely, because you carry our child.'

'You know?' She pulled back to look at him.

'Of course I do, sweetheart, for I am part of you. You must accept that I am. Death cannot stop my love. Or yours.'

She feasted her gaze upon him. He was as he had been that first night, when she and her sisters had still been in sanctuary at Westminster Abbey, and he had come to prove to her mother that her two sons were alive, not foully murdered in the Tower as his enemies would have the world believe. That was before he had been weighed with care and grief, when the lines and weariness had yet to show on his peerless face.

He was never meant to be king. Not at first. Her father died suddenly in April 1483, two and a half years ago now, leaving his realm to his twelve-year-old elder son. On his deathbed Edward IV named Richard, his loyal and only remaining brother, to be Lord Protector during the boy king's minority. The queen, Cicely's mother, had wanted *her* relatives to remain in the highest posts and appointments, and so fomented rebellion. She would have done anything to exclude Richard from power, but he proved his power and worth by easily overcoming the unrest and taking the new king, his nephew, into his protection.

The queen, fearful of his justifiable revenge, fled into sanctuary at Westminster Abbey, taking her younger son, the little Duke of York, always known as Dickon, and her daughters with her. Dickon had soon begged to be able to leave. And so he had, to join his elder brother in the Tower of London, which was as much a royal palace as it was a prison. They had been accommodated in comfort, as Richard had told Cicely herself. She also knew they had not been there for long, but had been taken somewhere else, to the Earl of Lincoln's manor of Friskney, near the coast in Lincolnshire, a place of safety where they were protected and well cared for by the Yorkist Thomas Kymbe. Twenty-three-year-old Jack de la Pole, Earl of Lincoln, was Cicely's unhappily married cousin, eldest son of Richard's sister, the Duchess of Suffolk, and had eventually been indicated as Richard's heir.

The boys had still been housed at the Tower when, just before the new little king's coronation, startling evidence emerged that Edward IV's marriage was unlawful because of his pre-contract to another. A consummated pre-contract was as binding as marriage, which meant that Edward had married bigamously. Richard had been as shocked as everyone else by the revelation.

Cicely's mother had never been queen after all, but merely Dame Grey, the widow of a Lancastrian lord . . . and Edward IV's mistress. Her children by him, including Cicely herself, were declared illegitimate, and Richard, to whom the succession rightly proceeded, became King Richard III. Cicely's brothers were not seen in public again, but Dame Grey and her daughters saw them, well and very much alive, before they were sent to safety at Friskney. Now it was being whispered that Richard had his nephews murdered in the Tower, and buried deep somewhere, never to be found again.

When Richard was killed at the Battle of Bosworth Field only last month, and Henry Tudor became king, Dame Grey was promised the title of Queen Dowager. This was because her marriage to Edward IV had to be acknowledged as legal after all if Henry was to honour his vow to unite the Houses of York and Lancaster by marrying Cicely's elder sister, Bess.

Cicely should have felt loathing towards Richard III, but could not. How could anyone loathe this shining man? This perfect man whose body was imperfect, but whose heart was so great? He extended a hand of friendship to his brother's daughters and their mother, and so Cicely Plantagenet had come to his court, there to fall more deeply in his thrall with every moment. Until, finally, she knew she loved him as no niece should ever love her uncle.

'But you do love this uncle, sweetheart, and this uncle loves you,' Richard said gently.

'You could always read my mind.'

'And now I can read it more than ever. I am within you, Cicely. This is not real.'

She would not let herself hear. She had not willed him into being, she had *not*! 'What can I do, Richard? There is a usurper on your throne—'

'Firstly, you must hide such hatred, Cicely. Look at me. You have to dissemble with a man like Henry Tudor, for there is no other way.'

'As *you* would dissemble? Richard, I know you would not do such a thing; you are too incorruptible and true to yourself to ever stoop to it.'

'Incorruptible?' He laughed a little. 'Maybe, but then *I* am not a young woman, with child, alone in a hostile court and needing her wits about her if she is to survive. Pay attention, Cicely, for I have to make you understand. You do not have the leisure of time. Plunging into the deepest of grief over me is *not* permissible. Do you not see? Henry Tudor sees demons in every shadow, and is lethally dangerous because of it. He has none of the lenience that brought me down, and as a king he is the better off for it. If he seems friendly, it is because he wishes to *appear* so, not because he *is* so. Today you sent away the ladies he provided. It was a mistake. You must welcome every such gesture. You are a king's daughter, a king's niece, and will soon be a king's senior sister-in-law. You *have* to behave as such.'

'I am also a king's lover.'

'Yes, you are that too, and always will be. This king would have had no other.' He smiled. 'Cicely, you must not think of me every time you see Henry Tudor, for he will know. He has already seen too much in your eyes.'

'Not think of you? That is impossible!' she cried, looking away because her tears flowed so hotly again.

He made her meet his eyes once more, and then touched her cheek, running a fingertip tenderly over her skin. 'My sweet Cicely, I love you so much, but this is a different England from the one we knew together. You still live, and must not fail me now. Yours is the finest spirit God ever created, and you have always meant far more to me than you should have. I am your uncle, our love is wrong, yet it exists. You have my child inside you, and while I feel joy that it is so, I also fear for you. I have left you in danger, and there is nothing I can do to put that right. Except be here like this whenever you need me. But I am not real, sweetheart, I am *you*.'

'Do not say that! You *are* real, and I need you!'

'Our child has first call upon you now,' he reminded her quietly.

'And I cannot hide such a very physical secret forever, nor do I have anyone to turn to. I cannot tell my sister that I secured the heart, mind and body of the man she wanted for herself. Bess loves you as I do, and would never forgive me if she learned that you and I . . .' Her voice trailed away. Poor Bess would now have to submit in Henry Tudor's bed. Yet it was Richard she had always wanted. Only Richard.

Cicely thought of the sister who had not hidden her love for Richard, and had caused a scandal that was of *her* doing, not his. It had become so intolerable that he had been obliged to deny everything in public. He, who had so recently lost his wife and only legitimate child, and was beset by treachery and threatened invasion, had felt the need to clear his name of vile insinuation. And it *had* been vile, for he had been accused of poisoning his ailing queen, to replace her with Bess, who was said to already grace his bed. It was so unutterably cruel, and all without basis. What might it have been if the scandal spreaders had discovered that he did indeed love one of his nieces? Not Bess, but Cicely, with whom he had definitely not shared a single improper kiss until *after* the all-too-natural death of his wife.

Richard smiled a little. 'I was an uncle beset by loving nieces, one I could only ever see as a niece, the other for whom I felt—feel—so much that it devours me. Bess is strong, Cicely. And hard. Oh, yes, there is something in her that almost makes me feel sorry for Henry Tudor. I still wish him in Hades, of course.'

'Hades is too good for him,' she said, managing a smile in return. 'Richard, I cannot speak to Bess or my mother, nor can I speak to John, not about this. How can I when he must never know I betrayed him with you, his father?'

'Oh, Cicely . . .' He embraced her again, his cheek against her hair.

She knew it grieved him as much as it did her. John of Gloucester was her other love, her cousin . . . and Richard's illegitimate son. She *did* love John, and had been promised to him in marriage, but it was a poor feeling beside the love she had for his father. What would John feel when her condition became known? He would certainly realise the child was not his, because she had conceived in June, and the only time she had lain with him had been at Sheriff Hutton on the late-August night they had comforted each other after learning of the tragedy at Bosworth.

Richard had sent his heirs and close blood to the castle in Yorkshire for safety, including her brothers from Friskney, with instructions that if Henry Tudor's invasion succeeded, they were all to escape across the North Sea to another of his sisters, the Duchess of Burgundy. Another boy sent to Sheriff Hutton was Cicely's cousin, the little Earl of Warwick, son and heir of the Duke of Clarence, who had been the middle brother between her father and Richard. Her father had executed and attainted Clarence for treason, and his children were excluded from the throne, which was why Richard, not Warwick, had been her father's rightful successor.

Warwick and her brothers had escaped in time after Bosworth, in the charge of Jack de la Pole. But she, Bess and John of Gloucester had not gone too. It had been Bess's fault, and hers, Cicely's, but not John's. He had stayed behind to protect them, so they were all three captured by the men Henry Tudor sent to secure what was expected to be five fugitives. Henry had not known about her brothers having been there too, and he still did not know if they lived or not.

John had come south with Bess and her from Sheriff Hutton, but had been taken away after Henry Tudor greeted them at Lambeth. Only a few short hours ago. So very brief a time, yet already it seemed like weeks. She had since learned that John had gone to the Tower, where her other cousins, Jack of Lincoln and the Earl of Warwick, were already held, having been taken prisoner at Bosworth. They should not have been at the battle, because Richard wanted them safe in Burgundy, but Jack could not stay away from Richard's side simply to save himself. Warwick had followed him. Of her brothers there was still no trace. Hopefully they were safe with their aunt, the Duchess of Burgundy.

'Richard, will Henry have my cousins put to death?' she whispered.

'His nature is to bide his time, but he cannot take chances with high-ranking Yorkists who have better claims to the throne than his. He only holds the crown by right of conquest, for he certainly does not have the blood right. I can only hope they are preserved and that something will overthrow Henry. John is wise enough to appear docile, and God knows, Warwick is too small to be a hothead yet, but Jack is proud and may be defiant.'

'If he is, he will not show it. I think you wrong him. He is careful and discreet, and was *very* kind to me at Sheriff Hutton. He guessed my secret and kept it close. I would trust him with my life.' Jack had perceived her love for Richard, and its fleshly consequences. He had vowed his silence, and she knew he would adhere to it.

'You hold him in *such* esteem? Well, I trust your instinct more than my own. I made him my heir because he has the legitimate blood. The rest is up to him.' Richard smiled regretfully. 'You always warned me about my ill-judged lenience with my enemies. I knew you were right, but I have never been a man to kill with ease, unless it was in the heat of battle. Or betrayal. I knew so much betrayal.'

'I would have killed your enemies for you, in cold

blood, because they wished you harm.'

'I believe you.' He smiled again. 'You have a little of your father in you. I only wish the same could be said of me. I used to worship him, but he changed, which is why I spent more and more time in the north. I make no apologies for saying this of him, Cicely, because I think you know it anyway.'

'But you remained loyal to him.'

'Until he died and I learned of the pre-contract. I could not ignore the facts, or remain loyal after that. I certainly could not allow his illegitimate son to ascend the throne when there was a legitimate heir. Me. The crown was mine by right, even though it was not what I sought.'

'The throne should still be yours now,' she said quietly. 'When I think of the king you would have been . . .'

'Would I ever have been allowed to be the just king I sought to be? I think not. I wanted to do right by the people, which did not please an aristocracy that enjoyed immense powers and privileges under your father, and that now hopes to enjoy them again under Henry. I was not what they wanted at all. So, I will probably be vilified. It is in Henry's interest to make a monster of me.'

'It is unfair.'

'What has fair to do with it? What is done is done, and now, for you, John, and the others, there is only survival. Bess will be Queen of England, I do not doubt it, and she will revel in it.'

'She loves you.'

'Not with her whole heart, not deep inside, where her real self is. Oh, she wanted me as her lover, but I do not think Bess *can* love truly, Cicely, not as you do.'

The words made her feel guilty again. About John, whom she had let down so grievously.

Richard knew her thoughts and pulled her near once more, to stroke her hair, which was so very like his own.

'I led you into everything. I knew how you loved me, even if *you* did not yet understand the nature of that love. You were—are—young, still only sixteen.' He paused and smiled. 'No, forgive me, you are in your seventeenth year, I think.'

'Of course.' She smiled too, for he had teased her in the past, and it soothed her so much that he did so again.

'Well, *I* was not that tender age, Cicely, I was considerably older and should have protected you. Instead I commenced your seduction.'

'You did not. Not really. I did some seducing of my own, and I know it. You have always made such sweet love to me, Richard. That first night together, you were so gentle and exciting, you thought of me, you drew me on, taught me and cherished me. I do not think any other man could have introduced me to such pleasures in such an incomparable way. *You* are incomparable, Richard, and you are mine. The fact that you are my uncle does not matter. I did not grow up with you, or see you so frequently that our shared blood was a natural and undeniable barrier. You entered my life, and I entered yours. We were strangers, and neither of us could have known what would happen between us. Yes, you are my uncle, but no, I do not view you as that. You are the man I love; nothing else matters.'

He kissed her lips again and then smiled. 'I was certainly too knowing and experienced for you, Cicely, and only too well aware of how to make you desire me more and more.'

'I may have been young and green, but I knew what I wanted. I had passions too, and did not know how to stop them. When my eyes were opened at last, it was like a great beam of light blazing through me. You hesitated, had second thoughts, did not want to commit the sin, but I *made* you give in to me, Richard, and I too knew what

I was doing. I followed my heart and made you follow yours.'

"And so we burn together, my sweet Cicely.'

She caught his right hand and held it to her cheek. It was the hand with the shortened little finger, the result of a childhood accident. She put the finger in her mouth and slid her tongue deliciously over it, before holding it tightly in her hand and closing her eyes. 'Oh, how I wish you had won the day at Bosworth, and—'

'But I did not, Cicely,' he broke in quietly.

'Jesu, how I know it.' She kissed that beloved little finger again.

'Cicely, you still have me. You always will. I am here now, because you willed it. I am your imagination.'

'No!'

His hand moved softly against her skin. 'Yes, sweetheart,' he whispered, 'and deep in your heart you know it well enough. I died at Bosworth, and so cannot be here with you now.'

'But you are! I can touch you, talk to you . . .'

'Maybe you are not ready to accept it, Cicely, but eventually you will *have* to. All you need to do is think of me, picture me, and what is not clear will become clear. You know me more than anyone else, you know how I would respond to something and what I would do as a consequence. Use this knowledge, but *please*, do not have my faults.'

'You have none,' she whispered, tears stinging her eyes again.

'Oh, I do. Many. But there *is* someone you can trust here in this court. I speak of Sir John Welles.'

Cicely drew back. 'He seems to be a friend, but how can he be? He is Henry Tudor's half-uncle.' Henry had despatched Welles to Sheriff Hutton castle, and he had been courteous and correct throughout, unlike his companion Sir Robert Willoughby, who had been all that was disagreeable.

She and Bess had been well treated, because Bess was to be Henry's queen, but John of Gloucester had not. Willoughby had seen to it that John's wrists had been cruelly bound for the long ride south, although Henry Tudor had personally cut the bonds when he saw. Henry had not been pleased. At least, it seemed so, but who could tell with him? His face seemed a mask, and his eyes were strange.

Henry needed to know if Cicely's brothers lived, because if he was to marry Bess, he had to change the law and make her legitimate again. That would legitimize her brothers too, and they would immediately have a far greater claim to the throne than Henry himself. If they were alive, a possibly unstoppable Yorkist rebellion would follow, so Henry had to be sure they were dead, preferably so that he could display their bodies. Should they be found alive, he would have to see to it they soon breathed no more.

Richard watched her face. 'Cicely, being Henry Tudor's uncle—half-uncle—does not make Welles dishonourable.'

'You think well of him?'

'Did he speak badly of me?' He already knew the answer, because she did.

She thought, and shook her head. 'No.'

'Trust him, Cicely, for he *is* a friend. He thinks more of you than he wishes.' Richard smiled again. 'I more than anyone know how to recognize the signs.'

'He merely tries to help me.'

'Out of the goodness of his heart? It is far more than that, Cicely. He desires you. He knows you are with child and he is almost certain I am the father. It is very dangerous knowledge, yet still he keeps faith with you, showing friendship and concern. *And* he has offered the same advice I give now. You must disguise your feelings about Henry. Welles knows his own nephew, Cicely, so please heed what he says.'

'Welles is Lady Stanley's half-brother, they share the same mother, so how can you be so sure he is a friend?' Margaret, Lady Stanley—born Beaufort—was Henry Tudor's mother, and a more scheming, ambitious, conscienceless, supposedly pious woman had yet to draw breath. She was a snake, and hated Bess for preferring Richard's court to staying in sanctuary to await 'rescue' by Henry Tudor. And she hated Cicely herself for daring to love Richard's son. Margaret did not know that Cicely Plantagenet loved Richard himself a thousand times more. The Almighty alone knew how much greater the woman's loathing would be if she did.

'Cicely, I am you and therefore I know your exchanges with Sir John Welles, and I know you lay with John at Sheriff Hutton.'

Her lips parted in dismay.

'You did it to comfort him, and comfort yourself. I know that. You can never be disloyal to me. What you do with your body is one thing, but your heart and mind will always be true.'

'I do love him, Richard, but—'

'But you love me more.'

'Yes.' She had *always* been able to talk to him, for he was so natural with her, always gentle, always patient and always truthful. Always prepared to smile and tolerate. Never had there been such a king, such a man, nor would there ever be again. They were kindred, in spirit as in blood. Was that not what he had once said to her?

'I also said that you are my soul's mirror, Cicely.'

'Can I hide nothing from you?'

'There are no closed pages now, Cicely. Nor were there ever very many. You are my book, as I was always yours.'

She smiled. 'But now you have an unfair advantage.'

He nodded. 'Indeed I do.'

'How can I possibly go on without you, Richard? I know you say I must, but if I am your soul's mirror, then you are mine.'

He pulled her into his arms again. He had a way of doing it, an incredibly intimate way that was due to his distorted back. It made his embrace so wonderfully attentive and dear, as if he wrapped his whole self around her, not just his arms. He could not embrace in any other way, but it always made her feel so very precious to him. And so she was. So she was.

'Be strong, my sweet Cicely.'

'You are going from me now, are you not?' She knew by his voice, by the note, that slight timbre, that she was about to be on her own again.

'You will see me again. When you need me, I will come.'

'Richard, I miss your physical love so very much.'

His lips were on hers once more, yearning, tender, filled with desire and emotion, but as she tried to embrace him, to keep him with her, he was no longer there. Yet he was all around her.

She could not—*would* not—believe he had not been real. She had felt him, kissed him and inhaled the scent of him. Surely mere imagination could not conjure such tangible things? She took a deep breath. Whatever had really just happened, the desolation of earlier had abated a little, and the draining sense of hopelessness and grief, of bewilderment and fear, had eased. She felt stronger, supported by his continuing love and understanding. Restored, but not entirely, because she could never be fully restored without the living man.

She pressed her hands to her belly, where his child quickened within her. She would confront whatever lay ahead, her Plantagenet head held high. She smiled then. Well, perhaps not too high. She would dissemble, as Richard had warned her to do. And he was right, she *would* always know what he would say to her, no matter how difficult her dilemma. He would *always* sustain her.

But she was not as strong as she thought, nor as composed and sensible. Nor did she remember to do as Richard told her.

Chapter Two

CICELY HAD ALWAYS been one to follow her instincts, and now, bolstered by being with Richard again, those instincts urged her to seek an audience with Henry Tudor. Twice now she had been told to beware of him, but she needed to get her own measure of the new king, and learn how to temper her future dealings with the man who had usurped Richard's throne.

She hesitated, because although she had met him she certainly did not *know* him, only what others said of him. But Richard was right, at Lambeth she had permitted Henry to see too much in her eyes. He probably knew she wished him dead, so she had to convince him otherwise. There was enough danger for her already, because of her child, without facing his personal enmity as well. Maybe he would not receive her anyway. Why should he? *He* was the one with the power, and she was still only Edward IV's by-blow.

She made no attempt to change her appearance for going to Henry. There was little she *could* do. Stupidly, because she did not wish to accept *anything* from this new king, she had dismissed her new ladies on arriving, without knowing when her wardrobe would arrive from Sheriff Hutton. And so she brushed her hair and then studied herself in a mirror. She was not tall, and had a small but rounded figure. Her eyes were grey, like

Richard's, but hers were flecked with brown. Her hair was also his, a rich, deep shade of chestnut. In the sun, the glints of red and gold became apparent. She chose not to wear it fashionably shaven back from her forehead, because Richard had liked it the way it was. And so did she.

Bess was more beautiful, at least in Cicely's opinion, but there was clearly something about the younger of the sisters that men found alluring. Maybe they felt the challenge of her pride. She had certainly never lacked for attention. Not even from Henry Tudor, who had made far more of meeting her than he had of Bess. Maybe it was because he sensed she had secrets of great interest to him. He seemed intuitive, or so she realized now, when she thought of him again.

Richard's name reached through her again, and she opened the little decorated purse on the belt around her waist. In it was a letter he had given to her the last time she had seen him in life. An expression of his love, it made her weep then, and still made her weep. She took it out and read again.

'My dearest, most beloved lady, I send this because I have to put down in writing the feelings I have for you. You are all around me, every moment of every day, and there is not an hour when I do not think of you as many times as that hour has minutes. Being parted from you is to be likened to purgatory, and I am but half a man because you are not with me. I am a king, yet lack that one jewel that will make me complete. I know that I am in your heart, and for this I cannot measure the honour I feel. Your sweet, forthright nature, your voice, your touch, your constant support, all of these make a slave of me. If our love is crossed by fate, I no longer care. It is an eternal love that will carry me to whatever lies ahead. No spirit could ever be more true than mine is to you. Be safe, my beloved. My heart and soul are forever in your keeping. Richard.'

'And mine are in yours, my dearest lord,' she whispered, folding the letter and kissing it before returning it to her purse.

She left her rooms to go to Henry. Westminster Palace was where she had been born, but it was alien to her now. The very stones of the building had seemed to change with the ruling House. Her courage almost failed as she neared the royal apartments that had once been Richard's, but thinking of him again renewed her courage as she reached Henry's guards. They wore Tudor colours, green, red and white, with the red dragon of Cadwallader and red rose of Lancaster.

'Cicely! Turn back, now! You will regret what results from it!' Richard's voice was within her—or was it her own belated wisdom?

Pikes were crossed against her, and she halted. 'I am the Lady Cicely Plantagenet, and humbly crave a moment of His Grace the king's pleasure,' she said in a clear voice, for the door was ajar and maybe someone could hear.

For a moment there was silence, but then Henry himself answered. 'Enter, Lady Cicely.'

The pikes were pulled aside and she went in.

It cut through her heart to see the royal apartments again. She had been with Richard here, and now strove not to look at the things that reminded her of him the most. Things she had seen him touch, places he had stood, where his smile had invited her to talk. The smile that had eventually invited her to do so much more.

Henry Tudor was alone by a window, the sunshine pouring over him. As if it blessed him, she thought disgustedly, hiding her opinion behind her bland expression. He was taller than Richard, and at twenty-nine three years younger, but even so he seemed older, and not in a pleasant way. He had never known his father, who died before his birth, and he had been exiled in Brittany since the age of fourteen. The next fourteen had been spent avoiding capture by her father or Richard. All this had made him what he now was. Or perhaps there were other things too, for she already knew how very intricate he was, because she had seen it in his eyes at Lambeth.

His hair was a nondescript reddish-brown, neither one colour nor the other, and fell in waves to the shoulders of a sumptuous purple doublet that was embroidered with gold and scarlet dragons. Richard's hair was—had been— thicker and heavier; Henry's seemed fragile, as if she could easily pull it from his scalp if she wished.

He had a face filled with suspicion, hooded, watchful, and his thin, pale features had none of Richard's appeal. His cheekbones were high and his chin small. His mouth was straight and wide, his lips thin. He would not have been entirely ill-looking, had not his nature so taken the upper hand. His clever, wintry-sea eyes were filled with distrust and guile. One of them had a disconcerting incli- nation to wander, but at the moment they both rested very levelly upon her as she sank into a deep curtsey and remained low, for she could not rise until he indicated.

'You surprise me, Lady Cicely.' He was quiet-spoken, his English accented with perhaps the slightest hint of French or Breton, but not greatly with Welsh. She was intrigued, for it was through his Welsh lineage that he sought to suggest descent from King Arthur himself.

'Your Grace?'

He still did not raise her. 'You surprise me that you have the audacity to come here like this.'

How should she answer? Follow your instincts, Cicely, she thought. 'I wish to apologize most humbly, Your Grace.'

'For coming here?'

'For having seemed to reject your kindness. It was not my intention.'

He left the window and came closer. 'Really? What have you rejected?'

The scent of cloves breathed over her as he put his fingers on her shoulder, a signal for her to stand, but he did not assist her as Richard would have. A hand beneath her elbow, a quick smile . . . Henry seemed devoid of such important little courtesies. The only king she could see in this room was Richard, and from *him* she gleaned strength.

He met her eyes. 'What kindness have you rejected?' he asked again.

'I have been disrespectful.'

'I am usually fairly observant, my lady, but confess I had not noticed such a failure on your part.'

'I dismissed the ladies you so kindly sent to me.'

'Ah. Do you really imagine I concern myself with such matters, Lady Cicely? My mother sent them, so I believe it is to her you should apologize.' He drew a long breath and turned away, rubbing an eyebrow as if deciding whether or not to believe the ladies to be her reason.

He still wore the ruby ring that must have been taken from Richard's dead finger at Bosworth. Resentment surged through her again, but she forced herself not to show anything at all. 'Your Grace, it is just that at Sheriff Hutton I had a single maid, Mary Kymbe, whom I shared at first with my sister, but who eventually came to serve mostly me. I was very happy with her.'

'My future sister-in-law with but one single maid? I do not think that is very appropriate, do you?'

'It is most inappropriate, Your Grace, but I am content for it to continue.'

'And your contentment must be protected, of course. Very well, you may have your Mary Kymbe, if that is your wish.'

'I am grateful, Your Grace, and mindful of the good will you show me.' She had noticed another of his rings, a small gold signet ring on his little finger. It depicted a man—a saint—with a leashed dragon at his feet. 'Who is that on your ring?' she asked, rather forwardly.

He looked at her, in two minds about whether to satisfy such unbecoming impudence. 'It is St Armel. I regard him as my patron saint. He was a Welshman who saved a Breton town from a marauding dragon. He led it to the top of a mountain and told it to jump off into the river far below. It did as he commanded, and was never seen again.'

She was about to ask more, but he changed the subject. 'You do not conform, my lady, which makes you most thought-provoking. You loved Richard, did you not?'

The question seemed to slip in naturally, but it was intended to disconcert. And it did. 'Yes, Your Grace. I loved him.' *If only you knew how much!*

He paused, and the seconds hung. 'My bride-to-be loved him too, or so I am told.'

Trepidation crept in. 'She was his niece too, Your Grace, so of course she loved him. He was a difficult man not to love.'

'Unlike me, is what I suppose you to mean?'

'I do not know you, Your Grace.' So you *are* aware of your shortcomings, she thought uncharitably.

'Lady Cicely, the rumours that abounded at Richard's court were conveyed to me. I know what happened. Your sister felt more for him than she should; perhaps she even went to his bed.'

'No! No, Your Grace, you have my word that she did not. Richard saw her as his niece and that was all. How can I convince you I tell the truth?'

'How vehement you are.'

'Yes, because I do not want you to think less of my sister than you might otherwise. She did love my uncle, but there was nothing wrong in it.' Oh, yes, there was, she

27

thought, it had been very wrong indeed. *As is* my *love for him.*

His eyes were thoughtful. 'I think the entire host of angels would find it hard to disbelieve you, Lady Cicely, but I am not—nor ever will be— an angel.'

'I do not seek anything but to persuade you of the truth.'

'You show no fear of me, my lady. Perhaps you should.'

She met his gaze. 'I *am* afraid of you, Your Grace.'

'There is far more to you than I am comfortable with, Lady Cicely. You were not commanded to come here, you simply took it upon yourself to do so. Tell me, do you come to make yourself a more attractive marriage prospect than your sister?'

She stared at him, so taken aback that she was lost for words, but then she found them. 'No, Your Grace! Such a thing has never entered my head!'

'And now that it has, you are appalled at the very notion. I had no idea the thought of my bed could be so abhorrent.'

It was a response that lost him the advantage, and she seized upon it. 'You would not wish me in your bed, Your Grace, for no doubt I would talk you to sleep.'

His lips parted, and she could see that in spite of himself, he was amused. 'You are talented at playing with conversation, Lady Cicely. You even play with me, and that, I can assure you, is not something to which I am accustomed or intend to become accustomed.'

No, but you enjoy it, she thought. Yes, he enjoyed her parries, even though he did not wish to. There was nothing sensuous in it—at least, she did not think so, although she suspected he was well acquainted with matters of the flesh. Yes, he took his pleasures, but she doubted if he considered his women, or bothered to share the final moments with them. He was no Richard. Henry

Tudor would think only of himself. God help Bess.

Henry studied her. 'If you were so very fond of Richard, should I be allowing you near me? You look at me and see his nemesis.'

'What would you have me say, Your Grace? That I hate you for bringing about his death?'

'Yes, that is indeed what I would have you say, my lady, for it would be the truth.'

He was being a cat to her mouse, and so she had to use guile of her own. Her conversations with Richard, so affectionate and quick, so witty and penetrating, so filled with shared secrets, had taught her well how to retort and deflect. Richard was her tutor in everything. Everything. 'Then I say it, Your Grace. Yes, I hate you for what you did at Bosworth Field.'

Henry drew a long breath. 'That's better, Lady Cicely, for now I know where I am with you.'

He gestured to her to be seated, and that was when she knew she really had engaged him. He was intrigued, and now she could try to banish any suspicions he might entertain towards her.

'My lady, I do not profess to know why you are really here, unless you have a dagger about your person.'

She smiled again, and more easily now because she had begun to get his measure. 'No, Your Grace. I *do* wish to apologize about the ladies, and—'

'And?'

'I wished to know more of you.'

'Ah, now we come to it. You fascinated one king and hope to fascinate his successor? Although, I imagine, not in a way that might lead to the royal bed.'

How right he was. 'The royal bed is my sister's destiny.' She almost called it Bess's awful fate.

'I am relieved you are not the elder sister, my lady, for I escape lightly.' He smiled, so fleetingly she wondered if she had seen it at all. Richard's smiles never disappeared like that; they lingered and caressed her with their warmth. This man had no warmth, and gave the impression of knowing little of caresses, least of all those that lingered.

'You veil your thoughts, my lady,' he said softly.

'You would not appreciate them,' she answered, not realizing in her naivety how very great the consequences her rashness today would eventually be.

He was a little perplexed to be answered in such a way. 'How very daring you are, Lady Cicely. I was told that you are more mature than your years, and it would seem you are. How old are you?'

'Sixteen.' *In my seventeenth year.*

'My mother gave birth to me when she was thirteen. My father was twenty-five, and apparently no respecter of age. But she has never hated him. Indeed, when the time comes, out of all her husbands, he is the one with whom she wishes to be buried.'

Something passed over his face, and she knew he was astonished he had said such a thing to her. She knew that look by now, for she had seen it often. People—men *and* women—found themselves confiding in her, and this king was no different. But just how close could she come to him? Into his confidence? It would be interesting to find out.

'Do you prize honesty, Your Grace?' she asked, still too bold for her own good.

'Occasionally.'

'I note the reservation.'

He rubbed his eyebrow again. 'Who are you to *note* anything concerning me?'

'Your future sister-in-law, Your Grace.'

'How could I forget it?' he murmured. 'Well, do you know enough of me now?'

'No.'

'Thanks be to God. I had heard how great a store Richard set by you, and begin to understand why. Well, *I* will not be doing the same as him, my lady, because one day that dagger *will* be there.'

'Not if you are a good king.'

'More insolence?'

At last she was a little more careful with him, but not enough. 'It is not insolence, Your Grace. At least, it is not meant to be. I admire honesty, and if you are indeed the king England needs, I will be glad.'

'For which I am to be grateful?'

'You would never bestow your gratitude upon me, Your Grace. You do not like or trust me, and why should you? I do not hide my support for my uncle, and if he were here again now, I would still go to him. If it is insolent—treasonous even—to say these things to you, of all men, then I cannot help it. I treasure sincerity.' By now she knew she had gone too far, but somehow she could not help herself. Nor was she still naïve. She had put herself in this scrape and must now do what she could to find a little favour. She wished she had listened to Richard, because she really had been silly. And was continuing to be.

He gave a laugh that was neither filled with nor devoid of true humour. 'Dear God, lady, I do not know whether to chop off your head or rush you to my bed!'

She did not respond. Neither prospect held any allure.

'If you treasure sincerity, Lady Cicely, you may as well know that your betrothal to John of Gloucester, such as it was, is at an end. He has already been informed.'

'I could not expect otherwise, Your Grace.'

'You do know that he is in the Tower, along with Lincoln and Warwick?'

'Yes, Your Grace.'

'Well, please remember that the Tower is a royal palace

as well as a prison and fortress. I am sure Richard would have said he sent your brothers to the palace, not the prison.'

She looked away, for fear he would see that she concealed things.

'You will no doubt be pleased to know Lincoln, Warwick and John of Gloucester will soon be given their liberty, because all three have sworn allegiance to me.'

'They have?' Even Jack?

'Yes, my lady. Not everyone in Richard's camp supported him to the abandonment of common sense. If they had, he would have defeated me. As I think I said before, he came within an inch of me. I have never seen such valour. For that I can only admire him. There was not much of him, but he fought like a giant.'

He was *all* that was admirable, she thought. Her beautiful, beloved, *betrayed* Richard.

'Do I take it that I have praised him suitably?' Henry observed her face.

'Yes, Your Grace.'

'Oh, Lady Cicely, there can sometimes be too much honesty. *I* am the king now, while he is very much dead. Remember that.'

'Yes, he is dead.' Something caught upon a nerve. 'May I ask something of you, Your Grace?'

'I do not care for the look in your eyes. I fear I am not about to like this question.'

'Why did you let your men abuse his body?'

He was taken aback, and remained silent for a moment. 'Would you believe me if I said I did not know until it was too late?'

She met his eyes squarely.

'Ah, I see your woeful lack of faith. Nevertheless, it is true. He has been buried with due rites by the Grey Friars in Leicester. I intend to provide a proper tomb for him, one that will honour him as he deserves. Nothing can alter the fact that he was the anointed king.'

'Yet you let them stab and desecrate his naked body, sling him hands-bound over a horse and then put him on display to be gaped at. It was cruel and ungracious of you.'

She knew she now went beyond all bounds of what she could and could not say to him, but she was unable to leave these things unsaid. At this moment, Henry Tudor brought out the very worst in her.

He put his hand to his chin and stroked his lips. 'You take great liberties with me, Lady Cicely.'

'I know. But this matters to me so much. Do you not see? I honoured him with all my heart, and cannot bear to think of how he died or what happened to him afterward. I crave your forgiveness for asking you about it,' she added belatedly.

'What you are saying is that your respect for me depends very much upon my answer.'

She lowered her eyes.

'What happened was a victorious army's euphoria. I truly did not know what was done to desecrate his body, my lady, but I stopped it once I learned. However, I *did* have him put on display, not his nakedness, for the lower part of his body was properly covered. It was his face that had to be shown, because the people had to know he was truly dead. I trust you will admit that he was very hard *not* to recognize. Slight he may have been, but with his crooked back and arresting features, forgettable he was not.'

She gazed at him, knowing he told the truth. 'Thank you, Your Grace.'

'I am not entirely bereft of conscience or chivalry, Lady Cicely, even though you prefer to think I am.'

'I do not prefer it, Your Grace.'

'Where are your brothers?' he asked suddenly.

'I do not know, Your Grace,' she answered, truthfully enough. They had been sent to Burgundy, but she did not know if they ever arrived. 'I believed they were still in the Tower,' she added, with total absence of truth.

'And I am expected to believe that?'

'Yes, Your Grace,' she added, with apparent candour.

'Oh, how charming and sweet you are when you wish to deceive. You know your brothers are not in the Tower, and I believe you also know their whereabouts. However, I will leave the matter for the moment.'

She was relieved, but again she hid it.

'You may also care to know,' he continued, 'that my uncle, Sir John Welles, speaks as highly of you as you did of him at Lambeth. Such agreeableness between two opposites seems a little unlikely.'

'Unlikely?'

'Yes. You are so strongly for Richard, yet my uncle came to you from me. Hardly a recommendation in your eyes, I would have thought.' He studied her again, with his disconcertingly inconsistent eyes. 'He pleads that you be treated well, although why he should think I would do otherwise rather escapes me for the moment. My mother, whose half-brother he is, supports his request. She always supports him, for he is her favourite. After her only son, of course.'

Sir John Welles had done so much on her behalf? Maybe Richard was right.

'I do not doubt that my other uncle, the Earl of Pembroke, would think highly of you as well.'

Jasper Tudor was the younger brother of Henry's father, and had not only brought Henry up but had been in exile with him in Brittany. Jasper was also one of the few men Henry trusted. At fifty-five he was in his prime, was to be created Duke of Bedford and to be prominent at Henry's coronation. He was one of the king's councillors and would soon marry Cicely's Woodville aunt, her mother's sister, Katherine. Katherine was the widow of the traitor Duke of Buckingham, whom Richard had ordered beheaded in Salisbury market place. Jasper's marriage was yet another attempt by Henry to join Lancaster and York. Honours would be heaped upon him, as Cicely supposed was only right for a paternal uncle who had been so unswervingly loyal throughout Henry's entire life.

'I have many questions to ask of you, my lady,' Henry continued, 'but now is not the time. Yes, you have caught me off guard, as I think you intended, but you may rest assured you will never be able to do so again. I now know what to expect where you are concerned.'

'And I know what to expect where you are concerned, Your Grace.' It was a flippant, immature remark that she regretted the moment it was uttered. She had never spoken to Richard like that, never been so idiotically childish.

'Have a care.'

'Forgive me, Your Grace. I apologize. Truly. From my heart.' There was nothing flippant in her words now. She should not have spoken as she did.

'I rather like it when you are repentant, Lady Cicely, for it cuts you down to a more suitable size.'

She met his eyes, but held her tongue.

He trapped her gaze. 'You are a challenge, and if you reply that you find me a challenge as well, so help me I *will* have your head.'

She remained silent.

'I think you had better go, before you try me too far.' He held out his hand to be kissed, and she got up to bow over it, but as she did, his fingers clamped cruelly around hers. The scent of cloves was suddenly not so pleasant. 'Never do again what you have today, my lady. You will not be admitted to my presence in future unless *I* send for you. Attempt it and you will make a fool of yourself.'

'Yes, Your Grace.'

'Would you have gone to Richard like this, I wonder? Without his summons?'

She had praised honesty, and so she would not turn from it now. 'Yes, Your Grace, I did. He never turned me away.'

There was the thinnest of smiles on Henry's lips. 'He ever was . . . fond of his nieces, shall we say? Or so I am given to understand.'

'Do not say that,' she whispered, 'for he had such honour.'

He studied her for a moment. 'Well, honour or not, my lady, he led you into bad habits where kings are concerned.'

Oh, such *wonderfully* bad habits, she thought, smiling inside.

Even now Henry's gaze was sharp. 'I will have those secrets one day, my lady. You may count upon it.' He took his hand away, signalling her dismissal.

As she returned to her rooms, she thought of Richard. 'You are angry with me, are you not,' she stated unhappily. 'I have been truly stupid.'

The empty air echoed with eloquence.

Chapter Three

Two days later, at mid-morning, Cicely was reunited briefly with her mother, the Queen Dowager, and with Bess, in whose temporary Westminster apartment the meeting took place. It became a confrontation of Cicely's own making, because she again permitted impulsiveness to plunge her into difficulty. Richard's death seemed to have robbed her of all maturity and common sense.

Bess's apartment had last been occupied by Richard's dying queen, Anne Neville. Cicely knew, as had Richard, that Anne had never loved him as completely she should, because her heart had always belonged to her brief but unworthy first husband, the Lancastrian Prince of Wales, son of Henry VI. She had been betrothed to Richard first, but for dynastic and political reasons had been taken from him when she was fourteen, and given to the arrogant, seventeen-year-old prince, who had not treated her well. But she had formed a passion, and lay willingly with him. It was a passion that had not faded throughout her life.

The prince had died at the Battle of Tewkesbury in 1471, where Richard, naturally, had fought on the opposing Yorkist side, in support of Cicely's triumphant father. Richard, so much the better man, had been the second husband, consigned to second place in all ways. And yet foolish Anne had believed he did not know it! Cicely, who had become quite close to Anne, could not quite forgive the ailing queen for this betrayal of his love. How could any woman not love him, and *only* him? But Anne herself eventually took second place. Cicely had him in the end, all of him, and the knowledge gladdened her heart.

But not even thoughts of Richard could make her feel well today. She had been sick again that morning, so very sick that she now felt drained and weak. Her maid Mary had tried hard to bring some colour to her cheeks, pinching and patting, but the awful pallor remained. Mary was young like her mistress, and rounded, kindly, with pretty brown hair and a pleasant face, and she had a considerable knowledge of herbs and other such things. She prepared Cicely a settling drink containing mint, but it had only been partly successful.

The Queen Dowager, wearing black robes and a tight white wimple—a harking back to Edward IV, not a sign of mourning for Richard—was anxious for herself as she took a seat by the smoke-blackened fireplace. She was not a woman to inspire affection in her children, being selfish, ambitious and false-hearted, but the beauty lingered that had brought their royal father to his knees. Now she was anxious because Richard was dead. *He* had forgiven her for so much, but Henry would not forgive her for coming out of sanctuary into Richard's protection. Henry had planned to invade and be seen to 'free' Bess from sanctuary to be his wife. He would still take her as his wife, but would he ever forgive her, or her mother, or indeed Cicely Plantagenet, for turning to the man Henry wished to portray as a murderous tyrant?

Bess, regal in a midnight-blue velvet gown, her red-gold hair swept up beneath a delicate but cumbersome headdress, as if she were already married, spoke first. 'Well, the only news I have is for you, Cicely. You and I are to be placed under Lady Stanley's protection, at

Coldharbour, our grandmother's Thameside mansion in the city. Well, it *was* our grandmother's house. Henry has turned out the College of Arms, which Richard permitted to be there, and has presented the property to his mother. Until I become queen, you and I are to stay there. Of course, no one must mention that such arrangements could legally be deemed to be abduction, and therefore a great impediment to marriage.'

Cicely's lips parted in astonishment. 'Really? This is true?'

'So I've been advised.'

'By whom?'

Bess shook her head. 'It does not matter, but I know I could easily claim to being coerced. And so could you, of course, since you are still on his list of possible brides. However, it would only delay the inevitable, and cause even more trouble.'

'*Trouble?* Bess, you seem to prefer going along with Henry's wishes rather than fight for what is right! The throne belongs to York! To Jack!'

'Enough, Cissy, my mind is made up,' Bess replied, clearly wishing she had not mentioned abduction. 'We go to Coldharbour and that is the end of it. At least, we will after the house has been completely renovated and refurnished from cellar to attic. Nothing but the very finest of everything for Lady Stanley.' Bess picked up a candlestick, glanced at it as if assessing its value, and then replaced it.

Cicely's heart sank. Bess had no intention of refusing, and now they both had to live under Margaret's protection. The prospect was dire. Coldharbour was a fine house in the city, rising up from the Thames and fronting Upper Thames Street. Cicely had been named after her grandmother, Cecily Neville, Duchess of York, now in religious retirement. It was insulting that serpentine Henry, who had slain Cecily's youngest son through treachery, had appropriated her house for his equally serpentine mother.

The Queen Dowager was anxious. 'And what of me, Bess?'

'I do not know.'

'Jesu, how I fear a tread at the door, a visit in the night,' her mother said, gripping the arms of her chair.

Bess paced up and down restlessly. 'Well, Mother, I will warrant you now wish with all your self-centred heart that Richard were still king. You, who loathed him and plotted against him, now know him to be a far more honourable man than Henry Tudor.'

'I admit it. I was wrong about Richard, but at least I have the comfort of knowing that I did tell him this. He did not die thinking I still hated him.'

Bess paused. 'Mother, I doubt if *you* were anywhere near his mind at Bosworth,' she said cuttingly. 'As to whether he was delighted with your belated conversion, I should think it did not matter to him in the least. He was never concerned with you and your comforts, only with his nieces and nephews.'

'Well, *you* did not behave like his niece, did you?' the Queen Dowager countered. 'As I—and the rest of the world—know well, you craved him so much you were incapable of making a secret of it. I wonder you did not attempt to fondle his cock in front of the entire court. Well, you had better make a secret of your ill-placed lust from now on, because Henry will not tolerate your stupidity, or your ungodly thoughts toward your own uncle.'

Cicely sat quietly, her eyes lowered, her hands clasped in the lap of her sage-green gown. If only they knew how very good ungodliness could be. One night of it with Richard was infinitely more exciting than the prospect of years of godliness with Henry Tudor.

She watched her sister. Richard was right, Bess *was* hard. It had commenced when her carnal desire for him had not been reciprocated. Desperate to win him, Bess had left her true self far behind.

The Queen Dowager sighed. 'Well, Henry needs to say that Richard had my boys killed, but he is unable to prove it without bodies, and *we* know they were still alive when Richard died. I pray they are safe and in Burgundy, as Richard intended.'

'How I would love to proclaim it from the steps of St Paul's,' Cicely murmured.

The Queen Dowager's lips twisted, her attention still on Bess. 'Well, your precious Henry is posed with a ticklish problem, is he not? I wonder he can sleep at night.'

'He is not my precious Henry! He does not want me and I certainly do not want him. He is everything that is ignoble.'

'No,' Cicely found herself blurting.

'No?' The others' eyes were turned upon her.

'I . . . have spoken with him. At some length,' she admitted, wishing yet again that she had held her stupid tongue. 'I accused him of being dishonourable for treating Richard's body as he did.'

'Oh, my God,' the Queen Dowager said faintly. 'You actually said that? Jesu, Cicely, he will have your silly head!'

'No, he will not, Mother. He told me he knew nothing of the treatment Richard's body received until it was too late. He told me Richard's nakedness was not displayed to all and sundry, only his upper body and face. And he told me Richard would have a fitting tomb, as became an anointed king. I believed him.'

'How does it come about that *you* are so amicable with him?' Bess demanded, a jealous note entering her voice. She did not want Henry himself, only to share his crown. Suddenly Cicely seemed a threat.

'Does it matter how it came about?' Cicely replied.

'I spoke with him, that is all. He also told me that John of Gloucester, Jack of Lincoln and the boy Warwick have sworn fealty to him and will soon be at liberty.'

Bess's eyes flickered in a manner not far removed from Henry's. 'My, little sister, you *have* been busy.'

'It was nothing, Bess,' Cicely protested, even though it had been something very much. She and Henry Tudor had tested each other, and neither had emerged entirely victorious.

Bess's dark blue gown rustled over the floor and freshly strewn fragrant herbs as she resumed her pacing. 'Well, *I* have not seen him at all. He rode at my side into London from Lambeth, and left me at the palace steps. He could not have been less courtly had he tried. I do not even know if he could see me at all. Only one of his eyes seemed to function. The other floated whither it would. Oh, he repulsed me.'

The Queen Dowager's lips pursed. 'Well, Bess, his mind is the difficulty, not what his eyes do. He must know about your passion for Richard. There was talk enough. He probably wonders if you come to him as less than a virgin.'

Cicely stood. 'Please, Mother, do not say such things. Richard did not do anything to Bess, and it is wrong of you to hint as much. Yes, Henry does suspect it, I know that to be so.'

Again her mother and sister stared at her, and Bess was furious. 'You and he discussed my *chastity*?'

'I reassured him that you were all you should be, Bess. And you are, as far as I know. I did not bring up the subject, he did. He interrogated me on many things, and I found out things from him. That is all it was: a probing conversation, I believe it could be termed.'

'My, my, Cissy, how easily you find it to worm yourself into the confidence of kings,' Bess breathed icily. 'You always had much more of Richard than I did.'

You have no idea how much more, Cicely thought.

'Where did this revealing conversation take place? Henry's bed? You would have me believe you are well in with him. Such a tawdry little triumph, Cissy.'

'It was a conversation, not a roll in the hay.' Now Cicely was angry as well. 'Actually, I think I can vouch that your initiation into his bed will not be long-lasting! He is a man who will take what he wants, when he wants, and how he wants. Your pleasure will not enter into it.'

The Queen Dowager chuckled. 'You know nothing, Cicely. Henry Tudor is no different from any other man. They *all* think only of themselves.'

'No, not all.'

Her mother looked intently at her. 'And how would you know that? Do not tell me you have been foolish enough to spread yourself beneath that *boy* John of Gloucester. If you think you know about *men*, you must . . .' She paused, her eyes narrowing shrewdly. 'Or do you already have experience of men? Who was it?'

Bess was riveted, seeing her sister as if for the first time.

Cicely did not answer. She was in a pit of her own digging. As John had once said of his father.

The Queen Dowager sat forward. 'Who have you lain with, Cicely?' she asked again.

'Do you really think I will tell you?'

'And what if you find yourself with a whelp inside you?' the Queen Dowager demanded.

Cicely fell silent.

Bess gazed at her, a myriad expressions crossing her pale, perfect face. 'Was it Jack? When he failed with me at Sheriff Hutton, did he tumble you instead?'

'There is no one,' Cicely answered, resisting the almost overpowering urge to clasp her stomach, to protect her child from their critical eyes.

The Queen Dowager got up suddenly, and came to slip a knowing hand over Cicely's belly. 'Jesu, you *are* with child!' she gasped, as if stung. *'Please* tell me it was not a common man!'

'Neither of you need be party to my problems. When I leave this room, you can both forget it all. You can look Henry Tudor in the eyes and play innocent. I am *not* innocent, nor can I conceal it for much longer. I do not care what happens to me, but I do care about my child. If either of you does anything to jeopardize its safety or wellbeing, I will curse you both. So leave me alone. I love my child, and I love its father. More than either of *you* will ever understand.'

With that she left, and her mother and sister gazed after her.

Not long after noon of that same day, on her way back to her rooms after walking in the palace's riverside garden, Cicely suddenly found herself face to face with Henry Tudor's mother. As always, Margaret, Lady Stanley, carried a book of hours. This one was Richard's, taken from his tent at Bosworth. How dare this toad of a woman even touch it!

Margaret's small, thin body was swathed in black. She wore a wimple that pulled her face back, but unlike the Queen Dowager she had never been a beauty and did not cut an impressive figure. Merely a threatening one. Like her son, who had his hooded expression from her. But to Cicely's astonishment, Margaret spoke warmly. 'Why, Lady Cicely, I trust I find you well?'

'Lady Stanley.' Cicely managed a curtsey. Lord Stanley was Margaret's fourth husband, and had turned traitor to Richard at Bosworth. Margaret had been born a Beaufort, the illegitimate line that had descended from John of Gaunt and which was specifically barred from the throne.

It was through her that Henry Tudor had any royal blood. Bastard royal blood, and not even paternal.

Margaret was concerned. 'Is something wrong, my dear? You are very pale.'

'I fear it is the curse we have to deal with every month.' The other's concern seemed genuine, which bothered Cicely even more. Margaret had always shown her dislike for Edward IV's two eldest daughters because of their adherence to Richard, yet now, suddenly, she was amiable. Such a change in this particular woman was alarming.

'It is indeed a curse. Perhaps you should join me on this bench for a while?'

Without waiting for a reply, Margaret conducted her to a stone bench set against the wall, beneath a window overlooking the Thames.

Cicely was mindful of the shunned ladies. 'Lady Stanley, I must crave forgiveness. Without thinking, I dismissed the ladies you so considerately provided.'

'I believe you are content with a single maid?'

'Yes, my lady.' Henry had to have told her.

'If that is your wish, it is no insult to me.'

'You are kind, my lady.'

'My dear, you and I have perhaps not been as properly acquainted as we should have been. It is mostly my fault, I admit, for I took it as a slight to my son that you and your sister were so loyal to Richard. But I feel I do know *you*, if not your sister.'

'You . . . know me?' Cicely was increasingly uneasy. What was all this? Kind concern from Henry Tudor's mother? What could Henry have said to her? It could not possibly bode well.

'Well, I know *more* of you. My brother speaks in your favour.'

Sir John Welles again! 'I am honoured, my lady. I confess I did not expect to like him so much. He has been all that is courteous and gallant toward me.'

Margaret almost preened. 'He is an honourable knight, my dear, and dear to me. If he praises you, then that is good enough for me. I am sorry to have been disagreeable toward you in the past, and I trust you and I can forge a friendship in the days to come.'

'I hope so too, my lady.' *No, I do not! But what else can I say?*

'I do not know if you have been told that you and your sister are to lodge with me until such time as your sister is married. I am to reside at Coldharbour. Well, this arrangement cannot take place until the house has been made habitable again, and in the meantime we all stay here. I look forward to us being together, Cicely.'

'What of my mother?'

Margaret stiffened. 'I think you will understand that the Queen Dowager and I do not like each other, my dear. Believe me, there would be bloodshed if she were beneath my roof. I do not know what is to become of her, but my son will treat her with due respect.'

Cicely gazed at her. 'How can you like me, my lady? I am loyal to Richard, and nothing can change that.'

'I have been in conversation with the king. It is not often that he is spoken to as you did. It did him good, I fancy. He can be . . . distant.'

And always would be, Cicely thought.

'Henry knows of your unswerving allegiance to your uncle. He does not like it, but he accepts it.'

'Accepts?' This grew more unlikely by the second.

'In as much as he can. My son is not a happy man, my dear, as I think you probably realized.'

Henry was unhappy? Yes, Cicely supposed he was, but she also supposed it was his own fault, for permitting himself to be so convoluted, and it was his mother's, because her ambition and ruthlessness had done him no favours. He was also malevolent, and *that* came naturally. 'The king has been very gracious to me, Lady Stanley. He told me what he intended for my uncle's tomb, and that had he known of it, he would not have permitted the desecration of his body.' She was permitting her stupid tongue to rattle again. Because of Richard.

'Your uncle still matters that much to you?'

Was there a narrowing of Margaret's eyes? A slight pinching of her lips? 'How could he not, my lady? He was my uncle and loved me as I loved him. He was kind to me, thoughtful and generous.'

Margaret gazed at her. 'You have a very stout heart, Lady Cicely.'

Cicely felt the closeness of tears. Let Margaret and her chilly son think what they would; she was no longer able to dissemble. She felt completely out of sorts and strange, and secretly prayed it did not herald a problem for her baby. But she knew much of it was grief.

After a moment, Margaret smiled. She actually smiled. Cicely could not believe it. 'When one's loyalty is truly engaged, there is little one can do about it. I remain loyal to my first husband, my son's father, who died when I was still thirteen and carrying his baby. He did not treat me as disgracefully as the stark facts might suggest, even though he was twice my age and should *not* have taken me to his bed. I was such a poor little thing, still a child, still frightened of everything. We may frown upon what he did, but he was kindness itself to me. He did not hurt me or treat me badly, nor was he a man who preferred children. Far from it. He had his reasons for doing as he did, and some of them were not entirely admirable, but he was not cruel or thoughtless. I adored him, Cicely, with all my silly child's heart, and I grieve for him still. Edmund Tudor was a prince to me, and we women do not easily forget such men. Childbirth did me no favours, however, because my body was too small. I remain too small, so if childbirth had come later, I believe it would still have had the same result.'

Cicely was transfixed. Margaret, Lady Stanley, was confessing such intimate things to her? Was there anyone who did *not* feel the urge to confide their innermost secrets to Cicely Plantagenet? It was becoming a curse!

Margaret put a hand on hers. 'I have misjudged you, my dear. My brother is not a man whose praise is easily won. That is enough for me. As is the fact that you quite confounded the king. Poor Henry, his is not an easy character. Not as was Richard's. *That* man could wheedle the Arch Fiend into becoming Christian.'

'Richard was simply a naturally charming man who did not misuse his undoubted effect upon others. Oh, you are bound to not agree, my lady, but I knew him. I was close to him, and saw him truthfully. Nothing and no one will ever induce me to speak badly of him. I fear his death is still too raw to me, because I cannot yet allow anyone to mention him without having to speak in his praise or defence. I crave your understanding if it offends you. Or the king.'

Margaret nodded. 'I admire your faith in him, my dear.'

'He deserved my faith, my lady. He earned every ounce of it.'

'But he could not keep his throne.'

'He was betrayed.' *By your husband, for one!*

Margaret chuckled. 'Oh, you share his courage and charm, my dear, although I would never have guessed it from the stony looks you and I have been in the habit of exchanging. I truly look forward to spending time with you at Coldharbour. Well, I must go to my son now.' She rose. 'Will you give your sister a little simple advice, Cicely?'

'That depends what it is, my lady.'

'I am not stupid, nor is my son. She has made it clear that she does not intend to approach their forthcoming marriage as anything other than a necessary evil. She is foolish. She has only to change her attitude to win his respect, if not his love. At the moment she has little more than his contempt, and that will not do at all. My son *is* susceptible to female charms, my dear, and the sooner your silly sister realizes it, the better.'

Cicely managed to nod agreement. Henry Tudor had clawed his way to the throne over Richard's bloodied body. He could be as miserable as a plucked duck for all she cared.

'If your sister sees sense now, before hatred sets in, there is a chance of happiness between them. Otherwise, any strife will be of her own making. Will you tell her that?'

'I will try, my lady, but my sister and I do not see eye to eye at the moment.'

'May I ask why?'

Cicely saw no reason not to tell the truth. 'Because I have spoken to the king and she has not.'

'So, there is hope for her yet. A little jealousy cannot be a bad thing.' Margaret smiled again. 'I think it would terrify him to think he had to take you on, my lady. He would never know what to expect next.'

Cicely almost wished she *was* to marry him. Oh, what a dance she would lead him. He would regret the day he ever returned to England!

Margaret lingered. 'May I hope that when next we meet, my dear, we can be well disposed toward each other?' she asked.

Cicely gazed at her for a long moment, and then nodded. 'Yes, my lady, you may.' *But your friendship will not last long once you discover the truth about me.*

When she finally reached her rooms, there was a page waiting to present a sealed note. She knew neither seal nor writing. Opening it, she read.

'My lady, I believe it is time you and I spoke in private, for there is much that needs to be said. I will walk in the palace garden at three of the afternoon. Jon Welles.'

So, he styled himself Jon? She refolded the note and nodded at the boy. 'Tell Sir Jon I will be there as he wishes.'

'My lady.'

The boy hastened away again, and as the door was shut behind him, Cicely closed her eyes and exhaled. Sir Jon Welles seemed to be at every corner of her life at the moment.

Chapter Four

WHEN THREE O'CLOCK came, Cicely was ready to meet Sir Jon Welles. Her wardrobe from Sheriff Hutton had now arrived, and she chose to wear a cream velvet gown with pendulous sleeves lined with crimson brocade. Her dark chestnut hair she left loose, as always.

The September air was unexpectedly warm, but at least it was not spring again, she thought. The appearance of daffodils and apple blossom always heralded death. Or so she felt. She walked past the window where she had heard her mother plotting Richard's downfall when he had been Lord Protector, and the apple tree where Bess had chased their little sister Bridget, and then she halted by the river wall, where she had once looked over and seen John of Gloucester's reflection appear alongside her own. That had been immediately after the spring-time death of Richard's legitimate son, and heir, little Edward of Middleham. How broken Richard had been. And alone, unsupported by his wife, who had collapsed completely. He was a king without an heir, with a wife who could no longer provide him with another. Or offer him the comfort he had so willingly given to her. How careworn he had been, and how this niece had loved him, although without knowing it for a love that crossed too many boundaries.

She sensed Sir Jon's approach, and turned. He was

young to be Henry's uncle, perhaps two or three years older than Richard. Oh, how she judged every man by Richard. A good-looking man, with bearing and presence, Jon Welles cut a handsome figure, dressed as he was in mustard velvet, with a soft black velvet hat that was devoid of a brooch. He was tall and spare, with a straight nose and thin lips that were neither hard nor set, and his long hair was prematurely grey at the temples, but otherwise brown and wiry. His eyes were an incredibly dark, vivid blue, with a steady gaze that invited trust. It was hard to believe he was Margaret's half-brother, because there was no resemblance at all. Perhaps he took after his father, not their shared mother, the Duchess of Somerset, whose third husband had been Lionel, sixth Baron Welles. Cicely knew Jon to be adroit, and was sure he had little difficulty dealing with any trouble that came his way.

'Lady Cicely.' He removed his hat and sketched a very courtly bow.

She accorded him a curtsey. 'Sir Jon? It is J-O-N, is it not?'

'My father wished me to be J-O-H-N, but my mother preferred Jonathan. The unfortunate result you see before you is a painful compromise.' He smiled.

'You wished to speak with me?'

He ignored the question and leaned back against the wall to look at her. 'How are you, my lady?' he enquired.

'I am well, as you see.'

'That is not what I meant.'

She blushed. 'My answer remains the same, sir, although . . .'

'Yes?'

'I would prefer to feel better in the mornings.'

He smiled. 'I am told that is the way of it. You have seen someone with knowledge? Someone who can make sure things are as they should be? Forgive me such impertinent interest, Lady Cicely, but your wellbeing is of concern to me.'

'I am not your responsibility, Sir Jon, as I think I reassured you at Sheriff Hutton.'

'I know what you reassured me, my lady, but that does not oblige me to walk away and pretend I know nothing. You are with child, and I think the father to be Richard Plantagenet.'

'Do you expect me to confirm that?'

'No, for I know you will not. Nevertheless, I am sure I am right. Yours is a very hazardous secret, my lady. The child of one Yorkist king and the grandchild of the other, with a mother who is the daughter and niece of both those kings? If a boy, he will be an uncommon magnet for future Yorkist rallying cries. If a girl, she will be an uncommon desirable bride for some ambitious magnate.'

'Do you intend to tell on me, Sir Jon?'

'What do you think I am, my lady, a petty schoolboy? If that had been my intent, I would have done it by now.'

'Forgive me, I did not mean to offend you. Sir Jon, I hardly know you, yet you have my as yet secret condition in your palm. If you wonder if that makes me anxious, let me assure you that it does. I have met your king now, so I know full well the hazards that loom.'

He smiled. 'Ah, yes, you have met Henry, and jolted him somewhat, from all accounts. Do you *enjoy* putting yourself in peril? I would not seek my nephew voluntarily, so what possessed you?'

'I needed to, well, to—'

'Estimate his character?' he supplied.

'Yes.'

'I grant you are intrepid, but please do not attempt such a thing again. Henry is a dog best left lying, not prodded by a pretty toe.'

'You have no need to warn me now, sir, for he left me in

no doubt that a repeat would be very unwise indeed.'

'He does not like to be caught off guard, because he likes to be the one doing it, my lady. To have it turned upon him is something for which he may well bear you a grudge.'

'Do you think he does? I did not think so.'

'Do not trust him, my lady. Keep your distance.'

'You still have not said why you wished to see me. Was it simply to enquire after my health?'

'No.' He glanced towards the palace, and Cicely saw Margaret standing at a window, watching. 'Take my hand, my lady,' he said.

'Your hand?'

'The thing with a thumb and four fingers at the end of the arm I now extend to you. Do as I say, if you please.'

Slowly she did as he requested. 'Why?' she asked.

'All will shortly be made clear,' he replied, glancing at the window again and then drawing her palm to his lips.

'How dare you take such a liberty, sir!' Cicely would have snatched her hand away had he not held it so tightly.

'It is no liberty, madam.' He turned her to face him. 'Now, behave as if you do not object,' he said, putting his hand to her chin and raising her face a little. 'Look soulfully into my eyes, if you please.'

'Certainly not!'

'You make this very difficult.'

'Make what very difficult?' she demanded.

'Your wooing.'

She stared at him. 'My *what*?'

He smiled and glanced surreptitiously at the window again. His half-sister had gone. He released Cicely's hand. 'Your moment of humiliation is at an end,' he murmured.

'What, *exactly*, do you wish of me, Sir Jon?' she said icily.

'Your consent to marriage, I think.'

She drew back. 'I ... must be misunderstanding you, sir.'

'No, you have my correct meaning. I assure you I will make a reasonably competent husband.' He said it with humour.

'For someone else, not me.'

'I think it has to be you, my lady. And I am not all that lowly for a Plantagenet princess. I am the king's uncle, and have extensive lands in Lincolnshire and Northamptonshire. I am Constable of Rockingham, Bolingbroke and Castle Donington, and have various other posts. My duties are many and varied, and I will have to travel a lot in order to attend to them. I will expect my wife to accompany me. That is the life I offer. For your protection. If you would rather be exposed to comment when your condition becomes impossible to hide, that is your business, but if you are married at the time of the birth, and if your husband acknowledges the child, your reputation is saved.'

'And you will be a laughing stock, sir, because I have been with child since June, whereas you and I met for the first time at the end of August.'

'I am aware of that, which is why I think you and I did first meet in Nottingham in June.'

'But we did not.'

He laughed. 'Well, I do realize it, my lady, but as it happens my whereabouts in June are known only to me. I could well have been in Nottingham, and I could well have seduced you from the straight and narrow path of virginity. Do not look at me like that, for I am not entirely bereft of ability in that respect.'

'I am sure you are not, sir, but nevertheless—'

'I will be able to marry you, my lady. There is no impediment. I have only to express such a wish to my half-sister for her to be eager for it. She will convey her eagerness to my nephew. I may not be Richard Plantagenet, or indeed his courtly son, but I will do for the purpose in question.'

'And you will rise much higher in royal circles, will you not? Brother-in-law to the queen and uncle to the king?'

He raised an eyebrow. 'A double-edged sword, unless your sister mends her ways. Be warned. The last thing you need is for my nephew to change his mind about her.'

'Change his mind? And choose *me* instead? Sir Jon, the king is certainly not interested in me. Annoyed with me, perhaps even downright angry, but that is all.'

'You do not know him. Going to him as you did was a very ill-advised notion in many more ways than one. Now you have pricked his interest, stimulated it even. You are not the usual pattern of princess or even court lady, and God alone knows, a man has only to look at you to want you. I would certainly not turn down the chance.'

'You transgress, Sir Jon. Besides, you were speaking of the king. To imagine he wants me is quite ridiculous.'

'Is it? You are like Richard in more than just colouring, my lady. You have his ability to engage others without very much trying.'

'I do not want Henry Tudor. Richard is irreplaceable, Sir Jon, and I loved him in a way that I do not think you would wish to know. I lay with him, and wanted to again and again. He brought me to life, and I could not have enough of him. I did things with him and to him that I never dreamed could be. He was a considerate, passionate, patient, exciting lover, and he taught me more in a very short time than most men could teach in their whole lives. He could sustain my pleasure until I could scarce breathe of it. Do you understand? I have loved someone else far too much to be worthy of becoming your wife, Sir Jon. I am not suitable, deserving or worthy.'

'If that was supposed to repel me, my lady, you do

not know men very well after all. The thought of what you have just described is . . . highly provocative. At this precise moment it would be entirely gratifying to get you between the coverlets. Provided you were willing, and could be persuaded to imagine I am Richard III.'

She blushed again. 'That was not my intention.'

He smiled. 'If you do not wish to excite ardour, the very last thing you should do is speak so eloquently of your carnal dealings with your own uncle. Men may outwardly pretend to be shocked and disapproving, and carve crosses through the air, but in truth they would be heartily aroused. We are a poor lot, driven by our lusts.'

'Including you?'

'I have my faults, like the rest of my sex, but that does not mean that I do not have your wellbeing in mind when I propose this marriage. It is still possible to protect your good name. If you say that you and I first met in Nottingham, and that we lay together there, I will confirm it. I will claim the child as my own and it will be born in wedlock. Is that not better than the alternative?'

'Sir Jon . . .' She looked at him. 'How can you want me? I have sinned very much, and the child I carry is that of my own uncle. How can you possibly even *think* of doing this?'

He reached out as if to touch her cheek, but then drew his hand away again. 'My lady, I may not appreciate the finer points of incest, but I do know I admire you. The defiance you showed at Sheriff Hutton was something to behold. So young, and yet so valiant. And when I saw how you shielded your unborn child, without even knowing you gave yourself away, I was even further impressed. I do not expect you to love me, nor indeed can you expect me to love you, but I *do* respect you. If I can help you when you need it, please accept my offer.'

'You are a very honourable man, Sir Jon Welles.'

'You know nothing of me. I could well turn out to be a monster who beats you and forces himself upon you night and day.'

'I do not think so, Sir Jon.' She searched his dark blue eyes. 'But a wife *is* supposed to warm her husband's bed, is she not?'

'Ah, well, we will leave that to fate. I will not make any demands of you. My proposition is merely to rescue you. That is all.' He straightened. 'I imagine you will need a little time to consider this. I know you will decide to accept me in the end, because to do otherwise would be disastrous, for you and Richard's child. If nothing else you will think of the latter. It is too early in your grief for you to be anything other than overwhelmed by your loss. I can wait for an answer, but do not leave it too long. Every day you delay in something like this makes it more difficult for you. And for me, because I will be perceived as being unwilling to attend to my responsibility to you.'

'You will have your answer soon, sir.'

Chapter Five

THAT NIGHT, AS Cicely lay in her bed, watching the shadows of the night lamp move against the bed hangings, she thought of Sir Jon's offer. What would Richard advise? Would he tell her only a fool would decline?

'Yes, he would, Cicely.'

He stood beside the bed, in the light of the night light on the table, and she opened her arms gladly as he leaned down to kiss her. His hair was against her skin, his lips were warm and giving, and his arms were loving. He was so blessedly real that she *knew* she held him again; held the man, not the image.

'You do not really need me here in order to clear your mind.' He drew gently away and straightened.

She sat up, wanting to say so much, but what came out was completely incongruous. 'Henry wears your ring.'

'And he sits on my throne, which is much more to the point.'

'And his vile mother has your book of hours.'

'May it make a true Christian of her.' He smiled.

She slipped slowly out of the bed, drinking in everything that made him so dear to her. 'I have so wanted to see your face and hear your voice again,' she said.

'Both are always with you, sweetheart,' he said gently, and then added, 'although you may not care for what this voice has to say to you tonight. For one thing, you *have* to curb your overt support for me. Bess showed so little restraint that it attracted attention. You are in danger of doing the same.'

'It is impossible *not* to defend you.'

'I am beyond defending, Cicely.'

'They tell lies of you!'

He smiled again. 'That is nothing new. There will always be lies about me. The events that led up to my reign, and continued through it, are bound to cause controversy. I knew it even as I made my decisions and then acted upon them. You are still the great private truth of my life, sweetheart, but it must remain private. Well, maybe known to a few.'

'Sir Jon?'

He nodded. 'And Jack and Francis Lovell.'

'And Robert Percy, whom *you* told. But they are the only ones. Not even Mary Kymbe knows you are the father of my child.'

'So, four people apart from us. It is not a safe secret. Cicely, and your mother will not leave you alone until you give her an answer. Nor, I hazard, will Bess.'

'I will tell them both it is Sir Jon's child.'

'Which response proves you have already made your decision,' he pointed out.

She looked at him. 'Bess will know I do not speak the truth about him.'

'To Hades with Bess, Cicely. She cannot *do* anything to you, because she mishandles Henry. Bess mishandles everything. She could secure him if she really put her mind to it. He does not wish to have a resentful wife, he would prefer some warmth. He is not the most uxorious man in the world, but we all want some warmth, Cicely, even him. Bess seems not to see it. She is not your equal, Cicely, nor ever will be.'

He gathered her close again. 'You must become Lady

Welles, Cicely, for that will protect you. I know you love me, and that you love my son John, whom you do not wish to hurt. But he has to be hurt. You have a child to protect now, a *defenceless* child, and your duty is to him.'

'Him? I carry a boy?' She looked quickly at him.

'You believe so, do you not?'

'Yes, I suppose I do.'

His wry little smile reappeared. 'And please, for the love of God, resist the temptation to call him Richard.'

'How could there be another name?'

'Easily. Just choose one.' He traced her lips again. 'You know what you must do now, Cicely. You do not need me to tell you.'

'I *do* need you. Always,' she whispered.

'And you will always have me, do you not understand it? Losing my living self has dulled that common sense and insight that makes you so exceptional. I once offered myself for your confidences, because *you* had always supported me when I needed you. And I did need you, Cicely, I make no pretence that it was otherwise. Sweetheart, I can no longer care for you physically. Sir Jon Welles can. And he will, although there is an obstacle that I think has been overlooked.'

'What do you mean?'

'There exists the ticklish matter of the marriage contract I had drawn up for you, with Ralph Scrope.'

She hated the very word Scrope, and could not believe she had once enjoyed Ralph's false smiles. He was a few years older than her, and all that had passed between them was a glance or two and some smiles, yet he had sought Richard's consent to a marriage, claiming she desired it and that her father had agreed. Ralph wanted the advantage of a Plantagenet bride, and the royal status she would bring to him. But she had soon dissuaded Richard from the match, even though, in the belief that she wanted Ralph, he had already had the documents prepared.

Because she had rejected him and then accepted John of Gloucester, Ralph had punished them by turning upon Richard and going over to his enemies. Ralph it was who had brought about the detainment at Sheriff Hutton.

Richard interrupted her thoughts. 'The contract was real enough, Cicely. I *did* have it drawn up.'

'But did you sign and seal it?'

He shook his head. 'I had given you my word there would not be any such marriage. My word is always my bond. The contract was supposed to have been destroyed. My secretary was trustworthy and would not have kept it, appended my seal or forged my name. Someone else did that, probably Scrope himself. I underestimated his capacity for revenge and treachery.'

Her lips parted, for it seemed so obvious. 'Where is the contract now, Richard?'

'I have no idea. The unlovable Willoughby may have it, but others were there when Henry's men took Nottingham Castle. Several of them believed it was genuine, and that you and Scrope were lawfully wed. Henry does not seem to know of it, for I think you would have heard if he did. You must warn Sir Jon, because if the document, for which there appears so much factual evidence, cannot be disproved, there will have to be an annulment. Such things take time, and with my seal and apparent signature, it may not be easy. It may also not be in time to legitimize your child. Our child.'

She reached for his right hand, just to feel the warmth of his flesh, and the shortened little finger she loved so much.

'I am not real, Cicely,' he said gently. 'I wish I were. Your mind gives me life. That is all.'

'I do so want your love again, your body.' She gazed at

him. 'I do not imagine this. Not *this*.'

'You do, sweetheart. Whatever you experience with me will be a phantasm. *I* am a phantasm.'

Her heart turned over with the force of her love. He aroused such feelings, such emotions, such . . . everything. How could his queen have preferred another?

'You wish to know about Anne?'

She nodded. 'I will never understand how she could not have cleaved to you, completely and unquestioningly.'

'Because *you* are the one who loves me like that, and I worship you for it.'

'But you are temptation in human form, and have me so enslaved that I scarcely know night from day. Why did you not *make* her love you? You could have done it.'

'Such unquestioning faith in my power to beguile? Yes, Cicely, I could have seduced her into loving me as I then so wished she did, but she made no real effort to forget her first husband, and it smothered something in me. I know now—because of you—that I did not love her enough.'

'But—'

'She made it too plain, although I do not think she realized how much she gave herself away. I remained a good husband to her, and to outward appearances we were happy and in love, but she was not truly in my heart any more than I was in hers. The marriage was a close friendship, and I *did* mourn her passing, but I had long since lost interest in tempting her from her indelible memories.'

'She believed you loved her completely.'

He smiled a little. 'I know, and I did not disabuse her of that impression.'

'It would have eased her conscience if you had.'

'More wisdom and advice, Cicely?'

'I spent many hours with her when she finally became really ill. She told me the truth, and she was so anxious for you, Richard. She asked me to stay close to you and support you. *Me!*'

'Were you in love with me then?'

'Not that I realized, but yes, I was.'

'If you did not realize, why do you feel guilty? Sweetheart, if I had told Anne how I really felt, it would have hurt her far, far more. Believe me, it would. I had known her since childhood, and understood her. She believed she gulled me, and that soothed and sustained her because she thought I was happy. I could not spoil that for her.' He paused. 'And as I know your next question will be to ask why I did not make sure Bess fell *out* of love with me, I will tell you that I *chose* not to.'

'Why? She made life intolerable for you.'

He smiled. 'If I had dealt with her as I should have done, it would have hurt *you*. She is your sister, and at the time you tried so hard to shield her. I thought too much of you to cause you pain through her. I could have taken her aside, said hurtful things, and left her in no doubt whatever that I did not want her. It would have been easy enough, but I . . . I made a mess of it all,' he finished a little dryly. 'Does that satisfy your curiosity?'

'Partly. I cannot think you could ever make a mess of things.'

He laughed aloud. 'Jesu, sweetheart, I made a mess of a *lot* of things. And look where it got me. In my makeshift grave at thirty-two. Please allow me down from the pedestal upon which you are so determined to place me.'

She smiled. 'I love you so,' she said softly.

'You may not when I have finished with you tonight. But first, Sir Jon Welles. I think we have established that you mean to accept him, but I wish to hear you say it.'

'Richard, if I proceed with him, I will be letting it be thought I conducted a traitorous love affair while at your court.'

'Then allow it to be thought. You are not in *my* court now, remember.'

'I would not want it believed, in *any* court, that I was so despicable to you.'

'Survival is what matters now, Cicely. It will not hurt me, because I know I had no finer, truer-hearted soul near me than you. I know you have not lain with Jon Welles, that you did not even meet him until Sheriff Hutton. So let it all wash over you, sweetheart. It is not important. *You* are important, and our son.' He looked at her. 'And there is another side to this, you know. You fear giving the wrong impression about what *you* supposedly did in Nottingham, but Sir Jon takes a far greater risk, because by saying he is the father of your child, he will be implying to Henry Tudor that he consorted with a highborn Yorkist lady who was actually within my household. Close to me by blood as well as friendship, someone *known* to be deep in my confidence.'

'Not how deep. At least, Henry does not know, but Sir Jon certainly does.'

He smiled. 'Think on, Cicely. Henry received no useful information about my plans, so he will wonder if his half-uncle was the one confiding the secrets. So Sir Jon does not propose lightly, because the moment he broaches it openly, he puts himself in jeopardy. He will need all his half-sister's support, believe me, because she is the only one with any influence over Henry. The only one, apart from Jasper Tudor, who holds back from such matters. I believe something happened in Brittany that has taught Jasper a signal lesson about when and when not to be drawn into Henry's private affairs. But that is immaterial now, because it is Jon Welles of whom we speak. He persists in taking risks for you, Cicely, and he does it out of regard. He has told you of his feelings, oh, maybe not to the full, but certainly enough to convey to you that he is honest in everything. Yes he desires you, but he *is* honourable. Margaret will lend her full support because she loves him enough to want him to have a wife who is both a king's daughter and the queen's sister. He, who is not royal himself, will become so through you.'

'That was my only attraction for Ralph.'

'But not for Jon Welles. He wants you for sincere reasons. Nothing less. So marry him. Make his chivalry worthwhile.'

She looked at his eyes in the lamplight. 'I will.'

'Good. Now I have to speak to you about Henry Tudor, who now recognizes you as a much warmer prospect than your sister.'

'No!' But she remembered Henry saying something of her trying to rival Bess.

Richard turned away. 'He would not have tolerated anyone else praising me as you did, vehemently, to his face, and then accusing him of dishonouring my body.'

'I could not help it.'

'Yes, you could, you simply gave in to impulse. You will have to do better. Few men can resist the erotic challenge you present. Sometimes there is a wanton look in your eyes, in the way you move and behave, that cries out what a damned good fuck you are!'

'Richard!' He had never used such a word to her before.

'Cicely, *I* look at you and it's certainly what I think. What I *know*! You are a creature of love, sweetheart, delightfully abandoned and sensuous, so willing to caress and coax, to give yourself to every fleshly pleasure, to share all the things men dream of. And men *know* it. It shines in everything you do. That eagerness, that need for satisfaction, that desire to pleasure and be pleasured, that exquisite anticipation and *sharing* of the final moment, when the man you are with gives his soul to you, not only his seed. That is how you are, Cicely, and there is nothing you can do about it.'

She could not take her eyes from him. 'You cannot really mean it, Richard,' she whispered.

'But I do. Jesu, you really have no idea, have you? I have *lain* with you, sweetheart, I *know* what I am talking about. You are joy itself. And now Henry has been exposed to your bewitchery.'

'He cannot possibly regard me in that way. I gave him no cause.' Could she *really* have had such an effect upon a man as cold and cynical as Henry Tudor?

'And you gave Scrope no cause, yet look what happened. Do you imagine Henry would have mentioned his bed so often if it were *not* in his mind? You are *definitely* not yourself at the moment, my love, for the Cicely I last lay with was more quick-witted and intuitive. Sorrow has taken away your edge. Henry's character is contorted, his emotions deliberately stifled, but that does not mean the man has no urges. Are you listening to what I am saying? Really listening?'

'Yes!' she cried. 'I listen to *everything* you say. When you first came to me here, you gave me such heart. I felt so supported and able to face the obstacles. But then . . . when you had gone, I became weak again.' She could not meet his eyes. 'Richard, I think I know best, but do not actually seem to know when to speak or when to hold my tongue. I am so emotional and illogical that I have become foolish. I know it.' There were tears in her eyes. 'And I am frightened. I am so ill in the mornings and sometimes during the day as well, and I feel so very strange. And . . . and it is *your* fault!'

He pulled her into his arms again, and ran his fingers gently through her hair. 'Yes, sweetheart, I rather suppose it *is* my fault, but I am afraid I cannot undo my part in your troubles.'

'Nor do I wish you to. Richard, being with you like this makes everything feel better.'

'And this is not real anyway,' he said gently.

'It is!'

He did not correct her again. 'Cicely, my sweetest love, you *can* manage without me. When things once overwhelmed me, I asked you what I should do. Do you remember? On the tower at Nottingham?'

She nodded.

'You said there was only one thing I could do, and that was be the king. There is also only one thing *you* can do now, Cicely, and that is guard yourself and our baby. You have no other choice. I am so very sorry that my love has left you like this. It was the one thing I truly feared for you, and now I cannot help you. Because . . . I – am – not – fact.' He spaced the words deliberately and emphatically.

'Please do not make me admit it, Richard. Please,' she whispered, her eyes bright with tears.

He gazed at her. 'You still break my heart,' he breathed.

She reached to take his hand and pulled it almost roughly to her lips. 'I am sorry to be so weak and helpless today. I will try never to be so again.'

His fingers curled lovingly around hers. 'You are neither weak nor helpless, Cicely, you are a Plantagenet, and *such* a Plantagenet. And do not apologize for something that is, after all, *my* fault.' He smiled.

'I seem to recall that experiencing your "fault" was very enjoyable. Too enjoyable, for you left me wanting you *all* the time.'

'I am fairly sprightly, considering my accursed back, but *all* the time might have been beyond even me.' He took her face in his hands. 'Promise you will not tangle with Henry again, or anything remotely resembling it.'

'How can I give you my word about things I do not yet know? You will have to be content with that answer,

Richard, because—as you keep saying—you are not real anyway.'

He looked at her for long moment. 'Oh, Cicely, you have an incredible capacity to captivate, but you do not yet know how to ration it.' He sank his fingers into the hair at her temple. 'Sweet reason does not seem to work with you right now, so you have to be taught a salutary lesson in what can be done with the gift you use so lightly. You need to be confronted with it, sweetheart, and I mean *really* confronted.'

'Richard?' She could only whisper his name.

'You have no notion at all of what attraction I am capable when I choose. I have never really exposed you to my ability to seduce and persuade, but for your own sake, your eyes need to be fully opened.' He moved away, went to lean back against the wall again and then faced her. 'Come to me and kiss me, Cicely,' he said, very softly, his lips curved with promise, his eyes dark and warm.

She could not move. He was fascinating, a beautiful, desirable prize that she wanted so very, very much . . . yet she could not take even one step towards him.

'Come to me and kiss me. Succumb to temptation, seduce me as you say I seduce you.'

'Richard?'

'Do it.'

Chapter Six

CICELY HESITATED, BUT was at last able to go to Richard. Gladness washed richly through her as she slipped her arms around him and lifted her lips to his. Her body sang the moment she held him, but if she expected her kiss to be returned, she was mistaken. He made no move at all, not even to straighten from the wall, but by his very stillness encouraged her to do as she would with him. And so she did.

She caressed him, adored him and stroked him—so intimately that she was lost in the bliss of it. Time and again she was overtaken by those familiar sensations, those waves of exquisite pleasure between her legs that being with him like this always wrought into life. She was incapable of *not* exulting in him, of *not* experiencing this voluptuous reward. Still he did nothing, only to simply give silent, motionless consent.

His body was hers, and yet was not. He offered himself, but she did not have the key that would unlock the barrier he placed between them. It was unbelievably erotic. He dominated her senses without doing anything at all, except be there, permitting her to touch him. He tantalized, lured, tempted . . . and gave unbelievable gratification without a single caress.

But she wanted more. So much more. She pleaded with her lips, begged with her body, *willed* him to embrace her, but still he did not. And yet somehow he conveyed everything. He was so much in command of her that she felt incapable of resistance. Or pride. She wanted him to return her passion, needed him to do it. He had never failed to hold her before, never made her strive for his love, and the feeling was intolerably affecting. She was enthralled by his incredibly sensuous sorcery.

She took his face in her hands to kiss his mouth. Kiss it so much that she crushed her own lips as well as his. Her love was so vibrant and imperative that she could not help herself. She used all the skills she possessed, remembered the things she had done with him in the past, tried *everything* she knew, and when he remained unmoved, she wept.

'Please, Richard, do not do this to me,' she sobbed. 'I love you, please hold me close. Please.'

He was harsh enough to let her tears fall, to see her distress and do nothing to ease it. A touch, a whispered word, would have rescued her, but he yielded nothing. Except his extraordinary capacity to make her want him. So very much. It was only when she sank tearfully to her knees and hid her face in her hands that he finally reclaimed her, pulling her up into his arms and holding her tightly.

She did not understand anything, nor did she care now. He was embracing her, loving her with his caresses, and that was the only thing that mattered. He imparted his desire in such a way that her tears fell still more. She had no will of her own. There was just *his* will, his choice. And now that he held her again, the feeling was so good it made her feel weak.

At last he kissed her. Putting gentle fingers to her chin and raising her mouth slowly to meet his. It was unbearably seductive. Again his lips, the mint freshness, the costmary on his clothes, the delight of his heart close to

71

hers. The elation that was *him*. She was helplessly under his spell. His kiss played mercilessly with her and plundered her strength. His caresses, seeming so light and gentle, aroused her passion to such a peak that her inner muscles submitted helplessly to a riot of pleasure.

Everything he did was calculated, cruel even, but these were kisses she would remember into eternity, for they finally demonstrated exactly how potent and completely spellbinding he really was. It was no mere impression, it was fact. This man could conquer with a smile, confine with a touch, and imprison completely with his eyes.

But he ended it and looked into her eyes. 'What would you not do for me now, Cicely?' he asked softly, smiling and pushing her hair back behind her ear. 'Mm? Is there anything?' He pulled her gently to his aroused loins. 'You feel how you excite me? How great my desire?' Then he kissed her lips again, weaving himself even further into her senses.

He knew so well how to coax her with the promise of his body. 'Go to Henry Tudor, Cicely. You can seduce him as you seduce me. Make him set Bess aside. He already wants you, so make sure of him.'

His voice was so very soft and tempting, so very loving, even while he asked her to go to his slayer. His eyes were unfathomable, but compelled her to obey.

Hesitantly, unhappily, she moved towards the door. She did not want to go, oh, how she did not, except that for Richard Plantagenet she would do anything. Anything.

But as she reached for the ring handle, he came quickly over and caught her hand. 'No, sweeting, no. I do not really wish you to do anything of the sort.' The spell was shattered as he made her face him. 'I love you, Cicely, and would not force anything like that upon you.'

She was so overwhelmed, so in bondage to him, that she could not assemble her thoughts, let alone her senses.

She began to cry, and tried to hide her face again.

'Oh, Jesu, I should not have done it,' he breathed, holding her tightly to him. 'Forgive me, sweetheart, please forgive me.' He kissed her hair, over and over.

She clung to him, helpless, drained and hardly aware of what had just happened.

'Oh, my poor, sweet Cicely, I have treated you badly tonight, but I had to make you understand, not me, but *yourself.* I could think of no other way.' He rested his forehead to hers. It was communion, affinity, intimacy, and she felt his immeasurable love.

'Cicely, tell me you forgive me.'

'I forgive you anything, everything. You know that. You can never stop me loving you.'

'I needed to show you what it is in my capacity to do. For those minutes I deliberately misused the gift that I have, and I did not need force, threats or any other such thing to influence you. I made you love me a hundred times more, and want me a thousand times more. You *would* have gone to Henry for me. Because you thought it was what *I* wanted.'

He put his fingers kindly to her chin and turned her face towards him. 'It is not magic, Cicely, but it *is* enchantment of a sort. *You* have this potential as well, do you understand? Never underestimate your ability to influence others, but use it judiciously. It will come so naturally to you that you will hardly know you do it. I could have had any woman I chose and you, my love, can have any man you choose. *Any* man. You could certainly have Henry Tudor if you so wished. And I am afraid you cannot apportion the blame for that to anyone but yourself.'

She would have spoken, but he put a forefinger to her lips. 'Cicely, going to him as you did was *bound* to result in him seeing you as you did not wish him to. You were unguarded, thinking only to make him look kindly upon you. You were innocent, at least, you thought you were innocent, and maybe you were at first. But you were not in the end, Cicely. You used the gift you hardly know you have, and that you certainly do not yet know how to properly control. It is *such* charm and desirableness, my dearest, and all too soon you will know exactly how to use it. But do *not* turn it lightly upon someone as dangerous as Henry Tudor.'

'I did not mean to turn anything on him.'

'No? Did you not go there intending to see how much you could influence him?'

She lowered her eyes quickly.

'Be careful with what you have, but never forget it is yours. You are able to make men want to have you, forgive you, trust you, or anything else you wish of them. You can charm women too. It is not often that a woman who has such an effect upon men can also endear herself to her own sex.'

He lowered his eyes for a moment. 'I was not wise during life, Cicely. I should have used what I knew I had in order to make certain of those around me. If I had, and if I had made calculated political decisions instead of adhering only to what I believed to be right and just, there would not have been a Bosworth. Without Bosworth, I could subsequently have applied myself to the right things. Instead I lost it all. So do not repeat my mistakes. Learn from me, because as God is my witness I am trying to teach you now.'

'Why did you not see that you should use it more? You are not a fool.'

'If I had deliberately misused my gift, I would have been a king with truly destructive charm, a user and a schemer, a trickster and a villain, hiding behind endearing smiles and kindly words. A man whose bent back really was an indication of the nature of his character.

That is not me, sweetheart, so maybe I *am* a fool. I certainly placed my trust where I should not. I think I was overwhelmed by everything that happened. From being Duke of Gloucester, content to rule sensibly in the north, I was suddenly, as if from a catapult, put on the throne itself, where life is anything but sensible. It was not what I wanted, Cicely, but it was what I had to accept. I could have been a good king, but I was not allowed to be. Circumstance overtook me. And so did death.'

She could have wept for him again. 'And . . . and now you think *my* character is such that I will use what I have? Am I so inferior a creature?'

His hand was over hers in a moment. *'Inferior?* Good God no, sweetheart, of course not. You simply have a little of your father in you. *He* had some of this charm, but he used it to always gain his own way. And he was often cruel and inconsiderate as he went about it. *You* would be cruel if you thought it would defend me. Is that not so?'

She nodded. 'Your enemies would have been dead before the day of Bosworth even dawned.'

'And you will be prepared to do it to protect our child, or anyone else you hold dear. You are strong, Cicely, and if it means seduction, you will do that too. God knows, you have the wherewithal to do it. You could bed Asmodeus himself if you set your mind to it. You say I am seduction personified, but you are too, sweetheart. I, above all, should know that.' He kissed her palm. 'Cicely, I can do no more than this. If I could, I would. You *must* be strong again. If you cannot do it for yourself, then do it for me. I need to know you are alert to the dangers, alert to the full extent of what you can do. Would you distress me by ignoring me now?'

'That is unfair.'

He smiled. 'Yes, of course it is. Which is why I say it.'

'I love you so,' she breathed.

'You are now to demonstrate that love by taking heed of everything I have said and done here tonight. *Everything*, sweetheart. You can rise above your present grief, and—'

'*Present* grief?' she cried. 'Richard, it is my *future* grief as well. The pain of losing you will never leave me. Never.'

His thumb smoothed her palm. 'Then you must make yourself strong. You—we—will have a fine son, a *healthy* son. I do not know what the future holds for him, but he *will* have a future. No sickly childhood and early demise for him. So, no more sinking beneath your bereavement, no more moping and silly impulses, and no more speaking and acting without thinking. I expect more of my sweet Cicely. Will you try for me?'

'Yes,' she whispered.

He put his hand to her cheek. 'You had to understand, Cicely. I am your mind and conscience now, not your living lover.' His hand moved from her cheek to her lips. 'The secret lies in how you use your gift, sweetheart. Never be vainglorious, for it is an ugly state.'

'But I am not vainglorious!'

'I know. I would not love you so very much if you were. But today you came close, and the temptation to succumb will always be there, Cicely. You drew things from Henry that he was shocked to have confessed, and now you have his mother in your palm as well. You have Sir Jon at your mercy, just as you had me. My wife confided in you, more than I probably would like, you knew Bess's every carnal thought of me. My son loves you to distraction, Jack would bed you in a moment, and Ralph Scrope wanted you so much he turned traitor for vengeance. Need I go on? It will never leave you, this power over others, this facility to engage their emotions, and you will need to cope with it. A single smile, a brief touch, even if it is careless, can do so very much.'

'You think I do not know that? There have been so many times when you have dominated me with a mere glance. You have actually *spoken* to me with your eyes. I heard you say my name across a great hall so crowded and noisy that it was impossible. But it happened.'

'I have never "used" anything upon you that I did not really feel, Cicely. Except tonight. Please know that. My emotions toward you have never been dishonest. However, they have been dishonest with others. I have smiled benevolently at Bess when I actually wished to look right through her. Sweetheart, I was your age when I discovered what I could do, so I know exactly how you feel now. It bewilders, angers, confuses, but it cannot be ignored. Never abuse it, for that will be to lose your way.'

'You make me a little frightened.'

'Do not be, sweetheart. It has never frightened me. I simply tell you all this to open your eyes to it. I recognized it in you at the abbey. How could I not? And how could I not have loved you for it? You touched my heart, and I felt I had waited for you all my life. But you were so young, and my *niece*!'

'They were not barriers, not in the end.'

'Death is the barrier now, sweetheart.'

Her lips pressed together mutinously, and fresh, even hotter tears stung her eyes. 'No,' she whispered. 'No.'

'Yes, my love, it is.' He raised her fingertips to his lips.

'Everything you have ever said to me has mattered. Everything, Richard. Every word, inflection, measure, quality. You could not draw breath without my sensing it. You understand what I mean, because you feel that way about me. Please do not understand me too well now, because I need to pretend. Do you not see that?'

'Oh, Cicely, what we could have been had I lived,' he said softly.

'Your voice strokes me. Just to *hear* you is to have your

arms around me again. I have only to think of you, in a quiet moment, and I am with you again.'

'Which shows you do not need to *see* me in front of you,' he reminded her a little dryly. 'And which also shows that you actually accept the truth about this. You *know* I am imagination. You know that what I did tonight is what you yourself have the power to do. You *know* it, Cicely. It simply comforts you more to conjure me and have *me* tell you. Show you.'

'Even while you punished me, you took me to paradise.'

'Tonight I could easily have sent you to Hell,' he reminded her.

'But what you did to me *before* sending me there was intolerably pleasurable.'

He smiled. 'It was intended to be, and it bound you completely because I decided to make you my prey. My sweetly vulnerable, unknowing, oh so sensuous prey. That is how it succeeds. And you, my love, will one day do this too. I know it, even if you do not.'

'If you were Mordred, Beelzebub and Judas fused into one, I would still love you. My heart can only be constant to you, Richard. I cannot be otherwise. You understand that constancy, that loyalty, that faithfulness.'

'Just who is seducing whom at this moment, my lady?' he asked softly. 'But remember, I am not real. You *invoke* me.'

'No.'

'Yes, sweetheart, and no matter how bitter a pill it is, you have to accept it.'

'But not yet. And certainly not now.'

Chapter Seven

CICELY WAITED FOR Sir Jon Welles in the garden again the next morning. She felt some trepidation. Before his offer of marriage she had been at ease with him, even though he was Henry's half-uncle, but now . . . now it was much more personal, and she was much more aware of herself than she had been before Richard had come to her in the night.

She chided herself. 'No, he did not come to you, Cicely. He is dead. Dead.' When she least wished for them, tears pricked her eyes again. She wanted to be in command of herself before Jon Welles, not beset by emotion.

Her mother had sent for her that morning, and for the first time ever, she, Cicely, had refused to comply. She did not relish being questioned and bullied to make her reveal that which she had no intention of revealing. There was nothing the Queen Dowager could do about this disobedience, but if Bess sent for her, Cicely knew she would have to go. As Henry's future queen, Bess had the power to summon her and expect compliance. Not that *she* would learn the truth either.

At last Sir Jon emerged from the palace. He wore brown, an unremarkable shade, but his tall, rather notable figure made much more of it. He had a certain attraction that she was very aware of, and when he smiled at her she felt herself relax. She could be at ease with him after all.

'My lady?' He bowed his head.

'Sir Jon.' She curtseyed. 'You are my Saint George, are you not?'

'See me as that if you wish.'

'I want you to know that your kindness to me far exceeds what I could ever hope. You have supported me from that very first moment at Sheriff Hutton. If I can ever offer support to you, I want you to know I will. Nothing will deter me.'

He gazed at her. 'Lady Cicely, you have a way of saying things, a way of looking that defies disbelief or distrust. I know you will do as you say, and I thank you for it.'

'It will be the least I can do, Sir Jon.'

'So, we will do well together?'

She smiled. 'Yes, I believe so. I accept your offer of marriage, and so do with both gratitude and gladness.'

He took her hand and drew it to his lips. 'Let neither of us ever feel regret. If, that is, we are permitted to wed.' He released her hand and leaned back against the wall.

'Permitted? What do you mean? There is surely no impediment. Do you refer to the contract with Ralph?'

'The contract?' He exhaled. 'Jesu, I had forgotten that.'

'You thought it was genuine, sir, even though it was not,' she reminded him.

'If you recall I believed the document to have been drawn up at Richard's command, and I believed that the seal was his, but I did *not* believe it was his signature. Richard was too educated and precise to write his name in such a scrawling fashion. No, someone else forged it, and did not know enough of his hand to make a good fist of it.'

'I think it will be found that Ralph himself was the culprit.'

Sir Jon nodded. 'It is as likely to be him as any.'

'So where is it now? Has it been disproved? Destroyed? Upheld?'

'I do not know, my lady. I suspect Willoughby took it; if so I have no idea what he did with it. I still do not think Henry knows of it.'

'I pray it has perished.'

He nodded. 'So do I, because if it reappears, and Henry decides to be obstructive, which is his wont, there is little chance of our being satisfactorily wed in time for your baby to be legitimate. We need the king's consent, and may have to marry before God and face Henry afterward. We'll need God's support. That is certain.' He smiled a little.

'I am aware of the great risk you take, Sir Jon.'

'I will weather it. But the Scrope contract is not the impediment to which I was referring. My actions yesterday, for the benefit of my sister at the window, mean that I have now been interrogated at length. Margaret has our full story, except that it is a lie, of course. She knows you are with child. Henry still does not, unless Margaret has chosen to tell him.'

'Does she wonder if you may have told me things you should not?'

His dark blue eyes swung to her. 'How perceptive you are.'

'Not perceptive, sir, because I know that Richard's friends and supporters will wonder if I did the same.'

'I had not thought of that.' He smiled. 'However, Margaret has faith in me, and after the initial shock accepts my assurance that I am loyal and that the child you carry is mine. She might wish we had waited before giving in to our apparently unstoppable passion, but she is pleased for me. My half-sister wants me to be higher in Henry's household. By marrying you, I will be. But it is actually Henry who presents the problem . . . the impediment.'

'Henry?' Her heart began to tighten unpleasantly.

'It seems he has expressed a wish to arrange a marriage for you.'

Her thoughts paused. 'A marriage? With whom?'

'He did not say. He said it to Margaret before I spoke to her and therefore, presumably, before knowing anything about us.' Sir Jon glanced at her. 'You clearly won his attention when you went to him.'

'But not in *that* way, surely? He asked me if I wished to make myself a more appealing marriage proposition, but I did not. Truly!'

He stretched out for her hand and squeezed her fingers, a natural and kindly action that encouraged her.

'Your nephew frightens me, Sir Jon.'

'He frightens everyone. Even himself, I fancy. He is everything of which he so falsely accuses Richard. Richard could sleep at night, at ease with his conscience. My nephew cannot. Henry Tudor is not . . . quite balanced.'

'What do you mean?'

'It is not important. I was saying that Richard could sleep, Henry finds it difficult.'

'I think you have a good opinion of my uncle?'

'Not as good as yours, I fancy. After all, he *did* have me arrested two or more years ago for plotting rebellion '

'Which you had. As I recall, you attempted to abduct my brothers from the Tower. What was your purpose? To be rid of them for Henry?'

'Good God, no! Henry was of no consequence then. This was right at the beginning, when Richard had just taken the throne that many still believed was actually his nephew's. Your brother was considered to be King Edward V, my lady.'

'But he was not, Sir Jon. The children of Edward IV are all illegitimate. And anyway, considering your crime, you were dealt with lightly. My uncle had you released.'

'True, albeit without what property I had at that time.' He smiled.

She smiled as well. 'So you have no reason to like him

particularly, any more than he had reason to like you. But even so, you do not seem overtly hostile to him.'

'I admired him. Albeit with great reluctance.'

'I felt no such reluctance, I can assure you. *No one* could think as well of him as me.'

'Ah, but he forgot himself entirely with you. Which I can understand.'

'We were speaking of his successor,' she reminded him.

'So we were. Henry will send for us both, my lady, and not together, so be aware. Be also aware that your so-called contract with Ralph Scrope *may* have come into his hands. And that Margaret may have told him you are with child. So, prepare yourself.'

Her heart plunged further. 'Can anyone be *prepared* to face him?'

'Probably not. Lady Cicely, I must pray Henry is convinced by his mother that I am a loyal uncle who did not give you anything to whisper to Richard. If he takes the other view, it will not go well for me.'

'Please do not say that.'

'You are concerned?'

She nodded. 'Of course I am. How could I not be?'

He considered her. 'You seem different today, my lady. Stronger, perhaps.'

'I am. I have been foolish, Sir Jon, indulging my grief, keeping it so close that it shadowed me completely. Now I am again the Cicely Plantagenet you first saw at Sheriff Hutton.'

'I am glad. I was sad to see you brought so very low. I understand, though, because your feelings for Richard are understandable.'

'He was irresistible to me.'

'And he should have known better.'

She smiled. 'You say you understand my love, Sir Jon, but I do not think you do. Have you ever experienced something so overpoweringly beautiful and brilliant that it transcends everything? Nothing else matters, just the two of you, and the love you share?'

He pursed his lips a little ruefully. 'No, I have not. Nothing even remotely close. Although I think I will before very much longer,' he added, but as an aside. Then he looked at her again. 'Did Richard know you carried his child?'

She almost submitted to her fantasy, but managed the truth. 'No, Sir Jon, he did not. There was very little he would not have done for me, so please do not despise him in any way for the plight I am in now. If he had lived, he would have protected me, done all he could for me. Never think ill of him.'

Sir Jon smiled. 'And you still commit the sin with every breath, do you not?' he said softly. 'You say his name and are in his arms again.'

She did not answer, for it was true.

'One thing I ask of you when—if—you become my wife. I will expect your fidelity. You may defy the words of Leviticus with Richard as often and to whatever degree you wish, but do not put horns on me with a living man. I have the right to at least ask this of you.'

'You have my word.' But she had to cross her fingers behind her back, because if Henry Tudor did indeed desire her, he would find a way of *making* her do as he wished.

'But is your word too easily given, Lady Cicely? Have you forgotten Richard's son, with whom you lay at Sheriff Hutton; I saw you creep from his door. Now you have learned he still lives and that he, Lincoln and Warwick will soon be released to appear at court. My nephew will *never* permit you to be close to Richard's son again. Besides which, I do not think that young man will appreciate the discrepancies in timing, do you? But even if he forgives you, the one way to ensure his execution is to be found with him. I trust you understand this? John of Gloucester is forbidden, and if you have affection for him, you will remember this. My lady, do not ever assuage your guilt by telling him you lay with his father. You will be doing it for yourself, without thought for him. If you wish to crush him beyond all redemption, that will be the way to do it. So spare him that. He has lost everything, although as yet he does not know how much, so the very least you can do for him is let him keep his memories and respect for Richard.'

Tears rushed to her eyes. 'Do not say such things, please.'

'I am sorry. I do not enjoy upsetting you.'

'I will never tell John the truth. Never. I could not be so cruel. You have my word.'

He nodded. 'Good. It is better by far to let him think you lay with me, that I somehow coerced you.'

'I will not let anyone think you *coerced* me, sir, not even John. You do not deserve it, because you have been all that is good to me. I will always respect you for it. I know I must confess *something* to him, and it will be that I went willingly to you.'

He smiled again. 'As you wish. In the meantime we must be convincing to others. That is why I took your hand yesterday. I saw my sister at that window and acted on impulse. It was an opportune moment and I became an opportunist. We *must* act as if we are lovers, or it will seem unlikely you surrendered to me willingly in Nottingham.'

'Are you sure I am worth the aggravation of this marriage? I am not a mere bride, I am so many other things too. And you will be taking another man's child as your "firstborn".'

'I know the problems I confront, Lady Cicely, especially the child, which I will claim as my own in a very public way.'

'Assuming the king permits us to wed, Sir Jon, I wonder if you will always be able to look upon me with kindness? I may stand in the way of your eventual true happiness. What if you meet a lady with whom you fall in love with as I did with Richard? What then?'

'Oh, I will weight you with stones and throw you into the River Witham. Nasty and tidal, and conveniently abutting my lands.'

She smiled. 'You may well wish to so dispose of me.'

'A wife who is so close to the throne must be properly cared for, my lady, and I will care for you. My word is given, and you may trust me to keep it. I have already said that I will make no demands of you. All I *will* ask is that in public at least, you behave as if you care for me just a little.'

'I do care for you, sir.'

He turned her to face him properly. 'Then I suggest you commence a demonstration right now, because some of my sister's ladies have come into the garden. It would be timely to give them something interesting to report to her. I trust you agree?'

'I do.'

'Be convincing, my lady,' he said softly.

'You wish for that?'

'I believe so.'

'Very well.' And so she kissed Richard, not Jon Welles. Oh, how she kissed him. It was so easy to do, because if she thought of Richard, she could do anything. *It will come so naturally to you that you will hardly know you do it . . .*

Sir Jon drew back, startled. 'Dear God above, he *did* teach you well!'

'It was what you wished, sir.'

'How very foolish of me.' But he suddenly put his hand to her chin, not unkindly, and made her look at him. 'I know what you just did, Cicely, and by doing it you proved to me that you can play me false, if never be false to Richard Plantagenet. I may have said, too lightly, that such pretence would be exciting to me, and to most men. It was said too carelessly, for while it did excite me, it also disturbed me. I find I am not a man to seek pleasure regardless of anything else. Please, do not ever do it to me again.'

She felt shame. 'Sir Jon, if I ever kiss you like that again, it will be because I mean it. You have my word. You know all there is to know of me. I have not hidden anything. You want me to behave—in public—as if we are lovers. I will. If you wish me to be restrained about it, I will. If you wish me to show passion, I will. But it will be at your behest. *Your* behest. I will never give you cause to wonder what I do or why I do it. I will be truthful with you. Always. Please know that.'

He nodded. 'I believe you.'

It was said so sincerely, and gently, that for a moment her new-found composure faltered. 'Hold me, please, because I am afraid.'

There was no hesitation. He did as she asked. 'I will keep you safe.'

'I will try to be a good wife to you, Sir Jon. Truly I will.'

He smiled. 'I think it time you called me Jon, do you not agree? And for me to call you Cicely? Under the circumstances, when we will be claiming an affection that is powerful enough to have led us to fall by the wayside, so to speak, then formality with names appears a little unlikely.'

She nodded, her face still pressed to him.

He held her close, imparting what comfort he could. 'Let me do all that is needed from now on. I will try to protect you, even to the point of endeavouring to dissuade my nephew from interrogating you, but I cannot promise success. If it is possible for us to marry in time for your child to be born legitimate, I will see that we are, even if it is without royal consent. Although, of course, the child will become a lowly Welles, and not a regal Plantagenet.' She felt his smile.

'Not so lowly, Jon. Not so lowly.'

'But if the false contract comes to light, and if Henry chooses to believe it, we will be between Scylla and Charybdis, Cicely, and whether I claim the child to be mine or not, he can see to it that you are disgraced.'

Chapter Eight

'Who was it, Cissy?' Bess stood angrily before her kneeling sister. 'John of Gloucester?'

'No. He does not even know I am with child. When he does, it will break his heart.'

'So, you *really* expect me to believe it was Sir Jon Welles, for whom you suddenly have this amazingly carnal attachment?'

'It is Sir Jon's child, Bess.'

'Conceived in Nottingham?'

'Yes.'

'So, you, who were closest of all to Richard, conducted an abandoned affair right under his nose, with a Lancastrian lord—Henry Tudor's *uncle*? No, Cissy. However, the name Scrope does occur to me.'

'Sweet God above, no! No! I have never even *kissed* Ralph Scrope, let alone lain with him! I would give him poison before I would give myself!'

Bess paused, and then nodded. 'Well, *that* was vehement enough to be the truth.' Her rosy velvet skirts dragged heavily as she began to pace to and fro.

A date for her marriage had still not been announced, because Henry did not intend to allow his reign to be seen to rely upon her Yorkist importance, yet it *did* so rely, for it was his promise to marry her that had won him the invaluable support of defecting Yorkists. He was determined to claim the throne by right of conquest and his own tenuous Lancastrian blood. He named Richard a usurper, even dating his sovereignty to a few days *before* Bosworth, thus making a traitor of anyone who supported or fought for the true and anointed King of England. Henry had no scruples, no honour and no ethics. He was an oppressor already, not simply in the making, and his coronation would take place at the end of this month of October. Just before Hallowtide.

So careful was he not to allow Bess any real political importance, that he had not even confirmed his intention to marry her. But he *was* aware that Cicely was with child, and it did not please him at all. Margaret had not informed him, but he learned quickly enough when Jon petitioned to be allowed to marry Cicely, and was obliged to indicate the need for some urgency.

Jon told her Henry's reaction had been one of such unutterable rage that he had hurled a candlestick across the room, damaging a costly tapestry. Henry told his bemused half-uncle there was to be no mention of such a match in public, nor any overt display of affection or attention. All dealings between Sir Jon Welles and the Lady Cicely Plantagenet were to appear strictly platonic. That had been the end of the matter, and Cicely was afraid that in spite of Jon's efforts to protect her, Henry Tudor would do all he could to prevent her union with his half-uncle.

John of Gloucester remained in the Tower, as did Jack and the boy Earl of Warwick. If they were still to be released, Henry gave no intimation of when. It was his pleasure to leave everyone wondering and waiting. About everything.

Cicely glanced at the window. It was very cold outside, the wind whipping wavelets on the Thames. A bleak day that suited England's bleak new king.

Bess demanded her attention. 'You have not answered me, Cissy.'

'Yes, I did deceive Richard. I love Sir Jon and lay willingly with him.'

'How can you be so *dishonest*?' Bess cried. 'You had never met Sir Jon before Sheriff Hutton. So your child cannot possibly be his.'

'You know nothing, Bess. I was not as you thought me.' Cicely knelt there, her hands clasped, her emerald-green gown spreading around her. The full gathers at the front still hid her condition, but sometimes, when she turned, it was unmistakable.

Bess came close. 'I cannot have ever really known you. I shared my secrets with you, but you did not share yours with me.'

'I had no secrets to share. Until Sir Jon.'

'Oh, you did, Cissy, you did. You lay with someone, and it was *not* Sir Jon Welles. You say it was not John of Gloucester, so who else was there to whom you were close enough? It *was* Jack, was it not?'

'No.'

Bess straightened again. 'Please tell me, Cissy, for the child will be my niece or nephew.'

'*Have a care, sweetheart, or you may find yourself tempted into the truth.*' Richard suddenly spoke so clearly in Cicely's head that she gasped.

'What is it, Cissy?'

'I . . . I cannot kneel like this, Bess. Please let me stand.'

'Yes, of course. Forgive my lack of thought.' Bess extended a hand and helped her to a chair near the fire, but lack of thought it had not been.

'Bess, I will never name anyone other than Sir Jon. He acknowledges the child and wishes to marry me. I am more than content to accept him.'

'No, Cissy, there is someone else in this, someone you

love very much indeed.'

'I loved Richard, but that does not mean he was my lover. You of all women should know that. My name will only be connected to Sir Jon's.'

'For your child's legitimacy. Not for love. And unless Henry gives his timely consent, you will not have the complete legality you seek.'

Cicely did not answer.

'In one way I thank God for your involvement with him, whatever that involvement actually is, because it precludes you from a much loftier match.'

'Loftier?'

'There has to be another reason why Henry will not marry me yet.'

Cicely's lips parted. 'Bess, there is no reason whatsoever for you to think such a thing! I have spoken to him twice now, once at Lambeth, and again since being here. That is all. He intends to marry *you*.'

Bess softened just a little. 'It is hard to forgive you for excluding me from this. I may not have been all I should have been to you when Richard was alive, but I *am* your sister and I *do* care about you.'

'And I care about you, Bess. Tell me of you now.' There, the subject was changed.

'Well, Henry has nothing to do with me. You still have the honour of being the sister he has spoken to the most.'

Cicely was startled. 'But—'

'If he leaves you wondering if you are to be married to Sir Jon, then he leaves me wondering about *my* situation as well.'

'Oh Bess, I do not know what to say. I mean, I knew he was delaying, but not that he virtually shuns you.'

'It is not virtual, but fact. Convince me I am having a very fortunate escape,' Bess replied wryly. 'He is hateful, Cissy, and I cannot bear the thought of him touching me.

I certainly do not want him . . . inside me.' She shuddered. 'You even know more of *that* than me, Cissy.'

'I know nothing whatsoever of having Henry Tudor inside me,' Cissy replied rather impishly, at last beginning to warm to Bess again.

Bess smiled. 'Well, at least I can be sure your baby is not *his*!'

'You certainly can.'

'What is it like, Cissy? Making love, I mean. Whoever you lay with, you clearly loved him. So what did you feel when you and he. . . ?'

'There are no words to describe how beautiful it was, Bess.'

'You are so fortunate. I do not think I will find it beautiful to have Henry's cold paws all over me.'

'Bess, do you recall the message I gave you from Lady Stanley?'

'That her beloved son is not without the capacity to love? I remember something of the sort.'

'Well, she is right. You are so lovely, and when you wish you are delightful company. You simply do not wish where he is concerned. Play up to him, smile, be warm, touch his hand, do *something*. Cold haughtiness simply will not do.'

'But *he* is so cold to me, Cissy.'

'Then do something about it.'

Bess gazed at her. 'As you would?'

'Yes. Bess, it would not be difficult to make him much more responsive.'

'Dear God, Cissy, you are younger than me, but know so very much more.'

'I am a whore. Does not our mother say so? She was always too cold with Father. Not that anyone could ever have kept *him* faithful anyway, I suppose.'

'She had what she wanted, Cissy. She was Queen of

England, and when it comes down to it, that really is *all* that matters. For me as well.'

Richard's words, Cicely thought. 'Do you really believe that, Bess?'

'Yes. It is all I want from Henry.'

'Do you not want to find happiness, Bess? Or do you think you will never find it again because of Richard?'

Bess was silent for a long moment. 'I do so wish I had shared at least one kiss with Richard, Cissy. One kiss. Was it so much to ask?'

'You were his niece, Bess.' Somehow Cicely managed to look steadily into her sister's eyes.

'So were you, but sometimes . . . sometimes I thought I saw something in his eyes when he looked at you.'

'Fondness. No more,' Cicely replied. 'He and I were friendly, Bess. We liked each other, we thought in similar ways. That was all.' I am fit only to be Sapphira, she thought.

'And you miss him as I do?'

Cicely felt the prick of salt and blinked it back. 'Yes, Bess, I do. So very much.' In that moment it was so hard not to touch her belly, not to cherish the beloved memory she had of Richard.

'So, you think I should apply *your* wiles on Henry?'

'Not *my* wiles, Bess, your own. Relax with him, smile, think shockingly carnal thoughts, lick him, stroke him, caress and kiss those masculine parts of him that matter so much.'

Bess gaped at her.

'If you do not even try,' Cicely continued, 'you will never forgive yourself, never know the joys you are missing.' Even with Henry, she thought, for there was something about him that suggested . . . she did not really know what it suggested, only that there was far more to him than appeared on the chill surface.

'You . . . you could do *that* with Henry?' Bess said
faintly.

Cicely thought of Henry Tudor, and smiled. 'Yes.
It would be quite exquisite to seduce him into giving
himself. You look so shocked, Bess. This is the way I
am made. I love it all. Do you not see? If you do nothing
now, a chance of contentment may be passed by and lost
forever.'

'Contentment with Henry Tudor? *Lick* him? Kiss his . . .
his *cock*? Never! I would be sick all over it.'

Cicely smiled sadly. 'Now *that* may indeed alienate him
once and for all.'

One of Bess's ladies hurried to them, and dropped a
deep curtsey to Bess. 'My lady, the king has sent a page.'

'Very well.'

'The king sends for the Lady Cicely, my lady.'

Cicely's spirits plummeted, and Bess's anger returned.
'You see, Cissy? Always it is you!'

Cicely was shown into Henry's presence. It was the same
room, and he even wore the same purple doublet, albeit
with the addition of ermine trimmings. He was nothing if
not determined to appear as royal as possible.

She sank to her knees again, her emerald skirts billow-
ing around her. How she prayed she was not destined to
be his mouse again, but she already sensed his whiskers
and claws.

He came closer. She could feel his cool eyes, recognize
his animosity. Although, *was* it animosity? She could not
tell, only that it was something she did not like.

'So, *cariad fach*, you have been keeping secrets from me.'

'Secrets, Your Grace?'

'Being so remiss as to give yourself to my uncle.'

'I love him, Your Grace.'

'Indeed? I doubt very much if my uncle sired your

95

child, my lady; indeed, I doubt very much that he was anywhere near Nottingham in June. Go into the heart of Richard's lair, risk all the gathering armies, capture and death in order to bed Richard's favourite niece? That does not sound like the uncle I know. He has too much sense, even if the niece in question is one as seductive as you, my lady. Unless, of course, you lured him to learn *my* secrets?'

'I wanted Sir Jon, Your Grace, not your secrets.'

'If that were true, my lady, the poor bastard did not stand a chance. I wonder he has any balls left. You would still have me believe you fucked him?'

'Yes, Your Grace.'

'Well, I do *not* believe it. So, whose child is it? John of Gloucester's? Do you carry Richard's grandchild?'

Oh, how good it would be to laugh in your face, Henry Tudor, she thought, but her eyes gave nothing away. 'No, Your Grace, the child is your uncle's, as he and I both affirm.'

Suddenly Henry's hand was beneath her chin, jerking her head up until she looked directly at him. 'I am displeased, my lady.'

'I do not understand, Your Grace! If I have angered you, I crave your forgiveness.' Jesu, how he hurt her. She could feel his fingernails digging into her skin, feel the brutality with which he forced her to keep looking at him. He caused tears she struggled to hide.

'Yes, you have angered me, more than I care to be. Who are you to think you can marry as you please? Who are you to get yourself with child and then dishonour my family? Dishonour my crown!'

His family? His *crown*? 'But Your Grace, it was while you were still in Brittany! Before Bosworth!' *Before you slew Richard and crushed my joy forever!*

'You think my being in Brittany makes a difference?'

He pulled her from her knees by increasing his grip on her chin.

She saw him through a shimmer of tears, trying to think how to extricate herself. Would charm really work this time? She raised a hand and placed it around his, as he held her. Then she tried to convey so very much from the contact, tried to make all the wonderful, warm feelings she could muster pass from her hand into his. 'Please, Your Grace,' she whispered, 'there was *never* any intention to dishonour you. You are my king, I am yours to do with as you choose.' Oh, the current of emotion she strove to transfer to him.

'But you are not mine, my lady. Not now. And I thought you such a virginal creature.'

She continued to look up at him, the truth beginning to creep in. He *had* entertained thoughts of her, and in the belief he would be the first! 'Please forgive me, for I cannot bear your anger. I would not displease you for the world.'

He hesitated, his grip softened, and so did the anger in his wayward eyes. He released her. 'Be seated, my lady, for I would not wish it to be said that I mistreated a woman who is with child.' He linked his fingers again, and tapped his lips. It was a strange habit, calculated to give him a few seconds to consider a response. 'I think you must forgive me, my lady. My conduct is reprehensible.'

The unexpected apology startled her, even though she knew it was design. He frightened her, because it was not possible to know how he would react to anything. Although he had certainly seemed to respond to her touch. Or had she simply imagined it? Or maybe he was letting her think it? She could not read him.

'My uncle pleads to marry you. You have him under your thumb, Lady Cicely.' He went to open a cupboard, and took out something small. A folded cloth? Something of the sort.

'Sir Jon is not a man to be under any woman's thumb, Your Grace.'

'Nor am I, my lady.'

She managed to meet his eyes. 'I do not presume to think so, Your Grace.'

He stood behind a table, thus separating himself from her. But he was not far away. Perhaps six feet. No more. 'Your ability to spellbind King Richard becomes more and more clear to me, Lady Cicely.'

'He was my most beloved uncle.'

'Ah, yes. You praise and support *him*, but you dare to question me.' He placed what he had taken from the cupboard on the table before him. He did it slowly, deliberately, and with every intention of inducing her to look.

She gazed at the familiar little embroidered kerchief she had given to Richard. It had been the first thing she had ever embroidered; its pattern was of the herb sweet cicely, and it was stained with blood. Richard's blood. He had it with him at Bosworth! She made herself glance away again, as if the kerchief was of no significance.

'Oh, neatly done, my lady.'

'Your Grace?'

'Neatly stitched,' he said, although she knew well it was not what he had meant. He referred to her self-control, not her needlework. She felt both hot and cold.

'It was found on the usurper's body, my lady. Next to where his heart should have been.'

She looked at him, her face devoid of emotion. Charm was now never further from her mind.

'Have a care, sweet Cicely, for you do not wish me to read you too well.'

'You are a cruel man, Henry Tudor.'

'Ah, I have touched a nerve at last. I feared you might elude me.'

'You have achieved the effect you wished, Your Grace.

I am more distressed than you can imagine, than you can have *hoped*. I make no secret that I gave the kerchief to my uncle, and if he had it next to his heart—his *great* heart—when he died, then I am glad. I trust it offered him comfort, as I would have done had I been there with him. You will *never* damn him in my eyes.'

Henry did not move. 'Such fervour, my lady? Such overpowering love? I cannot believe it was entirely platonic.'

She gazed him straight in the eyes. 'It was untarnished love, Your Grace.'

'Then God help Richard III if you *had* desired his body, for I vow you would have devoured his flesh and left only his bones.' He gave her a smile so thin it was almost emaciated. 'I believe he was on the point of taking a Spanish wife? Or was it Portuguese? One or the other.'

'No, Your Grace, he was not.'

'How sure you are. Did he discuss it with you?' He sat in the chair at the table, and sat back. His fluid movements trapped her attention.

'Yes. He had no intention of taking another wife, Your Grace. His advisers wished him to, but I know he had decided he would not.'

'His dynasty was to die with him?'

'Yes.'

He surveyed her. 'You are always so convincing where he is concerned, my lady.'

'Because I know—knew—him intimately. I was often with him and we were at ease together. As it should be between a good uncle and his loving niece. When you accuse him of wickedness, you practise deceit. He was not wicked.'

Henry raised an eyebrow. 'So, you and Richard Plantagenet were intimate? Your word, I believe.'

'Have you ever loved, Your Grace?' She did not care if

she went too far. Showing her the kerchief was callous and brutal, and if she had despised him before, she abhorred him now.

'What has that to do with it?' he enquired, rubbing his face wearily with both hands, to conceal the fact that his eye was wandering a little. When he took his hands away, the eye was steady.

'If you have never loved, Your Grace, you cannot understand its amazing power.'

He drew a long breath. 'You begin to displease me, my lady. I am amusing myself with you, and you are endeavouring to spoil it.'

'I am a toy?'

'Maybe. Why not? I have nothing better to do today.'

'Except rule your kingdom.'

He paused. 'I suppose I asked for that,' he murmured, momentarily revealing again that he had some humour, although it seemed very dark.

He spoke again. 'You really are prepared to provoke me, are you not, my lady? Everyone else quakes at my glance, and so do you, to a certain extent, but then, if I prick you just a little, there you are, defiant and presumptuous.'

'*I* am presumptuous?'

He clasped his hands behind his head, and pushed at a table leg with his foot. 'Now, what, exactly, did that remark imply? That I *presumed* to take Richard's throne?'

She looked at him.

'Ah, so I am right. The fact that I conquered him in battle makes no difference. *He* is still your king. A little nonsensical, do you not think? A dead king serves no purpose to anyone.'

'May I have the kerchief, Your Grace?' *Let us see how* you *enjoy being disconcerted!*

He looked at her for a moment. 'In due course.'

'And may I also have your uncle, Your Grace?'

He took his hands from behind his head and sat forward again, his attention fully upon her. 'Jesu, my lady, I do not think I have ever met anyone like you before. Crossing swords with you is remarkably stimulating. If you did not already carry my uncle's child, you may be sure that you would soon be carrying mine. There, you see, I can do a little confounding as well. I am *definitely* to marry the wrong princess, and although you do not think it now, Lady Cicely, you and I could have done well enough together.'

'You think so?'

'I know so. You could not keep me here like this if it were otherwise. Therein lies your attraction.' He treated her to another cadaverous smile, and rose. 'You may have my uncle, my lady, although not until I choose to give you my royal consent. All in due course, mm? I trust he understands exactly what he is taking on. If I find you a challenge, he will find you an overwhelming battle.'

'I will honour him as my husband, Your Grace.'

'Maybe.' His eyes were hooded. 'And you may have your memento, my lady, blood and all.' He pushed the kerchief across the table towards her.

'May I say something, Your Grace?'

'Please do, for I fancy it will be well worth the hearing.'

'I hate you.'

'Yes, I rather think you do, but oh, just imagine the joys of making you love me instead.'

'There is very little to love.'

'You might be surprised.'

'I think not.'

'So, you hate me, you are rude to me, and you hold me in just about every contempt it is possible to find?'

She looked through him. If the cap fits, Henry Tudor, wear it, she thought.

'You are not very respectful to your king, my lady.'

'How can you expect me to be?' she whispered. 'How can you possibly imagine I will ever think kindly of you?'

'Because I do not deserve so much malice, my lady. I am many things, and will, no doubt, be many more, but in this . . .' He paused. 'You should not be as you are, Lady Cicely, because if I get under your skin, you certainly get under mine. And I do not like it.'

'Have I your permission to go, Your Grace?'

Resentment flashed into his seascape eyes, and he got up. 'No, madam! You may not! I should have left you alone. What is it that provokes me so? I have only to look at you and I behave very much out of character. You will run rings around my uncle.'

She recoiled, for it was a phrase Richard had used. 'Please, do not say that,' she said quickly.

In a moment Henry had come to her, his hands on the arms of her chair, his face close. 'Why?' Cloves drifted over her. 'Why, my lady? What is it that affects you so suddenly?'

'I will not tell you, Henry Tudor, not *you*!'

'Why?'

'You have to ask?'

'Yes.'

'I cannot confide anything in you. You loathe me and I loathe you. You are my king now, and I will serve you as you should be served, but do not ever expect me to like you. You took away someone so dear to me that I feel I am only half alive now. I cannot forgive you. Do you understand? Please say you do.'

He gazed at her, and then took her hand and drew her to her feet. 'You actually shame me, Lady Cicely, and that is something I never expected to experience. I had none, and *you* hand it to me.' He stepped back, looking closely at her. 'Regarding your marriage to my uncle, my lady.

Unfortunately, there is a little … difficulty. When is the child expected?'

'March.'

'Oh, dear.' He was enjoying himself again, at her expense, and she found she was holding her breath. He was going to mention the contract with Ralph. What else could it be?

'There is undoubtedly some question about whether you and Ralph Scrope were ever handfast in the strict meaning of it. Hmm. Now *that* is a point. Might *he* be the father of your child?'

'You may be sure that Ralph Scrope has never been near enough to me.'

Henry nodded. 'I can believe that. However, the contract *is* rather awkward. Richard's signature seems a little dubious, to say the least, but he did order the document and append his seal. Therefore I cannot give my consent until an annulment is forthcoming. I trust you understand?'

'I understand how you rejoice in telling me this. You do know you condemn your own blood to illegitimacy?' She regretted the words immediately.

'Now *that* has a familiar ring to it, my lady. I seem to recall your precious Richard doing something of the sort.'

'And how it curdles your spleen now. I wish you well of your search for my inconvenient brothers.'

Henry scratched his nose. 'Hm, you make a good argument, my lady. Let me think now. Ah, yes. Suppose I promise to destroy all record of the Scrope marriage and give you my consent, will you then tell me your brothers' whereabouts? There, is that not a handsome offer?'

She gazed at him. 'I wish I could accept it, Your Grace, but I do not know where they are.'

'What a little fibling, my lady. Tut, tut.'

'Your Grace, I really do *not* know where they are.'

'When did you last see them?'

'I do not remember.'

'Oh, yes, you do, Cicely, you remember very well indeed. Was it at Sheriff Hutton?'

'No.' She looked him in the eyes again.

For a very long moment he returned her gaze. 'Oh, my lady, *what* a bedfellow you must be. If Merlin were here now, this Uther would definitely be turned into my uncle's Cornwall.'

'This Ygraine would throw herself from a turret.'

He laughed, and it was a genuine laugh. 'Dear God above, I am almost tempted to marry you no matter what. The thought of sparring with you every night appeals to me *so* much, you have no idea.'

'The thought of there never having been a Bosworth appeals to me, Your Grace.'

He nodded. 'I do not think I need telling of that, Lady Cicely. Nor should you need reminding that I do not *have* to tolerate your attitude.' His unsettling eyes looked deep into hers. 'Because I have permitted liberties today does not necessarily mean I will tolerate them in future.'

You, Henry Tudor, are the one to have taken liberties today, she thought, remembering he had used her roughly. No doubt her chin still bore the marks of his fingers,

'My offer will not be long upon the table, my lady. Your child's legitimacy for your brothers' last-known whereabouts. I think it a reasonable enough bargain, under the circumstances.'

'I do not know where my brothers are, Your Grace, only that my uncle would not have done away with them.'

'And you know your uncle *so* well.'

'Yes.'

'Would that be in the biblical sense?'

'No, Your Grace, it would not.'

'What a pity I do not believe you. About your brothers'

whereabouts, I mean, of course.'

'Of course.'

They looked at each other, the power and cunning of the House of Lancaster, and the proud defiance of the House of York. The House of Lancaster smiled. 'You are dismissed, Lady Cicely. No, one moment.' He turned, took the kerchief from the table, and pressed into her hand. 'It is yours, my lady. Now you may go.'

She curtseyed again, as deeply and reverently as even Henry Tudor could desire, although in her heart she insulted him. But he matched her by walking away as if he had already forgotten her. And so she rose and began to return to her own rooms.

She tried to walk sedately, but the kerchief burned in her hand. It was hardened with blood, and through it she felt as if she too died with Richard. At last she halted, to press it to her shaking lips.

'It did comfort me, Cicely.' Richard's voice was inside her. 'It was from you, and so it meant everything.'

'But it did not protect you,' she whispered, aloud, not within.

'It gave me strength, sweetheart.'

'Not enough. Not enough!'

'That was not your fault, it was mine.'

'Are you angry with me for speaking to Henry as I did today? Yes, of course you are. I did not heed your words. I defied him, was rude to him, and I defended you too much. Far too much. I simply could not—would not!— ignore the way he slighted you.'

'No, sweetheart, I am not angry. He left you very little choice. He sent for you with every intention of provoking another skirmish. He wanted you to defy him. And you did. He loves the novelty you present, he made that plain enough. And he felt so much through your hand. He actually felt it. Now do you understand about your gift? You actually have him, you *do know that? If you were to be his queen, he would have you making your vows with the bed waiting alongside.'*

She wanted to give him a cross look, but he was not there to bestow it upon.

'Cicely, if it were not for my libidinous attentions, you would be his queen. I told you how strong an attraction you present, and how you make men want you. Henry Tudor is living proof of it.'

'I would rather he were the dead proof,' she replied. 'I would trip a rejoicing measure around his tomb, provided he had one, because if the cost came from *my* purse, he would be chopped up to feed the pigs. Boars. White ones.'

'I do love you, sweetheart.' She heard the smile in his voice. And the farewell.

'No! Do not go . . . !' But she was alone. Again.

Chapter Nine

HENRY'S OFFER TO Cicely was retracted only a day later. She had not told him about her brothers, when he suspected she at least knew *something*, and so he did what he could to make certain her child was born illegitimate. The Scrope contract was examined for its legality, and Henry privately instructed that it be found debatable and the outcome delayed as long as possible.

His decision to give the document even this much credence had not only dismayed Cicely and Jon, but Margaret as well. She did not wish her half-brother's child to be born out of wedlock, and pleaded with Henry to reconsider. He told her he suspected Cicely to be lawfully married to Ralph Scrope and with child by him, and so full examination of the contract was necessary. In this spitefulness he was encouraged by his other uncle, Jasper Tudor, who did not like his nephew's interest in Cicely Plantagenet. In fact, Jasper did not like anything about Cicely, and the antipathy was more than returned. From the moment they met, there had been instant suspicion between them.

Ralph, naturally enough, took mean pleasure in asserting the contract to be true. In Henry Tudor he had found a master after his own heart. Not that Henry had confidence in him. This new king suspected everyone. He could not help himself. His ability to trust had long since been stolen away.

Now, because of Cicely, Henry was also vindictive for the sake of it. He really resented the effect Richard III's second niece had upon him. She treated him as no other dared, and her spirit made him want her. Henry's natural state was to be measured, secretive, spidery and menacing. These were cool attributes, and they had served him well. But Cicely had made him confront his other side, which was jealous, curdled, rancid, perverse and passionate, all uncontrolled aspects of himself. Such disagreeable insight angered him, and if there was anything he could do to obstruct her happiness, he intended to do it.

Nor did Jon Welles escape his nephew's ire. If Jon loved Cicely, and if he had not only enjoyed her body, but been the first to do so, Henry had no intention of allowing them an easy path to the marriage bed. He despatched Jon to Norwich on a trumped-up errand, with instructions that he was to return on the eve of the coronation at the end of the month. Thus the new king ensured there could be no further anticipations of conjugal bliss.

Henry lodged at the Tower in the days before his coronation, set for the thirtieth day of October. It was a tradition to stay at the Tower; Richard had done the same. The coronation ceremony at Westminster Abbey was to be on Sunday, and on Saturday a great procession progressed from the Tower to Westminster Hall. There was tremendous pageantry, with fanfares, banners, horsemen, display and grandeur. Henry was bare-headed, wearing a long gown of purple velvet trimmed with ermine and a rich ornamental belt over his shoulder and down to his waist. He was preceded by two mounted noblemen, the newly created Earl of Derby—formerly Lord Stanley—and the Earl of Nottingham. Behind Henry were two more mounted earls, Oxford and Jack, Earl of Lincoln, Cicely's cousin and Richard's intended heir. Henry's armed courser of state, trapped in cloth-of-gold, followed.

Jasper Tudor was prominent as well, a dark-complexioned, dark-eyed Welshman with an air of assurance born of having dissimulated successfully for so many years. He wore dark blue, his hair was black and so was his horse. He bore no resemblance whatsoever to his royal nephew, who was like his Beaufort mother.

Henry did not look regal, only unsmiling and cold. Richard, slightly built or not, had great presence, and it had been clear to all that he was royal. He had *never* been cold. Born to high station, he had been the favourite, most trusted brother of Edward IV, and regality came naturally to him. Henry Tudor had not been born to such very high station, yet in a day's time he would be the anointed king, with Richard's crown upon his undeserving head. Henry still needed to assert himself, and so had let it be known he was no longer to be addressed as merely Your Grace, but as Your Majesty.

He was so occupied that Saturday night of 29 October 1485 that he did not notice his half-uncle's failure to return from Norwich at the appointed time. He had no idea that Jon was already in London, and on the point of entering into a secret marriage with Cicely. It was a marriage for which a royal licence was required, and Henry had said that the union could *not* take place until such consent had been granted. He could change his mind, he could do anything he pleased, and both Jon and Cicely knew they gambled a great deal on his ultimate response. In the meantime, even though it was not strictly necessary to make their vows before a priest in a house of God, they felt it best so to do. And so the Almighty oversaw their nuptials, even if Henry Tudor did not.

The clandestine little ceremony took place at the church of St Anthony, on the northern corner of St Sithe's Lane and Budge Row, in the heart of the city. The church was close to Jon's residence at Pasmer's Place, which was in St Sithe's Lane, and was where the new Lady Welles would spend her first few hours with her husband. It could only be hours, because Jon preferred not to further disobey Henry by failing to go to him at all.

Nor did Henry know his mother was a witness to the nuptials, as was the Queen Dowager, who had not wished to be anywhere near but had been commanded by Bess. It no longer did to defy Henry VII's future queen, who adopted more airs and graces by the day. Bess herself was not present because Henry kept her under constant watch, being ever hopeful of discovering something to give him an irrefutable reason not to marry her. She gave him no such excuse, but his agents watched her nevertheless.

It was hazardous to flout Henry Tudor's express wish, but as Cicely entered the church she knew it was right to become Lady Welles. Her dark chestnut hair was completely hidden by a gable headdress, and she carried a posy of late roses. There had not been a hard frost as yet, and the bush grew in a sheltered place that caught the sun. They were white roses. She would not have carried anything else. Nor would Sir Jon Welles have expected otherwise. He was marrying a Yorkist bride. But then, so would his nephew be, of course. Eventually.

She wore a new grey velvet gown that was based unashamedly on the clothes Richard had worn that Christmas at Westminster; the clothes she had 'seen' him wearing again so very recently. His white boar emblem had been judiciously replaced with the white rose of York, but the boar *was* there, she had stitched it herself, and it was hidden in the rich folds. The knowledge that it was all for Richard made her feel guilty to wear it to wed Jon, but the gown had been made for Henry's coronation, as an insult to *him*.

Richard was with her in other ways too, because in the new white velvet purse on her belt she had his letter, the bloodied kerchief and a little sapphire ring once given to her by John of Gloucester. She had tried to leave them all behind for this particular occasion, but could not finally bring herself to the point. Sometimes, just to touch Richard's letter made her feel strong again. And if she needed hatred to sustain her against Henry, she had only to touch the bloodied kerchief. For fond memories of a more innocent past, of young sweet first love, she could slip John's little sapphire on to her finger.

But there was another ring in the purse tonight, heavy and gold, and fixed with a large, very rare turquoise. It had belonged to her father, and left to her. She intended to put it on Jon's finger as they made their vows. Maybe it was a very Yorkist ring, but Jon, even though Lancastrian, was her beloved lord.

The church was only lit by a few candles , the sounds of the city were dulled by the thick walls, and the air was very still as she walked towards Jon, who waited at the altar with the priest, Margaret and the Queen Dowager. Cicely's mother suspected her child to be John of Gloucester's, and did not think of Richard, which she certainly would have done had it been Bess.

Margaret smiled, convinced the bride's baby was that of Jon Welles. She would have preferred the vows to have come first, but all would be well. She was confident she could bring Henry around. She could *always* bring him around. Besides, Henry himself would soon have a Yorkist bride, and with luck that union would also prove immediately fruitful. Two marriages that joined the Houses of Lancaster and York into the House of Tudor. Three, if one counted Jasper and Katherine Woodville. Margaret had only ever imagined and plotted for one such coupling.

But then Cicely halted, because she felt Richard so very strongly that she knew he was here. Her glance was drawn directly to him as he leaned against a pillar, facing her, wearing the very clothes she had copied so diligently. She gazed at him again, unable to do anything else. The posy fell from her fingers, and her heart so turned within her that she felt she would die of it. The violence of her love swooped out of the shadows to engulf her again. 'Richard?' she whispered.

He smiled, put a finger to his lips and then wagged it with mock sternness. His rings shone in the candlelight, as did the gold embroidery on his clothes. Surely everyone could see him? But there was only silence, and then a small stir from those near the altar.

'Cicely?' Jon came to retrieve the posy. 'What is it? Is something wrong?'

Still she looked at Richard, who nodded towards Jon. *'You have a husband to wed, sweetheart.'*

Jon was anxious. 'Cicely, if you are unwell. . . ?'

She looked quickly into his dark blue eyes. 'It is nothing. A trick of the shadows. I thought I saw . . . the king.' She glanced back at the pillar, knowing Richard would not be there now. She was right.

'Do you have the sight?' Jon teased.

'No, of course not.'

'Neither do I, my lady, so when I look over there and see no one, I am content there *is* no one.'

'Forgive me.' She took the posy from him, and for a moment his fingers wrapped around hers.

'Cicely, if you wish to withdraw from this, you can. I will not hold you to anything. But once our vows are taken—'

'There will be no going back. I know that.' She stretched up to kiss his cheek.

The priest waited nervously. He was a Lincolnshire man with connections to the Welles family, and if Sir Jon wished him to perform this ceremony, to which the only impediment was the king's full consent, then perform it he would, before getting himself swiftly out of London.

Jon put an arm around Cicely's shoulder and conducted her to the altar, where they took their vows. In the eyes of God, if not the King of England, Cicely Plantagenet became Lady Welles. And she had a wedding band and God's witness to prove it. Jon now wore the turquoise, and she was so glad of it. When he embraced her afterwards, she was content with what they did. Now they could both only pray that Henry would stay his hand. But did he even possess the capacity to forgive?

Margaret and the Queen Dowager, who loathed each other, returned to the Tower afterwards, where they were supposed to be at the banquet all along, while Jon and his new wife went to nearby Pasmer's Place. The house nestled among the clustering rooftops of the old city, above the Thames and below St. Paul's Cathedral, the tall spire of which rose impressively from the top of Ludgate Hill. It was a noble residence, rambling, with latticed casements and gabled roofs tiled with Lincolnshire stone, and it was partly gathered around a courtyard, with an access from St. Sithe's Lane. Finely furnished and decorated, it was envied by many a higher ranked lord and was the property of one Master John Pasmer, a member of the Company of Skinners and the Calais Staple. Pasmer was a fat jovial man and very successful merchant and skinner, who had once lived in the house, which was how it got its name, but now he owned a number of houses throughout London. Pasmer's Place was the finest.

The bridal couple dined alone, modestly, for there were only the two of them. They were not at ease together. What Jon's thoughts were, Cicely could not know. He gave no hint of them, certainly not whether or not he still intended to let her remain his wife in name only. If he wished to consummate the marriage, there was not a great deal she could do to stop him. She did not even know if she would *want* to stop him.

He intended to go to the Tower after they had eaten, but time passed and he was still there. At last she felt awkward. Did he wish to lie with her or not? 'Should I retire, Jon? What do you wish of me?'

'Retire, by all means. I will speak to you before I leave.'

Mary Kymbe attended her as she undressed in the bed-chamber that was to be hers from now on. The bed seemed to dominate the room as the maid brushed Cicely's long hair loose again. Then she heard Jon's tread at the door, and as he came in, he had to bow his head beneath the low lintel. He indicated to Mary to leave, and then closed the door. 'Well, my Lady Welles, here we are,' he said, leaning a shoulder against one of the bedposts and looking at her as she sat in front of the fire. He toyed with the turquoise.

'Yes. Here we are.' She rose. 'What do you think the king will do when he learns?

'A little late to wonder that, methinks. He is not endowed with a great deal of human kindness. And he seems pesky determined to be obstructive. I have no real idea why.'

It was said with the sort of faint smile that animated her buried guilt until it rose unstoppably through her, like new vigour into a dying man. She had been *wrong* to marry him, because she would now blight his life! Henry would never forgive it. She *had* to tell Jon everything about Henry. It was inconsiderate and insulting to do anything less.

'It is my fault that Henry is so set against us.' The words were uttered with such a heaviness of regret that they even seemed to weigh her tongue.

'Why?'

'I have . . . interested him far too much.'

Jon straightened. 'What you are saying?'

'The reason he reacted as he did, throwing the

candlestick, is that until he learned I was with child, he believed I was a virgin, and he told me he wanted me for himself.'

Jon gazed at her. 'And you did not think to inform me of this?'

'I . . . I had not really thought properly. Forgive me, Jon. And I fear there is more . . .'

He groaned. 'What *else* have you got as my wedding gift? Henry's intention to have me slowly hung, drawn and quartered?'

'No. He said he would discard the contract with Ralph if I would tell him where my brothers were. Jon, I do not know where they are, except . . .'

'Except. . . ?'

'That they escaped to Burgundy.'

Jon gazed at her, his lips pursed. 'How good of you to tell me. Do they not say better late than never?'

'Please do not be angry. I should have told you sooner, I know that. They were at Sheriff Hutton.'

'I found no trace of them. Everyone else, yes, but certainly not them.'

She hardly dared meet his eyes. 'That is because I had all evidence removed, just before you arrived.'

He regarded her. 'I see. You *were* an industrious little lady. And then you confronted me in the courtyard as if *I* were the Devil Incarnate?'

'Yes. I am sorry. But only sorry because of you, not because I confounded Henry. Or that dreadful Willoughby creature. My brothers were put on a ship for Burgundy, but that is all I know. Truly. There has been no word of them since. That is the truth, Jon. *All* that I know.'

'But can I believe you even at this juncture? Or are you misdirecting me yet again?'

'You can believe me. It *is* all I know of my brothers, and it is not sufficient to induce Henry to destroy the Scrope contract. And even if I *do* tell him, he will still believe I hide more.'

'At least he would be certain Richard had not had them killed in the Tower. It would warn him of the real danger of legitimizing the children of Edward IV.' Jon drew a heavy breath. 'Better you had taken his offer, Cicely.'

'And *volunteer* information of use to him? I am the wrong House to do that!'

'Cicely, you have just told *me*.'

'I trust you.'

'I am a Lancastrian and Henry's blood uncle, sweetheart, nor should you forget it.'

'But you honour my Yorkist secrets, Jon Welles,' she replied.

'So I do, God help me.'

She gazed at him. 'I *did* tell him Richard would not have put my brothers to death, I simply did not say it as if it were an absolutely undeniable fact. Forgive me, Jon, because I have let you down so much.'

'Well, I would have preferred not to know about your brothers, if for no other reason than I now feel a complete fool.'

'You are not, Jon. How were you to know they had been there? You were sent specifically for Bess, me, Jack, John and Warwick. On top of which, if I recall correctly, it was Willoughby's responsibility. You, as Henry's half-uncle, had been sent to extend his greetings to us, especially Bess.'

'Which duty I exceeded because of Willoughby's conduct. None of this makes me feel any better. But it *would* have been wiser for me to know the nature of Henry's personal interest in you.'

'Would it have changed your mind about marrying me?'

He gave a slight smile. 'No. I would not turn from you

simply because my half-nephew wishes to bed you. He cannot marry you, and he knows it. He is angry about it, yes, and I can now hazard a fairly accurate guess as to the extent of that anger when he discovers we have gone ahead without his approval. However, if he is too venomous towards us, he will arouse talk. He knows that as well as anyone else. He may boast of being able to do as he wishes, but he cannot *always* have his way. His arse is not yet firmly enough upon the throne for that. I believe he may well give his belated consent, and we will stay married.'

'That relies on the good nature we know he does not have.'

He searched her eyes. 'Why have you told me this now?'

'Because of the way you smiled at me.'

'The way I . . . *smiled* at you?' He ran a hand through his hair. 'Please tell me there is logic in here somewhere?'

She gave him a rueful little smile of her own. 'You have a good smile, Jon Welles, and it forced me to confront what I was doing to you.' She went closer, but not to touch him. 'There is still time for you to step away from this marriage.'

'And why would I wish to do that?'

'Because I am your burden. I remember all that was said between us in the palace gardens, but now, when it comes to the actual fact of what I bring to you, I cannot go on. The information about my brothers, even though so small, is something Henry would dearly like to know. It will prove that you are loyal. You will . . . placate him.'

'*Placate* him?' Jon's tone was suddenly very cool.

'You have crossed him because of me, and I have made my vows with you today without warning you of the extent of his interest. I am sorry, Jon, sorry to have ever entered your life and caused you such trouble. Please forgive me.'

He was silent for a long moment, and then reproached her. 'Cicely, you do me a grave disservice by suggesting I go to Henry to wheedle my way cravenly into his good books. I will not set you aside, for *any* reason, other than that *you* wish it. Certainly not in order to save my own hide. Is that clear?'

'Yes,' she whispered, hanging her head.

'I am more concerned now to know exactly how far things have gone with Henry. Has he touched you?'

She hesitated.

'Well? Has he?'

'Not as you may think. He pulled me to my feet by the chin. It hurt. But then he apologized.'

Jon had stiffened, and his eyes became like flint. 'He pulled you to your feet by the *chin*?' he breathed.

'Yes. Oh, make of him what you will, Jon, for it is impossible to know what he is thinking.' Or where he is looking, she thought, remembering the cast in Henry's eye.

'King or not, nephew or not, if he were here now I would rip his heart from his body!' Jon looked at her again. 'What did you actually say or do that made him so hot to have you? Beyond merely exist, I mean.'

'He wanted me to stand up to him, he taunted me, and so I did as he wished. I told him what I thought of him, I criticized and did not always show him the respect he warrants. Whatever I may have felt, he is still the king, but I told him I hated him for it, that I wished Richard were still here, that—'

'For pity's sake, Cicely, I have heard enough. I am amazed your silly head is still attached to your equally silly neck. No one speaks to Henry Tudor like that.'

'He goaded me to it, he really wanted me to confront him like that. It is the only reason he sent for me. To amuse himself.'

'He said that?'

'About amusing himself with me? Yes.'

Jon gazed at her for a long moment. 'I can well imagine you aroused more than just his interest, Cicely, because when you defend Richard and give someone a piece of your mind, you do it with such style, conviction, brilliant contempt and fervour that most men could bed you there and then. You stir men's senses and desires, Cicely. *I* wanted you at Sheriff Hutton, so I should know. Well, small wonder Henry has an itch for you rather than Bess. Fire between the coverlets, not ice.'

She bit her lip. 'I have not done any of this very well, have I?'

'No.'

She lowered her eyes, because of tears.

'Oh, God above, Cicely, do not cry. I cannot bear it when women cry.' He came close enough to raise her chin and make her look at him. 'I am your husband now, and will do all I can to preserve you, your child and my good self. I will begin tonight by telling him of the marriage. I was going to wait until after the coronation, but I think it best to tell him when he has so much else on his mind. He is better told disagreeable things when he is distracted by something more important.'

'Please do not let him know I've told you that he—'

'That he has a lustful itch for my wife? Oh, that will be the very first thing on my lips! Be sensible, Cicely. Tell him *that*?'

She flushed.

'Well you might go pink, madam, because you certainly have enough to go pink about. I will only tell him we are married. He will send for you, of that there can be little doubt. And he will treat you to a most disagreeable and demeaning interview, but he has no real option except to marry your sister.'

119

'I am sorry, Jon,' she said again, biting her lip as she struggled not to cry.

'I really do have my hands full with you, do I not? It seemed so simple when I first offered you this marriage, but suddenly I am in the lion's den. Is there anything else you have omitted to tell me?'

'Not that I can think of now.'

'Then please do not think too hard. What did you believe you saw in the church?' he asked suddenly. 'You said the king, but which king? Ah, the light that passes so swiftly through your eyes tells me all I need to know. You thought you saw Richard.'

'Yes, but I do know I could not have seen him,' she replied quietly.

'I trust so. Promise me one thing, Cicely. If this child is a boy, please do not ask me to let him be named Richard. I will not spend my life with an heir—son or daughter— who not only belongs to him and will most likely *look* like him but, if a boy, carries his name as well.'

Oh, the echoes. 'You must choose the name, Jon, for the child will be born and brought up as yours. *Your* son or daughter.'

He nodded. 'If that can be achieved, I will be glad of it.'

'If? What do you mean?' She felt a sudden sense of foreboding.

'I mean nothing, Cicely. Do not look for things that are not there.'

'Will you stay with me tonight? Here, in this room?"

'So that you can *apologize* to me? I think my answer to that is no, Cicely.'

'Not to apologize, Jon, but because I want to show you how grateful I—'

'So now it is gratitude? Sweet God, Cicely, you really do know how to offend me.'

She was appalled. 'I did not mean it in that way.'

'Yes, Cicely, actually I think you did. Oh, not deliberately, just thoughtlessly. I have kept my side of this bargain, and will continue to do so. And, as originally made clear, I see no reason for us to pretend in private, but I will still expect you to be faithful.'

'If that is your wish.'

'It is. And let us be honest, Cicely, even if I *did* take you into my bed, there would be one too many there. Do you not agree? Richard Plantagenet would be present. In spirit, of course, but present all the same. He has an unfair advantage over a mere mortal like me. How can *anyone* compare with him, mm? Young, handsome, tragic, brave, betrayed, bereaved, beloved, cultured, powerful, just, loyal, intelligent, sensitive, unbelievably engaging, gifted and endowed with more attraction in his big toe than I have in my entire body. Jesu, what a list. And he could fight like a warrior, converse like an archangel, negotiate like a king, and dance like a courtier. Not even the imperfection of his body detracted from his incredible appeal. He did not only wear a crown, he wore a damned halo! Dear God, he is an impossible figure to contend with.'

'He was not a saint, Jon. He lay with me.'

'Ah, Leviticus again, Chapter Eighteen. If you were my niece, *I* would lie with you as well.'

'You are my husband, sir, and I would welcome you to lie with me, but you do not wish to.'

The reply wrought a change in him, for he went to the door suddenly. 'I cannot juggle words with you any longer. I have to go now. Good night, Cicely.' Inclining his head, he left.

Chapter Ten

CICELY DID NOT attend the coronation. She was unwell, and it was no sham. From the moment of awakening she felt sick, and *was* sick. It was quite impossible to attend the great service in Westminster Abbey because she was obliged to remain in bed at Pasmer's Place. Thus she also missed the state banquet at Westminster Hall. When she awakened on the morning after the coronation, she was feeling much better. At least she did once a less serious bout of sickness had subsided.

She had not seen Jon since he left Pasmer's Place, although he had sent a brief note that Henry had been informed of their marriage. The information had been received without a single word, except Jon's dismissal from the royal presence. Other than that, Jon had been kept close with extra duties that denied him the chance to return to his house and new wife. The last part of the message urged her, if she was able, to attend the eve of All Hallows merrymaking in the palace at the Tower.

'Be there if you can, my lady, for it will reflect badly upon you if you are not. There is not to be a disguising, so dress only for court, that is all. Whatever you do, you have my support. Jon.'

When the evening came she felt able to go as Jon wished, and so she dressed in her coronation gown and headdress, beneath a fur-lined cloak and hood, and was conveyed by river to the Tower, where everything was alight with torches and banners. She did not want to accept that Henry Tudor was now as anointed a king as Richard had been, or that the pageant and ceremony had been as magnificent. Whatever he did, however much he spent upon his own glorification, he could *never* be a king—or man—in Richard's mould.

She was received with all due respect at the Tower. A lot of noise greeted her in the hall: minstrels, fools, tumblers and dancing. It was a sumptuous scene, with ample food and drink, and coloured banners, hangings and candles. There were no masks and disguises as was usual on the eve of All Hallows, but it still appeared that the whole of the nobility was present, and there seemed not an inch of space to be had. A lull descended as she was announced, not as Lady Welles but as Lady Cicely Plantagenet. Henry had clearly *not* accepted the marriage.

Her arrival was a matter of interest because it had proved impossible to suppress the whispers about the king's half-uncle and future sister-in-law. Margaret's ladies had witnessed so much in the garden at Westminster Palace, and every court loved a salacious story.

Henry, set-faced, was seated on a throne at the centre of the dais, aloof from those near him. The long trestle table was garlanded and white-clothed, and there were silver-gilt vessels, beautiful goblets and golden cutlery, choice foods and drinks, and beautifully arranged sprays of evergreens. A table fit for a king. He wore a long robe of royal blue velvet, trimmed with sumptuous ermine, and beneath it a doublet of cloth-of-gold. The livery collar across his shoulders was one she had seen Richard wear. It was rich with diamonds, pearls and sapphires, and to see it upon Henry Tudor was a grievous shame. It was even more of a shame to see Richard's gold circlet around his pale forehead.

Margaret, still black-clad and, in her way, as menacing as her son, sat on his right, her chair almost as grand as his. To her right was Jasper Tudor, swarthy in the darkest of crimsons, and clearly not particularly comfortable or interested in the revelry. He looked, Cicely thought, as if he were chewing a wasp.

To Henry's left sat Bess, on a lesser chair than her future mother-in-law. She would not warrant a throne until she was queen. She was very beautiful in oyster velvet and russet fur, but her face was as set as his.

The Queen Dowager was at one end of the dais, gazing straight ahead as if she were not really there at all. Jon was opposite her, and by his expressionless face he—like Jasper—wished he was somewhere else. Anywhere else. He wore pine-green, the sleeves of his doublet slashed with grey, and as soon as she was announced he rose to go to her. All eyes watched, and then glanced at the dais, where Henry's face was like thunder. Bess was ruddy with resentment as she watched the sister who so effortlessly—if unwillingly—commanded attention.

Jon bowed over Cicely's hand, and she sank into a curtsey. He smiled. 'I am glad you were able to come.'

'Even if I am apparently not recognized as your wife after all?'

'Even if.'

'I am here for *you*, Jon. No one else. And I can tell by the interest we cause that our secret is not as secret as Henry would wish. Well, I wear your ring and we exchanged vows before God, so perhaps you should kiss me? Let us give the world proof of our affection.'

He tilted her chin and kissed her on the lips. Chatter broke out because Henry suddenly rose from his throne and left the banquet. He did not speak to Bess or to anyone else, but walked out, leaving confusion behind him. Bess's bitterly accusing gaze was riveted to her sister.

Margaret sat forward to look at Jasper, who shrugged angrily and then hurled some meat to the congregated hounds that had long since gained the measure of his generosity. The Queen Dowager gazed around as if nothing had happened.

Jon presented his arm to Cicely. 'Come, Lady Welles— for that is what you are—we cannot allow the king to concern us.' He smiled again, and they proceeded to the dais, where she took the seat next to him. But hardly was she seated when a royal page came to her.

'The king requests your presence, Lady Welles.'

Her heart plummeted. 'Jon?'

'Go, sweetheart. There is nothing else for it.'

Slowly she rose again, aware that almost all eyes watched her follow the page through the very archway that Henry had used only moments earlier. The festivities tried to recommence, but everyone knew—or thought they knew—that at the very least she was about to be severely reprimanded for having married without the king's consent.

She was conducted deep into the Tower, away from the hall, away from the comfortable apartments, and eventually up winding, draughty steps to a narrow doorway that was lit by a wall torch. She could hear the croak of a raven somewhere. As the page opened the door, there was something about the poorly lit room beyond that made her loath to enter. Superstition and dread seemed to lie in wait, and she was conscious of the drag of her gown upon the rough boards as, unwillingly, she went in. The fact of it being the eve of All Hallows seemed fitting, for dark spirits really did seem to be all around her.

A horn lantern glowed on a shelf, revealing a table and several chairs, but nothing else. And yet she felt so much in that room. Something terrible had happened here, and its memory was in the stonework. She shivered, but it was not only the cold that made her wrap her arms around her belly, because the very air seemed menacing.

The page withdrew and closed the door. She almost expected to hear the key turn, but it did not. She glanced around, sensing the ghosts around her. Whose ghosts she did not know, but they were sad. If there was one ghost she wished to see now, it was Richard, but she strove not to think of him. Not now, for she needed to keep her wits and be ready for whatever Henry Tudor had in mind.

The door opened and he entered. His steps were quick and angry, and he closed the door behind him. 'Well, now, my lady,' he said, removing his circlet and placing it upon the table, almost as if he did not intend to confront her as the king. His rich clothes were at odds with the surroundings as he turned to face her. 'What have you to say to me?'

'That I am here at Your Majesty's summons.' She had gone to her knees the moment he entered, and kept her eyes fixed to the floor.

'You did not attend the coronation.'

'I was indisposed, Your Majesty. I crave your pardon.'

'Look at me.'

She obeyed, reluctantly.

He considered her for a long moment, 'Yes, you do not appear well. Perhaps I forget my gallantry.' He came to put a hand firmly under her elbow and help her to rise. No fingers gripping her chin this time. 'Please be seated, my lady.' He indicated one of the chairs, and the emerald on his finger caught a little light from the horn lantern.

As she obeyed, he suddenly asked, 'Do you sense your brothers here, my lady?'

'No, Your Majesty.' She knew her brothers had never been in this room, because Richard would *not* have kept them in such a place. He told her they had accommodation to fit their station as his nephews, and she believed him.

Henry studied her. 'What happened to them, my lady?'

'I do not know, Your Majesty. I only know that my uncle would not—did not—have them murdered.'

'Did not? So, you do know something.'

His eyes were both very focused upon her. There was no cast now, unless a die had fallen that she had not heard. She did not want Jon to be in possession of any information that this king did not also know, and so she protected her husband. 'I know they were sent to Burgundy. I do not know if they arrived there, their present whereabouts, their condition, or even if their ship made land safely anywhere. I really do not know more, save you will not find their bodies here.'

'Why did you not tell me this before? I asked you plainly enough. *Paid a'm gwythio'n rhy bell!*' Anger quivered through the Welsh words.

'I do not understand.'

'Do not push me too far! An explanation, *if* you please.'

How could she answer? By using her talents? What would Richard advise her now? A draught passed through the room, making cobwebs shiver, but it was only the night breeze through the slit window high in the wall.

'I await your answer, madam.'

'I did not tell you exactly, but I did say Richard would not have killed them.'

'And I am supposed to accept such a very fine distinction between what is and what is not? That is not good enough, my lady. You have already greatly offended me with your marriage and by being with child *before* the event, and now you think to continue offending me?'

'No. It is because I do not wish to continue my offence that I have told you now.'

He moved closer, and once again leaned down to put his hands on either arm of her chair. 'And you expect my gratitude?'

'Please do not do this, Your Majesty.'

'Do what?'

'Amuse yourself with me again.'

'Well, there is precious little chance of *that* now, is there not? You have become my . . . aunt? Ah, but such a close tie is not always an obstacle to a Plantagenet, is it? At least, not in the House of York.' He smiled his scrawny smile. 'Well, you are my aunt and you are not, for there was no royal licence, was there? A small oversight, do you not agree? I am now able to make considerable difficulty.'

You would anyway, she thought, but she remained silent, her eyes lowered, her hands clasped before her.

He straightened. 'Oh, dear, you *are* proving difficult tonight. I want your sparks, my lady. It has been a very long day, I am feeling excellent, and now you spoil it.'

'I am sorry, Your Majesty.'

Another of his rings caught the lantern light. Richard's ring, that large, blood-red ruby. 'Are you still afraid of me, my lady?'

'Yes, Your Majesty.'

'There is no need.'

She looked up quickly. No need? His eyes were hooded, his mouth was cruel, and he dangled her as if upon the most delicate of threads. Of *course* she needed to be afraid of him.

'Ah, the mutinous gleam in your eyes. You are still in there, my lady. I can see you.'

'You are unfair to treat me like this.'

'Of course, because that is my prerogative. I am your king, my lady. Oh, and your nephew, and soon to be your brother-in-law, I believe. Well, *perhaps* I am your nephew.' He bent to cup her chin in his palm, gently enough. 'Do you love him?'

'Sir Jon? Yes, I do.'

'You should not have married him without my consent.'

'You gave your consent, Your Majesty,' she reminded him, her guard slipping enough to answer him back.

'I said you could not marry until your contract with Scrope had been annulled.'

'There is nothing to be annulled, because I was never married to Ralph Scrope. Please believe me.'

'I do not *want* to believe you, Cicely. You have displeased me so much that I cannot let it pass. You do know how much you have displeased me?'

'I . . . believe so, yes.'

'Then tell me.'

He took his hand away and stood before her, a thumb looped over his rich belt, the other hand loose, fingers flexing, and she was suddenly aware of him in a very different way. Aware of his power, multiplicity, elegance . . . and masculinity. He was not only a king and her enemy, he was also a man of peculiar attraction, and the realization caught her unawares.

'Tell me,' he repeated.

'Your Grace—I mean, Your Majesty, I can only deduce things from what you have said.' She gazed at him, able at last to bring tears. Such pretty tears, they melted in her eyes and appealed to the nobility in him. At least, they would have done, had he possessed any. Not yet, at least.

'I wanted you to myself, Cicely, and one day I *will* have you, but your virginity is denied me forever. Oh, how sweet a thought to have been the first man to lie with you.'

She gazed at him, shocked by his forthrightness, but at the same time she knew she ought to be more offended. There was a change within her, and it was not at all what she wanted. He was at once arresting and terrifying, with an edge that suggested a fine balance under threat. 'Why do you say these things, Your Majesty? Nothing can be changed. I have never intended to anger you.' She used her gift as best she could, seeming gentle, concerned, tender-minded . . . everything that might help to soothe him. And herself.

'I say them because you affect me too much, my lady,' he answered quietly.

'Do you not fear I will use my attraction to my own advantage?'

'Dear God, lady, that is what I *hope* you will try! *Diawl!*' He almost laughed. 'The very thought has me standing! So I say again, my lady, I *will* have you.'

'What does "Dee-owl" mean?'

'A name for the Devil. To whom you will surely drive me.'

She tried to collect her thoughts. 'Please tell me you do not mean to harm my husband in order to have me.'

'Harm him? Jesu, Cicely, I would have my mother upon me like a ravening wolf. And my uncle Siasbar, who disapproves of you anyway.'

Jasper's name in Welsh lilted on his tongue. She was to learn that Welsh often came to him when he was less than settled.

'No, Cicely, I do not think I will hurt Jon, for in spite of his crime, I do actually hold him in affection. Whereas you—'

'Have done nothing,' she insisted anxiously. 'I have done nothing to you, Your Majesty. You choose to toy with me, that is all.'

'No, Cicely, it is not all. You came to me uninvited, you proceeded to argue with me and tell me what you thought of me. You said you would never forgive me for Richard's death, and that you would always hate me. And you did it with such—' He sought the word. 'You did it with such a flourish that you cannot possibly be surprised by the effect you had. You are not a silly girl; if you were I would not bother. You are different, Cicely. So different. Only sixteen, but with all the powers and wits of a mature woman. You can probably prevail upon any living man, especially kings. Is that what you did to Richard? Drive him to distraction with his need for you?'

'No! *Please*, I beg you, do not keep implying that Richard and I—'

'Were lovers? Well, were you? You always deny it, and I *never* believe you. I vow your she-cat defence of him is such that I just *know* he had you.'

'We loved each other, but we were not lovers.'

He pretended to scratch his eyebrow. 'You cannot go around as you do, my lady. You cannot treat me the same way as you do other men. I will not have it. And now you have married my uncle, against my wishes, *and* you carry "his" child. Had you set out to antagonize me, you could not have done it more effectively.'

'I was with child before I met you, Your Majesty. What do you *want* of me? If I have offended, it was not done deliberately, I swear. If you believe I have insulted you, or done anything with intent to cross you, I crave your pardon. I did not wish to do anything of the sort. Please believe me.' Again she summoned the tears, and used them as never before. They had to save her from this new scrape with him.

He gazed at her, and then gave something of a smile. 'I really do not know what to do about you, Cicely. You are indeed a novelty. You and my uncle have tried me sorely. I will therefore not recognize your marriage until such time as your pre-contract with Scrope is annulled.'

'What has never existed cannot be annulled, Your Majesty.'

'True, but that is immaterial when I am determined to thwart you. I can still see to it that, marriage or not, your child is not legitimate.' He waited, and then sighed disappointedly. 'Have I not just handed you, on a platter, a perfect opportunity for you to lash me with your tongue?

I laid myself open, and you did not see it. At least, you pretended not to.'

'What would you do if I did indeed lash you with my tongue?'

'I would enjoy it, that is what. You are denying me the pleasure of your spirit, and I am very disheartened by it.'

'I am afraid to do anything now, Your Majesty. I think too much of my husband, and—'

'Yes?'

'I actually think too much of you as well.' *Come, charm, rescue me.*

'Too much of *me*? When did that happen? Was I looking the other way?'

In spite of herself she had to smile. 'No, Your Majesty. You are my king.'

'Whether you like it or not?'

'Yes.'

'What can I do to make you think less of Richard?'

'Why would you wish to?'

'Because he has your regard and I do not.'

She gazed at him. 'You do not want my regard, Your Majesty. You do not really even like me. I annoy you, and you are annoyed that you are annoyed. You are certainly annoyed that you want me in your bed.'

'That is your considered opinion?'

'I am damned whatever I answer.' She met his eyes again. 'You do frighten me. I do not know what you are thinking or what you will do. One moment you are . . . almost approachable . . . the next you are cold and threatening. How can I *possibly* know you?'

'You are an enigma too, Cicely, and if I could turn time back and choose again, *you* would be my queen. No, do not look at me in that way. I am not an easy man, I know that well enough, but you could have had me eating from your palm.'

'Your Majesty—'

'Hear me out. After all, I am now the anointed king, so you must humour me.'

She tried not to smile again, but could not help herself. He could actually be amusing. And good company. Or was he simply laying a trap for her? It was impossible to know. Either way he presented unexpected and unwanted attraction.

'Cicely, I am not happy that I must have your sister.'

'Bess will be a good wife.'

'She will be a *dull* wife. My uncle is a very fortunate man.'

'Thank you.'

He shrugged. 'A compliment means nothing.'

'I think a compliment from you probably does.'

'Maybe.' He drew a long breath and turned away. 'Will you wish my reign well, Cicely?'

'Yes.'

'Really?'

'I do not want your reign to falter, Your Majesty, I want it to be good for England.'

'Even though I am not the real king? Not in your eyes, anyway.'

'I know that Richard is dead, Your Majesty, and that no amount of wishing will bring him back. You are the king now, and I pray that you will—'

'Yes?'

'That you will be worthy. Oh, forgive me, I did not mean that as it sounded. Every king should be worthy, because if he is not, he is not much of a king.'

He looked at her. 'No one else gives me this, Cicely. No one else tells me the truth. Oh, yes, I *do* recognize the truth now and then.' He smiled one of his transient smiles. 'We *could* have done well together, and I think you begin to realize it.'

'We could have tolerated each other. Perhaps.' But she knew he was right.

'A little more than mere toleration, I think.' He toyed with his cuff, his eyes lowered. 'I cannot let you live with my uncle at Pasmer's Place.'

'Not live with him?'

'You must be here at court, close to me, not under another roof entirely. My uncle can be here too, I do not care. I only care that you are not away from me.'

'But he is my husband, I have to accompany him on his duties.'

'No.'

'Your Majesty . . .'

'No!'

She flinched.

'I can only hope that you begin to bore me as your sister does, my lady, but until then, if I wish to speak with you, you are to be here. And I hate to tell you this, but I do not think I will ever be bored with you.'

'I am to be your sister-in-law and am already the wife of your uncle, for whom you claim to have affection.'

'Do you love him?' He came really close. 'Do you really? I do not think so, somehow. Nor do I believe the child you carry is his. He is helping you, perhaps because *he* loves *you*. Who knows why he does it? I only know that you have a secret that I wish to learn—and so I will. There is one name that occurs to me over and over, a name you defend whenever you hear it. If I discover that Richard Plantagenet fucked you, I will not show any mercy. Do you understand? If I ever become certain in my own mind that your child is *his*, I will not suffer such a dangerously strong Yorkist pretender to my throne. Boy *or* girl, because a girl would attract a very powerful, potentially trouble-some husband.'

'Pretender? Your Majesty, my child is *your* uncle's, not

mine, and if it is a boy it will succeed to his Welles birthright. That is, unless you wish to bar any such inheritance. You can do whatever you like. Such is your power.'

'But my power will not extend to what I really want. You, Cicely.'

'And you will have me. One day. When you finally decide. There is nothing I can do about that. You will make certain you have me. You will threaten my husband, my child, my sisters, my mother, whoever is convenient for the purpose. And I will come to you to protect them.'

'But you will not love me.'

'Nor will you love me. You desire me, that is all, and—through duress—you will see that I do whatever you wish of me.'

He laughed. 'Whatever I wish? Dear God, I will have to start my list now.'

Again she was forced to smile, although she loathed herself for it. His humour was not always dark and unfathomable. 'Your Majesty, you are . . .'

'Yes?'

'Impossible.'

'Another royal prerogative.' He put his hand to her cheek suddenly. 'You have to forgive me for all this, Cicely. I cannot help myself.'

The tenderness in his touch seemed to sting her, and she drew back. 'Yes, you can! You relish it. Have you not already told me that? One moment you are gentle, the next you are filled with malice.'

'It is all your fault.'

'Yes, well, you *would* say that, would you not?' She took his hand suddenly, something she would not have dared to do before. 'Please do not do anything to hurt my child. I promise I will do *anything* you wish of me, but my child—'

His fingers were around hers, and she could feel

Richard's ring. 'Is safe enough. Unless its parentage becomes an unavoidable issue.'

'It will not.' She could not have seemed more open and sincere had she been Veritas herself. She used her wiles now, because so much depended upon it. She did not want Henry Tudor to feel as he did, and she regretted having gone to him, but it was too late now. Maybe he was still the wrong man for charm, maybe he always would be, but she *did* know she was now vulnerable to him in more ways than one.

'I will have to think about whether I believe you or not, Cicely.'

'You really should not call me that. You cannot address me by name and then be formal with my sister. It is not right.'

'I am hardly likely to be this familiar in company.'

'But you are the king, you can do what you want, is that not what you keep reminding me?' she replied, trying to pull her fingers away, but he would not let her.

'Cicely, if I wish to make you come to me and submit to whatever I wish, I will threaten the Earls of Lincoln and Warwick, and Richard's bastard son, John of Gloucester. They are still here, in the Tower, completely at my disposal.'

'May I see them?'

'No.'

'Your Majesty—'

'No is not a very long word, my lady, and its meaning is fairly straightforward.'

She lowered her eyes quickly.

'Cicely, they will suffer greatly if you do not comply with everything I wish from now on. I was going to free them at Christmas, but now I think it can wait until the spring. May. Yes, May is a good month, is it not? They will be freed then, sufficiently beyond the birth of your child for you to come to me. Their safety and freedom will depend upon you.'

He released her and glanced around the room, in such a way that she felt the hairs stir at the back of her neck. There was some frightful significance to this chamber. It had nothing to do with her brothers, but was something else entirely, something that aroused aversion.

Henry felt it too, but then a cough overtook him. For a moment she thought it would become quite a fit of coughing, but instead it passed. He had braced himself for more, clearly expecting much greater distress, and his relief when it did not happen was quite visible. She watched him. 'Is something wrong, Your Majesty? Shall I bring you some wine?'

'No, and no. But thank you. Go now. I am sure you know your way back to the banquet.'

She hesitated, thus failing yet again to obey him without question. 'What happened in this room?' she asked, trying not to shudder.

'Nothing that need concern you.'

'You should not stay here. Especially not tonight, the eve of All Hallows.'

'Concern for me? Am I not more evil than evil itself?'

'This is a wicked room, Your Majesty.'

'Oh, yes. Indeed it is.'

'Do not stay here. Leave with me,' she said suddenly. Not even Henry Tudor should be alone here tonight. She did not know why the feeling of dread had suddenly descended over her. Only that it had.

'I did nothing here, Cicely, nor did Richard. It was your own father. He was more cruel than any.'

'I do not want to know. Please do not tell me. Please.'

'Do you smell the fragrance of malmsey? It clings still, or so I am told. I confess I cannot detect it.'

'Malmsey?' she whispered, beginning to understand.

He met her eyes. 'Your father killed his traitorous brother Clarence in this room. With his own hands.'

'No,' she whispered. 'I do not believe you. My father would not murder his own brother.' George, Duke of Clarence, had been her uncle as much as Richard. He had not shown Richard's undivided loyalty to Edward IV, but he had always been kind enough to her. He had betrayed her father, more than once, and had been married to Isabel Neville, elder sister of Richard's queen. He believed the throne should have gone to him, and in the end he had been imprisoned here in the Tower, dying mysteriously in 1478, at the age of only twenty-eight. There had been many rumours of *how* he died, and being drowned in a large butt of malmsey wine was but one.

'Cicely, your father would kill with ease if said brother were to become too troublesome, and Clarence was certainly that. If I wish to model myself upon a cruel man, that man would be Edward IV. I know what was done here because someone kept a record. Who it was I do not know, only that it came to light when I was having this place searched for information concerning your brothers. The witness identified this exact room.' He encompassed their surroundings. 'Your beloved Richard did not know. I doubt if even he would have continued to support your father if he had. Although, it has to be said that he *might* have been complicit. Edward knew how to reward his youngest brother.'

She could no longer hide her shudders. 'Please, let us leave.'

'Together? How charming.'

'Please, Henry.' His first name slipped out. Her sudden fear made her forget herself, but then he had been calling her Cicely for a while now.

'How lovely you are when you plead, and with my name on your lips.'

'I am sorry for my presumptuousness. The familiarity was not intended to offend.'

'I do not know if you offend me or not, Cicely, only that I cannot leave you alone. I should, dear God, I should, but you have something that I crave so very much.' He rubbed an eye again. 'Such sweet torment,' he murmured. 'Very well, my lady, by all means let us return to the banquet together.'

'Without the symbol of your sovereignty?' She glanced at the circlet, which still sat upon the table where he had placed it.

'I am surprised you remind me, Cicely,' he said, taking it and resting it carefully on his head. 'Perhaps I should have requested *you* to do this.'

'It would not make you more of a king.'

'That remark has a rather double-edged quality.' He offered his arm, and she rested her hand over his. Again she felt Richard's ring. Again she hesitated. 'What will you do about my marriage?'

'I will leave it alone. But you will not be known as Lady Welles until I decide to give my public consent. Which will *not* be before your lying-in.'

'You are spiteful?'

'Yes. And still suspicious. But better you are married to my half-uncle than to some powerful lord who might use you to win support to challenge me.'

'If that is how you feel, why did you not simply say so?'

'And end our conversation before it had begun? Certainly not. Kiss me, and you will have my word. In blood, if you wish.'

Chapter Eleven

CICELY GAZED AT Henry Tudor. This was a moment when she had to show him she was not already conquered. She knew it as certainly as if Richard had told her. 'No,' she said. But she wanted to kiss him.

'No?' It was clearly not the response he had expected, and she could see how he tried to gauge her. 'Another provocative challenge, Cicely?'

She did not respond.

'You tantalize so exquisitely well. A sixteen-year-old should not know how to do it with such sophistication. Your touch is so delicate but knowing, so effortlessly instinctive. Your eventual tally of conquests will be something to behold.'

'Another compliment?'

He gave a faint smile. 'It was merely an observation.'

She gazed at him in the glow of the lantern. Somehow he had managed to take back the advantage. He played the game so very adroitly, and with such subtle attraction that she was now the one faced with the unexpected. If he enjoyed sparring with her, she began to do the same, and it was not what she wanted at all.

'You are lost for words, Cicely?'

'I am not sure.'

'So, this new Bosworth hangs in the balance?'

'I am not necessarily Richard,' she replied.

'For once.'

'The battle may go on for some time, Your Majesty.'

'I do hope so.'

She trapped his gaze. 'And the victory may not be worth the strife.'

'Oh, it will be.'

For a long moment she merely returned his look. She had to emerge from this room the victor. But how? Her following action was not what she foresaw, for it was another impulse that she may well come to regret, but she *knew* it would achieve what she wanted. And she *did* want. She stood on tiptoe to link her arms around his neck and kiss him. She wanted to imagine he was Richard, but he remained Henry Tudor. Her lips were parted, her body pressed to his ... but the moment she intended to be little more than casual took on more meaning than she could help. The scent of cloves was all around her, on his garments and his breath. It was pleasant, not heady or overpowering, but seductive, and he was unexpectedly good to kiss.

He embraced her and prolonged the kiss, moving his mouth richly against hers. It was not a clumsy or thoughtless kiss, and it knew so much that it disturbed the symmetry of her convictions about him.

Now *he* was the one who did not conform, and he stole the victory, making her want to go further ... much further. She could not, *would* not surrender to her sensuousness. Or his. There must be more of a battle, but at this most sensual of moments, his power was too great.

He took his time, but eventually drew back. 'Oh, how you struggle with yourself, sweetheart. That was not what you expected, was it? So, are you still so sure you can name your price? Or might I have a price of my own?'

'You have already named your price, sir. The lives of those I love.'

He smiled. 'Then I have added a surcharge.'

Yes, he had. What an engrossing viper he was, she thought, realizing she knew less of him and more of herself than she had a minute or so before. 'And I merely put down a deposit,' she said.

'Oh, how I look forward to the paying of the balance.'

And so did she. God help her, so did she. But she would *never* let him know.

He gazed at her. 'Never kiss my uncle in front of me again, Cicely. Never.'

'You are unfair.'

'I know. Promise me, Cicely.'

'I promise, Your Majesty.'

'Henry. When we are alone I am just Henry.'

She looked into his eyes. 'I promise, Henry.'

'Now that we have reached some understanding, I think we should return to the gathering.' He offered her his arm again.

She hesitated. 'You should not have brought me here, Henry.'

He put a fingertip to her lips and drew it gently along them. 'I do things, Cicely. You will have to forgive me.'

'What do you mean?'

'I cannot explain, for I do not have the answer myself.' He met her eyes. 'No, do not ask me more. Please.'

Please? There was something almost humble in that single word. Almost. Not quite, for it was Henry Tudor who said it.

'Come.' He extended his arm again and she rested her hand over his.

The noise of the junketing drifted towards them as they walked together, but he halted again before they reached the brightness and festivities. 'You are mine, Cicely. Never forget it.'

'I cannot be yours, Henry,' she said softly.

'In every way but a wedding band, you *are* mine, and you will stay mine. There is no argument, no room for compromise or conditions. I want you and will have you. As I choose, when I choose. Is that clear enough for you?'

'Henry—'

'Is that clear enough for you?' he repeated.

'Yes.'

'I will wait until maternal nature has taken its proper course, but after that, you will come to me.'

'Yes.'

'I can promise talent enough.' He smiled a little.

'Yes, I realize that.'

'I am sure you do. Oh, well, let us give them all something more to whisper about. I think I will smile. That will make ears prick and eyes widen.'

'And make them all think you have straddled me.'

'So it will.'

'You really do not care, do you? You have now damaged what is left of my reputation and slighted my husband's honour. You have also insulted my sister.'

He caught her hand and raised the palm to his lips. '*She* insults *me* with every glance, sweetheart, but your glances fire me with passion. Which of those facts do you imagine I appreciate more? As for my uncle, he married you without my consent, and for that he must endure the consequences.'

'Do not be cruel to him, Henry. He *is* dear to me.'

'I know, and he by some miracle fathered a child on you in June, at Nottingham, right under Richard's refined royal nose. Sir Jon Welles has married you to protect you, and to conceal the identity of your child's real father. Which of *those* facts do you think I believe most?'

She pressed her lips together and said nothing.

'I thought as much,' he said, and conducted her into the hall, smiling as he did so. There was the expected pause in the celebrations as everyone noticed what a rare good mood the king now appeared to be in. And all eyes rested upon Cicely, whose exertions they all imagined.

Henry escorted her to Jon, who stood to bow the moment they approached. His face gave nothing away as Henry ushered Cicely into her husband's keeping, but then retained her hand.

'I return your lady, my uncle. I congratulate you upon your conquest, and could almost wish myself in your place.' Henry's smile was bland.

Jon was his equal in blandness. 'I am flattered, Your Majesty, as I am sure my lady is as well.'

Henry's fingers clenched momentarily over hers, but then he surrendered her hand to his uncle's and went back to the throne that presided over the gathering, exalting him. He did not glance towards her again, but sat there, being the king.

Jon ushered her to sit down, and leaned closer. 'Are you all right, Cicely?'

'Yes, but I have now told him about my brothers having gone to Burgundy, so you are no longer in possession of a secret that is not known to him.'

'What of the itch in the royal scrotum?'

'I do not think he is as eager to scratch it as he was before. My condition dampens his ardour.' She felt a great need to lie, because she wanted to shield this man as much as she could, just as he tried to shield her, but she was dismayed by the ease with which lying came to her. She had promised to always be honest with him and faithful to him, yet here she was, already being dishonest and already contemplating unfaithfulness. But Jon had to be safe, and so she did not hesitate. If he thought she was no longer of interest to Henry, he would be more natural in the king's company. That was what mattered to her now. 'This is a horrible court,' she said then.

Jon nodded. 'Because it is a Lancastrian court. No, actually I fancy it is the first Tudor court.' He glanced at her. 'But most of all it is not Richard's court, is it?'

'It is where you are, Jon, and for that alone I will endure it.'

'Cicely—'

'Please hear me out, Jon. Henry has made it plain to me that he will not let me leave court. I am not to be permitted to live at Pasmer's Place with you, or travel with you when you attend to your duties. But you will be welcome to stay at court with me.'

'And you say his itch has *diminished*?'

'It is punishment, Jon, no more than that. He intends to let our marriage stand, and will give his royal consent, but not in time for your name to give my child your full protection. He is set upon that.'

'No wonder he smiled when he returned. He enjoys mean victories.'

'Jon, he told me he holds you in affection.'

'Did he, by God? Well, the feeling is not reciprocated.' He smiled a little ruefully. 'He is my nephew and my king, and I dislike him intensely.'

Oh, Jon, you would abhor him still more if you knew what intentions he really has towards me, she thought. She could not tell anyone. She would give herself to Henry and say nothing.

Jon took her hand. 'You have to be very careful with him, Cicely. It is no exaggeration to say he is dangerous.'

'I . . . begin to know it.'

'What happened?' he asked quickly.

'Nothing, truly. It was something he said. About not being able to help himself.'

John nodded. 'It is the truth, sweetheart. Always remember it, and always, *always* take care with him. It is perilously easy to lose his friendship. You are my wife, and I care very much.'

She gripped his hand, almost crushing his fingers against the turquoise ring. 'You have made it plain you do not intend to be my husband in the full sense of it, and—'

'Cicely, I did not intend to give you the impression that I will always shun you.'

'Nevertheless, you did, and I can understand why. I have never meant to hurt you, Jon. Nothing could be further from my mind. Please believe me.'

'I do.'

She gazed at him. 'You are such a good man, Jon. I am indeed fortunate to have you. Well, to have your name and protection, if not you yourself.'

'I will not share you with Richard, sweetheart. That is all. His hold is too great. Nor will I desert you, if that is what you still fear. We will do what we can to keep out of Henry's way. Let him enjoy the diversions of kingship. It will keep him busy, for I do not believe he has any idea how hard his predecessor worked at his responsibilities. I am told Richard was always half-hidden beneath letters, petitions, legal squabbles and just about everything that can be set down in the written word. The most Henry has been buried behind is a mound of his personal account books. He counts his money to perfection.'

She glanced past him, and found Henry's eyes upon her.

The following morning, All Saints' Day, when the atmosphere of the coronation still diffused the London air, and the weather was overcast and lowering, something took place that finally drove a deep wedge between Cicely and Bess. It happened because Bess sent for her sister, and Mary Kymbe had not fastened Cicely's purse to her belt as well as she should.

The meeting started off well enough, because Bess

intended to smooth things between them. Had Henry reassured her in some way? Cicely could think of no other explanation after the daggers Bess's gazes had thrust into her at the Tower.

Bess soon came to the point, and it concerned how Henry had departed from the coronation banquet. 'What happened, Cissy? Am I to wonder if you grace Henry's bed as well as your husband's?'

Cicely rose from her chair, gathering the heavy folds of her pale green velvet gown. 'Certainly not, Bess! He was angry because Jon and I had married without his full consent. He intends to be sure the child I carry is illegitimate. It was spite. That was why he made me speak to him in a horrid room where he said Father had murdered our uncle Clarence with his own hands.'

Bess stared at her.

'Be honest, Bess, we know Father was not the gleaming hero we used to believe. I now believe him to have been quite capable of personally extinguishing his own brother. Anyway, you wished to know why Henry sent for me, now you do.' She thought she had stepped swiftly and successfully aside from the question.

Bess rose as well. She was as slender as ever, and as beautiful, her salmon-shaded brocade gown shining even though there was no sunlight. 'And that was his only reason for sending for you?'

'He wished to taunt me in general. It is his way, Bess.'

'You are clearly of the opinion that you know all about him. Does he want you?'

'No.' Cicely moved around the room a little, for she felt particularly uncomfortable and unwell today. 'Why cannot we be friends as we once were?'

'Because you hide things from me, Cissy. Because you had more of Richard than I did, because you have Sir Jon Welles eager to protect you, because you are clearly so very glad to be with child, and because you now begin to have more of Henry as well. I am the eldest, the most important and the most beautiful, yet *you* have everything. When you returned with Henry last night, and there were sly whispers about kings and nieces, can you imagine how that made me feel?'

'Do you honestly believe I would become Henry's lover? Well, do you? You think I would go willingly into his bed?' Cicely paused amid her fibs. Henry was perhaps not quite as deserving of such vehemence, nor was she entirely innocent—in thought, at least.

'You see, Cissy? You have to pause to think,' Bess said quietly.

'Sometimes he chooses to be amusing, and he is good company, Bess. That is why I know that if you only put yourself out—'

'You know men so well, do you not?' Bess broke in. 'Tell me, how many have you lain with? Three? Four? Half a dozen?'

'Clearly at least one more than you, Bess.'

Bess's lips compressed. 'How amusing, to be sure. You have become mistress of the cutting rejoinder, have you not? What did you and Richard say and do in private, Cissy?'

'He was our uncle. That is all.' Cicely did not look away from her sister's eyes, did not show anything that would have told how deceitful she was.

'I wish Henry would let you go to your husband, I wish he would tell you both to go to Lincolnshire and stay there for ever. I begin to hate you, Cissy, truly I do.'

'Oh, Bess . . .'

'You eclipse me at every corner, Cissy, and yet look at you. You have no looks worth crowing over, you have far too much to say for yourself, and you have made a low marriage.'

Cicely was incensed at that. '*Low* marriage? I am the wife of the king's uncle, and that is certainly not low! Just because you think only of being queen, it does not give you the right to say such things.'

She turned to go, but her belt caught on the corner of a table and gave way. Her purse fell to the floor and burst open among the herbs. The bloodied kerchief and Richard's letter fell out. She bent quickly, but Bess pounced.

'What are these?' she cried, snatching them up and then staring as she recognized Richard's writing. 'He wrote to you, Cissy? Why?'

'Please give it back, Bess. You really do not wish to read it.'

'Oh, but I do.' Bess moved away, unfolded the letter and began to read it aloud. '*My dearest, most beloved lady, I send this because I have to put down in writing the feelings I have for you. You are all around me, every moment of every day, and there is not an hour when I do not think of you as many times as that hour has minutes.*' Bess paused, for a moment too shocked to go on, but then found her tongue again, although her voice trembled. '*Being parted from you is to be likened to purgatory, and I am but half a man because you are not with me. I am a king, yet lack that one jewel that will make me complete. I know that I am in your heart, and for this I cannot measure the honour I feel. Your sweet, forthright nature, your voice, your touch, your constant support, all of these make a slave of me. If our love is crossed by fate, I no longer care. It is an eternal love that will carry me to whatever lies ahead.*' Tears shimmered in her eyes. '*No spirit could ever be more true than mine is to you. Be safe, my beloved. My heart and soul are forever in your keeping. Richard.*'

His name fell into an echoing silence. Cicely stood with her eyes closed, waiting for Bess to say or do something. Anything but stand there without a sound.

At last Bess folded the letter again, her hands shaking

so much she could hardly manage to do it. 'You – had - Richard?' she whispered at last. '*You* had Richard? You stole the only man I will ever truly love. You comforted me, advised me, looked after me, when all the time you were lying with him yourself? Oh, *how* you must have laughed at me!'

'No, Bess.'

'You have his letter with you constantly, do you not? He spurned me because he said he could not countenance lying with his own niece . . . and then he lay with you, Cicely. You carry *his* child? Yes, of course it is. What a fool I have been.' Bess closed her eyes, but her tears fell. 'Does your husband know? Clearly he is aware the child is not his, because he was nowhere near Nottingham in June.'

'He married me to protect me and give the child legitimacy. He is a good man, Bess, a man of honour who only seeks to shield me from my own folly. He knows nothing of who fathered my child, but is prepared to say it is his own. For me, he does it for me.'

'Because you seem able to bewitch men to get what you want!'

Cicely did not respond.

Bess's anguish overflowed again. 'How *could* you, Cicely? How could you do it? How could you take him from me?'

'I took him from no one. He was a free agent, Bess, a widower. I certainly did not take him from you, because you did not *have* him!'

'So you admit that you lay with him?'

'I will answer you, Bess, but if any of this goes further, I will deny it all. And my husband will stand by me. Yes, I lay with Richard.'

'Is the child his?'

'Yes, but my husband does *not* know that.' She would shield Jon from such a suspicion.

150

Bess reached for a chair and sat down weakly. 'You did not only have more of Richard than me, you had *all* of him. All of him.'

'Yes.'

Bess glanced at the kerchief. 'And this is *his* blood?'

'Yes. He carried it at Bosworth. Henry took great delight in letting me know.'

'*Henry* knows of this?'

'Of the kerchief? Yes. Of the rest, no. He suspects, but that is all. Allow me to bear Richard a child? It would be far too dangerous to him. He only knows that I love Richard as my uncle. That is all. He guessed about the kerchief because it is embroidered with sweet cicely.'

'I cannot look at you, Cissy. I cannot look at you and bear to know that you had Richard's physical love. Was it good, Cissy? Was he worth the having?'

'Yes. I will never love anyone as I love him.'

'How long were you lovers? When did it start?'

'Just before we left Nottingham for Sheriff Hutton.'

Bess managed to look at her. 'I remember that leave-taking, Cissy. I should have known. How could I have *failed* to understand what I saw before me? The way he held you went far beyond the affection of a fond uncle.'

'Yes, it did.' Cicely fought back tears as she recalled those moments.

'You have broken my heart, Cissy. You have no idea how you have crushed me.'

'Bess, you are to be *Henry's* queen. *He* is the one you must look to now. Richard has gone, and there is nothing that will bring him back. Not to you, or to me.'

'You still have him, Cissy, for you carry his child within you. I really do hate you now. I hate you so much that I can scarce think of you, let alone look at you. All this time, when my tears fell and my heart broke, *you* were in his arms, kissing him, being loved by him, being joined to him in that way I could only dream of. You had him, Cissy. You had . . . *him*!'

'I am sorry you are hurt, Bess. But I am not sorry for being in his heart, nor do I apologize for wanting to be there, for rejoicing in being there, or for bearing the fruit of my sin. At first I did not know how I really felt about him, Bess. Truly I did not. My affection for him had always been too great, always gone beyond common sense, but I believed it was because I adored him as his niece. He was impossible not to adore, there was something about him. You know it so well, Bess. For so slight a man he managed to stand head and shoulders above all the rest. He certainly stood above Father. There will never be another man like Richard. Never. I love him so much that sometimes I think I will die of it. But he is the one who is dead.' She could not hold back the silent tears. She did not sob, her voice did not catch, but she wept.

'How eloquent, Cicely,' Bess said quietly. Coldly.

'I only speak the truth, and there was a time when you would have agreed with every word. I did not see my feelings for their true nature until the eve of our departure for Sheriff Hutton. It was just after he had told us we were to go there. You went out of the room, but he called me back. That was when my eyes were opened at last, Bess.'

'And he suddenly took you into his bed there and then? Come now, Cicely, it must have started before then.'

'It did not, Bess. I was honest in my dealings with you. When I offered you comfort and tried to help you, it was not false.'

'But it has been false ever since.'

'I too have only my memories now, Bess. You longed for him, yearned for him, without ever having him. I long for him and yearn for him because I *did* have him. Believe me, it is far, far worse.'

Bess looked at the letter and then at the fire.

'Please do not do that, Bess! Please. I will go on my knees, but please give my letter back to me.'

For a long moment Bess hung upon her decision, but then held it out. 'Take it. Take the kerchief as well. Take everything. Then there will be nothing left for you to take.'

Cicely put them back in the purse, which she then made sure to fasten securely to the belt. Soon it looked as if nothing had happened, but something momentous had ruptured the closeness of Edward IV's eldest daughters.

Bess watched her. 'Does John of Gloucester know?'

'No.'

'Well, it will be a tasty morsel for me to place before him.'

Cicely gazed at her. 'You would do that?'

'Why not?'

'Please, Bess, if you feel anything for him, do not do it.'

'I want to hurt you as you have hurt me, Cissy.'

'You would only hurt John. I am beyond hurt, Bess.'

'Are you? What of your child, Cissy?'

Cicely studied her. 'What of it?'

'Do you expect me to hold my tongue about the father?'

'Yes, Bess, I do. Richard would wish it of you too.'

'I do not owe Richard anything. Not now.'

'You do! He was not false to you, Bess, he was false to himself. He did not want to love me as he should not. Jesu, do you think it was easy? We sinned, Bess, we were incestuous, and although I did not struggle with my conscience, he struggled with his.'

'But he overcame his scruples, it would seem.'

'Think of it that way if you wish, but you wrong him very much. You wrong yourself as well, because you still love him. You will not do anything that will hurt his child. If you do, you are not true to yourself any more than to him.'

153

'Clever, silken words, Cissy. How talented you are with them. Jesu, when I think of how we used to be together.'

'We can be again, Bess.'

'No, Cissy. I do not ever wish to see you again, do you understand? I hate you so much I wish you were dead, and Richard's child with you. I will not have you at my wedding, nor will I suffer you at my coronation. If you *ever* show your face before me again I will complain to Henry.'

Much good *that* will do you, Cicely thought. Henry would take great delight in overruling his loathed bride's wishes. 'Please, Bess, do not do this. Richard is dead, and we both loved him.'

'Get out.'

'Do I have your word that you will hold your tongue about all of this?'

Bess looked at her without replying.

'Then remember that I will deny it all, and there is nothing you can do about it. I will swear before God, before Henry, that I am innocent of every charge you bring against me. Henry will believe me, Bess, because I can make him do so. And my husband will support me and swear that we lay together at Nottingham in June. And if you think to expose the contents of my purse for all to see, there will be nothing in it from now on. These things that I hold so precious and dear will be elsewhere, impossible to find. So, please, Bess, just think a little. I have not done such a terrible thing to you, nor do I want us to be estranged. If you ever wish us to be friends again, I will be glad of it.'

She gazed at Bess, who looked away.

'Goodbye, Bess.'

Chapter Twelve

It was Christmas, and there were celebrations in Westminster Hall, with music, feasting, dancing, acrobats, carolling and every other entertainment. There were men on stilts, rope dancers, morris men, fools and a colourful Lord of Misrule on a donkey. Seasonal greenery decked the walls, and there was a smell of warm spiced wine. But there was no Richard, no Queen Anne, no John of Gloucester, no Jack of Lincoln; not one of the beloved faces that had made Richard's court so wonderful to Cicely. Now the faces were those she despised, Richard's enemies and treacherous friends, those he should have eliminated, as her father would have done. As she herself would still do, had she been able. But then, Sir Jon Welles had been among Richard's enemies, and she could never raise a hand against *him*.

Bess, to be married on the eighteenth day of January coming, was seated on the dais with Henry, but again on a lower chair than Margaret. And lower than Jasper Tudor, now Duke of Bedford and married. Only his new duchess—lacking the precious Tudor blood, Cicely supposed—sat on a level with the future Queen of England. Cicely's elder sister was very beautiful, in a silver gown embroidered with the white rose of York, red rose of Lancaster, and red Cadwallader dragons. It was a political gown, a *Tudor* gown, a statement of Henry's ambition, and it would have been exquisitely appropriate for his new reign, had not Bess herself been so stiff, miserable and pale.

Having decided not to rebel in any way or make trouble over the fate allotted to her, she was now in Margaret's household at the newly refurbished Coldharbour. Marriage to Jon had saved Cicely from the same fate. He had confirmed to her that if Bess wished to claim being abducted to her future mother-in-law's residence, she would certainly have grounds. It was Bess herself who still chose not to. Her eyes were upon the crown, and that was all that mattered to her.

Margaret and Bess did not like each other, but then, Bess did not like anyone very much at the moment, least of all her future husband and his mother. And Cicely, Lady Welles, to whom she had not spoken since the revelation about Richard. Bess had not done anything with her new knowledge. Perhaps she knew that Cicely could indeed sway Henry.

He was impassive tonight, wearing black, the costliest of dyes, to which he resorted a great deal, but with much gold and ermine. His long hair fell about his shoulders, for he had yet to have it even trimmed. Cicely noticed how deliberately remote and uncaring he was towards Bess. It was a continued assertion that his claim to the crown was by right of conquest, not any union with York. And it was punishment for the way she conducted herself towards him.

Henry also wore a new, very rich livery collar that was much more extravagant than his predecessor would have worn. Richard was no idler in such matters, but had more taste, style and discrimination, Cicely thought. In her opinion the new collar was pretentious, especially given Henry's rather closed manner and character. And his evident parsimony. Clearly *he* had not paid for it! At the same time she was surprised by the collar, because it really seemed out of character for a man as naturally elegant as Henry Tudor.

Cicely herself wore light-brown velvet, trimmed with cream fur, and her hair was concealed beneath an attractive but cumbersome headdress. Well, not entirely concealed, for her natural hairline was revealed. Oh, how she disliked headdresses, and longed to wear her hair free again. But she was married now. That she was with child could no longer be doubted by anyone, and she felt as if she lumbered, rather than walked. She sat with Jon, well away from the dais, and was glad of it.

The thought of speaking with Henry again was daunting, although she would do it if he left her no option. So far he had not given an indication of any such intention. She had not encountered him since that night at the Tower, nor had he sent for her, even though she had given him reason to by petitioning him to let her see John, Jack and Warwick. She might as well have not bothered, for he declined her polite entreaties, and she imagined he took great glee in doing so.

Holding Jon's hand, she observed the scene, in particular a strange little man—almost resembling an imp—standing just behind Henry, who every so often indicated certain people in the hall. Always a group, never someone alone, and always where there was earnest conversation. There was something about the way the little man proceeded to watch whoever it was. His lips moved as if he repeated something, and then he would presume to touch the king's arm, and Henry sat back to hear whatever he had to say.

Something Mary had once said now slipped unbidden into Cicely's mind. *'I have an aunt who is deaf, my lady. She was not always so, and can speak as well as you and me, but she cannot hear at all. She watches people's lips when they speak, and knows exactly what they say.'*

The imp was like Mary Kymbe's aunt! Henry was using him to spy on the entire hall, right in front of everyone, and *she*, Cicely, might be the only person present who realized it! The sudden knowledge struck through her like a clarion. 'Jon?' She leaned closer to him, and made sure her lips were not visible to the imp. 'Lean closer, and keep your face turned away from Henry.'

'Why?' But he did as she asked.

Using her goblet as a screen, she told him what she had observed, and reminded him of Mary's aunt. 'Do not say a single word you would not say to Henry himself, because that little imp behind him will repeat everything.'

He was silent for a moment, watching the man surreptitiously, although without appearing to do so. 'Henry must be seeing murder in every shadow.'

'Good. I hope he finds it.'

He looked at her. 'Do you wish to leave? You have only to say you feel unwell.'

'Well, I would, but Henry would be very displeased.'

'Cicely, he is *always* displeased,' he replied, his head still turned from the imp.

'I am sorry to be of such interest to the king, and such anathema to Bess. It all makes your position so difficult.'

'At least I now know what I deal with. Do I take it your sister is aware of the nature of Henry's attention to you?'

'She only has a vague suspicion.' Cicely had not told him the real reason for her falling out with Bess. How could she? He did not know she kept mementos of Richard, and had even carried them in her purse at their wedding. She no longer did so, of course, for fear of Bess, but they were safe. To tell Jon would hurt and anger him. She did not want to cause him either.

He saw how she glanced at her sister. 'Do not fret over her, Cicely. She is not worth it.'

'She is still my sister.'

He made sure his lips could not be read. 'Aye, and a remarkably selfish one. She and my nephew deserve each other. *My* sister will remain the realm's most important and influential lady, Cicely, because Bess has not the wit to court Henry's affection. Richard would never have loved her, even had she not been his niece. He had the discernment to love you,' he added, and then spoke of Henry again. 'I have been watching him, and Jasper. The latter looks most unsettled, more so than usual. He hates occasions such as this, but tonight he seems particularly bothered. Henry looks like the cat about to claw the largest pike from the river, so I have the distinct feeling he has something momentous set to happen tonight, and that Jasper knows but thoroughly disapproves.'

'Jasper disapproves of everything, especially me. What could it be, do you think?'

'I have not exactly been in Henry's confidence since marrying you.'

'But he does not shun you.'

'No. A member of the family is always useful, and my sister insists upon praising me at every turn. He does not like it, but he puts up with it. Cicely, the fact that you show me such high regard has transformed you in her estimation. If you love me, and I love you, she will always extend a welcome to you.'

'And if she discovers we are not in love after all?'

He looked at her. 'She will not. From me, anyway.'

'She *has* been good to me since learning about us,' Cicely admitted, 'but, in the past, it was not so. I did not like her.' And still do not, came the afterthought.

'You will have to relinquish your grip upon the past sooner or later, Cicely. Those days have gone.'

'I know. Jesu, I know.' She smiled. 'But they were happy days, Jon.'

'I will not ask you why, because I know already.'

She gazed at him. 'Will you kiss me?'

'Now?'

'Yes. Please.' To the Devil—no, to the *Diawl*—with Henry Tudor, she thought.

Jon leaned closer and put his lips to hers. She reached up to hold his face, pulling his mouth closer and kissing it more sweetly than she had expected to. It made her blush, and she released him again.

'What was that for?' he asked.

She smiled. 'Christmas.'

'A kiss for the season?'

'Jon, I—' She broke off as a tall young man in his early twenties appeared in the main doorway of the hall, flanked by guards. Although he was not bound, he was not free either. He commanded her full attention, for he was her handsome, dark-eyed, dark-haired cousin. Jack de la Pole, 1st Earl of Lincoln.

He had not been particularly well treated. Not *ill* treated, just not shown the respect of his rank. Once—and still—regarded as Richard's chosen heir, he cut a fine figure, even though his hair was unkempt and he was in need of a shave. He was always attractive and debonair, and rather well endowed when it came to virility, so there was never a lack of ladies wishing to be bedded by him. He had long been one of the most sought-after lovers at court. And, from all accounts, was well worth running to ground. Or mattress. His dark blue clothes she had seen before, but he was thinner now, and they no longer fitted as they once had. By the way his guards kept away from him as best they could, she thought he had been brought straight from a noisome part of the Tower, not the royal apartments. Even so, dishevelled as he was, his royal blood could not be denied.

Jack was very dear to Cicely. He was an inveterate flirt,

but never unkind, and was also steadfast, courageous, considerate and honest. He had held Richard in high esteem and would have followed him anywhere. To Cicely he was the rightful king because Richard had wished him to be so, and it was so good to see him again that she longed to greet him with a cousinly kiss and hold him close for a moment.

Henry or not, she began to rise from her seat, but Jon held her back. 'No, Cicely. This is Henry's moment, do you not see it? He has been waiting for your cousin to be brought, and now waits for your reaction. And for pity's sake, remember the imp.' He made her settle back again.

There was a stir in the hall as more and more people realized Jack was there. The music and merriment faltered and a gradual silence fell as he began to cross the floor towards the dais.

Henry did not move, but sat rather casually on his throne, an elbow on the arm, his hand to his mouth, and it was not until Jack knelt at the foot of the dais that the king sat forward. 'Well, my lord of Lincoln, I believe you have sworn fealty to me?'

'I have, Your Majesty.'

There were gasps, and Cicely lowered her eyes, knowing how much it would have cost Jack to do such a thing.

Henry descended the steps of the dais and raised Jack from his knees. 'Welcome, my lord. I trust you will give me no cause to doubt you?'

'I will not, Your Majesty.'

Henry glanced towards her, as she sat at the end of the dais. 'Lady Cicely—or is it Lady Welles?—I think you should tread a measure with your cousin, to assure him of his welcome.'

She was rooted, but Jon squeezed her fingers harshly. 'Do it, Cicely, but take great care. Great care.'

She got up slowly, trying to appear unconcerned. She

felt Bess's enmity, and Jasper Tudor's, and then the whole court's attention as she made her way down towards Jack, who accorded her a deep, respectful bow.

'My lady.'

'Cousin.' She inclined her head and then was mindful to sink into a deep curtsey to Henry. To her surprise, and the surprise of everyone else, he came to raise her with exceeding courtesy, even bending to kiss her cheek. Cloves. So pleasant, so unsettling.

'I envy my uncle more each day,' he said, knowing it would be heard. Then he indicated that the music and dancing should recommence. 'Dance, my lords, my ladies,' he said, and returned to his throne.

As couples came quickly on to the floor to form lines, Jack extended a hand to Cicely and wrapped his fingers warmly around hers as they joined one of the lines. 'Please forgive me for the aroma of the Tower's murkier regions. The niceties of a bath have not been accorded me in some time. So, you are now Lady Welles? May I ask which Lord Welles has been granted such a prize as his lady?' he enquired as they took their places to wait for the measure to commence.

'My husband is Sir Jon Welles.'

Jack paused. 'Henry's uncle? And my Lincolnshire neighbour?'

Her fingers tightened with warning, and she turned to hide what she said. 'Do you see the imp behind Henry? I am certain he reads lips and relays what people say, thinking themselves private.'

'I understand.' He stepped a little closer and lowered his voice. 'Were you forced into the marriage?'

'No. I married Jon gladly, Jack. He is a friend to me, and he protects me. Do not think ill of him. The baby is his; I lay with him at Nottingham. Do you understand my meaning?'

He met her eyes. 'I believe I do.'

'It is important, Jack. He risks much for me and a careless word from you—'

'Will never pass my lips, Cicely. You know that.' He smiled. Warmly.

'Do not flirt with me either, Jack. It is dangerous.'

'*Dangerous?*'

'Yes. I will not tell you why, but you must take care. The only man here whom you can be sure of trusting is my husband, but please do not burden him with anything treasonous. I hold him in too high a regard to allow him to be jeopardized.'

Jack gazed at her, a little surprised. 'You *love* him? So soon after Richard you can love another?'

'I do not love my husband, Jack, but I do respect and appreciate him. No one will ever replace Richard. You know me too well to believe otherwise. I carry him in my heart and body, which my husband knows but protects me anyway.'

'Jesu, Cicely, you have changed beyond all recognition.'

'For the better, I trust?' She smiled, moving as the measure began.

'Oh, yes. If I could have bedded you before, I could do it twice as lustily now,' he replied, turning as she moved around him.

'Be very careful now you are at court, Jack. If you wish to live, you must not put a foot wrong, not only in the dance.'

'Do you suspect me of duplicity, Coz?'

'Oh, yes. You have no intention of remaining loyal to Henry. I know you, Lord Lincoln.'

They circled gracefully, and as they came together again, she asked about John of Gloucester. 'How is he, Jack? Does he know I am with child?'

'No, nor can he even know you are married.'

'I cannot bear to think how I have disappointed him.'

'Cicely, he is not as you remember him.'

'Not? Why?'

'He has been tortured.'

Her steps faltered and she halted, indifferent to the confusion she caused among the dancers behind.

Jack glanced around nervously. 'Cicely?'

She could not move, and her face had gone so suddenly pale that Jack feared she would faint, and so he put a supportive arm around her waist. There were gasps as she sank a little against him, and once again the merriment halted. The noise dwindled into a swirl of conversation as Henry sat forward but did not say anything. The imp's gaze did not waver from the scene of the disturbance, darting from first one pair of lips to another.

Jon hastened over, and Jack was relieved to relinquish her. 'What happened, my lord?' Jon asked him.

'I do not really know.'

'What did you say?' Jon glanced at the dais. 'And beware, for your lips will be read.'

'I have already been warned.' Jack moved closer and spoke very softly and invisibly to the imp. 'Forgive the Tower stench, sir, it cannot be helped. No royal apartment for me, I fear. However, I told Cicely that John of Gloucester has been tortured.'

'Why in God's own name did you do that?'

Jack flushed. 'Because she asked me about him and because he will be brought here tonight, as I have been. I attempted to prepare her. I did not for a moment think—'

'You should have done. She is six months with child and has not been well.'

Jack nodded. 'I deserve the rebuke, my lord.'

Jon looked at him with the briefest of smiles. 'I am harsh, my lord. But she means a great deal to me.' He lifted Cicely from her feet and carried her to a vacant seat at the side of the hall.

Jack hesitated, and then followed, feeling culpable even though he was sure he had done the right thing. To have left her unknowing until John was actually brought to the hall would have been far worse for her. He glanced accusingly at Bess, who had not moved at all to assist her sister. Jasper remained where he was, his face and expression dark. Jack had been questioned by him at the Tower, and could tell that the new Duke of Bedford not only knew what was yet to come, but was angry about it.

When Cicely was seated, Jon snapped his fingers for wine to be brought, and then held the goblet to her lips. 'You *have* to be strong, sweetheart,' he said gently, his vivid blue eyes filled with concern.

She managed a smile. 'I am sorry, Jon. It was suddenly too much.' She looked up at Jack. 'I do not blame you, Jack, because I know that if you could have left it unsaid, you would. He is bad, is he not?'

'He does not know me, sweetheart.'

On the dais, Bess suddenly caused a new disturbance. She asked something of Henry, who nodded with some annoyance. Accompanied by the Duchess of Bedford— who clearly did not want to go too but felt obliged to—she walked stony-faced from the hall, followed by the ladies Margaret had assigned to her. It was a calculated snub to Cicely, and everyone present knew it. Including Henry.

Margaret, now Countess of Derby, came to her half-brother's wife. Her ladies came with her, and in a moment Cicely was surrounded. Jon and Jack withdrew hastily and stood together, their backs to the dais.

'We meet again, my lord of Lincoln, although not as enemies this time,' Jon said, inclining his head.

Jack smiled. 'I trust we can be amicable Lincolnshire neighbours, Sir Jon, even though we support opposing roses.'

Jon returned the smile. 'I see no reason why not, my lord. My wife is clearly fond of you, which is a recommendation in my eyes.'

'And I am fond of her. We are friendly cousins, that is all. Not for want of wishing on my part.' Jack grinned.

Jon nodded. 'Knowing your reputation, I warn you not to show my wife undue attention.'

'I protest, sir, for I have not—'

'I do not imply that you have, my lord, but in my wife's case you would arouse resentment from a quarter you really would prefer not to.'

Jack gazed at him, light suddenly dawning. *'Henry?'*

'Yes.'

'I thought he was entirely without carnal urges.'

'You are very wrong, sir, so just beware. He was very well aware of the fair sex in Brittany. Too damned aware, as it happens. And please remember that he is my nephew.'

'Sir Jon, I think maybe you should remove your lady from the hall before John of Gloucester is brought.'

'He is that bad?'

'Yes. He was as well as me until they began to pay him particular attention. I do not know why.' Jack looked past Jon at the entrance. 'For the love of God,' he breathed.

Jon turned, and his lips parted in dismay, for Richard's illegitimate son was there, and was a pathetic shadow of his former self. His powder-blue velvet clothes were those he had worn at Sheriff Hutton, but they hung pitifully. His eyes were dark-shadowed, and he gazed at nothing in particular. He was empty, with no trace now of the vital, charming young man he had once been. And of whom Richard had been so proud.

Chapter Thirteen

RICHARD'S MUCH-LOVED SON was eighteen now, tall, with long, silver-fair hair and his father's grey eyes, once so expressive, but now vacant. His hair was cast in shade by the entrance, so that his resemblance to his father was quite startling. But what had been done to him was abominably savage—another tragedy for Richard.

Jon was appalled, and glanced quickly at Cicely, still too surrounded by ladies to know. 'He has indeed been singled out,' he said to Jack.

'I had no idea he had been reduced to this.' Jack was quite overcome as he watched John being almost bundled across the floor by the inconsiderate guards. 'The king came one day recently, and was closeted alone with him. After that, John was misused. I imagine now that Henry's interest in Cicely is at the heart of it.'

Neither of them could bear to watch John's humiliation, and as one they went to help him. There was an uncomfortable atmosphere in the hall. Richard's son was in no condition to be dragged here like a cheap trophy. Some watched with distaste, some with great discomfort. The only ones to gloat were those who hated the House of York beyond all measure. Even Margaret was clearly shocked, as were her ladies when they at last turned.

Jasper leapt to his feet. '*Harri! Er mwyn y Tad!*' he cried.

Henry's eyes flashed at him. '*Gwylia dy dafod!*'

Jasper left, without a bow or seeking permission. Cicely would later learn that he had said, 'Harry! For God's own sake!' Henry had replied, 'Guard your tongue!'

Cicely finally saw John, and was overwhelmed with dismay and pain. Her beloved John, who in 1484 had won her fifteen-year-old heart with his smiles and gentleness, and with whom she had lain that one night at Sheriff Hutton, when they learned of Bosworth. How could anyone have done such terrible things to him?

Jon and Jack assisted John to the foot of the dais, where they had to help him to kneel. He did not speak, and swayed so much that Jack had to place a steadying hand on his shoulder. Jon remembered how handsome, spirited and noble John of Gloucester had been, and could have wept for him.

Henry was punishing Richard's son for having aspired to Cicely's hand. White-hot jealousy had driven him to this. It had ripped through his customarily restrained nature and riven his honour, and he knew too late that he had done his reputation no good by this act. He waved the guards to remove John, and this time they actually helped him, rather than shove him along when he did not know what was happening. His grey eyes, once so warm and clear, did not recognize anything or anyone. He certainly did not know the young woman he had loved, even though he looked directly at her.

When he had gone again, Cicely rose slowly to her feet. The hall almost echoed as she crossed the floor towards the dais. Everyone knew she had once been intended for John of Gloucester, and that she had not been averse to the match. And everyone knew by her eyes and the proud tilt of her chin, that she was not about to prostrate herself to Henry Tudor.

Henry knew it too, and also rose, slowly, like an unfolding cat. There was warning in every sinew, but still the mouse approached.

Jon did nothing to halt her. What could he say? He shared her outrage and knew her so well. Nothing would stop her when her Plantagenet fury and pride was aroused to such a pitch. Jack gazed at the floor. He was a Plantagenet too, and silently supported her as she at last halted before the dais. She did not curtsey, she did not even incline her head; she simply looked at Henry with such loathing and contempt that he should have withered on the spot.

'My lady?' He spoke softly, but the great hall took up the sound.

She did not reply, but continued to look at him.

'If you have something to say, my lady, I advise you to say it,' Henry said, his voice cold and clipped.

Still her lips remained closed.

Henry rubbed the lid of his wandering eye. 'Madam, you try my patience.'

She turned her back on him and upon his throne, and walked from the hall before he had finished speaking. She flouted all the rules of how to behave in the presence of the king. Her gown streamed over the stone flags, and the veil of her headdress floated and fluttered as she proceeded out of the royal presence. It was a magnificent departure, and dealt Henry many insults at once.

The hall remained utterly silent as he gazed thoughtfully after her. That was all he did, except to gesture for the merriment to resume, which it did, but very unevenly. He returned to his throne and slumped there, his mouth stern, his eyes as hooded as ever.

Jack glanced at Jon, remembering to deny the imp a view of his lips. 'By God, he *does* want her. Poor Cicely.'

'She hardly knows how she fans the flames with almost everything she does.'

Jack nodded. 'She is her father's daughter. Edward IV

could be the same, but with cruelty alongside the charm.'

'Yes, but she is Richard's niece as well, and *he* it is to whom she looks the most. Damn the man.'

Jack looked at him. 'A very difficult rival to defeat, I would think.'

'Ah, yes, you know it all, of course.'

'Not all. Merely that they loved each other in a way that—'

'Mocked the Bible?'

'She thinks much more of you than you realize, Sir Jon. Believe me. She told me so tonight, and I know her well enough to recognize the truth.'

'He is still between us, and I do not think he will ever relent.'

Jack smiled. 'She is who must relent, Sir Jon, and she will. Eventually. If you want her without him, you may have to wait.'

Jon glanced at him. 'At least I do not have to battle *you* as well.'

'Believe me, I would like to think you did.' Jack grinned. 'Just think, Sir Jon, if you and I had faced at Bosworth, we would have hacked the very flesh off each other.'

'Richard very nearly did hack Henry's flesh,' Jon murmured. 'I often wish he had.' He nodded at Jack. 'But now, I must go to her.'

Outside, in the cold Christmas night, Cicely halted to draw a long, shuddering breath. She shook with the force of her emotions, her fury, her distress, her utter disbelief that Henry Tudor had allowed such a thing to be done. No, not merely allowed it, but ordered it. If he had *not* issued such an order, no one would have dared to do what was done to John of Gloucester. Or had Henry done it himself? As her father had when it came to his brother Clarence?

'Oh, Richard,' she whispered, 'if ever I needed you, it is now. And you need me.'

For a moment, just a moment, she was sure she felt his hand upon her shoulder, and the faint scent of the costmary. She closed her eyes. 'Hold me,' she whispered. 'Hold me before I die of this new grief.'

There was a tread behind her. She turned, Richard's name on her lips, but it was Jon. The name hung there, half said, and then slipped away again.

Jon put his palm to her cheek. 'How are you now? The better for making a fool of the king in front of his court?'

'I would do it again.'

'I know.' He had her cloak, which he put carefully around her. 'That was quite a scene, Cicely.'

'What he has done is unforgivable.'

'Yes.'

'John's only crime is to be Richard's son.'

'No, Cicely, his crime was to have had his father's permission to marry you, and for you to have been eager for it. Henry's interest in you has not waned, as you seem to believe. And he does not like to be subjected to such a powerful attraction.'

'I knew John before I even set eyes upon Henry Tudor.'

'You think that alters it?'

She bowed her head. 'I want to kill him.'

Jon glanced around uneasily, but there was no one else there. 'Be more guarded, Cicely, because what you have just said is treason. It is *treason* to speak of killing the king, do you understand?'

'Yes, but I would still like to rip his divergent *squinty* eyes from their sockets! I would like to slice his cock like a parsnip and boil it!' She struggled to compose herself. 'Why did he leave John in such a pitiful state? Why did he not have mercy enough to kill him?' Tears filled her eyes. 'It is inhuman,' she whispered.

He gathered her to him, a comforting gesture, no more. 'I wish I could say something to ease you, Cicely, but there is nothing. I, more than anyone, know how close you were to John.'

'Only once.'

'I realize that. You loved them both, father and son, but it was the father who meant the most.'

'What would Richard feel if he knew this? It would break his heart.'

'Cicely, he is no longer here to suffer more grief.'

But he is *here, Jon, he is with me all the time* . . .

'Your only consolation now must be that Jack at least is welcomed into Henry's fold.'

She remembered Henry's threats. 'Is he? What if Jack is to suffer as John has? Can you imagine him? Not knowing, understanding, seeming to see? Jack is so vigorous, so full of humour and purpose.'

'I think Henry is a little chastened. He realizes his actions tonight have been seen as more than ignoble. I have warned you that he is . . . dangerous. He acts sometimes, and then, when it is too late, he regrets what he has done. And never forget that sometimes it is beyond his control. He cannot *help* what he does. Now, if Jack treads safely, he will survive. I pray so, for I like him.'

She was able to smile a little. 'It is impossible *not* to like him.'

'How many virile Yorkist lords do I have to contend with?'

'I do not love Jack that way, you have my word upon it. I am just very fond of him. He is noble. And so are you.'

'If I am that, Cicely, you have to take more care that I do not face execution.'

The words were said quietly, and she looked up at him in dismay. 'Well, let us list my sins in Henry's eyes. You, a princess of the House of York, became with child, supposedly by me, out of wedlock. I have made a noise about marrying you, an event Henry does not wish at all, and I have made it worse by making you my wife anyway, without a royal licence, and maybe even when you are already married to Scrope. I have been to John of Gloucester's aid, in front of Henry, and I stood by, giving my silent support when you outfaced him. Again in front of the court. Now I have come out here to you, once more without his permission. Between us, we have affronted him a great deal, and whereas you provoke and stimulate him, I have most certainly *crossed* him. Do you not think so?'

'When you list it like that . . .'

'There is no other way to consider it, Cicely. And I am about to fall foul of him still more by taking you to Pasmer's Place, now, tonight, out of his way.'

'But that will make it far worse for you! He has told me I *must* stay here!'

'If he moves to stop it, I will see that you go to my sister at Coldharbour. *She* will shelter you. He will not attempt anything then. But I think Henry will stay his hand. I could see by his face tonight that he realizes he did not award himself a laurel wreath. Henry has turned John of Gloucester into a martyr in many Yorkist eyes. There is going to be considerable disapproval of this night's work, and while my nephew's view of things may be a little . . . odd, he is sharp enough when it comes to preserving his hide.'

'So is a cur.' She now loathed Henry so much that she could not be sensible, or civil. The nascent attraction she felt towards him in the Tower room had been exterminated by tonight's events.

'That is as may be, but it would be easy for him to remove me. Concocting false charges is not new to him.'

'And this is all because you have tried to help me. I am

so sorry, Jon, and even more sorry that I continue to do things that are not considerate of you.'

'If you were meek and mild, Cicely, you would not be the woman I am so eager to protect.' He made her look at him. 'This present situation with Henry has to be brought to an end.'

'How?'

He hesitated, for what seemed quite a time, knowing what he had to say but clearly very reluctant to actually say it. 'We need to be well away from him for a while. I will seek his permission to return to Lincolnshire, and to take you with me. I have to go to Wyberton soon anyway, there is business there to which I must attend. I will ask him publicly if I may take you with me, citing your indisposition due to being with child. The benefit of fresh country air, and similar rural joys. After tonight, he may well find it politic to let us go.'

She looked at him. 'I can tell you do not really wish to take me to Lincolnshire, Jon, and not because you fear Henry.'

'You misread me, Cicely.'

'No, I do not. Why are you so very reluctant?'

He took her hand and drew it swiftly to his lips. 'You are mistaken,' he said again.

She had to accept, but she knew there was something important he was not telling her. 'So . . . you will remove me to Pasmer's Place tonight?'

'Yes.'

'Will you stay there with me?'

'I will be in the house, yes.'

She studied him in the torchlight. 'But not with me.'

'Not with you.'

'I am your wife, Jon, and I would dearly like you to be with me. *With* me.'

'No.'

'But *why*? Can you not see that I mean what I say?'

'You also meant the name I heard on your lips a few minutes ago, before you knew it was only me who approached.'

That night, as she lay alone in the bed at Pasmer's Place, she made Richard come to her. She knew she did it and knew she should not, but on such a night she needed him so much that it was unendurable. He was the only one she could turn to in this, the only one, and even though he was not real, she *would* have him with her again for a brief, imagined respite.

He lay next to her and held her close. She did not need words, only to be close to him, and be honest as with no other. Words were not needed. It was as if his heart were within her, beating with the same intolerable grief. The tenderness and honesty were too powerful, the love too humbling, and the comfort overwhelming.

At last she had to speak. 'Please do not say again that I invent you. Not tonight. And do not leave me before dawn. I ask nothing more than to sleep in your arms.'

'Then you shall, sweetheart. You shall.'

'Richard, I know that I must give you up, but first I must still cleave to you. Please say you understand.'

He kissed her softly. 'I understand. How can I not? For I *am* you.'

Chapter Fourteen

IT WAS ALMOST time to leave for Lincolnshire. Cicely waited in her bedchamber on the first floor, looking down into the brilliant January sunshine that filled the yard. Everything was in readiness for Sir Jon and Lady Welles to set off. There were attendants, saddle horses, men-at-arms, carts and packhorses. Not a huge procession, just enough to transport the household to the wilds of the east coast. Jon's banners were much in evidence—a rampant black lion on a yellow background.

There was also a covered litter, should Cicely feel too unwell to ride, but she did not wish to travel that way. Litters reminded her of Richard's queen, Anne, who had travelled in one when she left Westminster Palace with Richard on a royal progress, hoping to see her adored only child, the Prince of Wales. She had returned in a state of complete collapse because the prince had died suddenly, aged only ten. Richard had been grief-stricken as well, but may as well have returned alone. He was already a widower.

Cicely was not superstitious. At least, she thought she was not, but nothing would induce her to travel in a litter when she was with child. Providence would surely be tempted. Maybe *her* child would be lost, and maybe Jon would return to London a widower.

She still did not know why he was so loath to take her

to his lands. When asked again, he denied it so convincingly that she almost believed she had imagined it in the first place. But the doubt remained, and she would have to wait to see what Lincolnshire held.

In a week's time Bess would be married to Henry Tudor at Westminster Abbey. He would have delayed still longer had his advisers not warned he was alienating Yorkist support by not honouring his word to marry Edward IV's eldest daughter. He had also alienated many by what had been done—or allowed to be done—to John of Gloucester. And so he had agreed on the wedding date. He would go on a royal progress not long after the wedding, but Bess would not go too. On that he was adamant.

Cicely knew no details of the wedding arrangements, nor had she been invited, even though Margaret had attempted to persuade Bess. The sisters had still not spoken. The fissure between them had become a chasm, and was just another pressing reason to be glad to leave London.

She wore bluebell velvet trimmed with white fur, and there was a hooded, fur-lined grey cloak waiting over the back of a chair before the fire. She was at the window because she awaited Jon's return from some royal business at the Tower. She did not fear for him, because it was a duty he carried out weekly when he was in London. There was little threat of him being detained on some pretext or other, because Henry had granted his permission for them to leave the capital.

Cicely had to hold back tears when she thought of John of Gloucester. She longed to go to him, hold him and make him remember, but she knew it was pointless. He had become a body without a person inside. His father had become the opposite, a person without a body to occupy. Richard was elusive, only stepping out of the shadows when she begged. But sometimes she could not create him, and those were the times when she was most conscious of her loss.

There was a sudden disturbance in the yard, and she was roused from her thoughts as a cavalcade rode in and found no room because of the waiting train. Jon? No, it was not Jon, but Henry! Royal banners streamed, red roses, red dragons, royal colours and livery. Henry was on a fine roan mount, and managed it well enough as it capered around, unnerved to find itself suddenly confined. He was angered because several moments passed before a Pasmer's Place groom took the bridle to steady the uneasy animal enough for him to dismount safely in the press.

She heard him curse as he flung a leg over the pommel and jumped down. He wore black brocade beneath a sleeveless fur-edged black coat, and the elaborate livery collar he had first worn at Christmas. There was a fine brooch on his black velvet hat, and his long hair fluttered. He had clearly ridden briskly in the sunny if chill January air, but he was pale and appeared unexpectedly frail. He almost threw the reins at one of the servants, and then looked around, pulling his gauntlets tighter and flexing his fingers. He paused on seeing the litter, and then suddenly glanced directly up at her, almost as if sensing her. Their eyes met before she drew back.

Dismayed, she waited for Mary to rush up to inform her that the king was here, and sure enough, the maid was truly panic-stricken. 'My lady, it is the king—'

'And he is right behind you, wench,' Henry said, striding into the bedchamber, and bowing his head beneath the door lintel. 'My lady?' he said to Cicely.

'Your Majesty!' Cicely sank into a deep curtsey. 'I fear my lord is not here.'

'I am aware of that. It is you I wish to see.' He had removed his gauntlets, and slapped them impatiently against his palm as he jerked his head at Mary. 'Leave.'

The maid almost ran from the room, and to Cicely's increasing dismay, Henry closed the door behind her.

'You would have departed without a fond farewell, Cicely?'

'You did not summon me, Your Majesty.'

'Ah. An oversight.' He tossed the gauntlets on to a table. 'However, as I too will soon leave London, I thought I would accord *you* the respect of a proper farewell.'

'You do us a great honour.'

'So I do. I go on my progress after my wedding, but then you already know that.'

'Yes, Your Majesty.'

'Am I not to be Henry now?'

'It does not seem appropriate.'

'Fuck that. Call me Henry.'

'Will you take your queen with you after all?'

'No, I will not. She is as displeasing to me as ever.'

Cicely looked at him, and then away.

'Do I detect a little frostiness in your manner?'

'This is the first time I have seen you since Christmas, Your M— Henry.'

He rubbed his eyebrow. 'Christmas. Yes. Well, I suppose there is nothing I can say to rectify that situation.'

'Nothing at all.'

'I have upset everyone, including my mother and Siasbar. Jasper,' he corrected. He waited, clearly expecting far more from her, and then almost shrugged with disappointment. 'I believe I have set my cause back with you, but at least you speak to me, which is a vast improvement on the long, cold stare to which I was subjected that night.'

'I do not *wish* to speak to you now.'

'No?'

'No.'

'Oh, how I have missed this,' he murmured. 'You preoccupy me a great deal, Cicely.'

She did not respond.

'I am sorry you will not be attending my wedding. I fear my bride is quite determined to exclude you. I am curious. Why are you and she at such odds? I would like to think you have fought over me, but that is so unlikely as to be from the land of cuckoos.'

'Take heart, because—strangely enough—she resents it that you have singled me out.'

He looked at her. 'And?'

'And then she and I disagreed about something else, and that was that.'

'And the something else was. . . ?'

'Nothing.'

'The original something and nothing?'

'Yes, Henry.'

'Tell me the truth.'

She met his eyes. 'I would have thought you had more important things to do than delve into women's arguments.'

'Yet again I neglect my kingly duties to the realm?'

She forbore to reply.

'Well, in one important respect I have not neglected my duty.'

'What do you mean?'

'I mean your sister. She is certainly not a rewarding armful, I can tell you. She gave what she had, I took everything and left her to think about it.'

Cicely stared at him. 'You have . . . lain with Bess?'

'Well, it was more a quick dibble against the wall, but it achieved its purpose.'

Cicely continued to stare at him. 'You *raped* her?'

'Certainly not. What do you take me for? Now you insult me, Cicely. She was willing enough, but she was not you. Which is why it was over and done with apace.'

'Are you sure that was *her* fault?'

'Oh, how droll.'

'Why did you tell me this?'

His wandering eye was not fixed upon her as steadily as its fellow. 'I do not really know. You goad me, I think.'

'So, you still blame me?'

He tossed his hat down with the gauntlets and turned away, his reddish hair alight in the sunshine streaming through the window. 'I blame you for everything, Cicely.'

'Thank you.'

'Not at all.' He glanced around to incline his head with utter insincerity.

Cicely could not hold her tongue. 'And I blame *you* for what has been done to John of Gloucester.'

'Ha! At last! I am surprised you have taken so long to tell me. I expected decapitation within a few seconds at the most.'

'I almost came to like you. I found a morsel of what I presume to be the humour of the real Henry Tudor, and could even smile with you.'

'*And* enjoy me a little more than you expected,' he interposed.

She ignored the remark. 'I did not even wish to leave you alone in that remorseless room, but then . . . *then* you had to prove to the world what a monster you are. You accuse *Richard* of being such a creature. He certainly was not, but *you* most certainly are. You had John of Gloucester tortured until his mind could take no more, and then you paraded his pathetic husk before the court. As a Christmas entertainment! Maybe you even tortured him yourself! Did you? *Did* you?'

'Did you ever lie with him? Did you? *Did* you? Oh, do not answer, for I know it already. You lay with him, and he—or Richard—is the father of your child.'

'No, Henry. Sir Jon Welles is the father of my child.'

He faced her again. 'You appear to have been very free

with your favours, Cicely.'

'Not free enough, as far as you are concerned.' She wanted to fight him, to beat him with her fists, bite him, kick him!

He glanced away and then back again. 'You always test my temper, do you not? Always.'

'And you revel in it.'

His cold eyes lightened for a moment. 'So I do, *cariad*, so I do. If you were not so far gone with child, believe me I would have you on that bed in a blink of whichever of my eyes chooses to obey. I need to have you, to plunge so deep into you that I almost split you in two. Do you understand what I am saying?'

'Yes. That I am the object of your unspeakable lust. You are saying that when you next instruct me to come to court, you will force me into your bed. You know that I will come because you will threaten to do to Lord Lincoln what you did to John of Gloucester. You will probably threaten my husband as well, in spite of the affection you claim to have for him. He is your uncle, your mother's beloved brother, but you would not hesitate to torture him if you thought it would make me do all you wish.'

'How accurate you are, my lady.' He coughed suddenly, and turned away as he tried to control it.

She was puzzled, remembering he had done the same in that room in the Tower. And he struggled again to suppress it. 'Henry?' She had to touch his arm.

'I am all right.' His hand went briefly over hers, and then away again.

'You do not need to be as cold and stern as you are, Henry. You are the king now, and when you are married to my sister, and you have your first heir, you will be secure beyond all doubt.'

'I am secure anyway, Cicely, for I am king by right of conquest.'

'That is not the security I mean. I speak of your dynasty. You do not *want* to have to marry a Yorkist princess, my sister least of all. I imagine your very personal dislike for her is due to the scandalous rumours about her feelings for Richard. That alone would be enough to make you hate her, would it not? As well as the fact that to marry her you have had to re-legitimize her.'

'Which brings us back to your confounded brothers.'

'Indeed.'

He looked at her. 'I do not want your sister, Cicely, and it has nothing to do with whether or not she craved Richard.'

'She did not lie with him.' *No, I was the one who did that.*

'She and I are so ill-matched that I vow we can barely stay in the same room.'

'You merit each other. And now you *have* to marry her. Your thoughtless little dibble could well see her already with child. Another daughter of Edward IV deflowered before marriage.'

He smiled. 'Jesu, lady, you *are* a fighting hen! How does my uncle cope?'

'Very well, because I feel only love for him.'

'Really?' He drew a long breath. 'So, you keep the invective for me?'

'Yes.'

'I am flattered.'

'Do not be.' She turned away.

'Come, lady, you wish to spit your venom, so please feel free. You have my permission.' He folded his arms and waited.

She faced him again. 'You invite it?'

'It will come sooner or later; it may as well be now.'

'You are a disgrace to the crown of England, Henry Tudor. You do not deserve to wear it, and you certainly will not die a loved monarch. You are already twisted with fear and jealousy, you start at shadows and see treachery all around you. Well, perhaps seeing treachery is what you deserve, for your throne is founded upon it. And you look at many of those around you, knowing they once swore fealty to Richard, and you wonder greatly. What they did once, they could so very easily do again. Look what they did to *him*!'

'Dismemberment appears to be another of your many talents, Cicely. Oh, how you fascinate me. I could watch you all day, jostle words with you all day, and fuck you all night. Perhaps fuck you even while we jostle words. I actually bask in your loathing. I believe you are my hair shirt, there to provoke me and gratify me at the same time. And I stand here now, *telling* you how I feel. Unbelievable.' He examined his fingernails.

'Please explain to me why you do the things you do. I *know* that you abhor your own actions. You do, do you not? I could not see past your defences if that were not so. Why, Henry? Why were you so dishonourable and without mercy as to torture poor John of Gloucester?'

'Because he lay with you! He may have been the first! He, or his damned father, took what *I* wanted! I cannot torture Richard now, but I can and *will* torture his damned bastard!' He closed his eyes, and she knew he regretted the words. 'I did not mean that,' he said, turning away.

The temptation to tell him it was *Richard* who had been the first was almost cripplingly tempting. Just for the exquisite pleasure of seeing this man's face. 'I cannot give you a purity I no longer have, Henry.'

'And even if you could, you would not give it willingly.'

'And you are surprised?'

He met her eyes. 'No, I suppose not.'

He came closer, and the scent of cloves almost caressed her. 'I do not care that you feel as you do toward me, Cicely. I do not care that you *might* have warmed to me had I not revealed myself to be totally beyond redemption. I care only that I have you, and am able—quite literally—to relieve myself of this intolerable desire.'

'How romantically you express yourself.'

He put his hand to her face, a tender gesture that would have melted her soul if it had been Richard. 'Do not fight me too much, sweet Cicely, because I will not always let you win. I am not very virtuous, you see, but then I think you have already gathered that.' His thumb caressed, once again evoking memories of Richard.

'You are not very anything, Henry, least of all good.'

'Whereas you, my lady, appear to be very good indeed at lying on your back.'

Her hands clenched, and she almost struck him.

He smiled. 'Do it if it will make you feel better.'

'If it is what you want me to do, then you may be sure I will not.'

'Now, how was I able to predict *that* response? Have you not yet realized that every time you speak to me like that, you merely increase my desire?'

She met his eyes and said nothing.

'The deposit was not sufficient,' he said then. ' I must be more certain that the goods are worth the asking price.'

'This is not a market place, Your Majesty.'

'No, it is a bedroom, my lady. You see? I *still* think of beds when I am with you.'

'What, exactly, do you require by way of an increased deposit?'

'Another kiss will do, and not a little peck, such as you bestowed upon me at the Tower.' He smiled, and for half a heartbeat it reached his eyes.

She gazed at him. 'Are you really the same man who sat on that throne at Christmas and behaved so very unpleasantly?'

'I am always unpleasant, Cicely, or had you not noticed?'

'I had noticed how you pretend it, Henry. You simply find it entertaining to confound and instil fear, but it is your peculiar notion of false amusement that disturbs me more. Your real sense of humour, the one God gave you, is sharp and clever, and so very . . . affecting.' What a word to light upon where this man was concerned. 'But you hide yourself away, like a squirrel fearful of endless winter. You are the king, your reign should stretch before you for decades to come.'

'Should? It will.'

'But what will it entail? If you are like this now, I hardly dare imagine the awful man you will eventually be. Please do not continue like this. Please. As you twist yourself, so you will twist England with you. And you can step back from it *now*, before you sink further. Please, Henry.'

He looked at her, an unidentifiable expression lighting his eyes. 'Oh, Cicely, *what* you do to me.'

'Henry?'

'Kiss your king,' he said softly.

'No,' she whispered.

'Please.'

He entreated? He actually *entreated* her? She was suddenly trapped. She should know what to do. She should *know*! But she did not. Here he was, the King of England, Richard's fatal enemy, John of Gloucester's destroyer, her tormentor, and she did not know what to do. Because he asked her. Because he suddenly seemed more threatened than threatening. And because he again stirred desires within her.

'Is it so much to ask?' His voice was quiet.

'You are so very clever, are you not, Henry?' she whispered. 'You play upon everything that . . .'

She could not finish because she wanted to kiss him. Wanted to rescue the Henry Tudor that still dwelt inside him. It was the same feeling she had experienced in that Tower room, the abrupt recognition of being attracted to him, the need to protect him. Protect *him*? Now, after that had been done to John of Gloucester? How could she possibly find this man alluring in any way? Perhaps because there were two Henrys, one abhorrent, the other peculiarly engaging. Dear God, she was losing her own self in this! But whatever her own conflicting feelings, she dared not refuse him, because he bargained with Jack's life and sanity. And with Jon's.

'Must you debate to that extent?' he asked. 'A kiss is not so very much, is it?'

She knew she had lost this battle, not only because she had to obey him, but because she *wanted* to obey him. She was ashamed and confused, for this was the one man in all creation whom she should despise. He was the enemy of all she held dear, but she wanted to kiss him, and be kissed by him. And so she went close enough to put her arms around his neck and draw his head slowly down towards hers, until their parted lips brushed softly together, dry and then gently moist; moist and then richly seductive. She dwelt upon the moment, enjoying the brush of his hair against her arms and the way he submitted to what she did.

In her mind's eye she saw the awfulness of his jealousy, but then she also saw his almost touching smile, his curious blend of uncertainty and random charm, and yes, his fear. He was a heady blend, but he bartered with two men who were dear to her, and she must make herself well worth their lives.

Never again would she be able to smell or taste cloves without thinking of Henry Tudor. She knew how to kiss a man, how to please him and make him want more. Oh, how she knew it. Henry would never dream of dibbling Cicely Plantagenet against a wall, because he would want to prolong his pleasure with her.

She dragged her mouth luxuriously over his, slipping her tongue between his lips, and breathing softly through him as if to stir his soul. She kissed his neck and his throat, and then his closed eyes. Her hands found their knowing way over him, prying through his rich clothes and finding places she could hardly believe she touched. She had learned so well how to make love, taught by that other king and matchless lover. Such lessons, learned so eagerly. Now *this* king wanted her, as his lips and caresses told her more each second.

Her fingers pried erotically into his hair, twining at the nape of his neck, and slipping softly over his scalp, winding just a little until the pale auburn threads coiled over the back of her hand. He was Henry Tudor, not Richard, but for these seconds she stood on the brink between the two. Two kings, one so beloved she could hardly bear to think of him as she kissed the other. But Henry was desirable, and his kisses were skilled and enticing. She wished it were otherwise, to enable her to do this now without a conscience. But it was impossible. John of Gloucester shone before her, and guilt weighed. She failed Richard. In this one thing she failed him so very much.

And so she thought of vengeance as she exposed Henry to the gift that Richard had shown her so well how to use. She offered no pity to England's new king, nor did he seek it. Perhaps he even read her mind as he returned the kiss with a hunger that revealed just how deeply engaged his feelings were.

He inhaled the scent of her, and moved his cheek against hers as if it was something he had waited to do all his life. He did not seem to care how much he revealed of himself now. Nothing mattered, except that she gave him what he desperately yearned for.

Such emotion and desire seized him that she thought he might take her to the bed, whether or not she was six months with child, but when he pulled her further into his embrace, her unborn child was suddenly very much between them. He released her and drew back immediately, closing his eyes and pressing his lips tightly together as he forced himself to regain control.

'Have I offended you?' she asked, uncertain of the exact reason for his withdrawal. The child? There seemed no other possibility.

He turned to lean his hands upon the table, his head bowed so that his long hair fell forward to obscure his face from her. It was a moment or so before he straightened to look at her again. 'No, you have not offended me. You made me forget myself almost completely.'

'Is that not what you want of me?'

'Perhaps. I do not know what I want, Cicely. Yes, I do, I want you, in all your facets, and I am faced with the knowledge that at Lambeth I should have followed my instincts and chosen you instead of your sister. But no, that would not have done either, because you were already with child. And now you are married to my uncle as well. I simply cannot have you, can I? And I want you so very much. As if that were not enough, I must also accept that you despise me. You are bound to, are you not? I wish to God I had never touched John of Gloucester, but I did. Forgive me, Cicely, please forgive me such a disgusting crime. I would not do it now. Do you understand? I would not do it now.'

'Oh, Henry, I do not know what to say or do. At this moment you are the real Henry Tudor again, are you not? And I appreciate you more for it. Even with such a monstrous act to cast a shadow over everything, I cannot entirely shun you. It is not what I want. What I *want* is to plunge that feared dagger into your miserable heart.'

'Treason?' He smiled with a hint of ruefulness. 'What a relief. You alarmed me for a moment there. If you *like* me, you may not be rude to me.'

'What made you stop? Just now, why did you pull away from me?'

'You tempted me too much. I wanted to have you here, now, but I will not take a woman who is six months with child. A girl of only thirteen gave birth to me, a small girl who suffered greatly on account of it. Yes, Cicely, I do have scruples. But not enough of them to leave you alone in future. You know how to fuel a man's lust, do you not? Who taught you? If not Richard, then John of Gloucester? I think not; he is little more than a boy. My uncle? I am not convinced of that either. So who was it? Who introduced you so sweetly to the pleasures of the flesh? Lincoln?'

'No. The Earl of Lincoln is only my cousin. We get on well and like each other, but that is all.'

'Who then? Your husband? Jon Welles is *such* a satisfying lover?' He laughed.

'Why do you laugh? Do you think he is without attraction? If so, you are wrong. He is a very gallant, attentive, charming man, and this Plantagenet bird descended from the tree into his arms.'

'The branch must have broken.'

'No, I jumped.'

'It was Richard, I know that. I will always know that, and you will never admit it.' His strange eyes rested upon her. 'I have never before been so violated by a kiss. You certainly have a remarkable talent.'

'Is that not what you sensed from the very first time we met?'

He nodded. 'Yes. You are so very tempting and provocative, Cicely.'

'I am sorry to have upset your well-planned existence.'

'You have certainly done that.' He continued to look at

her. 'What must it be like to be loved by you? Not used by you, as you have just used me, but truly loved.'

'You will never know, Henry.'

'More is the pity, although I think I *will* know what it is like to satisfy you. Just without the involvement of your heart.'

'Or yours. Have done with this, Henry. I have shown you today what I can do. You will have everything I have to offer, I swear it. But you *must* stay your hand where my husband and cousin are concerned. If you do anything at all that touches shabbily or cruelly upon them, you will not receive the promised goods in the manner you hope. I will lie beneath you like a corpse, and my lips will not soften against yours. You will have to do all the work, even to the parting of my legs and the exposing of my breasts, and I can tell you now that it will not be a pleasurable experience for you. There will only be my limp, lifeless flesh, which description will soon apply to the royal cock!'

'So, that is to be my fate if I am a bad little Henry. But if I am a good little Henry?'

'I promise you a sweet fleshly experience you will remember forever. You have my word upon that.'

'Dear God, I almost faint at the prospect.' He linked his fingers and tapped his lips. 'You know how to bargain, Cicely.'

'And you know how to play very unfairly indeed. Aping vulnerability.' He did not ape it, and she knew it. He *was* vulnerable. Although who would ever believe it?

His smile came and went in the blink of an eye. 'It was quite unconscious, I assure you.' Their eyes met, and he came to her again. 'Whatever takes place between us in private, Cicely, I need to know you will never speak of it elsewhere.'

'Henry Tudor, do you *really* think I mean to go around with a bell, telling the world I am too intimate by far with my nephew and forthcoming brother-in-law?'

'When the forthcoming brother-in-law happens to be the man you hate most, you may well feel so tempted. What an opportunity to destroy my reputation.'

She gave him a look. 'And you, Henry, know *all* about destroying reputations, do you not? Just look what a fine job you have made of Richard. If I *did* try to do the same to you, it would be no more than you deserve.'

'That, unfortunately, is true.' He tilted her chin. 'You could become an obsession, sweetheart. Perhaps you already are.' He kissed her softly, working his lips to hers, drawing little responses she tried hard not to give. Experience marked everything he did now. Her senses swam, her body came to familiar wanton life, and desire almost overwhelmed her. Perhaps it would have done, had he not suddenly moved away from her.

He paused, his back to her, and drew a long steadying breath, which told her he had felt everything as she had. And was as shaken. 'The anticipation of being truly in your arms will surely kill me,' he murmured, and glanced back at her. 'I look at you, *cariad*, and see my fate.' Taking up his hat and gauntlets from the table, he went to the door, where he halted again.

'I wish you well of Lincolnshire, Cicely, for I do not think it will be the reassuring refuge that you expect. From me, maybe, but not from others.'

'What do you mean?'

'Oh, I will leave it to your husband to explain. He should have done already, I think, but clearly he has been a little remiss.'

'Riddles, Henry?'

'Not quite. Ask him, Cicely. Ask him why a daughter of York will be so loathed on his lands.'

She gazed at him. 'And that is all you will say to me now?'

'No, I will also advise you not to consider escaping me by dying in childbed, for I swear that if I have to exhume you in order to have you, I will.'

'More limp, lifeless flesh, Henry?'

'Better than no flesh at all, sweetheart. I bid you farewell, and God speed. I cannot tell you how much I look forward to your return. In the early summer, no doubt.' He inclined his head, and then strode out, leaving the door swinging on its hinges.

Chapter Fifteen

WYBERTON CASTLE WAS one of the seventeen or so
Lincolnshire manors held by Sir Jon Welles, and it was
only a mile ahead as he and Cicely rode slowly through the
bitter January twilight at the head of the train that had left
Pasmer's Place. Jon's colours fluttered proudly above the
riders, and the slow clatter of hooves was almost drowned
by the noise of the weather. Mary Kymbe rode behind
her mistress, keeping a watchful eye, because Cicely had
found the journey more difficult than expected. The final
weeks before the child was born promised to be trying.

This land was not welcoming, especially on a winter
dusk. It was flat, the darkening sky was huge, and there
was no shelter from the elements. Snowflakes were flung
on the breeze from the bleak expanses of the nearby Wash,
the stream alongside the slightly raised road was noisy
and overflowing, and the dry reeds rubbed together like
thrifty old hands.

Jon reined in, his entire manner suggestive of a heavy
conscience. 'Cicely—'

He was going to tell her at last. She could almost feel
his inner struggle and reluctance. 'Please tell me, Jon, for it
is clear you feel you must.'

He leaned across to take the bridle of her palfrey and
then manoeuvred them both out of the way of the train.
Mary waited discreetly nearby, beyond hearing as he

dismounted and lifted Cicely carefully down, holding her arms until he was sure she was able to stand alone. She had fainted once since leaving London, giving him as much of a fright as she had herself.

'You are steady?' he asked anxiously, gazing at her as the breeze fluttered the hood over her headdress, and several snowflakes caught on the fur-covered shoulders of her cloak.

'Yes.' Her gloved hand rested on his sleeve. 'What is all this, Jon?'

'I should have told you before, sweetheart, but turned craven, I fear.' His dark blue eyes were oddly tentative. 'Cicely, no lady who is staunch to York by birth and loyalty could ever be welcome here.'

'Why?'

'You are aware my family is Lancastrian? My father died in 1461 at the Battle of Towton, which, you know, was won by your father. My elder half-brother succeeded to the title and lands, but in 1470, when I was twenty or so, he and his son were beheaded at your father's command, and it was because of a plot that was *all* Yorkist scheming.'

'What happened?'

'They were at the centre of a rebellion that originated in the dislike, quarrelling and rivalry between my Lancastrian family, which had supported the old Earl of Warwick against your father, and a neighbouring Yorkist family, the de Burghs, who were always your father's allies. My brother was fool enough to put a de Burgh manor to flame, and de Burgh went to the king, whom he had once helped to escape from Warwick's clutches. Your father summoned my brother for an explanation. My brother went, having first instructed his son, my nephew, to cause as much trouble as possible if anything should happen to him.'

Cicely was astonished. 'What did he imagine his son

could do against my father's power?'

'I have no idea what he imagined, Cicely, except that my nephew stirred up rebellion because my brother was thrown into the Tower. Lincolnshire was soon at the point of boiling over, and then everything fell under the manipulation and power of the Earl of Warwick, the so-called Maker of Kings, and also under the influence of your late uncle, the Duke of Clarence, who was, of course, Warwick's son-in-law. They meant to preoccupy your father with the rebellion, and then strike at him themselves, the intention being to remove him from the throne and replace him with Clarence. At least, that was what Clarence believed; in fact, Warwick had other plans. It was not until the rebellion had become truly dangerous that your father realized these lords' involvement. He out-manoeuvred them, and they did not get the support they hoped, because very few men wished to replace Edward with his untrustworthy brother. Warwick and Clarence were forced to flee, and my nephew's motley army had to face your father on its own.'

'What did *you* do during all this, Jon?'

He paused. 'I absented myself from the proceedings. I thought my family had behaved with great stupidity and wished nothing to do with it.'

'I imagine you were wise.'

'I am still alive, if that is what you mean.'

'What happened next?'

Jon pressed his lips together ruefully. 'My nephew had mustered thirty thousand peasants, armed with staves and farm implements. They found themselves up against Edward IV's full might, including artillery. It was a fore-gone conclusion.'

Cicely was appalled. Thirty thousand might seem like a large force, but not when it was ill-equipped and facing her father.

'The battle, such as it was, took place in the next county, at Empingham in Rutland, and did not last long,' Jon went on. 'The royal cannons were fired and your father's army charged. The peasants scattered, discarding their coats because they displayed the badges of Warwick, Clarence and Welles. That is supposedly why the battle was known as Losecoat Field. Some believe it was a reference to the ancient Saxon name for the place. Whatever, it was nothing but slaughter. A large number of Lincolnshire men died that day, and there are many families who lost fathers, sons, uncles, nephews . . . and friends. It was fifteen years ago, but as fresh here as it was on the day. The quarrel between Welles and de Burgh had been taken over by a plot to replace one Yorkist brother with another, and the fates of the unfortunate Lincolnshire men embroiled in it all was of no consequence at all. The House of York is hated.'

'I was a baby at the time, Jon, yet must take the blame for the whole of my House?' She was indignant.

'I should have warned you before, but, well, I did not. I hoped to avoid bringing you here. Rockingham, maybe, but not Wyberton. But it is where I have important business to attend to, and thus you are here anyway. Now it is almost journey's end before I find my tongue.'

'Is this what you shrank from telling me the night you took me from court and back to Pasmer's Place?' she asked.

Again the hesitation. 'Yes.'

'Even Henry knew of it and would not tell me. I explained that he came to Pasmer's Place on the day we left.' She certainly had not related everything. 'He warned me that there was something you were not telling me. Is there anything else, Jon? Because if there is, I would rather know it now.' She smiled, for was this not a reversal of their conversation on their wedding night? But he was spared the need to answer because something else occurred to her. 'If you have only just had the return of your lands, and you have been in London, does it mean you have not been here for some time?'

'Well, not entirely. I was here when I should not have been, if you understand me. I had joined Henry in Brittany in 1483, after being in the Buckingham rebellion and the attempt to get your brothers out of the Tower, but I returned secretly eight months ago. Which is why I could safely say I was with you in Nottingham in June last year. I could well have been, you see. I made it my business to be here, there and everywhere, but always returning to Lincolnshire. I was sheltered by the people here while I found out all I could that might help Henry. I rejoined him when he invaded.'

'So . . . you plotted against Richard as well as fought against him at Bosworth?'

'Yes, I did, sweetheart, and I was one of Henry's captains at Bosworth. I cannot alter anything. Your father left me no choice but to remain Lancastrian.'

'You should have approached Richard. He was not my father.'

'He had nothing to do with those events, for he was far away in Wales, but he was still a Yorkist prince, faithful to Edward IV. Richard was about eighteen in 1470, already with a reputation for justice, but I did not intend to test him. With a name like Welles, how could I? And when Richard ascended the throne, he had me arrested for acting against him. I was not his supporter, so why should he lift a hand to help me?'

'He would have heard you honestly, and did eventually release you.'

'He took my property in 1483, and I did not regain it until after Bosworth, from Henry. But we will never know what Richard may or may not have done after Losecoat

Field.' He put a gauntleted hand to her chin and made her look at him again. 'All you need to remember is that I did not personally hack Richard to death. I was there, but I did not kill him. I was not even near him.'

'Did you see him die?'

'No, nor would I describe it to you if I had. Battles are grim, sweetheart.'

'You fought and schemed to put Henry on the throne of England, even though you knew he was . . . "uneven", as you term it?'

'Sweetheart, his problem has only recently become so apparent.'

She understood only too well. 'Since me, is that what you mean?'

'He was like it before, Cicely, but finds the throne no easy place to be. His whole character is against him. And yes, there is you. He is *very* susceptible to you and he really is *not* accustomed to emotions of the heart.'

Oh, yes, he is, she thought. Henry Tudor was far from inexperienced. Very far. But she could hardly say so to Jon. And so she returned to the subject of her reception at Wyberton. 'Does anyone here even know you have married me?'

'Word has been sent ahead, yes.'

She looked away. 'And the fact that you did not support your brother and nephew is not held against you?'

'No.' But again there was a hesitation.

She took his hand. 'I am your wife, Jon, but I will not be untrue to myself. I will not stand by in silence if offensive things are said of my family.'

'Nor would I expect you to. Jesu, Cicely, if you are prepared to confront Henry, you are *bound* to confront the lesser mortals here. All of them at once, no doubt.'

She smiled. 'You will have my loyalty, Jon. I will never speak out against you.'

'Cicely—' He struggled with something else after all.

'Yes?'

He met her eyes, words clearly burning on his lips, but then he smiled. 'Nothing. It is not important. Come, we must reach Wyberton. You need to eat and then rest.'

'Do you promise the castle will not be as cold inside as it is out here?'

'I trust so.'

'Jon . . .' She hesitated. 'Please hold me.'

He pulled her near and embraced her. She slipped her arms around him and rested her head against his shoulder. 'Will we ever be truly man and wife?'

'When you are ready, sweetheart, but not until then. Richard has you still, and I will not battle him.' He made her look up at him. 'But I do desire you, if that is what you wonder. I have never made a secret of it.' He bent his head to brush his lips over hers.

She clung to him for a long moment, because he was so strong and reassuring, and because she really wanted to. Then she kissed him fully, and it was no mere brush of the lips. 'I *will* have you in my bed, Jon Welles,' she said then.

'I hope so. But please. Cicely, remember that it will *not* be before I can be sure Richard is no longer in the way of our true felicity. Promise me you will remember this.'

'I promise.'

He assisted her back on to her palfrey, and then remounted. They moved to the front of the ponderous train, and he called for some mounted men-at-arms, under whose protection Sir Jon and Lady Welles rode on ahead to Wyberton. Mary followed. The snow swirled around them, hiding everything but the causeway immediately ahead.

The moated castle lay within a large enclosure half a mile east of the village of Wyberton, and presented a virtually impregnable curtain wall that guarded what lay within. Jon's fortress was forbidding as it rose above the flat landscape, with his banners still just visible in the almost faded light. Torches smoked, the flames torn by the breeze, and the gatehouse was well guarded as they crossed the drawbridge.

She was to learn that Wyberton Castle was damp and cold, its old walls soaking up the moisture from the wet land upon which it had stood for several hundred years. Sometimes, when the wind blew in freely from the North Sea, the draught seemed to find its way through every room, and at other times, after much rain, part of the fortress was prone to be flooded. But the sumptuously furnished private apartments she would always find pleasing. She knew she would not be popular here, but at least she had Mary's friendly face. And Jon's, of course.

They rode into the castle yard, where there was shelter from the blast of cold air. Jon dismounted and again helped Cicely from her palfrey. The lord of the castle and his lady were welcomed inside, and there seemed no outward hostility towards the new Lady Welles, although certainly some eyes avoided hers.

Jon was detained by his steward, a sturdily built, middle-aged man named Edward Grebby, always known as Ned. There were pressing matters, and Jon requested Cicely to retire to the rooms that had been prepared for her. 'You are tired now, and I do not wish to expect too much of you, sweetheart. Refreshment will be brought to you. There will be time enough tomorrow to present to you those you need to know.'

She waited deliberately, and when he did not move, she whispered, 'Are we not husband and wife, Jon? Do you not wish us to be affectionate in public?'

He smiled, took her hand and pulled her to him, raising her lips to meet his in a kiss to show all onlookers that Sir Jon and Lady Welles were in love.

Cicely closed her eyes, for it was pleasing. Perhaps she felt more for him than she realized. Or perhaps she would respond to any man who kissed her like this. Maybe she could not be saved.

He drew back, and whispered, 'Will that do?'

'It will.'

He drew her hand to his lips, turning it palm uppermost as a lover would. 'Sleep well, my lady.'

'Jon—'

'I have to attend to things, Cicely.'

It was a dismissal. Of sorts. Maybe it was not meant to be unkind but somehow it was. She could not help drawing back, a little wounded. It was foolish, and unreasonable, because she knew how important it was for a lord to oversee his estates. She could only blame her weariness and the heaviness of her child.

And so she and Mary followed the respectful manservant who conducted them to the upper floors of the south tower, where the private apartments and solar were situated. But something made Cicely pause to look back.

A young woman stood gazing up from the foot of the staircase, and she did not flinch from meeting the new Lady Welles' gaze. She was about twenty-five, tall and full-figured, with flaxen hair that was clearly visible because her head covering sat well back from her hairline. Her clothes were not rich, a dark green kirtle and a plain grey gown, but she carried herself like a queen. Her face was haughty, and her eyes conveyed a sense of . . . ill intent. Everything about her issued a challenge, and far more. Then she turned to walk away, her hips swinging, her hair briefly brightened by the light of a torch.

Cicely remained where she was for a moment, not realizing she was protecting her unborn child with one hand while the fingers of the other were crossed among the folds of her cloak. Who was the woman who was bold enough to confront the new lady of the castle? Was it simply on account of someone lost at Losecoat Field? Or something more? Something personal? Cicely sensed it was the latter.

Mary touched her arm. 'Take no notice, my lady. She does not matter.'

'She does, Mary. Whoever she is, I must beware of her.'

'You are tired, my lady. You should eat and drink, and then retire for the night. You will feel better in the morning.'

A good fire danced in the hearth of Cicely's bed-chamber. There was handsome furniture, rugs on the floor, tapestries on the walls and candles readily available. The large bed was hung with yellow-gold silk curtains, embroidered with a frieze of small black lions, and looked inviting after the journey. Boards and hangings at the narrow windows kept out the bitter cold of the Lincolnshire night, and two upright armchairs were by the fire. Cicely sat in one of them when she had changed her travelling clothes for a loose robe. The chair was hard, with much carving, but it still seemed comfortable after riding for so long.

It would be so good to see Richard now, she thought wistfully, but he had not come to her since she left London. Perhaps it was now *his* turn to be left behind. She leaned her head back, and smiled as she felt her child move. Mary was present, and so speaking aloud to him was not possible, but she thought it. In a whisper. *I love you, Richard Plantagenet, with all my heart and soul.* The fire shifted, flames leapt for a moment, and sparks fled up the chimney towards the raw, snow-filled night above.

There was a tap at the door that Mary hastened to answer. It was not Jon, as Cicely had fleetingly hoped, but the same manservant as before, bringing food and refreshment. Bread, cheese, a little ham, with a small jug of Rhenish wine.

Mary prepared to pour the wine, but then paused and sniffed it.

'Is something wrong, Mary?'

'I . . . do not know, my lady. I believe I smell spearmint.'

'In wine? Surely not.'

The maid set the jug aside. 'I may be wrong, my lady, indeed I hope I am, but pennyroyal smells of spearmint.'

Cicely rose slowly, her hands immediately protecting her baby. 'Pennyroyal? The herb that is taken to induce a miscarriage or abortion?'

'Yes, my lady. The oil is very poisonous indeed.'

Cicely gazed at the jug. 'You must be wrong.'

'I pray so, my lady. But the women in my family do know certain things. We are not witches,' she hastened to add, 'we merely know about herbs and such matters.'

'But, who would want to—' She broke off and looked at Mary. They were both thinking of the woman with flaxen hair. Cicely resumed her seat slowly, looking at the food, not daring to eat.

'I will bring another drink for you, my lady.' Mary poured the cup of suspect wine back into the jug and hurried away with both. It seemed an age before she returned, with some mead that she herself had drawn.

'This is safe, my lady. And so is the food.'

'You can be sure?'

'Yes. I know someone in the kitchens, a cook who is from my home in Friskney. He told me you could safely drink this mead and eat. He himself prepared the food and knows it has not been tampered with because he alone has the key to the pantry. He also told me . . .'

'Yes?'

'The woman at the foot of the steps is called Lucy Talby, my lady.' Mary lowered her eyes, clearly uncertain of whether or not to say more, but then she met Cicely's gaze again. 'Lucy is the midwife here at Wyberton, and is said to have the eye. Her mother was hung for a witch-hag at Boston, and she has a younger sister who is definitely believed to practise the craft. No one dares to use any other midwife than Lucy, because if they do it is believed she will overlook mother and child.'

'And *she* is to attend me?' Cicely's whole body was in the sudden clutch of dread. 'Never! I will not have it! I will return to London rather than have her attend me! My lord would surely not force such a creature upon me.'

Mary was upset for her. 'There is more, my lady. Mistress Talby is also . . . Sir Jon's mistress.'

Cicely was stricken, her faith in her husband in sudden turmoil. She had not for a moment considered he might have a mistress. Few husbands admitted such things to their spouses, but *this* mistress would be attending his wife in childbed! The baby. What of Richard's baby? Tears sprang to her eyes. What *had* she done by coming here? She would have been better off staying in London.

But then, from nowhere, she remembered something Richard had said. *You—we—will have a fine son, a healthy son. I do not know what the future holds for him, but he* will *have a future. No sickly childhood and early demise for him . . .* The tears could suddenly be blinked away and overcome. She knew Richard had not really said it, that she had only been telling herself what she so very much wanted to believe, but now, in the grip of such agitation and anxiety, she convinced herself he *had* said it. Cicely would do bloody battle with ten witches to protect his child. And she would emerge the victor!

Chapter Sixteen

CICELY NEXT SAW Jon in the crowded great hall the following morning, where everyone broke their fast together, and where thin January sunlight fingered in through the narrow windows. She paused in the archway before entering, wondering where her husband had slept. And with whom. He had exacted a promise from her that she would be faithful, yet *he* intended to do as he pleased. And he had never even lain with the wife upon whom he imposed such a restriction!

She knew that most men would do the same, but this was Jon Welles, who certainly was *not* 'most men', and she felt almost irrationally hurt and deceived. So overwhelmed was she by this sudden turn of events that she suddenly saw his abstinence in a very different light. It had nothing to do with her feelings for Richard but everything to do with his passion and devotion to his hag of a mistress!

Cicely tried to bring herself up sharply. She did not *know* anything for certain, and the fact that Lucy Talby had been his mistress before marriage did not necessarily signify she still was. Did it? With a deep breath, she caught up her heavy lavender velvet skirt and entered the hall, where all the chatter and other noise was silenced immediately. Everyone watched the new Lady Welles. Or was it only the daughter of despised King Edward IV they saw?

Jon rose and came down the hall to meet her. He was dressed for travelling, she noticed, in a long, dark-brown leather coat, fastened closely at the waist with a wide belt. There was fur at his collar, cuffs and hem. His head was bare. 'You slept well, Cicely?'

She gazed up into those dark blue eyes that until now had always reassured her, but which no longer did this morning. All she could think was that Lucy Talby would be in attendance at her travails, and that *he* had known it even as he decided to bring his wife here.

'Is something wrong, Cicely?' Jon took her hand. 'Perhaps you did not sleep well?'

'Did you, my lord? Sleep, I mean.' *No, you were probably too busy fucking your mistress.* The obscenity leapt into her thoughts, and she did not wish it away.

'Yes, I slept.' His brows drew together in puzzlement. 'You are clearly out of sorts with me.'

'How could that possibly be so? Have you done something else that you know would make me angry?'

'I wince, my lady. No doubt you will eventually explain, because I do not know what you mean. There is nothing else I should tell you, Cicely, except that I learned this morning I have to go urgently to Rockingham. I am Constable there, as you know.'

'You do not wish me to accompany you?'

'Cicely, the journey from London was almost too much for you, so if you imagine I would now subject you to another journey, all the way into Northamptonshire, you could not be more in error. '

'And so, instead, you leave me in this place?'

'You are safe here, Cicely. Please do not think otherwise.'

But the only thing that came to her mind in that moment was Rhenish wine that smelled of spearmint. 'Will you return soon?' she asked.

'I will endeavour to be here again when your time is due, if that is what you mean. You know I will not stay away any longer than necessary. But this is not the time for conversation, I fancy.' He drew her palm to his lips, as he had the night before. 'Come, I will present you to the hall, and then we will break our fast together.'

He offered his arm, and she managed a wan little smile as she slipped her hand over his. But the smile was abolished as she suddenly saw Lucy Talby, seated close to the dais, with that same haughty expression, that same animosity, but now with an air of victory, it seemed. And clad in blatant scarlet.

'I believe Mistress Talby is to attend me in childbed,' she said, as Jon conducted her along the dais towards the vacant chair beside his own.

He hesitated, but then walked on. 'And who told you that?'

'I believe it must be common knowledge. You may as well accept it now, sir. That woman will not touch me. Do you understand?'

'I will not argue with you here, Cicely.'

'There is nothing to argue about, Jon. She will not come near me.' She smiled, for no one else could hear what she said and she did not wish Lucy Talby to know there was anything amiss between Sir Jon and Lady Welles.

He looked at her again. 'We *will* have to talk of this, Cicely, but for the moment I intend to present you. I trust you will not make a fool of me?'

'You have already made that of me, Jon.' Again she smiled.

He turned to face the silent hall, and led her a step forward, raising their clasped hands. 'I present my dear wife, the Lady Cicely Plantagenet, now Lady Welles.'

Her identity, which must have been already known to everyone, nevertheless caused disquiet. Lucy's face became angry at the word 'dearest'. It became still angrier at what he said next.

Jon looked around at all faces. 'My lady is beloved to me, and must be treated with all due respect and honour. She must be welcomed to Wyberton, and to all my other manors. If I hear of any discourtesy or ill intent, I will not be merciful. You have all been duly warned. My lady is my *wife* and will soon present me with a child. Remember it.'

He made Cicely take another step forward, and then addressed the hall again. 'Show respect,' he commanded, and as one the entire hall stood to either bow or curtsey.

Lucy Talby complied, but may as well have not, because respect was absent.

As Jon assisted Cicely to sit, he leaned closer. 'We will speak in the solar directly after this meal.'

'Do we need to?'

'Oh, yes, Cicely, we do.'

Cicely faced her husband before the large fireplace in the solar. Here the light was brilliant, falling through the coloured glass of a large triple window, to lie in spangles across the floor. It had snowed heavily overnight, and the land beyond the window was white, an endless flat expanse that stretched away to the horizon in all directions.

He now had his brown leather hat, and slapped it against his thigh. 'What, exactly, is this about, Cicely?'

'That you have a jealous mistress who is reputed to be a witch and who is intended to attend me while I give birth.'

'Well, that is direct enough, I suppose.'

'It was meant to be.'

'Firstly, Lucy Talby is not my mistress, secondly she is not a witch, and thirdly she is the very best midwife hereabouts and therefore well able to attend you.'

'Oh, well, my fears are vanquished,' she answered acidly, sweeping her hands to encompass the room.

'Do not do this, Cicely, for there is no need.'

'No need? Jesu, you do not understand at all, do you? You made so much of making me promise never to take a lover, and yet here you are, back in the arms of your mistress, but denying it all, of course!'

'I am trying to make allowances for your condition, Cicely.'

'How good of you. How considerate and kind. How untruthful! I saw that woman's face this morning, Jon. She was the cat that spent the night licking your cream. And I saw her last night. She did not say anything but she challenged me for you. *You*, Jon, it had nothing to do with Losecoat Field. You spent last night with her, did you not?'

'Were you there?'

'You know I was not.'

'Then how do you know so much?'

She looked at him. 'Have you ever lain with her?'

'Yes.'

'How many times?'

'I do not know, Cicely, for I was not counting.'

'So, there were many times?'

'Yes.'

She turned away, fighting back tears. 'This was what you knew you still had to tell me yesterday, was not it?'

He did not answer.

'You knew people here believe she has the eye, and you had every intention of letting her attend at my birthing. You *knew*, Jon, and you did nothing to prevent it. Why did you not leave me in London? I would rather endure Henry than this.'

'You do not have to *endure* anything here, Cicely.' He

put his hat on the table and came to turn her to him again. 'I did *not* spend last night with Lucy Talby. She *was* my mistress, but is no more. Whether you believe that or not is entirely up to you. I certainly have not brought you here to endanger you. Why in God's own blessed name would I do that? I have offered you my protection and my name, and you shall have both. I did not offer you love, nor did you offer it to me. But know this. If I ever decide to break my vows by taking another woman to my bed, I will do so. Is that clear?'

'Yes.' Her chin came up. 'I can break vows too.'

'Break them with Richard as wantonly and often as you please, but not with a physical lover! You will *not* put horns on me! Do you hear? There will *not* be another bastard that I am expected to claim!' He drew a very long breath to quell his growing anger, and then spoke more gently. 'Cicely, I do not wish it to be like this between us. I do understand that you are tired, upset and probably frightened to be here. But there is no danger, I swear it.'

'So there was not a smell of spearmint in my wine last night?'

He looked blankly at her. 'Spearmint?'

'Pennyroyal, Jon. It is used to end a pregnancy.'

'I have no idea what you are talking about.'

'Someone tried to poison me, Jon. At least, that is my firm belief. And if Lucy Talby is a midwife—and a witch—she will know all about pennyroyal. *All* about it.'

He ran his hand through his hair. 'I do not believe I am hearing this.'

'And I do not believe I am forced to say it.'

'You have proof of anything?'

'No.'

'So it is all fancy?'

She lowered her eyes. No, it was not fancy, but she could not verify anything.

'I imagine you have been told that Lucy's unfortunate mother was hung as a witch?'

'Yes.'

He met her eyes. 'Three children were murdered in this area, and people recalled that Lucy's mother and her two daughters were skilled with potions, herbs and all such things. Lucy's mother was caught gathering—' He broke off.

'Yes?'

'Pennyroyal,' he admitted reluctantly. 'Cicely, it is used for a great many things, as you well know. There are numerous plants that can be both beneficial and fatal, it all depends upon the dose and form in which it is given. I concede that pennyroyal oil is very poisonous, but having the plant in one's garden does not make one a murderous witch! Lucy Talby does *not* have the eye, or indeed any other supernatural ability, but if it will ease your anxiety, I will see that a midwife is brought from Boston. And I will leave instructions that if you begin your travails in my absence, Lucy is *not* to attend you. Will that reassure you?'

'A little. But I do not want anyone from Boston, I wish for my maid's aunt to come from Friskney. Her name is Katherine Kymbe, and she is skilled in birthing.' Mistress Kymbe was the deaf lady who could read lips.

'I know her. So have her, if you wish. Tell your maid to instruct her accordingly. I will attend to all expenses.' He took Cicely gently by the upper arms. 'Please do not mistrust me, for as God is my witness I am not untrue to you.'

'I want to believe you, Jon.'

'Then do so.'

'Send Lucy Talby away.'

'I cannot do that.'

She pulled from his grasp. 'Why?'

'Because I owe it to her late father to take care of her

and her younger sister, Judith.' He released her and turned away.

'Why?' she asked again.

'Because he begged me as he lay dying.'

'Why did he beg such a thing?'

'Jesu, Cicely, you can be plaguey difficult.'

'Because *you* are plaguey evasive. Why, exactly, do you feel obliged to keep Lucy Talby in your household? Or is her sister here too? Do you have them both together? *À trois?*'

'I have neither of them in my bed, Cicely, although I have admitted that Lucy certainly occupied it for a while.' He turned to her again. 'I have been providing for them both because when William Talby saved me from death at your father's hand, he forfeited his own life. Because I *was* at Losecoat Field, Cicely.'

She was taken aback. 'You were. . . ? But why did you not say yesterday?'

'Because I did not want to admit to you that I went there specifically to try to kill your father.'

Numb, she could only look at him.

'Has your mind changed, Cicely? Am I no longer your honourable husband, but rather dishonourable after all?'

'No, I think. To both questions.' She sounded like Henry!

'Are you sure?'

She nodded. 'I want to trust you, Jon. After all you have done for me, I really do want to trust you. So tell me everything this time. Everything.'

'I was seen at Losecoat, but not recognized by the Yorkists, and William Talby not only saved me but aided my escape. In so doing he was fatally injured by an arrow in the neck. He lived long enough to beg me to care for his daughters. I owe him a great debt of honour, and so I do as he wished.'

'And made Lucy your mistress? That was *dis*honourable!'

'An unworthy retort, Cicely. I did not make her my mistress, she eventually did that herself. I merely let it happen. Now she has a post in the kitchens. It is her choice. Her sister still lives in the villages and has *never* been in my bed. And none of this is actually your business. I am not yet an unfaithful husband, although I fancy in your mind *you* have been a very unfaithful wife. So what right have you to criticize me?'

She did not meet his eyes. 'None at all, except that my unfaithfulness is only imagined.' *So far, Cicely, only so far . . .*

'I doubt the exact nature of it is any different.'

'Probably not, but the act itself is. Any *living* man, is what you said, and in that I have not failed you.' *Yet, Cicely. Yet.*

He fell silent.

She composed herself again. 'Jon, I *do* wish to have Katherine Kymbe. That at least you must understand. How can I possibly be attended at such a vital time by a woman who has shared your bed?'

'You really do know how to stretch my patience. Must I remind you that the child is not mine at all? It is Richard's. It will merely bear my name, for which you should be more grateful than you seem to be right now. As for complaining that someone else has shared my bed . . . Damn you for your contrariness. What should it matter to you when you have no real interest of your own in my bed?'

'That is not true, Jon! I have begged you to come to me, but you will not.'

'And you know why. Oh, I have no time for any more of this. You have my word that Lucy will not attend you and that Katherine Kymbe will be sent for.'

'And what power do I have in your absence?'

'The power of any lord's lady, Cicely, which does *not* include the right to summarily hang Lucy Talby! No matter how much Henry Tudor desires you, I cannot think his forbearance would stretch to the flouting of the King's Justice! So please be so kind as to keep your Yorkist Plantagenet wrath to yourself. I will speak to her and make it clear that she has no call upon me now. Which she knows already, but I will repeat it anyway. I will warn her not to do anything at all that may offend you. I can do no more than that, unless I take her with me to Rockingham?'

'Do not dare!'

'I did not think you would care for that. Do you prefer to return to Pasmer's Place? Which you are at liberty to do, if that is your preference.'

'And leave her the victory? I *would* hang her first!'

Jon smiled. 'Welcome back, Cicely.'

'I am not about to smile with you now, Jon.'

'As you wish. I have to leave for Rockingham within the hour, and I will do all I can to return as quickly as is possible. I will instruct my steward to watch over you and not allow any harm to befall you, but you *must* heed his advice, Cicely. He is a local man, born and bred, and knows all about these parts.' He drew a deep breath. 'May I ask that when I do return, we can begin again?'

She nodded. 'I pray so.'

'Then the very least I can do now is show you that you *do* matter to me, Cicely, and that you do realize there can be happiness between us.'

He drew her closer suddenly, and embraced her. If he was conscious of her child, as Henry had been, he gave no hint of it as he kissed her on the lips. It was a good kiss, a tender kiss, with parted lips and the promise of a warmly shared bed when the time was right. Then he took her face in his hands. 'Have more faith in me, Cicely.'

After bestowing another kiss upon the tip of her

nose, he took his hat and gloves and left her in the solar. That final tenderness had only upset her more, and did nothing to allay her suspicion. She had no right to expect or demand anything of him, even though she was so highborn, but she needed to be sure Lucy Talby no longer meant anything to him. And while that woman was here, his wife could not be assured of anything.

After a while she heard horses as preparations were made for him to set off for Rockingham. Could she let him leave like this? When she was so confused and upset and might dwell upon so much? No, she needed more faith and trust. And she needed to defeat Lucy Talby. Jon Welles was *her* husband, not the witch's! Catching her skirts, she swept down to the courtyard steps. A large company of mounted men-at-arms waited in the snow, with Jon's yellow-and-black banners and badge on full display. The steward, Ned Grebby, had taken upon himself the honour of waiting with Jon's horse.

Jon came out behind her, cloaked, pulling on his gauntlets. He paused. 'Cicely?'

'Take care, Jon, and be safe.'

'I will do my best.'

She put a quick hand on his arm. 'God speed, and come back to me soon. I too have no wish for things to be bad between us.'

He gazed at her. 'You confound me at every turn, Cicely.' He smiled, and bent to put his lips to hers again, and this time she held his arms, making him dwell upon the kiss. He drew back at last, his dark blue eyes puzzled. 'Would to God I understood you, sweetheart,' he said softly, and then continued down the steps.

But then something happened. He glanced up at a window on the opposite side of the courtyard, and there, watching everything, was Lucy Talby. He halted, still tightening his fingers in his gauntlet. Then he turned to look at Cicely and she saw bitter accusation in his eyes.

He believed she had waylaid him simply to make a possessive point to a rival! But she had not known Lucy was there. 'Jon? It is not as you think—'

He interrupted by turning his back and going to his waiting horse. Within moments he rode out of Wyberton Castle with his escort. He did not look at his wife.

Cicely's only consolation was that he had not looked at Lucy again either. She returned to her apartment and was glad to find Mary waiting for her. 'Oh, Mary, I wish I had never left London.'

'You are still tired, my lady, and it is never easy during the final months. My aunt always says so.'

'Mary, my lord is in agreement that your aunt should attend me. The child is due in March, as you know, so if you could inform her that she should be here with me at the end of February? My lord will meet all expenses and I will give you money to send to her for the outward journey.'

'Yes, my lady. I will request my brother Tom to bring her. I will like to see them both again, but especially Tom, who was estranged from our father for so long that he lived with cousins far away on the Isle of Wight. I did not see him for a long time.'

Cicely saw the pleasure on the maid's face. 'You are fond of him, are you not?'

'Oh, yes, my lady. He is everything a brother should be. And he has found happiness at last, for which I am truly pleased. Although—'

'Yes?'

'Well, his lady is not meant to be his, for she is married elsewhere. So they are sinful. She now expects Tom's child, but they cannot marry.'

How achingly familiar *that* sounded, Cicely thought. 'I am glad your brother is happy, Mary. But for now, I would be alone. My lord and I did not part on a happy note.'

'I am sorry, my lady, but I know he loves you. All will be well when he returns.'

'I pray you are right.'

When the maid had gone, Cicely stood in the centre of her bedchamber. 'Richard?'

There was only the crackle of the fire.

'Richard? Please,' she whispered, for the need to have his arms around her was so powerful that she could almost have fallen to her knees of it.

She closed her eyes, summoning him to her mind. She could see him, leaning back against the wall in the sanctuary of Westminster Abbey, smiling at her. 'Please, Richard, hold me. Please, for I cannot endure it here.'

His arms were around her, but if she opened her eyes she knew she would not see him. Yet he *was* there, for she was in that unrivalled embrace, held so close and dear that nothing else was of consequence.

'Why can I not see you?' she breathed.

But there was nothing there, just the imparted sensation of his embrace. And that faint, exquisitely evocative scent of costmary. Just a sweet memory. Of love. So much love.

Chapter Seventeen

THAT NIGHT, WHEN sleep eluded her, Cicely sat by the fire, wrapped in a blanket of soft honey-coloured furs. But as she gazed at the dying fire, where the logs glinted and glowed, there was a sound at the door, a stealthy sound that was not meant to be heard at all. She got up slowly, pulling the blanket closer. As she watched, the ring handle was turned, and the door swung open very slowly. Lucy Talby, she thought, and she was right.

Jon's mistress, former or present, came slowly in, and was surprised to be confronted. 'How alert you are, my lady.'

'How alert I clearly need to be.' Cicely held a candle to the fire and then set it on a table between them.

'He is mine. *You* shall not have him,' Lucy said.

'He? You refer to *my* husband?'

Lucy turned to close the door, but Cicely halted her.

'The door will stay open, Mistress Talby, for I believe there is a guard not far away. If I scream, I need to be sure he will hear.'

Lucy stepped into the room again. 'The daughter of a king would scream for help?'

'You may count upon it, Mistress Talby. You may also count upon it that I am as capable as you of being untruthful to achieve what I want.'

'The offspring of an unscrupulous monster is without

scruple herself? Not surprising, I suppose.'

'And you are the offspring of a man toward whom my husband feels an immense debt of gratitude, Mistress Talby. That is why you are here, or so I understand from my lord. You are certainly not here because he loves you. If he did, why did he marry me? Why did he get me with child?'

'But not in that order.' Lucy smiled coolly. 'He told you I am only here because of my father? No, my lady, I am here because your husband lusts for me. He comes to my bed because he cannot be so satisfied by anyone else. He fucks me until he can fuck no more, and after a while he needs to fuck me again. And he was here, with me, at the time you say he got you with child. How very agile he must be, to have you in Nottingham and me here in Wyberton at the same time.'

'The difference is that I *knew* about you, but you certainly did not know about me.' Cicely found the barbs so easily. When it came to words, she was well able to both defend and attack. She spread her hands to indicate the fullness of her belly. 'Well, clearly he managed somehow to be in Nottingham with me, Mistress Talby, for he is quite content to acknowledge this child as his. Why would he do that if it were not? I lay with him and each time was a more gratifying and rewarding experience than the one before. I exulted in his lovemaking, as I know he did in mine. He belongs to me, not you, and I intend to keep him.'

'You think your royal blood will hold such a man?'

Oh, I have held a king, the finest king England could ever have, and it is his *child I carry within me!* But those words remained close to Cicely's heart. 'My royal blood is very royal, and has advanced Sir Jon's fortunes, Mistress Talby. He knows better than to play me false, for I have influence at court. With Sir Jon's nephew, the king, and the king's lady mother. Why, my dearest sister is to be Queen of England. So do not be foolish enough to set yourself against me.'

'I will set myself against you. I already have. You are at my mercy now, my *royal* lady. Here, in the depths of Lincolnshire, *I* am the queen. And if you think you cannot only outwit me, but keep *him*, you are mistaken.'

'Has he not reminded you that you are no longer of interest to him?' Cicely was sure he had.

'No, my lady, he has not. Why would he? The very last thing he did before speaking to you as he left was fuck me.'

'Perhaps he merely told you to fuck yourself *away*, Mistress Talby.' Cicely smiled. 'You do not frighten me, or pull the wool over my silly eyes. I know life at court, and believe me, I have contended with those far cleverer and more influential than you. Tangle with me at your peril.' Cicely was astonished at herself. But then, she had taken on Henry Tudor in what had felt like mortal combat, and if she could do that, she could surely do anything. But it was all bravado now. Except that she had also been the lover of a king, and that king's great heart was within her.

'You are a revelation, Lady Welles, and certainly not as meek as you look.'

'Remember it, Mistress Talby, for I am not of a merciful disposition either; there is far too much of my father's blood in my veins. If I wish to be rid of you, I will see to it.'

Lucy stepped closer. 'You will have to take care of every measure you drink, every bite you eat, and every place you go. You will *never* be safe, and nor will your child.'

'Let me make it quite clear that *you* will not be attending me in childbed. The matter is not for discussion. You will be kept well away from me.'

'I am everywhere, Lady Welles, and I have powers against which you cannot possibly compete. If I wish to attend your birthing, I will do so.'

'You claim the black arts? I cannot imagine that my lord will approve. He is a Christian lord.'

'Is he? Think well on it, Lady Welles. I know him, and his Christian faith is not that deep. As you will discover soon enough.'

Cicely wished her gone. 'Does your sister live in Wyberton village?' she asked with seeming incongruity.

'Judith? Yes. In the cottage where we were born.'

'Where the Devil conjured you, for to be sure I do not think William Talby had much to do with it. Well, you had best return there until my husband returns to decide your fate. *I* do not feel obligated to permit you inside the walls of this castle. Either of you, so keep your sister away as well. Your father did not save *my* life. Whatever my lord may have promised him, I did not promise the same. If you attempt to stay within these walls, I will have you put in the deepest cell it possesses. And I will pray that it floods. In my lord's absence, I am mistress here, with the powers of my lord's lady. So go. Now. Or I *will* do it.'

She was rewarded by the other's hesitation.

'Very well, my lady, I will leave the castle, but that will not protect you from my malevolence. There will soon be only one witch in Wyberton, Lady Welles, and that will be you.'

Cicely did not know what she meant, nor did she care. The creature was clutching at straws, and would say *anything* she thought would unnerve her rival.

Lucy left, and the candle on the table was extinguished by the draught she caused. The muted firelight was restored as Cicely hurried to close the door. She cast around, saw a chair, and wedged it to prevent it being opened from the outside.

'That was quite a performance, sweet Cicely.'

Richard! She whirled about, her eyes alight, her lips parted with joy, her heart tugging. She had begged him to come, pleaded with him but he had not. Now, when she did not expect him, here he was.

He smiled, and extended his hand, as always he did. She ran to him, and he welcomed her into his arms. She was safe again, loved again, precious to him again. She hid her face in his hair, her lips adoring his neck, where that small pulse *proved* he lived. She loved him so much that she could barely breathe for it.

His fingers reached gently into her hair, stroking and comforting . . . and with unbearable sensuousness. She closed her eyes. 'I only feel whole when I am with you,' she whispered.

'I should not be like this with you. Not now. Because you need to be free of me.'

'No,' she answered quietly. 'That is a freedom I will never seek.'

'You cannot bind yourself to me forever, Cicely.'

'Please kiss me, Richard. Hold me close and kiss me.'

His fingers slid forward from the nape of her neck, to her cheek, and then to her chin, raising her lips to his. Oh, the sweet taste of mint, the softness of his mouth, his breath. He was so tender, so gentle and attentive, that to be kissed by him was to be kissed by heaven itself. But the Devil was there too, arousing, wickedly sensuous and promising a world of carnal pleasures. A world where she knew Richard Plantagenet could always take her. With one kiss he gave so very, very much. Even now, when she was so unwillingly aware that nothing was real. She held him close, savouring the beating of his heart.

'Yes, sweetheart, my heart beats, because you wish it so.'

Guilt tiptoed into her, and she drew gently away, still

holding his hands. 'You know how I kissed Henry Tudor? The desire I felt?'

'Of course I know.'

'I am disloyal.' Tears leapt to her eyes.

His fingers closed tightly around hers. 'No, sweetheart. He is . . . a complicated man and you demolished him with that kiss. He had no defence at all.'

Nor did I, she thought.

'The attraction you feel towards him, and your fear of his cruelty are things with which you will have to contend, Cicely. Men rarely change because their women wish it so. Kisses, caresses and sweet understanding do not alter the character within. Men may disguise it for a while, but that is all. Sooner or later the true spirit will out.'

'I really must become his lover, must I not?'

He met her eyes. 'Yes, sweetheart, and you must accept that the thought is not as daunting as you would like it to be.'

'I will pretend he is you.'

'That may not be possible.' Richard put his hand to her cheek. 'And where does Sir Jon fit into this pattern, mm?'

'Jon?'

'The name *is* known to you, I think?' He smiled.

'I am no longer sure what to feel about him.'

'Yes, you do. Do not give in to your jealousy.'

She flinched. 'Jealousy?'

'Well, is that not what it is? You cannot bear to think Lucy Talby has him when you do not.'

'No!'

'Yes, Cicely.'

She gazed at him. 'How can *you* say it so lightly?'

'You think I should be jealous?'

'Yes.'

He smiled. 'You convince yourself you can touch me,

224

but I am not flesh and blood. Everything I say is only what you know for yourself, even if you refuse to acknowledge it. You want your husband, and I am glad of it.'

'I am not allowed to have him. He will not permit it.'

'Then stop thinking of *me* all the time! Jesu, Cicely, he *knows* you do it, and no man can endure being second. I experienced *that* misery.'

'But I love you, and he is not you.'

'Nor is he the less for it. Damn you, Cicely, for doing to him what Anne did to me.'

She gazed at him. 'I do not . . .'

'No? I suggest you consider for a moment.'

'I believe he has already been untrue to me.'

'No, Cicely, you do *not* believe it. He was sincere when he said he was not unfaithful to you last night. You know it, sweetheart. Do not deny it, because *I* can see right through you. You angered him greatly this morning, both with your accusations and then when he supposed you to have kissed him deliberately, in order to be seen by Lucy Talby.'

'But I did not.'

'Maybe, but *he* does not know it, and now he has gone to Rockingham to attend to his duties. You know he will not lack for female attention. He is a man to attract it, both physically and because of who he is. He may well break his vows because of a kiss that to him was very question-able indeed.'

'Did you break your vows, Richard?'

'Not that would be worth mentioning, or the world would surely know of it.'

'So you did.'

'Cicely, I have told you before how very hurtful and difficult it is to always be second. Anne did it to me and I do not want you to do it to Sir Jon Welles. My son will never know that he lost you to me—that *I* allotted him second place—and for that I will always be grateful. Sir Jon already knows of my place in your heart, and he is even prepared to give his name to my child. Have you any real comprehension of how great a compliment and respect he shows you in this? Well, have you? And now, unless you do something about it, he will always be blighted by knowing his wife is in love with a dead man. Just as I knew it with Anne. It is humiliating and debilitating, sweetheart, and I do not think you wish to do that to him. Do you understand? Let *me* go and turn to *him*.'

'Could *you* put me from your mind if our places were reversed? Could you stop thinking of me, yearning to see and touch me, *craving* me? Could you, Richard?'

'Oh, Cicely, I should have left you alone when you came to my court. Instead I gave in to my love for you. I am far from proud of it but I cannot, with any honesty, regret it. I had always been discreet about everything I did, but with you, discretion became more difficult every day.' He smiled, and his love caressed her. 'Doing what is right is not always possible. It is something I always strove to do in life, but could not when it came to you. You invaded me, sweetheart, and you annihilated every principle of which I had once been so sure. I love you so very much, Cicely, and I always will, but our final goodbye *must* come soon. And if you will not say it, then I will.'

'No, please,' she implored.

'When you look at me with those beautiful dark eyes, I am almost always robbed of common sense.' He touched her cheek. 'Almost always.'

She closed her eyes and moved against his fingers. But suddenly they were no longer there. *He* was no longer there.

'Almost always, but not this time,' she whispered.

Chapter Eighteen

IT WAS FEBRUARY, the morning of the Feast of St Valentine, and the weather was good. There were catkins and pussy-willow on the marshes, and snowdrops wherever soil and shelter permitted. The wind was so light as to be nonexistent, and the skies were a glorious blue. The Wash glinted, for the spring tide was in, covering the broad mud flats and other levels that often made the sea an almost imagined thing.

In London, Bess was now Henry's queen and there were whispers that she was already with child. If it was true, Henry's careless pre-nuptial dibble had indeed borne fruit. But Bess would not be crowned for a while yet. Henry was continuing to show he was king by right of conquest, not the birthright of his wife. And now the king was on his royal progress around the realm, leaving Bess behind. No doubt she was foolish enough to be pleased by the separation, Cicely thought.

Jon had not returned from Rockingham although he had sent his wife several solicitous letters, but they had all been couched in conventional terms, without any hint of deeper affection. He seemed a stranger now. A stranger she missed very much.

She wondered what he would say when he learned Lucy Talby had been ejected unceremoniously from the castle. Let him usher the creature back if he would. His wife did not expect otherwise. But even with Lucy gone, Cicely, Lady Welles, dared not take any risks with food or drink. Mary had to make doubly sure that anything served to her mistress was safe. The friend in the kitchens was of the utmost importance in this. Once, only once, was something discovered, and even that may not have been Lucy's work. There was a strong smell of bitter almonds in a preserve of damsons. There should not have been almonds at all, and no one wished to sample the damsons. Bitter almonds suggested arsenic.

Lucy was not in the castle, but her influence was still everywhere. Numerous things had happened that seemed to stem from Cicely's arrival. The milk had curdled, the butter would not set, pigs had died mysteriously and Jon's banners at the castle had caught fire of their own accord. Crude depictions of the white rose of York appeared in a number of places in the area, and whenever there was a death, that same white rose was painted upon the door of the deceased. It was even said that fresh bloodstains had been found on the site of Losecoat Field, in the next county, although no one had been there to see.

Hatred for the House of York, already pernicious, now became deadly. People averted their eyes if Lady Welles came near, and many crossed themselves superstitiously if they thought of her, let alone heard her name. Lucy Talby was right, there was only one witch in Wyberton, and that was Edward IV's daughter. If Jon were to return, Cicely did not doubt it would all stop, because Lucy would not wish him to catch her in such activities. In the meantime, his wife was her target.

Cicely was incensed, and frightened. It did not do to be accused of witchcraft, and here, with the memory of Losecoat Field so very dominant, it was more dangerous still. So much was she her father's daughter that it crossed her mind to do as he would have, and dispose of Lucy

Talby in the dead of night. It was an extremely appealing solution but she knew she would not do it. However, planning the details was a very rewarding pastime when seated in the solar on a wet winter afternoon.

Her time was still a month away that Valentine morning, when, quite unexpectedly, Mary's aunt, Katherine Kymbe, arrived at Wyberton. She came escorted by Tom, Mary's brother, who was close to Richard's age, a tall but sturdy man, good-looking with a weather-beaten complexion, curls the colour of hazelnuts and light brown eyes. He was dressed modestly, without embroidery or other ornament, and he had a reassuringly calm manner. But there was also something stricken about him, as if he had suffered a very recent, very terrible loss. In fact, he was filled with grief.

Cicely had come out to the steps to greet the Kymbes in person, because she wished to please Mary. She wondered why they had come so early, for they had not been expected before the end of the month. But it was Tom Kymbe who held her attention. She had known too much sorrow not to recognize its hold upon another.

Mary saw his agony as well, and hurried to meet him. Cicely watched the reunion, the clinging together of brother and sister, the brother's pain, the sister sharing it. It was heartbreaking to watch. Then he kissed Mary's cheek, and turned to assist their elderly aunt out of the litter.

Mistress Kymbe was small and wizened, but still sprightly, and reminded Cicely of a thin little sparrow. She had brought a number of belongings with her, including one heavy bag with which she would not part. Nor would she surrender it to anyone else. Cicely noticed how Tom studiously avoided even glancing at it. She also saw how the old lady patted her niece's shoulder and nodded sympathetically. Something truly devastating had taken place in the Kymbe family.

'What has happened?' Cicely asked as Mary returned to her.

'Tom's lady, Felice, died in childbed two days ago, and the baby lived only hours.'

'Oh, no . . .' Cicely's heart went out to Tom Kymbe.

He gave nothing away of his thoughts as he conducted Mistress Kymbe to Lady Welles. The old midwife certainly had all her faculties; her eyes were sharp and bright, her tongue quick, and her knowledge of childbirth seemingly infinite. It was hard to remember that she was deaf, and could only converse by reading lips. Cicely did not doubt that whatever happened, Mary's aunt would be able to surmount any problem at a lying-in. And now she had arrived, there could also be certainty that Lucy Talby would not be called upon. For *any* reason.

Katherine struggled with the heavy bag on reaching the steps, and Tom, with clear reluctance, went to take it from her, but she shook her head fiercely, giving him such an odd look that Cicely was puzzled again. There was something here she did not understand, and she felt it would affect her in some way. Or was she simply allowing her condition and imagination too much rein? 'I did not expect you so soon, Mistress Kymbe,' she said, making sure she spoke clearly for her lips to be read correctly.

'I will be needed before you know it, my lady. The death of one ensures the swift birth of another.'

'I . . . do not understand.'

'Forgive me, my lady, but I know things. I sense them. I know I am needed here, now, and that there is a pressing reason to—'

'Enough!' Tom silenced her, and then apologized to Cicely. 'Forgive me, my lady, I do not mean to speak harshly before you.'

The old lady looked at him, and fell silent.

Cicely indicated to Mary to take the old lady inside, while she herself remained on the steps with Tom. She wanted to touch him, to show sympathy for his loss, and so she did, briefly, on his forearm. 'Mary has told me of your bereavement, Master Kymbe. I am so very sorry.'

'Thank you, my lady.'

'If there is anything I can do to—'

'Please, my lady. I would rather not speak of it.'

He struggled with emotion, and she said nothing more, but remained there with him, for she could hardly turn and walk away when she felt so very much for his situation. After a moment he had mastered himself again, and looked intently at her, dropping his voice to little more than a whisper. 'I am glad to have an opportunity to speak to you alone, my lady, for I am charged with a message.'

'Message?'

'From Sir Jon.'

Cicely was surprised. 'But why would he not send a message directly to me?'

'I do not know, my lady, only that it is of a . . . sensitive nature. I am to relate it to you by word of mouth.'

'If he can tell you, then it is not *that* delicate, I think,' she observed. 'What is it you have to tell me?'

'I cannot say here. Nothing must be overheard. My lord was most insistent upon this. And with good reason.'

He turned as a step sounded behind them. It was Ned Grebby, who bowed to her. 'Have you any commands for me, my lady?' The steward made this enquiry every morning, so this was no different. She saw how his glance went to Tom. There was mutual dislike between the two men.

'Yes, Master Grebby,' she replied. 'I wish very much to be out of the castle for a while. It would please me to ride along the marsh causeway, toward the Witham.'

The steward was appalled. 'My lady, Sir Jon would not

wish you to do anything that might endanger you. And the river is tidal and always hazardous.'

'I may not be much of a rider, sir, but I can manage a placid palfrey, of which I know there is at least one here. The causeway is flat and straight, without hazard, and I will not go as far as the river. I have a whole month to go, and the day is too fine and mild for me not to sample the land hereabouts. I will not go toward the village, so will not risk any further opportunities for Mistress Talby to make a witch of me.'

She felt the change in Tom. Why? Because she was suspected of witchcraft? Or because Lucy Talby had been mentioned?

The steward wanted to keep Lady Welles inside the castle. If she went outside, and something happened, he, Ned Grebby, would be the unfortunate recipient of Sir Jon's rage. 'My lady, I have been charged to take great care of you. And—forgive me—are you quite sure you should ride when your child is so close to being birthed?'

'I will be quite all right, sir.'

'But—'

'Enough, Master Grebby. My mind is made up.'

Tom looked at him. 'I will lend my company, sir. My sister will be present, so there cannot be any suggestion of impropriety. I will see that no harm comes to my lady.' He paused, and looked belatedly at Cicely. 'With your leave, my lady. Perhaps I speak out of turn?'

'You do not, Master Kymbe. I am grateful for your offer.'

The steward gave up. 'If that is truly your wish, my lady?'

'It is.'

Ned looked a little slyly at Tom. 'Then I will leave the matter to you, Master Kymbe.'

Tom returned the look. 'You do that, sir. Oh, and lest

I forget . . .' He reached inside his jacket and pulled out a sealed document. 'Sir Jon instructs me to give you this.'

'Sir Jon chooses *you* as his messenger?'

'It would seem so, Master Grebby, and if you object, you had best take it up with him on his return. Which is imminent.'

Cicely's heart leapt with relief. Jon was returning at last? How glad she was to hear it. More glad than she expected.

Cicely had to change clothes for the ride, and Mary was attending her. 'Mary, your aunt said something about the death of one meaning the swift birth of another.'

'It is an old saying, my lady. My aunt believes in it, and it has often proved correct. Tom's child has left the world, and so she feels maybe your child will come early into it. That is all.'

All? Cicely was anxious. Babies born before their term were always weak and sickly. Were they not?

'All will be well, my lady. I am sure of it. You are strong, and recovered now from the journey from London. You have not had the sick mornings for well over a week, and your cheeks are rosy. Your eyes sparkle too. There is nothing wrong. I have not been close to my aunt for so long without learning things.'

Cicely smiled. 'You make me feel better, Mary. I bless the day you came to me.' She stepped out of her gown. 'I think your brother and Master Grebby do not like each other.'

'They are second cousins, my lady, and they have *never* liked each other.'

Cicely was silent for a moment as she was helped into clothes more suitable for outdoors. 'What does Lucy Talby mean to your brother? Have they been sweethearts?'

The maid was horrified. 'Oh, *no*, my lady! It is believed

that Mistress Talby overlooked Felice and the baby.'

Cicely was appalled. 'But why?'

'Because Lucy was in love with Edwin de Burgh, who chose to marry Felice instead. The witch punished her.'

'So your brother believes in witchcraft?'

'I do not know, my lady. I would once have said he did not.'

'And now the witch's way to Edwin de Burgh is clear?'

'No, my lady, for Edwin died of the sweating sickness in Burgundy, not long before Bosworth.'

Cicely hesitated. 'Was Tom at Losecoat Field?'

Mary became hesitant.

'It is quite all right to tell me the truth, Mary. It will not change my regard, or bring trouble upon him. I am merely curious, that is all.'

'Yes, he was at Losecoat, my lady. He was not yet twenty, and did not hold with the feud that led to the battle, but he would never move from Sir Jon's side at such a time. They had always liked each other, from boys. Tom was almost killed, but fell beneath some thick bushes and was not found when your—when the king's forces searched for survivors. If they had discovered him, he too would have died there. William Talby was able to save Sir Jon.'

Cicely was puzzled. 'If your family is Lancastrian, how then was your name put before King Richard to be maid to my sister and me? I remember my uncle saying that your father was his supporter.'

'And so he was. My father had served with King Richard at the Battle of Tewkesbury, when the king was still Duke of Gloucester, of course. My father would never hear a word said against Richard, saying that although the duke was still very young—the same age as Tom—he was already a very valiant and just prince. He saw great good in Richard. It was Richard who granted Friskney manor to your cousin, the Earl of Lincoln. The earl knew my father well, but does not know Tom at all.'

'Perhaps it is just as well, if your brother is a Lancastrian.'

'Yes, my lady. The Earl of Lincoln holds a number of Lincolnshire manors. My father did not care for Tom's adherence to Sir Jon, and thus to the Lancastrian cause. There was a great rift between them, but my father gave his loyalty to King Richard and to Lord Lincoln, and it remained with them until the day he died.'

'Loyalty meant so much to Richard,' Cicely murmured almost absently.

'I know how difficult it is for you, my lady, being the wife of a Lancastrian nobleman . . . and the niece of King Richard.' The maid returned her gaze in a level manner that conveyed knowledge of the truth.

'You know about me, do you not?' Cicely said quietly.

'I have guessed, my lady. No more than that. It is something I will never divulge.'

'Please keep it close, Mary, for it is a very dangerous secret.'

Chapter Nineteen

CICELY RODE OUT gladly with Tom Kymbe and Mary. It was unexpectedly warm for February, perhaps because the salt air, although fresh and invigorating, was almost still. No chill was carried in from the sea, and there had not been rain in over a week, so the causeway was dry as they rode east, towards the River Witham. Several miles to the north-west loomed the great tower of St Botolph's church in Boston. It was called the Boston Stump, and was a famous landmark for many miles.

Looking back at the castle, Cicely saw that Jon's burnt banners had been replaced, but hung limply against their poles and over the walls. All around her was a terrain of bogs and marshes, with reeds and rushes that had their roots in a shifting, unstable mire where a few water channels provided navigation, for only the smallest boats. Curlews called across the marsh, waterfowl honked, and there was the sound of flowing water from the stream that now meandered across the boggy landscape. It was all so lonely, but also very beautiful.

Tom manoeuvred his horse alongside. 'My lady, the message I have to give is that my lord's half-sister, the Countess of Derby, has sent word to him that King Henry has been told something concerning your ... dealings with King Richard.'

Cicely reined in. 'Dealings?' she repeated.

'Their nature was not conveyed to me, my lady.'

Her mind raced. Who else knew the truth? They suddenly seemed legion. Jack? No, he would die rather than tell. John of Gloucester did not know anyway, nor could say even if he did. Sir Robert Percy, Richard's close friend, who certainly knew, had disappeared after Bosworth. As had Francis Lovell. Who else knew? An awful possibility crept in, ashamedly perhaps, but it could not be denied. Bess knew. Bess, now Henry's queen, could well have betrayed her sister's secret.

Tom continued, 'Sir Jon believes certain information has come into the king's possession through very devious means. He will be with you again tomorrow. Possibly even today, if he is able to make sufficient haste.'

'I pray it is today, Master Kymbe, for I need him very much.' Yes, she did need Jon Welles, and never more than at this moment. She could sense his honest concern for her in the words he had expressed to Tom. Oh, how she needed to put matters right between them. And she would. She would.

Tom felt awkward. 'I fear I have something else to convey to you, my lady. I am to tell you that a certain Ralph Scrope has been sent to Wyberton village.'

Her heart plunged. Not Ralph again! Why had she *ever* smiled at him? She had definitely been a child then, seeing only on the surface, carried along by the feelings that took her towards womanhood. Smiling at Ralph Scrope had produced such ruinous and extended consequences. . . .

Tom watched her face. 'I was given a description of him, and on my way here with my aunt I rode ahead to the village to see if there had indeed been anyone seen matching the information. He is there now, and by his accent is believed to be from the north. And he is consorting with Lucy Talby, and stays with her and her sister Judith in the cottage where the Talbys have always lived.'

'Fowls of the same foulness, Master Kymbe.'

'This Scrope is known to you?'

'He claims to be my husband, but he is not. All he has ever been is a thorn in my side.' She looked at him. 'Do you stay here now, Master Kymbe? Or return to Friskney?'

'Sir Jon instructs me to remain with you until his return.'

She gazed at him, and then drew a heavy breath. 'Well, I came out here to ride and then perhaps take a little walk, and that is what I shall do.' She moved her palfrey on again.

They reached a point where there were willows and bushes ahead, crowding the sides of the causeway and rustling pleasantly as a light breeze crept up. Cicely reined in again. 'I will walk now, Master Kymbe. If you please?'

He dismounted and came to assist her, lifting her down easily and being as sure as Jon had been that she was steady on her feet. 'Do you wish to be alone, my lady?'

'Yes.'

'Please do not leave the causeway. I know there are inviting paths that lead down to seemingly solid ground, but marshes are treacherous. The eye is deceived.' He smiled. It was a reassuring smile. Everything about him was comforting.

'I will be careful, sir.'

Mary glanced around uneasily. 'I do not like it here. Lights are seen at night, will-o'-the-wisp, jack-o'-lantern, and strange noises are heard. Wails and howls.'

Tom frowned. 'Jesu, Mary, there is no cause to say such things now, in broad daylight. Do you wish to frighten my lady?'

'I am not frightened, Master Kymbe,' Cicely said, 'merely curious. I have never seen will-o'-the-wisp.'

'Nor will you now, my lady, for it is daylight,' he answered firmly, still annoyed with his sister.

'I do realize that.' With a smile, Cicely turned to commence her little walk. No, her little waddle, for to be sure she possessed no grace at the moment. It was tiring carrying her child now, and she wished it to come into the world, a contented, healthy baby. She rested a loving hand against her swollen belly. Never would she regret this. Never. Because her love for Richard was too great.

'I wish you were walking with me now,' she whispered to him. He did not respond, but she knew he could hear. He was part of her. At all times.

The willows whispered gently, their leaves sometimes white, sometimes green as the little breeze played through them. Then she came upon one of the inviting paths of which Tom had warned. It did indeed look safe, and it led down to what was clearly firm ground, because there were more bushes and at least one small tree. A breeze had risen, and a pale flutter caught her eye among some of the bushes a little further out. What was it? A seagull? No, for it was the wrong shape. Much longer. And it was made of cloth.

But then she realized, by its form, length and width, what the cloth could well be. She *had* to go closer to see. Ignoring Tom's advice, she went down the path and on to the marsh. As she drew near, she proved right, for it was a baby's swaddling cloth, tied to a stick, like a streamer to a pole. As she pushed through the bushes towards it, she realized the stick had been plunged into a small mound that looked like a tiny grave. Someone had buried a newborn baby in this place? But why? Then she saw that on the branches all around there were trinkets and spells, ribbons and wooden images. All manner of sorcery. Cold dread settled over her, and she felt as if the breath were being sucked from her.

The breeze rustled the bushes and seagulls mewed overheard, so that she was only vaguely aware of Tom shouting to her from the causeway, but she was too absorbed in what she saw to take notice anyway. She moved even closer, and only then observed the lovers on the ground, engaged upon violent congress. They were not just any lovers, for one was Ralph Scrope, and the other Lucy Talby. Their lovemaking was passionate to the point of being frenzied, with Ralph driving in so hard and fast that his pale backside moved up and down like bellows. Lucy was spread beneath him, her wide-parted thighs fully revealed as she writhed and moaned, clawing at his back as if she would rip him into shreds.

Tom called again, much closer now, and Cicely glanced around to see he had ridden to the path and was dismounting to commence a hurried descent of the path. Mary waited anxiously on the causeway with the horses.

At last the lovers realized they were no longer alone, and scrambled apart as if scalded. Ralph hopped about, shoving his dwindling member out of sight and struggling to straighten his clothes. He was comely enough, with brown hair and hazel eyes, and Cicely had once found him pleasing. No more.

Lucy raised herself to a sitting position. She was naked to the waist, her heavy breasts thrusting forward. Her gown was still pulled up around her hips, and she made no attempt to close her thighs or hide her crotch. Her gloating expression spoke an entire book. *Your husband had me like this, my fine lady, so many times that he wore his own path. And now your enemy fucks me as well.*

Cicely recoiled as the silent words came clearly into her head, as if directed there. She turned deliberately to Ralph. 'In whose pay are you this time? I should beware, Mistress Talby, for this man changes allegiance as easily as he probably does his whores.'

'What should I care of his allegiance?' Lucy replied, 'It is his cock I am interested in.' The witch got up, with only

240

a passing gesture of making herself presentable.

Ralph took a threatening step forward towards Cicely. 'You are *my* wife, not the wife of Sir Jon Welles, and I will claim you yet! The king will find in my favour!'

'I do not think so, sir. If you think that, you do not know your latest king very well.'

'I will have you yet!'

'No, sir, you and I were never married, nor even hand-fast or linked in any way, except in your imagination. You forged Richard's signature and appended his seal. *You*, sir.'

His eyes gave his guilt away, but he remained defiant. 'It was not in *your* imagination that you got yourself with child! Who by? I think I know, for he wore a crown, did he not? I saw how you looked at him, even while you pretended to love his son!'

Cicely was dismayed. 'You are mad,' she whispered.

Ralph smiled. 'The present wearer of that crown suspects it, my lady. No, he more than merely suspects it, he is convinced of it.'

'Because *you* told him?'

'Yes, I told him, but he suspected it already.'

She gave no outward sign of the sudden panic that ran riot through her veins. 'You cannot have told him anything for a fact, sir, and so you will have to explain your falsehoods. This child is that of Sir Jon Welles, as I think King Henry knows well enough. I did not lie with *my* uncle, I lay with *King Henry's* uncle, although I confess King Richard was a *very* attractive man. Hard to resist, I would imagine. Unlike you, Ralph Scrope. *You* I could resist until doomsday itself.'

Ralph stepped forward, a hand raised to hit her, but then he saw Tom running towards them, and stepped back warily, reaching for his dagger. But his belt still lay on the ground where he had discarded it.

Even as he thought of bending for it, Tom was there, his own dagger weighed in his palm. He drew Cicely to safety behind him. 'Are you all right, my lady?'

'Yes.'

Tom returned his attention to Ralph. 'Scrope, you have threatened Lady Welles, and intended to subject her to violence. I will see that Sir Jon is informed. I do not doubt he will complain to his nephew the king of your dishonourable conduct.'

Ralph went pale. 'I did not threaten Lady Welles.'

'I saw your raised hand about to strike her.' Tom continued to weigh the dagger threateningly in his palm.

'You heard and saw *nothing*!'

In answer Tom suddenly hurled the dagger at Ralph's right foot. It found its mark. He screamed and fell down, clutching at his shattered, bleeding instep, not daring to remove the dagger because the blade had passed right through to pierce the ground.

As Ralph's agonized cries and sobs continued, Lucy looked steadily at Tom. 'How very accurate your aim, Master Kymbe, but you are otherwise singularly unobservant.'

'Unobservant?'

She nodded at the little mound, and the swaddling band. 'What do you think, Master Kymbe?' She smiled coldly.

His face changed and he stumbled back a step. Cicely knew instantly that the swaddling band had been prepared for *his* child. Lucy Talby *had* overlooked Felice de Burgh and caused the baby to be born dead!

Cicely put a steadying hand on his arm. 'Have a care, Master Kymbe, for she *wants* you to lose control. There is something, I know not what, that she can do with your anger.' She turned to Lucy. 'I intend to tell my husband about this, and it will not be just my word but Master

Kymbe's as well. And my maid's.' She indicated Mary, still waiting with the horses on the causeway. 'My lord has more than repaid any debt he once owed to your father, and will no longer tolerate you on his lands.'

'Oh, how clever you think you are. Sir Jon is not here, and when he does return, you will not be here either. Or the child that is not his anyway.'

Tom glanced quickly at Cicely.

Lucy spoke again. 'I have overlooked once, my lady, and can overlook again,' she said softly, fixing her gaze upon Cicely's belly.

Tom caught Cicely and turned her swiftly away so that her back was to the witch, then he shoved Lucy so violently that she fell back. He pinned her there, first removing one of her shoes and then the other. He hurled both as far into the marsh as he could, in opposite directions. Then he took Ralph's dagger from the belt on the ground and set about Lucy's hair, carving and cutting indiscriminately until there were flaxen tresses all around. 'There! Like Samson, you are weakened!' he cried.

She tried to fend him off, but he was so empowered by grief and bitterness that nothing could stop him. At last he scrambled away from her, the look in his eyes warning that killing her was well within his capability. 'Now, walk towards the Witham, and keep walking.'

'Without my shoes?' Her glance moved nervously to the shifting marsh, where there was so little firm ground and so much hidden water. 'And to the Witham?'

'Certes, without your shoes, madam. The marsh will be so soft and welcoming beneath your dainty feet. And so will the tide.'

Ralph was appalled. 'We will drown!'

'Well, now, *there* is a pleasant thought. May some vile serpent devour you both. Now, go!' He reached over to pluck his dagger roughly from Ralph's foot, causing shrieks that echoed across the open landscape.

Cicely watched in astonishment, for it was clear that Tom Kymbe, so calm and agreeable on the outside, was capable of great violence. She knew he was very close indeed to killing these two. Maybe he would have done so had she not been there to witness.

He wiped his dagger on the grass and then straightened. 'Go,' he said again. 'Now! Before I forget my lady is present!'

As one they clambered away, treading from the firm ground into the less certain surface of the waiting marsh, east, towards the river. Ralph cried out time and again because of the terrible wound to his foot, but Cicely felt no sympathy. Part of her wished Tom had so forgotten himself sufficiently to rid the world—and Cicely Plantagenet—of two such banes. They would not get as far as the river, let alone be able to enter it. Tom Kymbe knew that, and so did they.

Tom went beyond the bushes, to where the lovers' mounts had been concealed, and led them past Cicely toward the path, then he slapped them both hard on the rump. They galloped towards the causeway, struggled up it and then set off for their stables, their tails high.

Tom was suddenly overcome and returned to kick the little mound into oblivion. There was nothing beneath it. Tears shone in his eyes as he broke the stick in half, but as he held the swaddling cloth itself, a sudden gust of wind snatched it from him, and swept it high overhead. It flapped and twisted, and then vanished against the dazzle of the sun. Neither he nor Cicely saw where it landed.

She went to him and put a hand on his forearm again. 'Tom—Master Kymbe—I share your sorrow. Truly I do.'

'You have not lost a child, my lady,' he said, and then immediately regretted. 'Forget I spoke. I was not thinking. Please, my lady.' There was superstition in his eyes. A dread of having tempted providence.

'I did not hear you say anything, Master Kymbe. I will commend you to my husband, for he should know how you came to my aid. He will be grateful.'

'I do not need his gratitude, my lady, for it was you I protected.' He managed a smile. 'Forgive me again, for it is not my habit to weep in front of ladies.'

'You are grief-stricken, and if you weep, it is a sign of your strength, not your weakness.'

'You have a way with words, my lady.'

'I am my uncle's niece, sir.'

But as they rode back to the castle, Cicely felt a sudden sharp pain lance through her belly. A gasp was wrenched from her, and she bent forward. 'Sweet God . . . !' Had she been overlooked after all? Had Lucy Talby managed to cast her vile sorcery upon Lady Welles?

In a moment Tom had dismounted, lifted her across from her palfrey to his much larger horse, remounted, and put an arm firmly around her. 'I will see you safely home, my lady.'

She clasped her arms around herself, biting her lip as another jab of pain plunged through her. 'Be quick, Master Kymbe, for I think my baby is impatient!'

He kicked his heels and urged the horse into a canter, leaving Mary to lead Cicely's palfrey. The maid glanced back across the marsh, feeling nothing for Ralph Scrope and Lucy Talby, and then she rode slowly on towards the castle.

As Tom and Cicely clattered into the courtyard, they found it filled with Jon's returned cavalcade. He had just dismounted, and was talking to Ned. Both men turned as Tom's horse appeared.

Jon saw Cicely, and the look of urgency on Tom's face. He came to quickly raise his arms for her to slip down into them. She was weeping with the pain, and could hardly stand, so he swept her from her feet and carried her up the steps, calling out for assistance.

Cicely clung to him, her arms so tight around his neck that she must almost have felt like a vice. 'Why were you away so long, Jon? I missed you so.'

'I am here now, sweetheart.'

'I am frightened.'

'At this moment, I am frightened for you,' he replied.

Chapter Twenty

CICELY'S AGONY HAD not abated, but became far worse as the hours passed. Worse to the point of being insupportable. So much pain, so much demand, so much draining of her strength. It was close to midnight, still Valentine's Day, and she seemed no closer to giving birth than she had at the outset. The travails racked her body, and she was weak of them, sometimes crying—sometimes beyond crying.

The room was stifling. A great fire roared in the hearth and was continually stoked to make it blaze the more, for there had to be heat when a woman was in labour. Moths fluttered around the candles, and the windows were tightly closed and packed against draughts, to retain as much heat as possible. All knots, even those tying the bed hangings, had been undone, for it was feared such things could prevent the child's entry to the world.

A heavy birthing chair had been dragged before the fire in readiness. It was an ugly, cumbersome thing, with a horseshoe-shaped seat, through which the baby should be born. If it was ever born.

Women waited, needed to assist at such a time. They were from within the castle, but Cicely knew they saw only Losecoat Field when they looked at her. She did not want them to touch her, but now feared Katherine Kymbe could not manage such a difficult birth alone.

Katherine knew her work well, but even she was becoming concerned by the obstinacy of the child. She examined Cicely again, running knowing fingertips over her swollen belly and then inspecting between her legs. 'This is no enlarging yet,' she muttered. 'I do not understand. I should see the child's head by now.'

'What is wrong? Is something wrong?' Cicely cried, fresh panic surging through her. Then her breath caught with the agony of another contraction of what felt like every muscle she possessed. The pain did not simply grip her, it galloped over her like a hundred horses, all with nails for hooves.

She closed her eyes to stem the hot tears that stung her with their salt wretchedness, but then she felt Richard's fingers linking gently through hers. She gripped him as tightly as she could. 'You did this to me! *You* did! I think I *hate* you for it!' she cried aloud, drawing astonished attention.

'You love me too much to hate me, sweetheart.'

She began to sob with the cruel pain. How did some women bear ten or more children? Just one should have warned them to keep away from men!

Katherine gasped suddenly. 'She carries the child in the wrong position! See? It comes feet first!'

Cicely wanted to laugh in the midst of her tears. 'If you are right, Mistress Kymbe, I am truly my uncle's niece! Is that not what they now say of him?'

She drew his hand to her lips—*his* hand—and kissed it adoringly. 'I do not hate you, Richard, I love you with everything I am.'

Katherine read her lips. Richard? The women exchanged glances as well. Mary lowered her eyes.

'You will be safe, my dearest, and so will our child. Your suffering will soon be over. Have heart.'

'I have *your* heart,' Cicely breathed, stiffening in

readiness as she felt the pain returning. There was scarce any time between the contractions now, scarce any time to breathe, let alone endure the paroxysms. The pain convulsed through her, as if her inside would be outside, and she almost began to wish she could die, to be free of it.

Richard's fingers tightened. *'Never think it, Cicely! Never!'*

She clung to his hand. 'Tell me you love me. Tell me you will always love me.'

Again Katherine read her lips, and the ladies looked at one another again. Lady Welles was clearly not in her right mind. Had she gone mad of the pain?

'I love you, Cicely, and I always will. You know I am yours, only yours, and that if I could spare you this, I would. I am ashamed to have brought you to such a state, ashamed that as a man I can have all the pleasure but none of the pain. But I do know pain, sweetheart, pain that I can no longer be to you what you need of me. I cannot tell you how much you mean to me, how much you have warmed my heart and my soul, but my love will never fail you. Never. Be strong now, my dearest Cicely, for it is almost over.'

Oh, his skill with speaking of his love, her sovereign lord, her dearest lord. . . . She felt herself relax suddenly, unwilling to fight any longer, and Katherine gave a cry of relief.

'It comes at last, the child comes! Help me, we must lift her to the chair. This will not be easy for her, not with the child the wrong way around.'

The women hurried forward, and Cicely felt Richard release her hand as she was carried to the birthing chair. She was hardly aware as Katherine did all she could to help the child into the world. The pain was such that unconsciousness pressed close. She was not giving birth to a child, but to every organ! She screamed in the final moments, as Katherine at last drew the baby from her.

Cicely heard the midwife slap the child, and then its first wavering cry. The ladies forgot their suspicion of Lady Welles, and gathered around in delight as the baby was wiped and oiled, and then swaddled.

'You have a fine boy, my lady, a beautiful, strong, healthy child. A child of St. Valentine, for it is only now midnight. He is early, but you need not fear he will be weak.' Katherine gave the baby to Cicely, who hardly had the strength to hold him.

Cicely gazed through tears at the tiny, puckered face. Oh, how she wished to call him Richard, but she knew she could not. 'I would see my lord now,' she said.

Katherine disapproved. 'So soon? My lady, that is not the accepted way.'

'I would see my lord, now,' Cicely repeated, making certain her lips could not be misread.

The midwife nodded at Mary. 'Tell Sir Jon.'

It seemed an age before Cicely heard his step at the door, but then he entered. The women stood around disapprovingly, for men were definitely *not* welcomed at this early point, before the mother could be cleansed.

Cicely smiled as he came to the bedside. 'You have a son, Jon.'

He looked into her tired eyes. 'You should sleep, sweetheart.' He touched her face gently, and the turquoise caught the firelight, shooting with green, gold and blue.

'He *will* be yours,' she whispered.

'I know that is your wish, sweetheart.'

She saw something in his eyes. 'What is it? Is something wrong?'

'Nothing is wrong, sweetheart. Nothing at all.'

But she knew there was, and needed reassurance. 'Kiss me, Jon. Please.'

He bent over the child to put his lips to hers. 'I love you, Cicely, please know that I do.'

She gazed up at him. 'You love me?'

'God help me, yes, I do.'

She closed her eyes again, for it seemed the room swam a little. She needed to rest. There was a name she breathed as she sank into sleep, but no one knew what it was. She did not awaken as she was carried back to the bed. She did not stir as Jon gave the baby to the women, or when he kissed her again. When he had gone the women cleansed her and changed her, but she slept throughout.

It was still dark when she awakened. The room was firelit, and there was no one there. Not even Mary.

'There *is* someone here, sweetheart.'

She turned her head. Richard was at the bedside, and he bent to take her hand. 'How are you, sweeting?'

'The better for seeing you again.'

'So, I am not hated now?' He smiled that smile, and she looked away.

'Do not make me want you *now*, Richard, for I vow I will kill you.'

He laughed. 'Yes, I believe you would.' He went to the crib. 'We have a son?'

'You knew that already.'

'So I did. You see? He is healthy and will live.'

She watched him. He was still so very beautiful to her eyes, the most beloved prince God had ever created.

'I am not quite *that*, sweetheart, nor should you think it. I am very human indeed, with all the weaknesses that state entails.' He looked down at the baby again. 'We did well, I think?'

'What is to become of him, Richard?'

'I only know that he will live.'

'You would not lie to me?'

'Cicely, do you not believe your king?'

'My king led me astray,' she reminded him. 'But no, my

251

king would not lie to me, he would simply be judicious with the truth.'

He came back to her and she saw something in his eyes. She had seen it earlier, in Jon's eyes. What was it? 'Richard? There is something wrong, I can feel it.'

'You must do as your husband tells you, Cicely.'

She gazed at him. 'You are going to leave me now, are you not?' she whispered. 'Now, of *all* days, you are going from me. Why do you not crush my heart as well? You could not do more.'

'I came to you tonight to be with you and our son, just once. Together. I wanted to affirm my love, for you and for him, but from now on you must turn to Sir Jon. Do not be his Anne, and do not make *me* the instrument of his misery. That is why I will not come to you again. You must not summon me. You *must* not. I demand your vow on this.'

All the moments of their love moved before her now. Every kiss and caress, every tenderness and shared understanding. She knew again that very first kiss, when she had at last realized her feelings for him. And that first night, when she had given her chastity so very gladly. It was all with her again now. He came to her and put his hand to her cheek. She felt him. Jesu, how alive he seemed. She could even catch his fingers and press them to her lips. She *wanted* to be the greatest fool in all Creation.

'And so you will be if you do not relinquish me.' Richard smiled gently.

'I wish I could hide my thoughts.'

He smiled. 'Not from me, sweetheart. Never from me. Cicely, your husband has now told you of his love, he confessed it truly, and I will not stand in the way of that love. You are his wife and are not indifferent to him; indeed you like and need him. What more do you want? You cannot have me. I am dead. *Dead*, Cicely. And I will no

252

longer assist you to make his life the torment I endured. Please tell me you understand.'

She saw him in a blur. 'I know you are right,' she whispered. 'I know it.'

'And have known it in your heart all along.'

'Yes.' Her fingers clenched over his. 'One last kiss? Please?'

'No, sweetheart. If I do that, I will lose my resolve. We both know it. One of us has to make this decision, and it must be me.'

She heard the slight break in his voice, and could hardly bear it. 'Then go, now,' she whispered, closing her eyes, 'before my courage fails.' She did not need to open her eyes to know he was no longer there. But he was still in her mind's eye. Her Richard. As clear and shining as ever.

Dawn was in the offing when Jon came to her. She had awakened only moments before, as if anticipating his approach.

'How are you now?' he asked, coming to the bedside and taking her hand.

'Tired.' She smiled, linking her fingers through his. 'I am so glad you have returned. Please believe that I did not kiss you that time because of Lucy Talby, I did not know she was watching. It matters to me that our marriage is made complete. I want to be one with you, Jon Welles, and when I am able to lie with you, when I have been churched and am strong again, I will *beg* you to let me come to you.'

'And what of Richard?'

'He must be put in the past. I know that. Now. I did not before.' But all she could see was Richard's smile, and the look of love in his eyes. She strove to banish the image. 'I am truly happy to be with you now, Jon.'

'You may soon wish you were not.' He sat on the edge of the bed, close to her. 'You already know that Henry's suspicions are now stronger than before?'

'Yes. It was Ralph Scrope who told him. He said it out of mischief, for he did not actually *know* anything. But Henry cannot be certain, Jon. Ralph was not even in Nottingham when I lay with Richard. Henry can still only suspect, and I will continue to deny everything except that my son is yours.'

'Well, Scrope and Lucy are beyond causing any more trouble.'

'Beyond?'

'I have taken the necessary steps. They were found on the marsh, alive, but are no more.' He looked away. 'I too can murder to protect those who are dear to me. You are dear to me. Your son is dear to me, sweetheart, simply because he is *your* son. That is enough for me.'

'Oh, Jon . . .'

'Love forces decisions on us all, Cicely.'

How well she understood the truth of that. 'I am sorry I was so foolish before you left.'

'You have nothing to apologize for.' He smiled, but then became serious again. 'Cicely, it would seem Henry does give credence to what Scrope told him, but my sister continues to believe I am the father. I will not change what I have said to both of them, but . . .' He looked at her. 'Henry will not wish Yorkist factions to learn there is a male child with Richard as his father and you as his mother. Sweetheart, Henry has to be rid of the threat.'

Her lips parted and she snatched her hand away as she tried to haul herself up against the pillows. 'Rid? *Murder* him? Is that what you mean?'

He made her lie back again. 'It is what Henry has to do, Cicely, and he is bound to act soon. Your child is far too close to the throne.'

'Where are you leading me now, Jon? I know it will break my heart, whatever it is.'

He drew her hand to his lips, and then clasped it tightly. 'The only way I know to be sure of the baby's safety, is . . . to say that he died after birth.'

She struggled to sit up again. 'Died? But he is healthy!' Her eyes were wide, her heart thundered, and she felt dread deep within. 'Jon?'

'And he *will* live, sweetheart.' Jon gathered her close. 'I intend to send him to Friskney with Tom Kymbe, now, before first light, to be brought up as *his* child. The child he has just lost, the child whose body Katherine Kymbe brought here, will be placed in your—our—son's crib. Tom it was who thought of it. He knew from my message that our child was not mine after all. No, I did *not* state as much to him, he inferred it from my words and saw what had to be done. I did not know his notion until I spoke to him after he had returned from the causeway with you. His son will take the place of yours, and will be buried as my son.'

'No!'

'It must be done, sweetheart.'

Tears trickled down her cheeks. 'Please do not do this, Jon. Please, I beg of you. Not my baby. I cannot lose my baby.' *I cannot forfeit* him *as well as his father!*

Jon kissed her hair. 'Forgive me, sweetheart, but I *must* save him, do you not see? It is because of Richard that Tom must take the boy back to Friskney, and treat him as his own child. Tom can do it. The deaths of his lady and his child are not known, for he has not yet informed of them. His lady's demise he can do nothing about, but your child—our child—*can* take his son's name and identity. I will provide for him. Your baby will not lack for anything.'

She struggled to be sensible. 'But, Jon, the ladies here know the baby is well and healthy.'

'They will know they are wrong when they find only a little body in the crib. By then Tom will be well on his way back to Friskney. Mistress Kymbe will take care of him there, for as long as she is still able. Then another will be found. Perchance Tom will find himself a wife.'

'The Kymbes will have my child, while I do not? I cannot bear to think of that, Jon.'

He held her more tightly. 'Tom is a good man, and does not live at the other end of the earth. You will be able to see your boy, Cicely. I do not expect you to give him up completely, just help me to do what I can to keep him safe. You cannot know how it pains me to do this to you, but *please* tell me you understand and accept.'

She tried to compose herself, tried to accept what was happening. 'Jon, this will break my heart.'

He stroked her hair. 'I know, sweetheart, but the child's well-being must come first.'

'I have hardly held him in my arms.'

'Do you wish to hold him now?'

'Yes,' she whispered.

He propped her up a little more on the pillows, and then brought the tiny bundle to her. She cradled her baby, her tears falling upon his little face. He did not like it, and grizzled, but she smiled. 'My tears are because you are to be sent from me, my little boy, but sent to safety.' She looked at Jon. 'What name will you give him?'

'Tom's son was named in honour of my father, who was Lionel. He was always known as Leo, and so Leo is the chosen name. I am happy with that, Cicely.'

'He should be Leo Welles, Jon.'

'No, sweetheart, because he is Leo Plantagenet.'

She gazed at him, and then kissed the baby's forehead before calling upon all her willpower to hold him out to Jon. 'Tell Master Kymbe that I trust him, Jon.'

'Do you forgive me?'

She nodded. 'You know that I do, because I know you are right.'

Jon touched her cheek, as Richard would have done, and then turned. 'Mistress Kymbe?'

Katherine Kymbe was in the doorway with the bag Cicely had seen when she arrived. She watched the old lady put the bag down and then take out a little form wrapped in a blanket. When the blanket was unwrapped, Cicely saw that the dead child was bound with exactly the same swaddling bands as her baby. Tom Kymbe's son was placed in the crib. Taking up the bag again, she curtseyed to Jon. 'I will wait outside, my lord.'

Jon nodded, and then looked down at Cicely again. 'It is as good as done, sweetheart.'

'I feel so for Tom Kymbe.'

'And he for you, sweetheart.'

'Then take my baby to him, Jon. I know well my little boy will be safe and loved.' And very well protected, she thought, remembering Tom's actions out on the marsh.

He bent to kiss her on the lips, and then left. Leo Plantagenet went with him.

She lay back against the pillows and closed her eyes. Her heart was so devastated that she could not feel anything. It was as if she was only acting, and at any moment the performance would end. She wanted to call Richard. Surely he would not be so hard as to abandon her now? When their baby had been taken from her? For a moment his name trembled upon her lips, but she did not say it. She must turn to Jon from now on. And be the wife she had just promised to be.

Chapter Twenty-One

CICELY WAS FEELING well again. Truly well. Her body had recovered from childbirth, she had been churched, and now it was late May. She was seventeen. No, she was now in her eighteenth year. She smiled, hearing Richard's teasing tone, and even seeing the sparkle in his eyes.

She had not tried to summon him, although there had been times when she had come so very close. But the thought of him not responding was even worse than the distress that drove her to the point of wanting to see and touch him. Sometimes, when she longed most for her baby, it was Richard's comfort she needed.

All had not gone well on Henry's progress, for there had been a rebellion, led by Richard's close friend and supporter Francis Lovell, with two members of the high-ranking Stafford family. It had been ill-timed and unsuccessful. The elder Stafford had been executed, the younger spared. Francis Lovell had escaped, it was believed to Burgundy, where he was with Richard's other close friend, Robert Percy, who alone had accompanied Richard to the hunting tower near Sheriff Hutton. To be with Cicely for a few stolen hours.

On first learning of the uprising, she feared Jack had been with the rebels, but it seemed he was with Henry. Against Francis? It did not seem possible. Perhaps he had been involved, but not found out. That seemed more like the Jack she knew. She was relieved he was still alive, and that Francis had escaped. What was happening now she did not know, except that Henry was more secure upon Richard's throne.

There had been no word from him, but just as she began to wonder if Ralph's information about her baby had not been taken seriously after all, there were reports that a man wearing the king's livery had requested to see the registers. He would have found a correct entry, confirming the birth and death of the son of Sir Jon and Lady Welles.

Tonight, however, it was of Jon Welles that she must think. It was time to be a true wife to him. If he would have her. He had made no demands of her, not complained or shown impatience, but had been a courteous and attentive husband. She had not mentioned Richard to him again, but only spoke of her child, at Friskney, not thirteen miles away across the Witham as the crow flew. Further by horse, for the way was inland through Boston, where the first bridge was to be found. She received word of him, and knew he prospered, but until she had been churched she had not been able to leave the castle. Now, perhaps, with the fine spring weather, Jon might take her there. Perhaps.

She stood in her bedchamber as Mary helped her to don her night robe, so very white and costly, embroidered with sweet cicely and tied at the throat by silver satin ribbons. Her hair was brushed loose, and it spilled down over her shoulders in a dark chestnut cascade. She had smoothed rose oil over her body, and her breath tasted of mint. How could it not? Mint was the flavour of true lovemaking, and tonight she wished to make true love to Jon Welles.

'Am I ready, Mary?' she asked.

The maid smiled. 'Oh, yes, my lady.'

Cicely took a deep breath. 'Is my lord in his apartments?'

'Yes, my lady. He said he had papers to attend to. There was a messenger from the king.'

Cicely paused as a cool sensation passed slowly down her spine. A message from Henry? Catching up her skirts, she hurried barefoot from her rooms, along the draughty, torch-lit passage to Jon's door. There she halted. Should she knock? Did he have someone with him? Oh, shades of that first night she had gone to Richard. Then, too, she had halted at the door, tormented with indecision. She had entered on that occasion, and must do so again now.

She tapped and did not know he was there until the door opened abruptly. He was a little dishevelled, his doublet undone, as was the shirt he wore beneath. The room behind him was lit only by a single candle, on the table, where numerous documents and papers and writing implements were in confusion. It made her think of another table, different papers . . . another man.

'Cicely?' His glance moved over her. 'I see this is not a formal visit?'

'It certainly is not, my lord.'

He stood aside and swept an arm to invite her in. Then he closed the door and leaned back against it. 'You may not wish to continue with your intention, sweetheart, because my dear nephew has instructed us to go to Westminster next month, when he will have returned from his progress.'

Her lips parted and her heart sank. 'So soon?'

'I am prepared to invent an excuse, something that will keep you here.'

'And let you go without me? Never. We are man and wife, Jon Welles, and if you go to London, so do I.' She smiled. 'I have to face him some time, and it may as well be next month.'

'He desires you, Cicely.'

'There is nothing either of us can do about *that*.' She felt oddly strong. She would go to Henry, do as he wished, and allay his suspicions. She would do whatever was necessary to protect her husband, her child and her cousin. And in the meantime, she would get Jon Welles into bed, whether he wished it or not!

'Are you my husband, sir?'

'What manner of question is that?'

'A seductive one. I am not an innocent, Jon. I know how to please a man, and tonight I wish to please you. To show you just how very innocent I am not.'

She moved closer, but he took her by the arms. 'I am not Richard.' The words betrayed his uncertainty.

'Nor do I wish you to be. I am *your* wife, Jon, and I have come tonight to be in your bed. If you will let me.'

'Jesu, lady, have I married a siren?'

'Do you want me, Jon?'

'Will I enjoy it more if I make you strive to win me around?'

She smiled. 'Is that what you wish?'

'Further postpone the moment for which I have been waiting? I do not have the willpower.'

She moved closer. 'We are alone, Jon, just we two. I promise you.'

'If you play me false now, Cicely, I—'

'I do not play you false. Please, Jon, I have come here honestly, because I want you. Can you not see how much this means to me? I want to make wicked love to you, I want to do things to you that I will need to confess and atone for.'

'Hellfire, madam, I only hope I am up to it.'

'Oh, I think you are already, Jon Welles.' She slid a hand down over his thigh and then slowly, tantalizingly, to his stiffening erection. 'Yes, sir, you are definitely up to it.'

'Have you no shame?'

'I have left shame at the door.'

He smiled. 'Fie on you.'

'Fie on *you*, sir.' She began to push his doublet from his shoulders, until he took it off for her.

'How much do you wish me to remove?' he asked lightly, invitingly.

'Everything. I would see what manner of man you are beneath your fine clothes.'

'I am just a man, as any other.'

She shook her head. 'No, Jon Welles, you are not as any other, you are my husband.'

And so he took off his clothes, and then stood before her. His shoulders were broad, and his body tapering to slender hips. There were dark hairs on his chest, thicker than Richard's, and his loins were ... a match, she thought. His body was muscular, but not overtly so, and he was tall and straight, without that damaged spine that had made Richard so very dear. But Richard had no place in this bedchamber.

She undid the ribbons at her throat, and the night robe slithered down to settle gently around her feet.

He gazed at her in the softly moving candlelight. The shadows glided over her, finding her breasts and small waist, her curving hips and slender thighs. 'You are so beautiful, Cicely.'

'And I belong to you, my lord.' She moved closer and reached up to put her arms around his neck, stretching up to kiss him, gently at first, for their previous kisses had not been shared with an intention to consummate their marriage. But this was different.

His arms enclosed her, and he returned the kiss with an ardour that drew her on, and she moved her body against his arousal. Oh, it felt so good. So very good. Because it was Jon. Images of him passed through her mind, from those first minutes in the courtyard at Sheriff Hutton, to his strength when she had to meet Henry at Lambeth. He had always been there, always offering his support, and she loved him for it. Yes, she loved him. It was not like the love she felt for Richard, because nothing could be like that, but it was strong and would be constant. Because he was constant to her.

She needed to be made love to again, and to make love, and it was right that it was with him. Her excitement began to mount, and she teased his mouth, nibbling at his lower lip, touching her tongue to his, losing herself in the pleasure of it. She heard the change in his breathing, felt his increasing response. The desire he had felt for her since Sheriff Hutton was pouring through his veins, and was to be satisfied at last.

She drew back. 'Not yet, my lord, not yet.' She sank slowly to her knees and took his erection in her hands. Then she adored it with her lips and tongue, toying with it, coaxing it, and at last took it into her mouth.

'Sweet God,' he breathed.

She savoured him, and it was sheer enjoyment to her. She loved to make love, and Jon Welles was . . . precious to her. He meant so much that she wanted to pleasure him and be pleasured by him. Her body convulsed with the gratification she felt from this act. This incredible intimacy, first shared with . . .

Jon caught hold of his member, gripping the tip tightly. 'I would show a little more masculine stamina, my lady, but you make it pesky difficult.'

She knelt there, looking up at him, her hair spilling around her. 'Do you have a bed, my lord?'

'I do, madam. I only sleep on a board when I am off to war.'

'In your armour?'

He smiled. 'It has been known to some extent, my

lady, but if you think I am about to don all *that*, you are mistaken.'

'I am able to imagine whatever I choose.' She rose. 'The bed?'

He pointed towards a curtained archway.

'Are you not going to carry me off to have your wicked reward? Is that not what knights do once they have rescued their damsel?'

'Some knights, maybe. Just how wicked do you wish me to be?'

'Masterfully wicked, Jon.'

'Very well, what my lady wishes, my lady will have.' He caught her from her feet, as if she were mere gossamer, and carried her through to the bedchamber, where a large bed, hung with blue silk, stood against the far wall. He laid her very gently on the coverlet.

'That was not masterful, sir.'

He picked her up again and virtually threw her down again. 'Will that do?'

'Much better.' She held her hands out to him. Oh, this was so good. He was so different from Richard, and she liked the difference. It was just a difference, no more. Richard had given her pleasure that was so intense, exquisite, and on a level so sublime that he caught hold of her soul and held it forever. *He* would command her until time itself was ended. She had not thought she would be blessed by love again. But here was Jon Welles, with challenge in his eyes and a very visible need to make fierce love to her! And she *wanted* that fierce love.

He got on the bed with her, and she smiled. 'I am at your mercy, my sweet lord.'

'I rather think it is the other way around.'

'No. It is shared.' She gazed at him. 'You are so very dear to me,' she whispered.

'Then let me demonstrate *my* share,' he said softly,

moving close beside her and then leaning over to kiss her. He took command, cherishing her lips, caressing them with his, cajoling them, sucking gently upon them, sliding his tongue to hers, allowing her no escape as he tempted her further into erotic delight.

She gave in to that temptation, returning his desire. Her eyes were closed with the ravishment of it. Oh, how she had yearned for this, and yet had not realized it. Jon Welles held her now, and she was so ready to be made love to again, by a man who cherished her. And this man did. How he did.

Jon kissed her breasts, cupping them tenderly and dragging his lips all over them. His hand moved between her legs, delighting her senses still more.

She stroked his face. 'Come into me, Jon. Please come into me. I must be one with you. There is no need for words now, only for a union that should have happened on our wedding night.'

At last she felt him between her legs, strong, hard, urgent. She arched and gasped as he pushed into her. For a moment, just a moment, she caught the faint, other-worldly fragrance of costmary, but then it was Jon Welles who thrust passionately into her as he was swept towards final surrender to her.

When he came it was with a force that gave her so much delight and fulfilment that she hardly knew where her senses took her. It was not over in a few seconds, but continued, diminishing so gradually that she felt she floated. She continued to move against him, adoring his lips and his throat, still making love, still unwilling to let these moments end.

At last . . . at last he had to draw away and lie back beside her. 'Sweet God above,' he breathed. 'I feel I have made love for the first time.'

She straddled him and leaned down to kiss him again,

lovingly, reassuringly. 'Because you *have* made love for the first time, my lord. To me, and I could storm you again already. I could love you all night, and still want more. Do you understand? I need physical love. It is what I yearn for. The act of love, the feeling of you inside me, the sweet moment when you yield your seed. I have a whore's heart and a whore's body, and like nothing more than to *be* a whore. With you. My husband.'

'And I a poor, defenceless Lancastrian boy.'

She sat up again and looked almost lazily into his dark blue eyes. 'Defenceless? I think not. You are a very strong man, Jon, in mind and in body. You can deal with me, I think. If I decide to let you.'

'So, that is the way of it? I must take the crumbs?'

She drew back a little. 'Do not say that.'

'Why?'

'Bess used to say it. She would take the crumbs rather than nothing at all.'

He knew it concerned Richard.

She smiled again. 'We should not be a happy match, should we? I so strong for York, you for Lancaster.'

'My ferocious Yorkist kitten?'

She smiled, for he had called her that at Sheriff Hutton. 'Quite a kitten.'

'Indeed. I trust I will never feel your claws, Cicely.'

She bent to kiss him again. 'You will not. But Henry may.'

He held her gently away. 'Please, Cicely, do not tangle with him any more than you have to. Promise me, sweetheart, for I do not wish to lose you. You will have to contend with much from him.'

She moved away to kneel beside him. 'I know that note in your voice. There is something you have not told me.'

He sat up as well, and put a hand upon her thigh. 'Yes, there is. I have only learned of it tonight. From Henry.'

She tilted her head to look at him. 'What is it?'

'The court is soon to adjourn to Winchester, where Henry intends his child to be born. King Arthur's city, Cicely. Henry intends to harness memories of Avalon, the Knights of the Round Table and the Holy Grail.'

That sounded like Henry, she thought. 'You have not yet said why you are loath to tell me all this.'

He drew a long breath. 'We are to join the court when it moves to Winchester in August. And when the baby is born—Henry is relying on it being a boy, who can be named Arthur—*you* are to carry it at the christening.'

Her lips parted. 'Me?'

'As the queen's eldest sister, I imagine.'

'Or as a mother Henry believes has just lost a child.'

Jon nodded. 'There is that possibility, but maybe it was not *his* notion.'

'Bess? No, this has Henry's mark.' She looked away, for suddenly it almost seemed she *had* lost her child.

'Sweetheart, if you wish to see Leo, you have only to say, but we should not go to Friskney, not yet, because it might cause speculation. For me to make a special visit, especially with you, would certainly be noticed.'

'Then how can I see him?'

'Tom Kymbe can bring him to you, to show Mary her "nephew". That would be natural enough.'

'Would he do that?'

'Of course.'

'Then . . . please?'

'I will see that word is sent. It will have to be when we return to London.' Jon caressed her thigh. 'I am sorry, sweetheart.'

'Why?'

'Because I share Henry's blood.'

She stretched out a hand. 'Come to me again, Jon.'

He smiled. 'You are indeed a whore, sweetheart,' he

said softly, taking the hand.

'A *Yorkist* whore,' she corrected him, 'and this time I intend to decimate your Lancastrian fortifications.'

'My dear lady, you demolished *them* a long time ago.'

'Should I be pitiless?'

'Oh, I do pray so.'

Chapter Twenty-Two

CICELY KNELT BEFORE Bess in the queen's apartments at
Westminster Palace. It was mid-May, and Henry's wife was
supposed to be four months with child, but it was clear to
her sister, and therefore to almost everyone, that she was
more than that. Cicely knew Henry would not be asserting his marital rights now, for he would not take a woman
who was with child. He would probably not go near Bess
again until it was time to beget the next Tudor heir.

She watched Bess, who paced as she had before. The
queen was splendid in golden brocade with black fur
trimming, and her lovely face framed by a headdress with
a veil that fell down her back, but if she was happy with
her regal lot in life, she gave no hint of it. Instead she was
sullen and hard.

'So, Cicely, you lost Richard's child. How very careless
of you, and how dismissive you appear to be.'

'Dismissive?'

'You do not wear black.' Bess indicated Cicely's lavender gown.

'Richard did not wear black for his son by Anne,'
Cicely reminded her.

'He had his reasons. What is yours, Cicely?'

That my son is not dead? 'That wearing black never really
makes any difference to the depth of grief. It is merely
display for the benefit of others. My baby is not with me,

Bess, and I wish he were. Wearing black will not change that.' She selected the words with care, because Leo was most certainly not dead.

Bess looked at her for a long moment. 'I am not quite sure what you are saying, Cicely, for it seems almost . . . ambiguous.'

Cicely did not respond.

'So, Richard is forgotten, his child is forgotten, and you now cling to Sir Jon Welles?'

'I cling to Sir Jon, yes, but what else you say is not true.'

'How easily you bestow your favours.'

Cicely wished no more of this. What Bess dealt out, Bess could receive. She looked deliberately at her sister's belly, and then at her eyes. 'Was it good to be taken against a wall, Bess? Was it a satisfying experience?'

Bess's lips parted and she recoiled. 'How. . . ? Henry? *Henry* told you?'

'He enjoys to shock and distress, or have you not realized it yet? He thought it amusing to tell me.'

'And I suppose you *were* amused?'

'Bess, I am not your enemy. Please. I am your sister and I would never do anything to hurt you.'

'You hurt me beyond all redemption when you took Richard from me.'

'Why do you insist upon saying that? I did *not* take him from you, Bess, because you never had him in the first place!' Cicely got up without leave. 'I did not do anything with intent to cause you pain, Bess. I . . . loved him. That is all.'

'All? But he loved you, did he not? Well? You had him, and I mean it in whatever way you choose to interpret. You lay with him. With . . . *him*.' Bess turned away. 'Dear God, how I hate you, Cissy.'

'Bess, I cannot help what happened. You of *all* women know what it was—is—to love Richard. It was wrong to feel that way, I know it. He knew it.'

'He resisted me, but not you.'

'He loved you as his niece, Bess.'

'*You* were his niece too!'

Cicely suddenly felt tearful. 'Please, Bess, can we not be friends again? I hate to be estranged from you. Yes, I had his love, and I would *never* wish it otherwise. But I need your love too. I want it to be as we were before. Please, Bess. We need each other, I think.'

'I cannot, Cissy. Not yet. I am married to the wrong king, you see. I have Henry, but it is Richard I still want.'

'Richard is dead, Bess. You cannot have him. Nor can I.' Cicely lowered her eyes. 'So you and I must remain at odds? Very well. I cannot make you like me again. How should I address you now? As Your Majesty?'

'Henry reserves *that* for himself. I am still Your Grace.'

'It was good enough for Richard, and he was a far greater man and king than Henry Tudor will ever be,' Cicely reminded her.

'Yes, it was good enough for him, and he was everything you say.' There was a long silence, and then Bess looked at her again, her lovely blue eyes alight with tears. 'Dear God, Cissy, I have missed you so.' The Queen of England ran to her sister, flung her arms around her, and began to sob. 'I am so wretched, Cissy, so wretched that I wish I were dead!'

'Please do not say that, sweeting. Please.' Cicely returned the embrace, whispering that last word because she was weeping too.

'Henry does not care for me at all. I know *nothing* of love, of tenderness or true desire. I know that you do, because you lay with Richard, and everything that I am tells me how very fortunate you are. You now know love in all its sweet facets and moods, whereas I . . . know only Henry Tudor's rough servicing against a wall!'

Cicely held her tightly.

Bess paused, and then drew back. 'I have never said anything about you to Henry, you do know that, do you not? I knew who had fathered your baby, but not a word passed my lips. If he has learned anything, it was not through me. I could not do that, Cissy, no matter how hurt and jealous I was. And . . . I am so sorry you lost your little boy. You cannot *know* how sorry I am, but at least you have found some measure of happiness with Sir Jon, although as he is Margaret's half-brother, I cannot imagine how you can even like him.'

Cicely smiled. 'You do not know him. He is very different from his sister, and is so good to me.'

'Where is he now? I know he came south with you, but have not seen him.'

'He has been sent to Winchester.' Cicely looked away, for Jon had hardly been allowed to set foot in London before he was sent off again. As yet Henry had not summoned her. She had not even seen him, but his tentacles seemed to be all around her. The waiting was agonizing, but she prayed that he would summon her soon, and do what he would, before Jon returned. She did not want Jon to know, nor would she say. She would tell him Henry had not shown any interest. She looked at her unhappy sister. 'Oh, Bess, I do wish Henry could be good to you.'

'Even I know he will never be a great lover. I have only to *see* him to know that! How he even knows what I look like I do not know, for his eyes still swivel. You may be thankful that *you* do not have to go to his bed.'

'I am. Very thankful.' Cicely lowered her eyes.

'I did not want him to choose you to carry my baby at the christening. I railed against it, but it seemed the more I objected, the greater his pleasure became to insist upon it. But now I am glad he prevailed, Cissy. You will be my child's most senior aunt, and no matter that Henry will

272

be the father, I know you will be kind and affectionate.' Bess laughed. 'Half an hour ago I would not have *believed* I would ever say such a thing. Or be reunited with you.'

'I am glad we are reunited.'

Bess looked at her. 'I am not the Bess of before. I have become hardened and selfish, fighting Henry over everything. It is not the way, I know that. You would have him taking those crumbs from the ground at your feet. Oh, those crumbs. I destroyed everything so much that in the end it was all I had from Richard. Do you remember?'

'Yes, of course I do.'

'I was such a fool. Well, I will not be a fool again. I will not *beg* anything from Henry Tudor. I will simply spend his money.'

Cicely was startled. 'His money? I will warrant you do not get much of *that*!'

'I have discovered a taste for greyhounds and playing cards. A very expensive taste. He has to pay for it all. He does not like it, but he does it. He fears to upset me so much that I lose his precious heir. His *Arthur*! What he will do if I produce a daughter I really do not know. I suppose he will ram me up against the nearest wall and do his kingly duty again.'

'Is it really that bad?'

'Yes.'

Cicely wondered if even Henry Tudor, who had been so incredibly sensuous with her, could really be so brutish with Bess. But then, see what he had done to John of Gloucester. It had been vicious. But how full of loathing Henry was when speaking of Bess. And vice versa.

Bess glanced at her. 'He will send for you soon.'

'He has said so?'

'No, but I know it. Men cannot stay away from you, can they? They are bees, and you are an irresistible honey-pot. Even Henry Tudor feels it.'

'Henry does not want me, Bess,' Cicely replied with almost glib untruthfulness. She to deceive in this. How could she possibly do anything else? 'He likes to torment me, Bess, and probably for the same reason he does you. We both think too much of Richard and he cannot forgive that.'

Bess nodded.

Cicely loathed herself, because she knew there was far more to Henry's attention to her than she was saying. Unless he had changed very much while she had been in Lincolnshire.

Her hope of being no longer of interest to Henry was soon dashed. Not long after, at nightfall, he summoned her to his apartments.

On the way there she came face-to-face with Jasper Tudor, who treated her to his usual glower. She smiled sweetly and dropped him a curtsey. 'How pleasant to encounter you, my lord.'

He grunted something and started to walk on.

But she spoke again, her smile even sweeter. 'Really? How very charming and gallant of you to say so. You are a real adornment to the court, and *such* an embellishment to the reputation of your homeland.'

He paused and turned. 'I wish I could say the same of you, my lady.'

She was not abashed by what was meant to be a crushing snub. 'Oh, I will *never* be like you, Your Grace, for which I am, of course, exceedingly thankful.' Head held high, she walked on, and felt the glower following her.

Under Henry's rule, the royal apartments were not well lit. It did not matter to him whether or not he created a good daily impression, only that he spent as little as possible. He was a man of the grand gesture, but not the day-to-day style and refinement that had been Richard's mark. Henry did not like to spend money on unnecessary light, and so he did not. He would rather strain his eyes than open his purse strings.

His manner was calculatedly intimidating as he stood by a paper-cluttered table without looking up from the document he was studying. His doublet was black brocade, rich and intricate, with a thick, jewel-studded belt that emphasized his slender waist. The emerald was on his finger. It was the only ring he wore.

She sank to her knees in a whisper of silver-stitched violet brocade and lowered her eyes respectfully. 'You wished to see me, Your Majesty?' To call him Henry now might be a little foolish.

He looked at her then, and once again she saw his pale, arresting face. Not good-looking at all, with those high cheek bones, almost hollow cheeks, prominent nose and small chin. His arched eyebrows and hooded, strangely divergent eyes gave him such a cold, menacing air, and his wide mouth was unsmiling. But she now knew what that mouth could do to her composure.

He pushed his long hair back from his face. 'You appear restored, my lady, and as delightful as ever.'

'Thank you, Your Majesty.'

'I am sorry you have suffered so sad a loss.' Had he actually pointed at the brocade she wore, he could not have drawn more attention to the absence of black.

'Please do not speak of loss, Your Majesty.'

'It was Richard's child, was it not?'

'Richard's? You know it was not, Your Majesty, for I have protested my innocence on more than one occasion. The child was that of your half-uncle.'

'With whom I am told you are very close.'

'Yes.'

'How fortunate he is. You will have to marry him again, of course, for which ceremony I will give my royal approval. Eventually. It has now been determined there never was a marriage with Scrope, as I believe you kept telling me. I should have listened. It will be annulled anyway, to be sure of an end to it.'

'So I will be believed to have been married twice?'

'What difference does it make? Marriage is marriage. There is no stigma.'

'There is to me. I despised Ralph Scrope more than you can ever understand.'

'Ah, yes. The past tense. You would now be his widow anyway, would you not?'

'You do know he consorted with a witch? Together they turned sorcery upon me, to destroy my unborn child.'

Henry looked at her. 'I was unaware of this.'

Her dark eyes were wide. 'Your Majesty, perhaps you should hope *you* were not also the object of their wicked necromancy.'

'I do not believe in such things.'

'Nor did I, but I lost my child.'

'Not through witchcraft, I hazard a guess.'

She returned to the matter of a remarriage. 'If you wish me to take my vows a second time with Sir Jon, Your Majesty, then so be it, but please, I beg you, do not expect me to welcome the Duke of Bedford as a guest.'

'Jasper? Why?'

'Because we loathe the sight of each other. He thinks I am a very bad influence on you. He does not appear to know that you can be a perfectly effective bad influence on yourself. I do wish you would tell him so, for I have so many daggers in me—front, back, sides and no doubt the soles of my feet—that I find it hard to move.'

'Jasper means well,' he answered, with a hint of a smile. Only a hint.

'Not to me, so please, Henry, do not inflict him on me, or me on him.'

'As you wish.' He bent to raise her by her elbow, and suddenly she was face to face with him. There was nothing indirect in his eyes now, for both were very much upon her. 'I trust that, having vented your spleen on Jasper, you are not going to be meek and mild with me?'

'I must show full respect for your rank, Your Majesty.' His touch kindled an unwanted warmth within her.

'Full respect? That will be a change.'

'You have brought me here, Your Majesty, and I am at your disposal.'

'How very dull of you, Cicely. Will you at least snarl at me?'

She gazed at him, conscious of his closeness, his voice, his presence. His virility. Yes, she was *so* conscious of that. 'But I am incestuous, is that not what you think?'

'I struggle immensely with my Christian principles.'

'You have some?'

'I do not always have them with me.'

She had to look away. That humour could always sway her, and she so wished it otherwise.

'I have decided not to honour your uncle with a fine tomb after all,' he said then.

She met his gaze again. 'Why am I not surprised?'

'Because, sad to say, you now know a little of me.'

'I know you to be shabby,' she retorted. Did her voice shake a little? Was he aware of it? Yes, he would be, for he was aware of *everything*.

'Oh, excellent. At last you have your tongue fresh from the whetstone.'

'Do you wish us to fight our way to the bed?'

'The thought has a certain appeal,' he answered. 'Oh, do not fear I mean to leave your precious uncle in a mean grave. I will set a suitable monument over England's anointed king. I simply cannot resist goading you, for the sheer exhilaration of your forthright response.'

'I have another quarrel with you, Henry.' She intended to catch him unawares, but she failed.

'Oh, first names at last. I begin to get quite excited.'

'You treat my sister badly.'

He paused. 'And what business is it of yours?'

'It is every bit my business. She is my sister.'

'Your *fond* sister?'

'Yes, fond, for we have made up our differences.'

'Again?'

'Again. I may have promised to make your possession of my body the most carnally rewarding of experiences, but while you do wrong by my sister, I too can be untrustworthy.'

'Yet you persist in demanding truthfulness and sincerity from *me*? How very contrary.' He rubbed an eyebrow. 'So, now we must haggle over my queen? Very well. What is it you wish of me? That I pretend to cherish her?'

'Why not? It is surely not beyond your capabilities. You are Henry Tudor, King of England, and clearly skilled between the coverlets. Or perhaps I give you too much credit.'

'You will soon find out if you do or not, Cicely. As for your sister, she is the most miserable, emotionless woman it has ever been my misfortune to fuck!'

'She speaks highly of you too. Walls are so romantic.'

A light passed through his eyes. 'You think me a brute?'

'I *know* you are. Any man who can treat a woman like that is a brute.'

'Then change me, Cicely, turn me into the chivalrous hero you clearly think I *ought* to be.'

'Chivalrous? I wonder *you* can even say the word.'

'You still think you know everything about me, do you not? You think that because I desire you, I will be grateful for your charity. Well, the one who has to hope for charity

278

is you. I want you to make love to me tonight, Cicely, and I will yield a great deal if you convince me with your kisses.'

'I know I can please you until you will not know which way you face. I can make you want me so much that you will beg me to relieve you of your load. If, indeed, you can hold on to it that long!'

'War is declared?'

'A challenge has been issued. Whether you pick up the gauntlet is entirely up to you. But know this, I *will* make you beg.' She intended to use everything she knew upon him, and, God help her, she looked forward to it.

He smiled. 'Then let us begin.'

'Without preamble?'

He laughed. 'Cicely, merely *talking* to you is all the pre-amble I can endure. I want to be inside you, and I am not wasting time on foolish nothings.'

'There speaks the royal lover.'

He moved behind her and removed her headdress, dis-carding it upon a table. Then he loosened her hair until it fell about his hands. For a moment he paused, moving his fingers into its warmth. 'Even your hair is temptation, Cicely.'

'Should I say the same of yours?' She turned her head, into the lure of cloves, and before she knew it he kissed her on the mouth, there, as she looked around to deliver the retort. His hand was to her throat, smoothing and caressing her as he dwelt upon the moment. A clever little kiss, from lips that knew so much.

Then, as if nothing had happened, he began to calmly unfasten her gown. 'What delights am I about to uncover, my sweet lady? I hope you live up to my many daydreams.'

'And will you live up to mine?'

'I cannot promise a beautiful body, but this is a meeting

of minds as well, I think.'

'My mind remains my own,' she said softly.

'No, it does not. You speak back to me, insult me, are untruthful to my face, and I love every moment. You are such a prize, Cicely, such a prize.'

'Do you *really* see me like that?'

'Oh, yes.'

Her gown slipped to the floor and she was naked.

Chapter Twenty-Three

Henry stepped back to look at her from head to toe. 'Fully clothed, you are astonishingly desirable, Cicely, but without any clothes at all, you steal my very breath. I imagine you have already been told that. By your husband, by John of Gloucester, and, I think, by Richard.'

'I keep telling you that I have never lain with my uncle,' she repeated. 'Ralph Scrope lied to you.'

'You are the liar,' he breathed. 'Every time you speak Richard's name, your desire for him is as naked as you stand before me at this moment. Well, I am your king now, and, thank God, I am not your uncle.' He began to take off his clothes.

'No, you are my nephew and brother-in-law.'

'Both only by marriage, for which I am sure a little secular and ecclesiastic dexterity would soon absolve me. Provided it could be overlooked that I fucked you before setting aside my inconvenient wife. Cicely, you are simply the woman I have to possess at all costs. The fact that you happen to be married to my mother's half-brother, and are also my wife's sister, is a matter of indifference to me. My morals are . . . selective.'

She watched him, suddenly unable to believe she was about to be bedded by Henry Tudor. It had the feel of a dream. But she knew it was not, and when he was naked too, she gazed at him. He was calm, unaroused, it seemed. He had a good body, pale, with reddish hair on his chest, loins and under his arms, and she concealed the thrill she felt to see him thus. That body was about to make demands of hers. Invade hers. She looked up into his eyes, which met hers very steadily indeed. There was no strangeness about them now. And oh, those cloves, moving softly around her. Like an invisible embrace. His embrace.

'Where shall we begin, my lady?' he asked quietly.

She started to move past him to the bed, but he caught her wrist. 'No, not just yet. I require a little intimate attention first.' He pulled her hand down to his genitals, where quiescence had begun to give way to something much more forceful.

Such contact electrified her. That part of him, the one part that could give her the pleasures and ecstasies of lovemaking. Her pulse was beginning to race with anticipation, and as her fingers enclosed him, she exulted in the way he hardened and lengthened. How good it would be to go down on her knees now and take that male joy into her mouth and do all the things she adored to do. She wanted him!

But if she obeyed him without question, she would have lost the battle before it had even begun. 'I have been on my knees to you once since entering this room, and will not go on them again. I will do what you wish, but in the comfort of the royal bed.'

He hesitated, as tempted as she to make a point, but then he gestured towards the bed in question. 'As you wish.'

'I do not wish it at all, sir, you do.' *Oh, you liar, Cicely Plantagenet.*

'There is no answer to that.'

'I am sure you can think of one,' she answered.

He raised an eyebrow and nodded. 'Yes, so I can, but

this may not be an opportune moment.'

She hesitated. 'I know I cannot trust you in this, Henry.'

'Why?'

'I fear you may tell Jon. Please, Henry, swear to me that you will not.'

'You think me *that* ignoble? Who could possibly have made you so cynical? Your charming uncle, perhaps? Now *there* was a man who could probably inveigle his way around Medusa.'

'Whereas no one would credit you with similar talents,' she answered, intending to provoke him.

He raised an eyebrow. 'Such a thought would so beggar credence?'

'You know it would, but then, who again would believe you were blackmailing me into your bed with threats to the lives of others? Who would possibly imagine that cold, emotionless Henry Tudor would be so besotted and libidinous that he would do anything he could to get on top of me? It does not chime with the Henry everyone sees, the one who has to handle his horn every night to gain some relief from it. His Majesty the King, so silently threatening, so devoid of human kindness and so twisted by his own darkness that he can hardly bear to look into the light.'

'An amazingly incisive assessment. You are wrong about the horn, however.'

She looked at him. 'I will sing hosannas when Satan hauls you down to join him.'

'But in the meantime, Satan will have to wait, because you are going to make sweet love to me. I beseech the Great Lord of the Dark to make you as rewarding an armful as even he would wish.'

'Oh, yes, I *am* such an armful, Henry. I love the pleasures of the flesh, Henry, I love its enthralment and its exquisite gratifications. Does that excite you? Oh, yes,

I can see that it does. You do have human blood in your veins after all. So, come to bed with me, Henry, and let me show you what I can do.' She climbed on to the bed and lay back. 'I dare you, Henry Tudor. I dare you to take me and think you can do it solely on *your* terms. King you may be, but not tonight, even in your own bed.' *Such bravado, Cicely.*

'You begin to terrify me.'

She glanced down at his loins. 'Terrify? I think not, for you throb before my very eyes. Come, Henry, let us start with a kiss, and *not* one of your clever, scheming busses that mean nothing at all, even to you.'

'I have yet to *buss* you. I would not be so disrespectful.'

'You would be as disrespectful to me as you pleased, whenever you pleased and however you pleased. I am not such a gull to think otherwise.'

He got on to the bed and leaned over her. 'If you only knew how often I have been here in this bed with you, Cicely Plantagenet.'

'And now you are, in the flesh, and your right hand may have a rest.'

He smiled. 'What an embarrassing thought.'

'But true, I fancy.'

'Make love to me, Cicely,' he said softly.

She hesitated, for to touch him now would be to commence the lovemaking that both tantalized and filled her with detestation. Then, slowly, she slipped a hand behind his head and drew his lips towards hers. Desire flooded through her the moment their mouths touched. She was not repelled at all, she really and truly desired him! Her hands moved over his pale body, and she fondled him, lured him, gave him delight with skills that were both natural and learned. And as she adored Henry with her caresses, her kisses threatened to draw his very heart from its place. If he had a heart. Well, *something* was beating in his breast, so she could only suppose he was mortal. Whatever his form, she worshipped him with her body, played havoc with his senses, and showed him what a kiss could be. Not that he needed showing, for he returned her skills. He could never aspire to be Richard's match, but came closer than she would ever have credited him capable.

She lost herself indulged in the giving and taking of pleasure, moving sensuously against him, loving, exciting offering him delights. And she moved down his body, for that one magical intimacy, the worshipping of his masculinity. She adored it with kisses and caresses, loved its taste and the thought of its potency, and the texture . . . warm iron within warm velvet. She assaulted it with sensuousness, and each pleasure she gave him was echoed within her own body. She abandoned herself to the ecstasy of things that should *never* be shared with Henry Tudor. She heard him groan with the relentless gratification. He was so hard he seemed almost in pain from it, and he succumbed to his senses as she caressed him to the very edge of endurance, before pausing, only to do it again. And then again.

He not only withstood the tender onslaught, but was able to sustain the enjoyment, until at last he pleaded with her to stop. 'For pity's sake! And you accuse *me* of cruelty?'

'I told you I would make you beg, Henry,' she whispered, her lips against the tip of his erection. Oh, how her tongue worked upon him, how her lips played and kissed, how her fingers teased and stroked. But she too found erotic luxury in these minutes, because he was a generous lover, taking care to pleasure her as she pleasured him.

At last she had to kneel up. Her eyes were dark and her final need so great that if he had denied her now she would have wept of it. 'I think, Your Majesty, that the House of York should ascend the throne again.' She bestrode him, a knee on either side of his hips. 'There, the white rose is supreme once more, Henry. Where is your red rose now? Your red dragon? Your royal standard? Ah, yes, I believe I have found the royal standard.' Her breath caught as she felt him against her secret places.

'Yes,' he gasped, 'you would indeed appear to have found it. God's blood, woman, you *do* enjoy this!'

As she eased herself onto him, until he was deep inside her, she had to close her eyes to savour every sweet, trembling sense of it. Such delight, such heart-stopping delight . . . When she thought of how cold and distant he had been at first, it was almost beyond credence that he was now beneath her like this. Beneath her, inside her and returning her caresses. She moved slowly up and down, each movement drawing him towards the peak he tried so desperately to delay. 'Do you not enjoy it too, Henry?' she whispered, at last bending down to whisper against his ear, while continuing to move slowly on his virility.

'I will tell you, if I live long enough,' he replied softly, his fingers pushing lovingly into her hair.

'Take me now, Henry,' she breathed, 'make love to me now, for it is *your* turn to do the pleasuring. Do what you will with me.'

He slid her over until she was on her back, spread-eagled and at his mercy. 'The House of York appears to be overthrown yet again, my lady,' he breathed.

'So it does. Just how ardently are you going to complete the defeat?'

He smiled. 'Oh, I think I will decide as I proceed,' he said softly, bending to kiss her breasts. It was not simply a kiss, but an act of love in itself, as was the way he kissed her abdomen and then the springy hair at her groin. Then . . . then he moved further down, kissing every part of her.

It was so good to acquiesce, to let him take her over completely. His lips and tongue were as knowing and fulfilling as hers, and the way he stroked her body made her feel he stroked her soul. What a fool she had been—and Bess still was—to ever think Henry Tudor would never think of the woman to whom he made love. How wrong she had been, for he possessed such sensuality that she felt he truly loved her. That she was all that mattered to him. She almost felt the same towards him. If it were not for Richard, perhaps she would.

This Henry Tudor was very far from being a brute, and she could not hate him. But she could—and did—hate herself, because traitorous, unacceptable, perfidious, *irresistible* reward undulated relentlessly through her. That familiar, exquisite, rippling joy, known first with Richard, shared again with his son and then with her husband . . . but now with Richard's conqueror! She should push this man away, deny him the climax he sought, deny *herself* that climax. But she could not, because she wanted to share it with him. Share every second of his surrender to her. And hers to him.

And when at last he entered her, there was no selfishness for he made sure he did not forsake her or leave her behind. And when he knew she was at a peak, he prolonged it for her. But at last he had to come, and the emotion was so intense that he cried out. His eyes were closed, his face flushed, his hair damp, and like Richard at this same moment, he was beautiful to see. She felt everything with him. Everything.

Eventually, the acute gratification began to die away, and he sank down against her, stretched her arms above her head and linked his fingers tightly between hers. Then he buried his face in her hair. It was so tender and revealing, telling her that Henry Tudor was not as invulnerable as he pretended. And that perhaps what he felt for her really did go beyond mere desire. Certainly, for these moments, he sheltered honestly against her, and she, God help her, felt honest enjoyment in such closeness to him.

He lay thus for a long while, but then found the will to move, and lay on his back beside her. 'That was, without question, the best fuck I have ever had,' he said at last.

'Should I thank you for the compliment?'

He looked at her, and touched her dishevelled hair. 'No, but it *was* a compliment.'

'And so gallantly said.'

'I am not a man of gallantry.' He waited, and when she did not answer, he smiled. 'Now you disappoint me again. Where is the stinging retaliation?'

'You delivered it yourself. You are *not* a man of gallantry.' It was not true, for the consideration his love-making had just shown her had been very gallant indeed.

'That is more like it.' He glanced at her. 'You are right, you *were* born for pleasure, your own as much as that of the fortunate fellow you lie with.'

'I still despise you.' *Oh, Cicely, that is no longer true either . . .*

He nodded. 'At least I know you enjoyed it more than you wanted.'

She looked away. 'I marvel at your stamina.'

'So do I. Jesu, woman, you know how to make love.' He looked at her. 'It *was* Richard, was it not? The man you lay with first? The one who wrought all this in you?'

'Do you wish for the truth, or would you prefer me to lie?'

He did not say anything for a moment. 'What a very willing pupil and niece you were, to be sure.'

'That would be to say he was the most exquisitely talented, unbearably desirable and unbelievably gratifying of teachers, would it not?' She smiled. 'Maybe he was, but I would be deceitful to claim such intimate knowledge of his carnal talents. I have no idea what he was like in a bed. Or against a wall. The truth is that I did *not* give myself to Richard. Nor did he show any such interest. I do wish you would believe me and stop suggesting I was guilty of repeated incest.' Such blatant, *blatant* lies! 'Was that my attraction, Henry? The fact that you thought I had lain with my uncle? I am sorry to disappoint, but at least you have only discovered the unexciting truth *after* I have shown you what it is to bed me.'

'*I* bedded *you*? That is not quite my recollection.'

'I did warn you.' *And you warned me. Yes, I know it, Henry.*

'Yet you *look* so sweet and innocent.'

'I cannot say the same of you.'

He smiled a little. 'No, probably not.'

'You have a cold, vulpine, tight-mouthed, *mean* face, Henry.'

'Why, thank you.'

'And I hope my sister buys a hundred greyhounds and loses a very great deal at cards.'

He looked at her again. 'She certainly does the latter. The former has not yet become too ridiculously costly. I imagine *you* would purchase every greyhound in England, even the ones with three legs, and then lose much more at cards, just to spite me. You would probably wager Westminster Palace itself on the turn of an ace.'

'For spite? Oh, yes, I would.'

He reached to take a strand of her hair, and she pulled sharply away. 'No! Do not do that!'

He leaned up quickly. 'This is where we were once before, as I recall. Who was it, Cicely? Why does it affect you so?' He watched her carefully.

'My father. *He* used to do it to annoy me.'

'Your . . . father?' Quite rightly, he did not believe her, for it had Richard of whom she was again reminded. As Henry suspected, but she would never admit.

'Yes.'

He got off the bed. 'Come, I will dress you.'

'I am dismissed?'

'I have had enough honesty, Cicely. For the time being.'

She got up as well, and he turned suddenly, pulling her close and kissing her almost tenderly. Yes, it *was* tender! Their lips melted together again. She could not resist him, because she did not want to. He had made love to her, not simply taken her, used her for his own satisfaction. He had made love, and he was very, very good at it. Who would ever have thought that Henry Tudor had such erotic talents? Who would have thought so much about what had happened here tonight?

He smoothed her hair back from her face and ran a gentle fingertip down her cheek. 'I am sorry for the hurt I have done you, Cicely, but I would not undo it. Do you understand? I would face Richard at Bosworth again, and if it took renewed treachery to defeat him, I would still accept the victory. But I *do* wish it had not hurt you so. You are unique, as the owner of this cold, vulpine, tight-mouthed, *mean* face knows well. I will not hurt Lincoln or my uncle.'

'But you will keep the threat to hand.'

'Of course. I would be foolish not to. As for my queen, I will be kinder, and not continue to treat her as I am at present accused of doing. Provided she spares my purse. I will do it for you, not for her, because her deep animosity has probably alienated me forever.'

'Make love to her as you made love to me tonight, Henry, and she will soon not hate you.'

'I will do my duty, that is all.' He turned to gather her gown from the floor. 'Does that make me a good little Henry, or a bad little Henry?'

'Neither. You are simply the king. And a shabby one at that.'

'Shabby? *Now* what have I done?'

'You have insisted that I carry Bess's child at its christening. Why, Henry? To make me hold a baby when you know I have just . . . lost my own?'

He looked at her. 'Is that what you think?'

'What else can I think?'

'Perhaps that I simply wish to see *my* baby, my *son*, in *your* arms?'

Her lips parted. 'No.'

'Then give it a little thought. I want *you* to carry my son at his christening. It matters to me. That is all. The rest of it is of no consequence.'

'And you are the king.'

'You had noticed?' He began to help her with her gown.

'I have noticed much about you, Henry, and much of what I see is not admirable. I have just lain with you to save the lives of my husband and cousin. I did not lie with you out of affection or even anything approaching it.' *But I lie to you now, because already I want you to kiss me again, hold me again, make such love to me again.*

'I know exactly how you felt with me not long since. What you still feel now. You may not like your reaction to me, but you cannot deny it. You need what I can give you, *cariad*, just as I need what you can give me. Put us together and fire is kindled.' His hands paused upon her naked shoulders, and for a moment she was in the hunting tower again, and Richard was attending her. The salt of guilt stung her eyes and she closed them, because tonight she had found immeasurable physical reward in the arms of his adversary. She had been unfaithful to Jon, after promising him fidelity, she had pushed thoughts of Richard aside, and John of Gloucester. And she had played Bess false. Again. With this second king.

'Tears? Surely I was not *that* overwhelmingly pleasing?' Henry closed the fastenings of the gown, and then studied her. 'There is so much I wish to learn of you, Cicely, both inside and out. All those secrets that I know you keep close to your sweet breasts.'

'I have no secrets. You know everything.'

'You surely do not expect me to believe *that*!' He began to dress himself again. 'One thing puzzles me,' he said then, as he attended to the comfortable arrangement of his spent loins. 'You have omitted all mention of John of Gloucester.'

She turned slowly. 'You enjoy being hurtful, do you not? You gave away too much of the real Henry Tudor on that bed, and so you punish me. God forbid you should punish yourself. I loved Richard and his son, and lost them both because of you. Richard I can almost bear—almost—because he died honourably and with great courage, in battle, defending his realm and everything else he held dear, but John was your personal victim, Henry, and is now what *you* have made of him. There was no glory, no battle, no clash of weapons, just your inconceivable savagery and lack of conscience.'

'Cicely, there was nothing calculated about what I did to John of Gloucester. It was on the spur of the moment, an act that was *not* in my character, no matter what you may think. It was monstrous jealousy, and it poured like acid through my blood. It corroded my judgement and made me less of a man for it. I regret it. He had been granted your hand, Cicely, you loved him—he had probably *fucked* you!—and I could not see clearly because of it. And although I know you do not want it, I *do* offer my apology.'

'*Apology?* Of what use is that to *him*?' Tears filled her eyes again.

He folded his fingers together and tapped them to his lips. 'I believe enough has been said, my lady.'

'Now the distance is put between us?'

'You put it there.'

'No, *you* did, Henry. You had to be despicable again,

did not you?'

'Perhaps because *mine* is the conscience, Cicely. I will not let you know me. I will keep you out. Oh, I have given myself away in many instances, mostly tonight, I realize that, but then so have you, I think. I will *not* let you go. I will want you again, and again, because you light such a flame in me that I rejoice in the scorching heat.'

'And if I refuse you?'

'You will always come to me and be with me, Cicely.' He gave a hint of a smile. 'Oh, that haughty, challenging look, that pride and defiance. Confronting your uncle at Bosworth was *nothing* compared to confronting you on a bed. You stir my blood so very much. So go, my lady, before I decide I must have you again, right now.'

As she went to the door, he spoke again, softly. 'Thank you, Cicely.'

She turned to study him, and saw sincerity in his gaze. 'Perhaps I should thank you too,' she answered.

'Perhaps. I want you to know that was one of the two most exquisite experiences of my life.'

'And the other?'

'Gaining the crown at Bosworth. But I will not tell you which matters most.'

Chapter Twenty-Four

BESS HAD SENT a message that she wished to walk with her sister in the palace garden, and so Cicely waited by the wall, where the river lapped the stonework. It was a week since she had lain with Henry, and she had not heard anything from him since. She had not even seen him. Jon was still detained in Winchester, and there was no freedom for her here. She could not even ride out, because Henry ordered that the queen's sister had to have an escort of a dozen men-at-arms, with all the trappings of her royal position.

She continued to wait, pacing slowly. There was no sign of Bess. The spring breeze fluttered the gauzy veil of her headdress, and her lime silk gown dragged on the grass, where the daffodils had now disappeared, to return again next spring. There were so many memories here in the garden, but not of Richard. She had never been with him here, only in the palace. She *had* been with John, though.

She drew a long breath, and thought instead of her husband, whom she missed so much, and whom she set completely apart from Henry, in a corner of her heart and body that the king would never reach. It was where her faithful self still dwelt. Oh, how she tried to justify herself. She had lain with Henry, and enjoyed it far, far too much. She would enjoy the next time too, and the time after that.

When Jon returned, she would lie with *him* again, and enjoy him as she had before. And she would give him all the pleasure she could—and more—not only because she loved him, but to assuage her guilt.

There was a tread behind her, and she turned, expecting to see Bess, but instead it was her cousin. 'Jack? What brings you out here? Surely not the sun and air?'

He seemed puzzled. 'I rather thought *you* brought me out here? I received a note.' He bowed over her hand. His wine-red doublet was slashed with gold satin, and his black hose clung almost wilfully to his perfect legs and hips. There was a soft charcoal velvet hat on his long, wayward curls, with an amethyst brooch that went so very well with the same stone on his finger. He did not reek of the Tower now, but was fresh with thyme.

'You are as fragrant as a herb garden, sir,' she said. 'I still cannot believe Henry imprisoned you, a royal earl, in a miserable part of the Tower. Why not the royal apartments? It was your right.'

'Henry is not concerned with my rights at the moment, sweetheart.'

'Thyme suits you.' She leaned closer to sniff. 'In your hair as well?'

'I washed *everything*, believe me.'

'I can well imagine. If I were not already taken, I might offer to smooth all of you with a scented oil.'

He grinned. 'What an arousing thought.' Then he hesitated. 'Sweetheart, I was very sorry to hear of your baby. I know how much it must have meant to you.'

She hesitated. Should she tell him? She *wanted* to tell him. 'Jack, my baby—' She broke off, for there, seated beneath an apple tree about ten yards away, was Henry's imp, and he was watching their lips very carefully.

She caught Jack's sleeve and made him turn to lean on the wall, looking out at the river. 'We have a spying imp,' she said quietly. 'No, do not look around, for I do not wish anyone to realize we are aware. I am here because, supposedly, Bess wishes to walk with me. This meeting between you and me has been designed, most likely for Henry to learn if we plot anything. Or if I will embark upon an affair with you.'

He smiled. 'If Henry spies upon you, he clearly still has an itch.'

'This may not be anything to do with that, Jack, more that he is watching for any sign of planned rebellion by the House of York. But yes, he has an itch for me.' She did not add that in the end it had been an itch she had more than enjoyed alleviating.

'There is something on your mind, sweetheart?' Jack was watching the nuances flit across her face. 'I confess your expression is most intriguing.'

She smiled. 'Nothing you need to know about, Jack de la Pole.'

'Which means I would *like* to know, very much. However, if you mean to be disagreeably tight-lipped . . .'

'I do, but there *is* something I wish you to know. Jack, my little boy did not die. Richard's son is well and healthy,' she whispered, putting her hand on his, although it could only have been seen from the river, and there were no craft close by.

He gazed at her, his dark eyes alight. 'Truly?'

'Yes. I will not tell you how or where he is, just that he . . . is. I have not seen him since only a few hours after he was born, but I know he is safe, and with someone I trust. Someone my husband trusts. I would have seen him again by now, but he had a snuffle and the lady caring for him decided it was best he did not travel. He is well now, though; word was sent.'

'So, we do after all have Richard's son, by a highborn Yorkist princess?'

'Yes. But Jack—'

'I know. I am to leave him alone. I will. Until he is of an age to understand his heritage. You must at least allow me that, Cicely.'

'I cannot stop you, Jack. I will tell him of his father, make no mistake of that, but the decision about it *must* be his, and his alone.' She lowered her eyes. 'I will also make sure that he fully appreciates and respects Jon Welles, who may not be of the House of York, but is one of the most honourable men I have ever met.'

Jack smiled. 'I will keep faith with you. You are astonishingly strong, Cicely. I see more and more why Richard cast caution aside for you.'

She looked away, because suddenly the pain of her loss brushed close again.

Jack drew her hand to his lips. 'You had his heart, Coz, and that will always carry you. Just remember it.'

She studied him again. 'You always seem to know what to say.'

He pretended to be offended. 'You do not have to sound so taken aback.'

'I was praising you, sir.'

'Then I forgive you.'

'Have you seen John again?' she asked after a moment.

'He does not know me. Oh, he is treated well enough now, when it is too late. Tudor is a barbarian.'

'Yes. But he does have a conscience.'

Jack's eyes met hers. 'And how would you know that?'

She returned his gaze, and said nothing. But her face felt hot and she knew she blushed.

'Jesu, you have been in his bed?'

'Jack, if I had not gone to him, *you* might now be as John is.'

He straightened. 'You went to him to save *me*?'

'And Jon—who does *not* know, nor must he ever! I

would protect you both, as I believe you would do for me, Jack. You and I are of the House of York, are we not?' She smiled.

'Oh, Cicely . . .'

'I have told you because I am afraid you may tread unwarily with him, Jack. He is so very poisonous. You *must* take care, and always seem loyal to him, even though you are not.'

'I already take care, sweetheart. Believe me.'

She gazed at him. 'I do so like being with you again, Jack. It reminds me of . . . other days.'

He nodded. 'I echo that feeling.'

She watched his handsome face. 'There *is* something planned, is there not?'

'Perhaps it is best I do not answer that, except with a denial.'

'*Please* be careful. I cannot lose you as well.'

He changed the subject. 'So, soon we will all be whisked away to Winchester, eh? To await the birth of the new Arthur? Dear God, Tudor has grand notions of his rather mundane ancestry. Still, every member of the House of York is to be there. And the House of Lancaster too, one supposes.'

'The House of Tudor,' she corrected. 'I think it will not be long before Lancaster is forgotten and Jasper has become the second lord of the realm.'

'No doubt, although I fancy Jasper wishes to sit back from the reins of government.'

'The further back the better, as far as I am concerned. The middle of Cardigan Bay during a terrible storm would be perfect.' She looked at Jack. 'Did you know I am to carry the baby at the christening?'

'Yes, and very pretty you will look too. I was so angry when I heard, believing you had lost your own baby, but now— Well, the joke is upon Henry, methinks.'

'Jack, I do want to help you, but I will not put my husband at risk.'

He smiled. 'I know, sweetheart, nor will I seek your help. But I *will* seek your company and your counsel. Besides, from what you have said of Henry, you already do more than your fair share for the House of York.'

'Oh, Jack, there are kings and there are kings.'

'Yes, and you, my lady, have very personal experience of two of them.'

'Which Bess does *not* know, Jack, nor are you to make the mistake of thinking she does. She knows of Richard, and my child, but believes the latter lies buried at Wyberton. You and Jon are the only ones at court who know.' She thought better of mentioning Mary Kymbe.

'I would not speak of such a thing to Bess anyway. I certainly do not seek her out.' He gazed over the river. 'I know she loved Richard and loathes Henry, but I cannot sympathize. Oh, I flirted with her at Sheriff Hutton, but it was merely to pass the time, and I have lost all respect for her since then. When I left there with your brothers and Warwick, it was Bess's fault that you, she and John would not accompany me. I will not forgive her for that stubborn selfishness. She simply would not leave while she believed Richard to still be alive. Yet *he* wished her to leave. He wished us *all* to leave. If it were not for her, John might still be free, still able to recognize and reason.'

'I was as guilty as Bess, Jack, for I would not leave without her. And be fair, even if John had gone with you, he would not have gone to Burgundy any more than you did. The boys probably went willingly enough, although how Warwick remained behind I do not know.'

'I thought he *was* with them. I only realized too late that he had somehow disembarked. But your brothers *did* go, Cicely, and to the best of my knowledge are now safe at your aunt's court in Burgundy. Word would have reached me by now if they had not arrived. I think.' He paused. 'Does Henry know about your brothers?'

'He knows they set off for Burgundy, but that is all. It is all *I* know.' She glanced at him. 'I told him, Jack. I did it because of Jon. Oh, the whys do not really matter, just that I gave up the fact of their survival during Richard's reign.'

'So he knows he has legitimized them while they most probably still live? Oh, joy, I love the sweet irony.'

'But they will not live long if his agents find them, and then he will blame Richard for their deaths and all else that is bad he can think of.'

Jack glanced at her. 'I will clear Richard's name, sweetheart. If it is the last thing I do, I will restore him to true honour.' Something made him turn around, and he straightened from the wall. 'Sir Jon!'

She whirled about, her breath catching as she saw her husband's tall, journey-worn figure approaching between the apple trees. She was happy! So happy, just to see him again! Jack was forgotten as she ran to him. 'Jon! Oh, Jon!' She flung herself into his arms, and put her mouth to his in a kiss that could surely leave him in no doubt of her delight. She held him, her arms tightly around his neck, her body pressing to his as she savoured the reunion, relishing the feel of him, the taste of him, the unkempt, travel-weary scent of him. Everything else was forgotten as she made the sweetest love to him with her lips.

At last he held her back slightly. 'Jesu, lady, would you have me roll you here on the grass?' He smiled.

'Yes, oh, yes! Jon Welles, I have missed you so!'

He kissed her forehead. 'And I you, Lady Welles.'

'Why were you so long?'

'There was one excuse after another to keep me there.'

He met her eyes, and she knew he feared that Henry had made sure of his absence for a very personal purpose.

'I am quite all right, Jon,' she said softly, choosing

words calculated to reassure him that nothing had happened. She was aware of Jack, but knew he would not betray her.

Jon smiled. 'Good.' Then he looked at Jack. 'My lord of Lincoln?'

'Sir Jon. Would that I was in your boots at this moment.' Jack came closer, and then turned a little to conceal his mouth from Henry's little spy. 'Beware of imps under apple trees, Sir Jon.'

Cicely caught Jon's hand, aware that the veil of her headdress had floated around in such a way that whatever she said could not be observed. 'Jack and I did not meet by accident, Jon, nor did we arrange a meeting. We were both lured here on a pretext. It has to be Henry's work, because the imp has been set to watch every word we say. We have been careful to conceal our mouths. Henry must be alert for any hint of a Yorkist plot. That is all we can think.'

Jon looked intently at Jack. 'And *is* there any sign of such a plot, my lord?'

'No.'

'Do not involve my wife.'

'There is nothing in which to involve her, Sir Jon.'

'You had best not be lying to me.'

Jack shook his head. 'I do not lie.'

But Cicely knew he did. Swearing fealty to Henry Tudor meant nothing to the trueborn heir of the House of York.

Jack bowed. 'I think perhaps my presence is superfluous at the moment. I will leave you to your conjugal pleasantries.'

Cicely kissed his cheek. 'Be careful, Jack .'

He smiled. 'Would I be anything else?' Seeing the look in her eyes he laughed. 'Perhaps it is best not to answer that, my lady.' He bowed to Jon, and then walked away towards the palace, and as he passed beneath a certain window, Cicely was suddenly back in April 1483, three long years ago now, where she had first heard her mother plotting against Richard, then only the Duke of Gloucester, but intended by the dying King Edward IV to be Lord Protector of England during the minority of the new king, Edward V. Even now that fateful window stood open to the spring air.

She smiled at Jon, making sure this time that the imp could read every word. 'Come to my bed, sir.'

'Now?'

'Yes. I need to be with you.'

'I am expected to go straight to the king.'

'But *I* must have you first, Jon. The king can wait.'

His dark blue eyes were quizzical. 'Have you really missed me *that* much?'

'It would seem I have, my lord. I certainly know how very glad I am to have you with me again. So glad that you have my blood rushing and my body all a-stir.'

Leaving the imp to ponder what he had been allowed to read, Jon took Cicely back to the apartment that had been set aside for them. Mary left them alone immediately, and Cicely slipped her arms around her husband's lean waist. 'I am true in this, Jon, I do need you. Now. Because I have been without you long enough to know how very much you mean to me.'

'I should go away more often if my return is to be so welcomed, but perhaps I should take a little time to make myself cleaner and more presentable for the bedchamber? I have come straight to you from a long ride and am far from—'

'No! I want you as you are, sweaty, dirty from the road, and wonderfully male.'

He laughed. 'Very well, madam, that is exactly how you shall have me!' he declared as she placed herself in readiness on the bed. 'Just how wonderfully male do you wish me to be? Ardent? Rampant? Or frantic with lust?'

'The latter, if you please.'

He flung off his coat, loosed his virility, got on the bed, thigh boots and all, to pull up her gown and shove her legs apart. 'Right, madam. Your desire is mine as well.'

He straddled her, his member rigid and his eyes dark. 'Not even a little finesse?'

'None at all,' she whispered. 'Come into me now, Jon! Now, please!'

And so he did, and she writhed with the pleasure of it. She begged him to take his satisfaction, to thrust into her as he willed. Her excitement was beyond control. She did not know why she felt as she did, only that seeing him again had driven all other thought from her mind. She wanted him so much that she was convulsed with pleasure. Her lips demanded of his, her hands explored him, and his name was on her lips. Over and over. This was nothing like being with Henry. This was Jon, the husband she now knew she adored.

She ground her hips to his, tightened her muscles hungrily around him, and arched herself to meet his strokes. Wilder and wilder her emotions ran. She kissed him, licked his skin, adored him, almost fought with herself to have him. There was no thought of others now, for this was her marriage bed and Jon Welles was all that mattered.

His strokes matched her urgency. He was past thought, swept up by her hunger. He could not contain himself for long, not like this, and suddenly he reached a peak that jolted through him so intensely that he could hardly breathe. He gasped at the sheer force of it, and gathered her to him, the better to hold her onto his erection, even after he had been drained.

She clung to him, still moving richly against him and stealing more waves of that delicious pleasure she enjoyed so much. But at last even she was sated, filled with warmth and contentment, and she allowed him to roll on to his back. Then she leaned over to put her lips softly to his again, and breathe the wonderful scent of him.

He returned her kiss and then smiled. 'I feel as if I have been in a battle and somehow achieved victory.' He cupped her breast and smoothed his thumb over the nipple. 'Dare I ask what that was about?'

'I saw you again.'

'You . . . saw me?'

'Yes. That is all. I was so overjoyed that I just had to have you. Without delay. And it was good, Jon, so very good.'

'I am pleased to have been of service.'

'It was more than that, Jon. Much more. You cannot know how I feel just to have you back again. I cannot bear it when you are away. You reassured and comforted me from the moment you came to Sheriff Hutton. I turned to you then, and you have never failed me and never questioned my feelings. You knew how my heart was given elsewhere, knew what that other love meant to me, but still you stood by me. Now I return your love, Jon. I did not know how much until I saw you again. I had to be with you, I had to have you. Does that sound foolish?'

He smiled. 'Sweetheart, the day I fully understand women will be the day of reckoning. But, I confess, your ardour took me by surprise.'

'It was meant to. I wanted to excite you to the same level as *my* excitement. I had to have you like that.'

'Well, you succeeded.' He put his hands behind his head, his long legs stretched out.

She looked at his thigh boots, and then slipped seductive fingers inside one, to caress him. 'You have fine legs, Jon Welles, and these boots are particularly . . . well fitted. And unconscionably high. It looks so very, well, interesting when your, um, cock is exposed to my lustful eyes. There it slumbers, intent upon regaining its potency at its own leisure. I cannot allow that.'

'Jesu, lady, you will have me like a log again if you say much more.'

She smiled, and wriggled around to slip her arms around his hips and rest her cheek against his maleness. She breathed deeply. 'You will soon wish you had stayed in Winchester,' she murmured, kissing his genitals and pushing her face into them. Dear God, how she loved to be with him like this.

'You underestimate me, I think,' he said softly.

'I do hope so.'

He caressed her hair. 'I know you still love Richard, sweetheart.'

'Jon—'

'Hear me out. I know you love him, and I do not want to detract from that. But I also know that you love me enough. I can be happy with that.'

'But I do not want you to think . . . that you are second best. That is *not* what you are to me. You are my new love, Jon, the love who is with me now, who can be physically joined to me now. You are my *present* love.' She moved up to look into his eyes. 'I am a very fortunate woman, Jon Welles.'

'I trust you are about to show your gratitude?'

'Oh, yes, for I have you on a bed, and I am not about to let you go too soon.'

'Not even when the king has requested my immediate presence?'

'Especially not then.' She stopped any further words with another kiss.

Chapter Twenty-Five

LATER THAT DAY, when Jon had been ensconced with Henry for more than two hours, Margaret, Countess of Derby, came to Cicely. She was, as ever, clad in black, with a white wimple that pinched her small face even more than it was already, giving her thin lips a permanently disapproving set.

So far, because of her affection for Jon, his half-sister had shown herself as a friend to this daughter of Edward IV and niece of Richard III, but there would always be an element of doubt and suspicion. On both sides. And perhaps Margaret was suspicious now. Certainly there was something about her that made Cicely suddenly wary.

'Lady Welles . . . Cicely, I am so very grieved for you, and for my brother. To have lost your child so very sadly . . . I also grieve because I have lost a nephew.' Margaret came close enough to take Cicely's hand and clasp it earnestly. Her grim black skirts brushed audibly against Cicely's lime brocade in what seemed like an indictment regarding the absence of black.

'You are very kind, my lady.' Cicely still found it very hard to warm to Henry's mother, because the woman had been instrumental in plotting against Richard, of fomenting so much unrest and treachery that she may as well have killed him herself at Bosworth. But more of a response was needed yet. 'Lady Margaret, I am very grateful to you for . . . sending word to my husband when he was at Rockingham. I wish you to know that whatever Ralph Scrope told the king about my closeness to Richard, it was not true. My child was the child of Jon Welles, not my uncle.'

'Jon has told me so, Cicely, and I believe him. Therefore I believe you. And so, I think, does the king.'

Cicely doubted that very much. Henry would *always* suspect, partly because he genuinely disbelieved her protests of innocence, and partly because, even as he despised Richard, it excited him to think of her willing incest. He could not leave the matter alone.

'I must warn you, Cicely, that you have a foe in my brother-in-law, Jasper Tudor.'

'I realize that. If looks were daggers, I would have been stabbed to death long since.'

'He mistrusts you because you were so close to Richard.'

'I, on the other hand, merely dislike the Duke of Bedford for his own sweet sake.' Cicely had been ignored and cut by Jasper Tudor once too often.

'He is a good man, loyal to Henry throughout his life.'

'I am supposed to be impressed?' Cicely was chill.

Margaret's eyebrows twitched. 'It is my earnest hope that I can bring about a better relationship between you and—'

'I would rather you did not. I have no desire at all to make the further acquaintance of someone who is so biased against me. Everything is my fault, Henry is a cherub. Do *you* think the king is a cherub? No, I thought not. The Duke of Bedford is therefore totally ridiculous, as I am likely to tell him to his face if I have the opportunity,'

'I believe you would too. Well, there is not a great deal I can say after that. Jasper is not accustomed to being berated by a woman.'

'He soon would be if I were around him much.'

Margaret smiled a little, and then gestured for a page to bring her some wine, before seating herself by the fireplace, even though there was no fire. It was still sunny outside, and the Thames was as crowded as ever. 'I trust you are content to be in London again, Cicely? I do not believe Wyberton is one of my brother's most amiable residences.'

'It is not, my lady, although the private apartments are pleasing enough. Especially when Jon is with me.'

Margaret studied her. 'So my brother is still pleasing to you, Cicely? I know that he loves you, but I must always be concerned that the reverse may not apply.'

Cicely was startled. 'Lady Margaret, I *do* return his affection, more than you realize. Why would you think otherwise?'

'Because you have been observed keeping a tryst with the Earl of Lincoln.'

'Well, that is to the point, my lady. May I remind you that the earl is my close cousin?'

'How close, exactly?'

'Not close in the way I think *you* suggest. There is nothing between the Earl of Lincoln and me. He was sent a message, purporting to be from me, that we should meet in the palace garden. I received a message, purporting to be from the queen, to meet with *her* in the garden. Someone made certain my cousin and I were seen, apparently keeping an assignation. It was not my doing, nor was it his.'

Margaret continued to study her. 'Who would do such a thing?'

'Anyone who wished to be rid of the Earl of Lincoln would very much have a motive, Lady Margaret. He was, after all, Richard's heir. No longer, of course, should my brothers still live.'

'Ah, yes, we come to Richard again. That man is my curse, I swear.'

'He is certainly Henry's curse. But why yours? You have everything you ever wished for, my lady. Your son is on the throne, he will soon be the father of a child whose blood will unite York and Lancaster, and he is monarch by right of conquest. What more can you desire?'

'The complete elimination of the House of York.'

'Then you wish to eliminate me? I represent that House, my lady, and the fact cannot be changed. It is a matter of blood and lineage. I am proud of my ancestry, Lady Margaret, as I know you are of yours. I am also a good wife to Jon. I love him very much, because he is a fine and honourable man, well worthy of my respect and affection. I would never willingly do anything to hurt or shame him. I certainly would not form an immoral connection with my cousin. Nor would the Earl of Lincoln disgrace his own vow of fealty to the king.' As she said this she somehow managed to look Margaret innocently in the eyes.

'My dear, I look at Jack of Lincoln and see a young lord of incredible appeal, as was his uncle. Your Richard.'

Cicely smiled. 'He was not *my* Richard, my lady, but I loved him as if he were. Oh, no, do not look shocked, for I do not mean that I would have lain with him. But he had something that bound people to him. His motto may have been *Loyalty Binds Me,* but we were all bound *to him* as well. You met him, my lady, so you know exactly what I mean. You hated him, I can understand that, but you would be dishonest if you said you were not affected by him in other ways. If he had been a Lancastrian king, you would have served him more than willingly. Tell me I am wrong. Tell me your only real reason for plotting against Richard was that he represented the wrong House. As a man he was unequalled.'

Margaret drew a long breath. 'He was a usurper, my dear. An astonishing man, I admit, but a usurper nevertheless. However, I have not come here to discuss him.'

'Do you still doubt my love for Sir Jon?'

Margaret sipped her wine, and then set the cup aside. Her elbows were upon the arms of her chair and her hands placed together before her mouth, which she tapped with them. It was exactly what her son would have done at such a juncture. 'Cicely, you must not underestimate the extent of my love for my half-brother. I would shield him with my very life, and if you cause him pain of any description, I will see you dead.'

'And if *you* cause him pain, my lady, I will see *you* dead.'

'Ah, the Plantagenet in you is to the fore again.'

'Of course it is, Lady Margaret, what else do you expect? I love my husband. I love him honestly, and I know it would grieve him very much if he ever discovered you have come here like this.'

'You are right, of course. I would not have come if I thought there was even any vague chance of him being present. Forgive me, my dear, I did not want to say the things I have, but I think the Earl of Lincoln is a very comely proposition for any young woman, especially one upon whom he looks with such favour.'

Cicely laughed. 'Lady Margaret, Jack of Lincoln looks at *every* woman with favour. He has trouble keeping the ample contents of his hose within said hose. He is incorrigible. A rascal and born seducer, if ever there was one. It means nothing that he smiles at me, and it certainly means nothing if I return his smiles. We are fond of each other. How could I not like someone with such a wicked smile, an even wickeder sense of humour and more kindness in him than you could ever imagine? He has never made an advance toward me, he simply flirts with me.

There is nothing in it.'

'I do trust so.'

'Lady Margaret, I respect your concern for my husband, whom I think we both love very deeply. When he comes to my bed tonight, I will keep him very busy, you may count upon it. And if he seems tired when next you see him, it will not be on account of the king's business.'

Margaret's lips parted and her eyes widened. 'You speak to *me* of such things?'

'Why not? You would have lain with your first husband in exactly the same way, had he lived. Well, you would, would not you? There would be no piety or everlasting mourning, just the sheer bliss of being bedded by Edmund Tudor.' It was said gently, but firmly.

Margaret looked away. 'You are right, of course. I will always miss him. A few months, that is all we had together. I, a child, he a warrior lord. He was so tall and handsome with long, fair hair and the bluest of eyes. Nothing like Jasper at all. He would hold my little hand and kiss it, smile at me and tease me, but so kindly. He was certainly my prince. Nothing can ever change that, and when I lie beside him again in death, I will be happy. Edmund Tudor was ... so very dear to me.' Margaret's eyes met Cicely's again. 'So I understand love, my dear. I understand it very well indeed.'

'Yes, I think you do, my lady.'

Margaret gave a little laugh. 'Of course, Edmund did not live long enough to change, to become anything I would not have liked. A little as it is with your uncle, Cicely. When they die young, we can never know what the future man may have become, good or bad, just or unjust, kind or unkind.'

Your precious Henry will be bad, unjust and very unkind, Cicely thought. Unless he reforms remarkably. But then she remembered his lovemaking, such rare, beautiful lovemaking . . .

'My son still thinks very highly of you, Cicely.'

'He does?'

'Well, he went out of his way to tell me he would consent to your remarriage with my brother. Considerably out of his way.'

'What do you mean, Lady Margaret?'

'That he came to Coldharbour to tell me in person. Believe me, that is not at all like him. He spoke of you in such a way that I—'

'Yes?'

Margaret met her eyes. 'That I believe he feels he is married to the wrong sister.'

Cicely gazed back at her. 'I doubt he thinks that, my lady, for I stand up to him a little too much. I do not think he would appreciate such a wife.'

'On the contrary, Cicely, I think he would. Take care, my dear, because although I love my son very much indeed, I know—as do you—that he thinks of you as he should not. He is the king . . . and I know what was done to John of Gloucester.'

At last Henry's mother had come to the real reason for her visit. 'You fear for Jon?' Cicely whispered, feeling suddenly very cold. Had something happened?

'Yes, my dear. And for your cousin, whose sudden and mysterious demise or torture would surely unite far too many Yorkists.'

'I am forbidden to the king, and he to me, because we are married to others. ' Cicely paused. 'Do you fear for my sister as well?'

'Cicely, I do not know *what* I fear, just that I am very uneasy.'

'So, you think Henry VII will do away with his wife in order to marry his sister-in-law? Why, is that not close to what was so falsely put around about Richard III?'

'Do you think I find it easy to say these things to you, Cicely? Henry means the world and more to me, because I am his mother. But that does not mean I cannot see his faults. There was a time when I would have said he had none, but my eyes were opened at Christmas, when he exhibited Richard's irreparably damaged son. I have been guilty of many cruelties in my time, and there have been cruelties done to me, but that was a terrible thing. I was forced to think of Henry anew. That is why I have come to you with all this. First I had to reassure myself concerning the Earl of Lincoln, and also that you do truly love my brother. I am completely content on both points, Cicely, and so I confide all this in you. Leave Jack of Lincoln well alone. He must live, do you not see? His sudden demise or torture will bring about rebellion. But with Lincoln gone, who might the Yorkists have to lead them? There could be such bloodshed, such jostling and threats. Such *horrors*. It is better that he lives and there is harmony because he stays with my son.'

Better still that he lived and took back Richard's stolen throne, Cicely thought.

'So, if you are tricked into meeting him again, my dear, depart immediately. Advise him of the same. There must be peace now. Your cousin must be made to see it.'

'Lady Margaret, far be it from me to point out that Richard too wanted peace, but you were not prepared to seek it with *him*, were you? You only hope for it now because your son is on the throne. The House of York has been put in the position the House of Lancaster was then. Perhaps it will feel it has no alternative but to follow your example.'

'That is how the grim struggle will continue, Cicely. It has to stop somewhere.'

'Preferably at the point that has been reached now.' Cicely lowered her eyes, knowing that Jack would *never* remain passive in Henry's England.

Margaret moved the subject on prudently. 'Cicely, I do not know what actually passes between you and my son, just that there is something. Its seriousness is not certain, and for the sake of my brother's happiness, I pray it soon passes. Please, I beg you, do not say or do anything that will put Jon at risk.'

'I already do all I can to protect him, Lady Margaret. As I think you have guessed.'

Margaret met her eyes. 'Yes, I had guessed. Does my brother know?'

'He knows nothing. I do whatever your son wishes of me, and I will continue to do it until he tires of me. He has no need to do away with Jon, Jack or with Bess, for he has me already.'

'Maybe that is not enough. Maybe only having you as his queen will do for him. I have never seen this side of him before, Cicely. Oh, I had little contact with him for years on end when he was in exile in Brittany, but I still thought I knew him. He is my only child, how could I not know him? But the fact is, I do *not* know him. I wield influence with him, and he listens to me, but there is a side of him that will *never* listen. I think you possess that side, my dear.'

'What else can I do, Lady Margaret? I give myself to him in order to shield those dear to me. I know not what else there is.'

'Nor I, Cicely. Nor I.'

'There is one way in which you can help me.'

'Say it.'

'If there is ever a time when Jon suspects what I do, if I can say I was with you, maybe it will ease his suspicions.'

'I will back you, my dear. Have no fear of that. I will always work to keep my brother safe. And my son, for I do not wish him to be like this. You certainly have turned his head, but what are your feelings towards him?'

Cicely paused. 'Perhaps you do not really wish to know.'

'I will tell you what you feel. You loathe him for everything he has done, but there are times when you see something else in him, and it draws you. Am I right?'

'Yes.'

'I cannot blame his father for the way my son is, because Edmund died before Henry was born, but I can blame myself. I—together with Jasper—made him what he is, Cicely. There are many deaths to be laid at my door. Too many. My hatred, duplicity, plotting and ambition have created the Henry you see now. I would not let him be his own self. And Jasper kept making sure it continued in Brittany. My poor Henry has never been left in peace. Now, when it is far too late, I have a terrible conscience. Do not plot against him, Cicely. Do not support any Yorkist uprising. If you do, I will shield him and do all I can to destroy you.'

'I would not expect anything less, my lady.'

Margaret smiled. 'Try to find the good in him.'

'It is not for an exchange of pleasantries and searching conversation that he sends for me, Lady Margaret.' What an untruth, because Henry wanted those things, as well as to have her beneath him on a bed.

'I have had many husbands, Cicely, but I believe you know infinitely more than me when it comes to all things carnal. You are not only your father's daughter, you are also your uncle's niece, with all *his* charm and bewitchment. Yes, I know what sort of man Richard was, how he was honest and could enchant all those around him with a single smile. Those smiles would have wrung the heart of the Devil. You are like Richard, and my son does not stand a chance. My dear, you have him in your palm.'

'He has been there several times already, my lady.'

Margaret's lips twitched. 'That is perhaps a little more than I wished to know.' She stood and moved towards the door, and then turned. 'The court will leave for Winchester next week, and my brother will be charged to escort the queen and other ladies. You will not be with them, nor will I. We will follow a day later. Everyone will be told that I have something with which you can assist me concerning my favourite estate at Collyweston, which is being refurnished and redecorated as was Coldharbour. I will say I wish to consult you because I value your taste and discernment. I imagine you guess what business will really occupy you for that day.'

'I can hazard well enough, Lady Margaret.'

'You and I will then leave Coldharbour together, along with the king and his gentlemen. Yes, I am conniving with my son in this. I ask you to forgive me.' Margaret met her eyes. 'I too wish to shield my brother, my dear, and in this I know I do.'

'Jon is uppermost in my thoughts too, my lady, as is my cousin of Lincoln.'

Margaret looked away. 'I can imagine what has been threatened, Cicely.'

'I will give Henry whatever he wants. He will not lack the attention or gratification he seeks.' Nor will I, Cicely thought guiltily. *Nor will I*. 'You and I each have two men we wish to protect; you have your brother and your son, I have my husband and my cousin. I think we need a pact, Lady Margaret, because our goals, from now on, are the same.'

'Who would have thought it?' Margaret replied.

'Some fool or other.'

Chapter Twenty-Six

JON HAD GONE to Winchester, the court, queen and ladies had gone there as well, but Cicely remained at Westminster Palace. Alone, waiting for Henry to send for her. Margaret was at Coldharbour.

It was the middle of the afternoon, small white clouds scudded west across a dazzling azure sky, and gulls swooped over the Thames. Cicely watched them from her apartment window. She wore a gown of kingfisher blue, and her headdress was on the table behind her. Her hair fell loose, because her head had ached earlier, and the thought of such a weight had not been pleasant.

She closed her eyes. What was her little boy doing now? Was he asleep in his crib? Suckling? Crying? Or was someone cradling him and singing him a lullaby? She longed to see him, but knew it would be some time yet. She was now afraid to let him be brought to London, afraid of Henry's watchful intuition. It all depended upon whether he lost interest in her or not. If he did, she and Jon would be able to return to Lincolnshire after the christening. But if Henry still wanted her . . . who could say how long he would keep her close?

She smiled in spite of this, her eyes still closed. Richard would approve of her now. She knew he would. She was stronger and more capable because she had been forced to think for herself. How good it would be to talk to him, to let him know how she had changed. She knew he would not really be with her, that he was something she held within herself. Had she *made* him stay away from her? Had her own conscience denied her his comfort? Yes. She believed so. And now she could not bring him back.

Losing him forever was now fact in every way, and she remembered a poem he had written, and that she had found in one of his books at Sheriff Hutton. He had written it of his original love for Anne, who became his queen but never gave him her entire heart.

To be without you is to fade a little within
To not hear your voice is to lose the sweetness of music
To forfeit your smile is to be plunged into darkness
To never feel your touch is to lose all sense of being
To know you have gone forever is to steal away all joy.

Her eyes opened suddenly as she sensed someone else close by. She had been in this very room when Richard had first returned to her. He had been leaning against the wall, behind her, to her left, where the sunlight streamed upon a tapestry. Was he there now? Had he come to her again after all? She whispered his name. 'Richard?'

'I do know how you feel, sweetheart.'

His hands were upon her shoulders, gentle but firm. So very tangible. The shock kept her where she was, but only for a moment. She turned, and he smiled. In a moment she was in his arms again, in that embrace, holding him, feeling his heart beating, the brush of his lips, the stroke of his fingers. Adrift in him, breathing him, absorbing him, she loved him so much that she felt weak. She trembled as he kissed her again. Such a kiss, second to none, and as beloved as everything about him. His lips alone could soothe and stir her like this, play with her senses, seduce her mind and her body.

She would not be foolish this time, she would not weep and beg him to stay, tell him she needed him, nor any of the other things she had always done before. It was enough that he was here, enough that he held her again. He transcended everyone and everything.

How could any one man—*this* man—affect her so very much? With him there was a fleshly delight that was at the very heart of sin. As well as at the heart of joy. 'I love you so much,' she whispered, 'and I am so glad you have come to me again. But why? Why now?'

'Because you no longer put me before your husband, and now accept everything for what it is. You are your own woman.' He smiled, and put a gentle finger to her lips. 'You will never forfeit my love.'

'Nor you mine.'

'You know now that you must keep me separate. You have your life, and you have your imagination. Be sure I remain the latter.'

'I do not put my husband in second place. Please know that I do not.'

'I do know it, sweetheart.' He looked towards the door. 'You must go now.'

As he spoke, there was a tap.

'Enter,' she called, for Richard had already gone from her.

A page entered. 'My lady, the king requires your presence.'

Within minutes, she was admitted to the royal apartments. Sunlight streamed over Henry as he sat at the same table, surrounded by documents, the smell of melted wax and candle smoke hung in the air. He was richly dressed in cloth-of-gold and black velvet, having not long come from granting an audience to the Venetian ambassador, and the golden circlet lay on the table on a pile of papers, as did his three, apparently favourite rings, the signet with St. Armel, Richard's ruby and the emerald. He did not smile, and his eyes offered nothing. It was always thus when she came into his presence.

The door closed behind her, and she went to her knees before the table. Still he said nothing. She was in no mood to be toyed with. 'If you do not let me rise, Your Majesty, I will walk out.'

He tossed his quill down, splashing whatever he was writing. 'Yes, I believe it.' He came to help her up, and then looked at her hair. 'No headdress? And before your king?'

'Forgive me. I . . . had forgotten.' She had. Completely.

'I like it that you do not shave your forehead,' he said suddenly.

The words echoed from the past. Richard had liked it too. His warmth still rushed through her. Needing distraction, she went to look at the rings, even slipping the emerald on her finger. She could not bear to touch the ruby, even though she longed to wear a jewel Richard had worn. Instead she spoke of the signet ring. 'When I first saw St Armel's leashed dragon on your signet, I thought it was a play upon your situation.'

Henry's brows drew together. 'I am afraid I do not understand'

'Well, it is leashed, and I wondered if you felt leashed as well. As did Richard II. His white hart badge had a crown around its neck, because he felt imprisoned and controlled.' She studied the emerald. Light caught through it like sunlight slanting through clear green water.

He watched her. 'Why in God's own name would I feel leashed?'

'I do not know. Except perhaps . . .'

'Yes?'

'That being on the throne is not the great joy you expected it to be. Perhaps it is Henry Tudor himself who is leashed, not King Henry VII.'

'You play with words a little too subtly, *cariad*. In fact, you confound yourself. I am not leashed, I merely choose St. Armel as my patron saint.'

'But you *are* leashed, Henry. You cannot be your real self any more, can you?'

'I can with you, Cicely,' he said gently.

'You have a wife and I have a husband,' she answered.

'My wife will not be joining us, so *please* assure me Jon Welles has not been invited either.'

Here he was again, the Henry she did not want to like. 'We will have each other's undivided attention.'

He touched her hair, gently, seductively. Everything about him was seductive. 'Please do not be cruel today, Henry.'

'I promise,' he answered softly, moving behind her to begin unfastening her gown. She felt his lips upon her shoulder—where Richard's hands had rested—and upon the nape of her neck, and she closed her eyes. Her gown slid down, and he cupped her breasts from behind, teasing and stroking her nipples. She leaned her head back for him to kiss her cheek. He did, softly and enticingly.

'I think my sister may yet find she is a very fortunate woman,' she said softly.

'I will have to pretend she is you.'

We all pretend, Henry. She turned to him. 'Put on your gold circlet. You are dressed in cloth-of-gold, as the King of England should be, and I wish to see gold across your brow as well.'

'Should I send for the sceptre and orb?' he asked dryly.

'Why, I think you already have a sceptre, and at least one orb. No, you have two!'

'How fortuitous.'

'Indeed so, Your Majesty.' She brought the circlet from the table, and reached up to put it on his head. There it rested, gleaming richly against his reddish hair and the pallor of his forehead. She met his eyes, so steady and clear now. 'There, you are king, Henry Tudor.'

'Because a princess of York has deigned to crown me?'

'A *naked* princess of York,' she corrected, 'whose lips are about to anoint you. All over.'

'And I must stand here, subduing my fevered dick while she does it?'

'No, Henry, you are only to subdue it until I have divested you of your rich clothes. Which I intend to do slowly. You cut a fine figure in your royal garb, Henry, and you have a good body and such grace, but you would be *so* much improved if you would smile a little more. Your smile makes such a difference to you.'

'Smiles do not benefit kings, not in the end. Richard discovered that, did he not?'

'Yes, he did, because he would not deny his own self, Henry, whereas you certainly do. You could pass your pleasant self in a passageway and not notice, except perhaps to wonder who the fool was that dared to smile.' She paused. 'But you are the sovereign now, not Richard, and you want me, I think.'

'I admit to a passing interest in your person, my lady.'

She began to undo his garments, all the trappings of royalty, the rich cloth and adornments that marked him as the monarch. Just as such things had once marked Richard. She did everything at leisure, pressing to him as she pushed both doublet and undershirt from his shoulders. Then, not touching his hose or footwear, she slid her arms around his waist and moved her breasts against him. Her lips searched for his, and found them. He crushed her close, and she could feel his eagerness pressing into her.

But then suddenly he gripped her upper arm, hard enough to really cause pain. 'Do not play with me in this, Cicely, for no matter how much I want you, I *will* destroy you!'

Unnerved by the unpleasant change in him, she tried to pull away. 'I only play with lovemaking, and it is because I enjoy it so much! Please, you are hurting me! I mean nothing unkindly. Unkindness I leave to you.'

He released her, clearly disturbed by his own reaction. It had caught him without warning, and its ferocity had temporarily robbed him of his virility. He removed the circlet and tossed it aside. It fell with a hollow ring, and then rolled away into a corner, where it lay among dark shadows. There seemed something oddly prophetic about it, as if the fate that had brought Richard down also lay in wait for his successor.

Henry clearly thought so, for he turned away from her, and ran his fingers through his hair a second time. He was still in the bitter clutch of suspicion and vulnerability, and his body shook with it.

'Henry?' He frightened her now, for cruelty seemed to glisten upon him. She ventured to touch his arm, but he shook her away. 'Would you rather I went?' she asked then, uncertain what to do.

'Jesu, woman, you *are* aggravating!' He faced her again. 'Go? No, I want *you*! Not what you offer me because you have to. I want all of you, Cicely, and the need in me is maiming. I cannot breathe without thinking of you. I cannot walk a step without you being there with me. And all this when you only come to me because I have made you do it. You will never come to me because you want to be with me, will you?'

She gazed at him. 'Henry, I do not know what to say to you. Of course I have come because you command it so. I cannot come to you uninvited because you have forbidden it. What else can you expect of me?'

He closed his eyes for a long moment, and she could almost see the rage slipping out of him again. Then he caught her hand and pulled her to him, wrapping his arms tightly around her and hiding his face against her hair. 'I did not mean to hurt you. Forgive me. Forgive me.'

His distress was moving. 'I know you did not mean it. I am not indifferent to you, Henry. You already know that. When we made love, it was so good, for us both, I think. I admit to coming here today at your behest, but I also admit to coming here hoping you will love me again as you did before.'

'How can you even *like* me? I am your enemy and you are mine. We both know it.'

'I like half of you, Henry, for the other half can be . . . so very heartless. You know it yourself, because that is what you want to be. In fact, you wish you were entirely without heart, and you resent me because I prevent it.'

He drew away. 'Possibly.'

'There is much about you that frightens me,' she went on, 'but also so much that draws me.'

'Oh, Cicely . . .' He stroked the flesh he had bruised only moments before. It was another apology, although silent.

'Henry, I am ashamed of wanting you as much as I do at this moment,' she said frankly. Why pretend? He was an exciting and knowing lover, and her wanton nature responded to his mere closeness. She could not help the way she had been created. Was she a slut? Yes, right now, Henry Tudor aroused the wanton in her, and *such* thoughts. Such thoughts. 'I want you to make love to me again, Henry,' she whispered.

He gazed at her. 'Can there ever be another like you, Cicely? I find it hard to believe so.'

'Perhaps it is as well, Henry, for I think you would soon buckle under the strain of dealing with two of me.'

'I would make a game and courageous effort, be sure of that. Now, where would you like to make love? I am at your command.

'On the bed, on your back and at my complete mercy.'

'Are you sure you do not have that dagger?'

'Where do you imagine I might be hiding it?'

'I trust I do not discover the painful way.'

'I would walk a little strangely if it were hidden *there*, Your Majesty.'

He smiled and led her to the bed. Throwing off his shoes, he lay down. 'Very well, I am on my back and at your command.'

She gazed down at him. His hair had spread over the pillow, his lean body possessed not an ounce of fat, and even only lying there, he had such elegance that he might almost have been posing. Except that he was not. It was natural. Effortless. There was something about him, a catlike laziness that belied the swiftness of his mind and the torment of character against which he struggled every day of his life. Henry Tudor was all that she should loathe, and deservedly so, yet she felt his unexpected fragility.

It was not a fatal flaw, as Richard's lenience and trust had been, nor was it even close to being as dear, but it was there nevertheless. She was drawn to such men as this, powerful men who were also susceptible and who needed her. Richard, her husband, John of Gloucester, Henry . . . and, perhaps, Jack. Yes, perhaps Jack, whose kisses she had sometimes wished to sample.

She got on the bed as well, and knelt facing him. 'My, how very pleased you are to see me,' she murmured, placing her hand on his virility, which strained the front of his hose.

'It has been thinking about you since the last time it nuzzled its ardent way around you, lady,'

'Then it must think a little longer,' she whispered. 'Do not do anything now, Henry Tudor, for the House of York is going to do some nuzzling of its own, and you are forbidden to make a single movement.' She leaned over to kiss him gently, sucking his lower lip, running her tongue around inside it, curling her tongue against his and drawing upon it as if she would be joined to him that way as well. She kissed his ear, breathing softly into it, licking it, making him shiver. His throat did not escape, for she kissed it, savoured it, played her lips tenderly against his pulse.

Then she stretched his arms above his head and eased herself on top of him, her lips still trailing kisses over his supple skin, her parted thighs allowing his eager virility close enough to touch its goal, but not slip within. She moved herself gently against it, brushing softly, tantalizingly, almost cruelly against the tip. His pleasure was intense, and so was hers. Such constant gratification, but not the ultimate climax. That must be postponed, kept in check for the final moments of union.

She heard him whisper in Welsh. *'Rwyn dy garu di . . . rwyn dy angen di . . .'* She did not need to know what he said, because she could tell he used endearments. The knowledge felt good. Almost too good.

His eyes were closed, his face was flushed, and he was so very warm and pliable, so responsive and given to his senses. There was no side to him now, no veil, no restraint or control, just a man who surrendered completely to his great sensuality. He was an enigma, a paradox, and he excited everything that she was.

But she did not have it all her own way, for he pushed her on to her back again and then gave her body his full, ardent and knowing attention. Now his were the kisses that burned and enticed. His were the lips that explored, arousing her to many gentle climaxes that flowed and ebbed, and then flowed again. There was true feeling in everything he did, and it ravished her body, heart and soul. But this was Henry Tudor, the king who presented such a cold, threatening, dangerous exterior. The man she loathed for all that he had taken from her! If she were not in his arms now, she would never have believed it possible to indulge in such passionate joy with him. Not with him.

Only Richard could give her more than this. When it came to lovemaking, the outcome of Bosworth was reversed, for the vanquished was by far the easy victor. But this king was not entirely routed . . .

Henry took her from delight to delight, so aware of how to please and tease, to lead on and on towards a promise of such ecstasy that she felt she must surely die of it. The temptation to indulge in almost unthinkable acts was there, and into some of them . . . some of them . . . she trespassed willingly. As she had with Richard, with whom nothing was unthinkable.

Finally, he leaned over her, and looked down into her eyes. 'Oh, Cicely, I feel so much at this moment that I think heaven must have claimed me.' Then he smiled with that exquisitely wry charm. 'Do not even *think* of a witty Yorkist reply. Not now.'

'Love me truly now, Henry. Please, for I want you so much.'

He pushed into her at last, and with him came such acute delight that her muscles closed convulsively around him, holding him tightly as he moved in and out, long, rich strokes that no long attempted to merely play. She shared it all, for they were in complete harmony, and as his strokes quickened towards a climax, she was embraced by sweet, sweet love. When he came, the flame of it seared through her. She was weightless, on the edge of consciousness, completely ablaze with passion and joy. She wanted it to go on and on. But no man could go on and on, and all too soon, it seemed, he was utterly spent, and sank against her, slowly stretching her arms above her head as he liked to do so much. Then he buried his face in her hair and lay there, his body relaxed, his manner trusting and defence-less. He could be incredibly loving, this icy Tudor to whom vicious cruelty could come in the splitting of a second. If he were to give *this* side of himself to Bess, all would soon be well in his marriage, because surely not even Bess could resist for long. Unless her blood really had turned to ice, never to melt again. But he showed this aspect of himself to no one, except the woman he lay with now.

She rested her cheek to his. 'That was so beautiful, Henry,' she whispered, still hardly able to accept that lying with him was so astonishingly erotic and rewarding. He had truly been her lover, indulging and appreciating her as much as any woman could need. Whatever she had wanted he had given, without needing to be prompted. He simply knew. Oh, silly, silly Bess, to be missing such a joy. He kissed her cheek, and then leaned up on an elbow. 'Most men dream of such a woman as you, *cariad*, someone who adores to do all the things we long for. I knew you at first glimpse. It would be perilously easy to fall in love with you.'

'You are a consummate lover, Henry.'

'This is me, Cicely. You are supposed to issue insults, not compliments.'

She smiled. 'Very well. You are like an ill-cooked sirloin, tough as an old leather boot on the outside, but soft and juicy inside.'

'That was an insult?'

She smiled again. 'Who have you practised on, Henry? You know a great deal about a woman's body, so there must have been someone very important.'

'Does it matter?'

'No, not if you do not wish to say. It is not my business.'

'That is true. Just as it is not my business who taught you, because I *know* it was not my uncle or John of Gloucester.'

'I am content with you at this moment, Henry. Please let me stay so.'

He lay on to his back and rested an arm behind his head. His other hand reached for hers. 'I intend to keep you here, with me, tonight.'

'I do not think that is a good idea. If such a thing were to be discovered—'

'I do not think I care if it is.'

'Then you are selfish. *I* care, very much. I do not wish my husband or my sister to learn of what takes place between you and me.'

'Cicely, I cannot make you my wife, unless I murder my way to you, but nor can I leave unknown my attachment to you. I would make you my mistress.'

She sat up, appalled. '*Mistress?* No! I am a king's daughter and will *never* allow that! I lie with you anyway, Henry. There is no need to humiliate me by adding the word mistress to my name.'

'Since when has it been humiliating to be a king's mistress?'

'Since my mother was proved to be *only* that to my father. No, do not look at me so savagely. You know as well as I do that my parents were never married. You can overturn whatever entitlement, declaration and law you wish, but the fact remains. My father was pre-contracted to Lady Eleanor Talbot—no, Butler, was she not a widow?—who did not die until four years *after* my parents' supposed marriage. I have been made a bastard by my father's lust for my mother, and I will not let you consign me to her fate.'

He regarded her. 'I would not consign you to any *fate*, Cicely. Please. If it upsets you that much, I pray you forget I mentioned it.'

She did not respond. He would mention it again. At some point. Because it was his only way of securing her solely for himself. Unless, as he said, he murdered his way to her.

He changed the subject. 'Do you still say you do not know where your brothers are?' he asked then.

She paused, dismayed to sense a fresh trap. 'I know no more now than I did when I last spoke of this with you.'

'I wondered if perhaps the gallant Earl of Lincoln had news for you.'

'Stop it, Henry! *Please* leave your suspicious nature elsewhere when you take me to your bed! Jack has told me nothing because he *knows* nothing. If either of my brothers should come to claim the throne, you will have to respond to it as my uncle had to with you. York and Lancaster can never be truly united until there are no males left of *royal* Yorkist blood.' *Including my son by Richard.*

She held his gaze. 'Either you are prepared to take many lives to achieve such security, and thus gain the revilement you are so happy to pile unjustly upon Richard, or you will have to live with suspense and threat. And if you kill Jack, *I* will kill *you.* I do not care that we can make wondrous love together, I do not care that you desire me, or that I can lie here beside you now and—sometimes— actually like you. If you strike down my cousin, or anyone else in my family, or if you *touch* Jon as a punishment to me, you will have to kill me as well.'

'You know well how to touch a nerve, Cicely.'

'So do you! Please, Henry, do *not* pursue this, and do not choose the wrong course. If you have all that blood on your hands, your conscience will always be clawing your intestines. You know that already, but I can see in your eyes that you do not *want* to do what is right for others, only what is right for you.'

'Richard was too weak.'

'He was not weak, Henry, he simply tried to do what he believed to be honourable.'

'And so you ask me to do the same, and bring another Bosworth down upon myself?'

'You should have thought of it all before you invaded. You knew you had no immediate claim to the throne, that there were many others of closer blood. Your only hope was to defeat Richard and take the throne by that act. Yes, one way or another you managed to gain the support, but by its very nature you are now frightened of those same men, or their sons, proving their treachery all over again. I do not envy you, Henry.'

He rubbed an eyelid. 'You are always so damnably to the point, Cicely.'

'You should not have spoiled this, Henry. What is wrong with you? Why do you do it?' She felt the closeness of tears, and fought against them.

'I appear to have said the wrong thing.'

'You *know* you have.'

'Mentioning your brothers was an impulse immediately regretted.' He smiled a little.

'And you thought you wanted me for your *wife*?'

'There are advantages and disadvantages to that proposition.'

'Indeed so, Henry, and which way would the balance tip, I wonder?'

He took her hand. 'Can we forget my lapse?'

'Not really.'

He exhaled slowly. 'I truly cannot help the way I am, Cicely. It has become the way I protect myself.'

'How can I believe you? You will say whatever you want. Its veracity or relevance is hardly of consequence. The art of misleading has become your scripture.'

'I think you are right.'

She snatched her hand from his. 'Oh, Henry, you make me so angry!'

'I cannot be like Richard,' he said suddenly.

'Richard? What do you mean?'

He met her eyes. 'I cannot be all that he was. It is not in me to be charming, amusing—'

'Now *that* is wrong! You have charm enough when you decide to employ it, and you can be very amusing, even though you mostly smother it at birth.'

He smiled. 'Dear God above, I do love being with you. You keep me on my toes.'

'Or on your back.'

'Infinitely better.'

He had her liking him again! How did he do it? She had never known anyone who was so much two men in one. There was the dread Tudor monarch, and there was . . . the Henry who lay next to her now. She ran a hand over his thigh to the forest of hairs at his loins, kneading him just a little. 'I do not know what to think of you, Henry. I do so want to know only this pleasing side of you, but your other side will keep driving me away again. You do understand, do you not? I am trying to be honest with you.'

'I cannot be honest with anyone, sweetheart.'

'Oh, yes, you can! You were honest not long since, when you made love to me. That was *all* honesty, Henry Tudor. You know it was. You shared yourself with me for those minutes.'

He looked away. 'Your lovemaking is high treason. You robbed me of everything and I had no way of stopping you. You put me into bondage, and then raped my soul.'

She gazed at him.

'Cicely?'

'I am trying to gauge whether those words actually came from you, or whether you read it in a romance.'

He laughed. 'Jesu, lady, you have a tongue on you.'

'And it services you well, I think.'

His eyes almost caressed her. 'It has certainly licked its

way into parts of me I hardly knew existed.'

'I like the taste of cloves.'

'Ah, that explains it.' He smiled again. 'So, you will not be my mistress?'

He had returned to it more swiftly than she had guessed. 'I am already, am I not? Just not overtly.'

He caught her hand again. 'I did not mean to insult you when I asked, Cicely. It did not occur to me that you would view it that way. It should have done, of course. Perhaps I did not *want* it to occur to me.' He drew her fingertips to his lips.

She looked down at him. 'How long will it go on, Henry? You wanting me like this?'

'Until I have you out of my blood, I imagine.'

'That might be a very long time indeed.'

'Yes, I believe it will.'

'It *cannot* continue without end, Henry.'

'Why not? Can you give me one good reason why I should not have you as and when I want you?'

'Well, I am your sister-in-law and your aunt-by-marriage, and we are adulterous.'

'Admitted awkwardnesses.'

'Are you kind to Bess now?'

'After my fashion.'

She was vexed. 'That means you are not. I know full well that you are capable of better than that. And you promised you would improve.'

'I have improved. Jesu, Cicely, you give me no credit. I *am* pleasant with her now. Why, I even sleep in her bed occasionally! Sleep it is, because you already know my feelings about actually lying with a woman who is with child. It is something I will never do, and you at least should respect that.'

'I consider myself duly chastised.'

'Good. Cicely, do you know what it is like to try to

sleep alongside someone who prays for your death?'

'No, but Bess would not—'

'Can you be sure of that?' His gaze held hers. 'I wish I had your confidence, *cariad*, but I know what she thinks and what she wishes. My prompt demise is certainly one of her greatest priorities.'

'You are wrong, I am sure.' But how could she know? Bess certainly despised him. But *that* much? 'Henry, my sister does not need much from you, just the knowledge that you care. You *can* care, I know it.'

'Because I care for you?'

'Oh, you do not catch me that way. If I say yes, you will tell me you do not.'

'As you wish.'

She leaned over him. 'Henry. . . ?'

'Are you about to wheedle?'

'Certainly not. Unless . . .'

'I knew it.'

'Very well. I was going to offer you another unimaginably gratifying roll upon the bed, but now I will not bother.'

'Oh, *why* am I not married to you?' he groaned.

'Because Sir Jon Welles reached me first.'

He put his palm to her cheek. 'I do not like to be enthralled by the House of York.'

'Then send it away.'

His hand moved around the side of her face and into the hair at the back of her neck, and he drew her lips down to his again. But before he kissed her, he whispered. 'And I have not overlooked the fact that you still have my prized emerald on your delightful but thieving little Yorkist finger.'

Chapter Twenty-Seven

IT WAS HIGH summer, and so hot that the air shimmered and the horizons danced. Henry wished his queen to give birth to his heir at Camelot itself. Winchester may not have been any such thing, but it certainly *had* been the seat of the ancient Kings of Britain, and Henry was determined to establish that his line was descended from Arthur. He was placing a great deal of faith in the expected child being a boy. A girl would not do at all and might even make him look foolish.

Winchester overflowed with splendour. The arrival of the court had taken all possible accommodation, as well as every house for miles around. There were encampments, banners, horses, sumptuous tents and pavilions, and lords and ladies of such rank and finery that perhaps Winchester did indeed become Camelot again.

Bess felt the strain of it. So much depended upon her baby being a boy that her health suffered as a consequence. She fell victim to the ague, sometimes hot and fevered, sometimes cold and unable to stop shivering. Cicely stayed close to her, as did their mother, the Queen Dowager, who was to be the baby's godmother. She had come from virtual seclusion at Sheen, where she still had charge of her three youngest daughters, Ann, Katherine and Bridget, who had been left behind.

Henry did not trust his mother-in-law. She had come

willingly out of sanctuary in 1484, bringing her children, and had welcomed Richard's protection. Henry trusted no one who had changed sides before. Often he did not trust anyone who had never changed sides. He simply could not trust.

Margaret was kept very busy with all the preparations. She had charge of the royal lying-in chamber, and was organizing the pageantry of the baptism. For Bess, the ever-increasing pressure made it worse by the hour. What if she had a daughter? What if the child were not perfect? What if, God forbid, it was born dead?

Cicely tried hard to comfort and soothe, but Bess believed there was the example of Cicely's own dead child to prove such fears were justified. Cicely longed to reassure her that Leo was alive and healthy, but it was just too dangerous. Only Jon and Jack knew the truth of it, and her trust in them was as unshakable as her trust in Richard.

Jack was in Winchester, and had a role in the christening. Together with Jon, he would walk beside her as she carried the baby to the church. It would be such a procession, with so many lords having roles to play. All very formal, very reverent and ablaze with pomp.

The more the pressure of it, the more Bess sank, but it was impossible to ease her burden. Henry had been prevailed upon to spend time with her and be amiable, which, to give him his due, he had done to the best of his ability. Well, to the best of the ability he was prepared to offer. Cicely knew—to her great guilt and sadness—that if *she* had been Bess, he would have offered infinitely more. There were times when she found it difficult to even look Bess in the eyes, because Henry showed no sign yet of releasing his queen's sister from the carnal bondage he imposed.

When Bess was asleep one afternoon, propped up on numerous rich pillows in a bed of such grandeur that she looked lost in it, Cicely went to find Jon, but found Jack instead.

He was in the great hall, involved in a rather heated discussion with Jasper Tudor about some duty or other, but he abandoned it the moment he saw her. Jasper did not care for either the Earl of Lincoln or Lady Welles, or indeed anything that reeked of the House of York, and his face bore its usual scowl as he stalked out of the great hall like an angry cockerel.

As Jack approached her, Cicely had to concede again that he was a truly engaging figure, nor could she help but think what a king he would make. Another magnetically charming Yorkist king.

He allowed his knowing glance to move approvingly over her as well. 'How now, my lady? I do pray you seek me?'

'I seek my husband.'

'That is excessively dull of you, and entirely lacking in romance.' He put an arm around her waist and planted a warm kiss upon her cheek. To others it would seem like a friendly kiss between cousins, but she sensed it to be more. Something had happened.

He pretended to sigh dramatically. 'Oh, to have you spread beneath me, Lady Welles.'

'Would it be an unforgettable experience?'

'Hm, methinks thou hast a barbed tongue.'

She smiled. 'Now, why would you immediately leap to such a conclusion? Can you possibly be *that* uncertain of your attraction?'

'In your case, yes, most probably. I should have pursued you more intently at Sheriff Hutton, when I had the chance.'

'Another missed opportunity.'

'Yes.'

They both knew they were speaking of something else

337

entirely. Of Sheriff Hutton.

'Something is about to happen, is not it, Jack? I can feel it. You are going to flee?'

He smiled.

'That is all the answer I need. Do not tell me anything more. Please.'

'Would you come with me?'

'*Me?*' She was startled.

'You may be married to a Lancastrian lord, Cicely, but you are York through and through. Tell me I am wrong and I will not say any more.'

'Of course you are not wrong, Jack, but I will not come with you.'

'The thought of my ardent kisses does not lure you?' He grinned. 'Come now, sweetheart, Richard was your lover and you have his child. You should *not* be here in Henry Tudor's court.'

'Jack, please. You know my situation.'

'That Henry desires you? He would not be normal if he did not! *I* desire you.'

She smiled and looked away.

Jack watched her face. 'What is it, Cicely? What are you thinking?'

'I wish I could say that lying with him is an abominable experience, but it is not.' She glanced at him again.

'You can lie *willingly* with that twist-eyed, twist-minded, misbegotten maggot?'

She put a finger to her lips. 'Certainly not with the huge reluctance I *should* feel. I am being honest with you. There are times when, God help me, I can actually like him. And he is far better on a bed than I imagined.'

'This *is* still Henry Tudor we speak of?'

She smiled. 'Yes.'

'Then he is clearly Janus.'

'Yes. But I am not untrue to York, least of all to you.'

'Take care with your marriage, sweetheart, because you tread a very precarious line. Sir Jon Welles is far too good a husband to risk losing.'

'There speaks the expert on marriage?'

He smiled. 'I may not have done well in my own, Cicely, but that does give me insight.'

'I have no control over Henry. He will say and do whatever he pleases, and if it pleases him to destroy what I have with Jon, he will do it without hesitation. And if he chooses to trump up a charge against you and execute you, he will. I could not endure that. Your death will leave York without a natural and capable leader. You *must* be careful, Jack. At the moment you are absolutely irreplaceable. You always will be to me. I love you, Jack, so very much. You and Jon both mean everything to me.'

He put his hand gently to her cheek. 'And my feelings for you are the same, sweetheart. But how in God's own dear name can you actually *like* this paltry Tudor?'

'I do not know, but I do.'

'I could serve you far better, sweeting,' he said softly, his eyes dark.

The unspoken attraction that had long been between them came to the surface momentarily, but then melted away again as he laughed. 'Women! Creatures of no discernment.'

They laughed together.

Jon was eventually found in a small turret room where he had retreated to write some important letters to Ned Grebby at Wyberton. He looked up in surprise and pleasure when she entered.

'Why, Lady Welles, you are a vast improvement on Ned Grebby.' He got up and came to embrace her. He kissed her on the lips, and then kissed her again. 'I think I begin to forget how to write,' he said softly.

'I have never been taken over a table, sir.'

'No? Well, we must rectify such a glaring omission.' He bolted the door, dashed his letters, ink, quills and all to one side, and then seated her on the edge of the table, before freeing the urgent erection that leapt from his loins. 'Will this do, my lady?' he asked.

'It looks delightfully potent and promising, my lord. I do hope you will be suitably deft with it?'

He smiled, hauled up her skirts and drew her gently forward until it would be easily able to enter her. Then he kissed her again, before pulling her right on to him.

They made swift but rewarding love, enjoying full reward, and then they clung together afterwards, he leaning against her, she still on the table, her legs wrapped tightly around his hips to keep him inside her. 'I love you, Sir Jon Welles,' she whispered. 'I really do love you.'

'And I you, sweetheart,' he whispered, turning his head to catch her lips to his.

She closed her eyes as she returned the kiss, and then smiled at him. 'I cannot believe I am so fortunate as to be your wife. I do wish we could go home to Lincolnshire.'

'Home? Is that how you think of it?'

'If you are there, yes, I do.'

He embraced her still more. 'When all this pomp is done here, I will beseech the king for permission to leave.'

She closed her eyes, because she knew it was very unlikely indeed that Henry would agree. But she could hope.

Someone tried to turn the ring handle of the door, and they pulled apart hastily. 'Jon? Are you there? Why have you bolted the door?' It was Margaret.

'Jesu!' Jon gasped, stepping away to straighten his clothes. Cicely slid hastily from the table and shook out her skirts. Then he went to open the door.

Margaret hastened in like an anxious black crow. She

had not ceased hastening everywhere since arriving in Winchester, but there seemed something extra in her manner now. She paused on seeing Cicely, clearly dismayed, and then turned to look at Jon. 'Well, I believe I can now understand the bolt,' she murmured.

Jon spread his hands. 'There are times when privacy is very much to be desired.'

'Yes, I imagine there are.' The way Margaret's eyes encompassed Cicely raised Henry's image.

'You wished to see me?' Jon indicated the only chair.

'Ah, well . . .' Margaret accepted and then glanced at Cicely again, this time with almost tangible wariness.

Jon watched her. 'I am sure that whatever you wish to say can be said in front of my wife.'

'That may not be so.'

'What? That you cannot say it? Or that she is not my wife?'

'That I cannot speak openly.' Margaret turned to Cicely. 'With all due respect, my lady, you are still a Yorkist.'

Jon straightened. 'What is this, Margaret? You cannot possibly believe Cicely would—'

'She is thick with Lincoln, Jon.'

Cicely came forward. 'Thick? What do you mean?' She suspected that Jasper the Cockerel had not stalked completely out of the hall.

'You were observed today, in the great hall, hugging and laughing, kissing, and seeming to discuss something dangerous.'

Jon's lips parted. 'Dangerous?' He glanced at Cicely, whose face bore an expression that lay somewhere between dismay and guilt.

Margaret thought the same. 'What is afoot, Cicely?'

'Nothing. Truly. I happened upon my cousin when I was looking for you, Jon. We talked a while, that is all. It is impossible not to talk and laugh with him. You should know that. And of course we kissed. We do sometimes. It means nothing. We were in the great hall, for Jesu's sake, with many people around. Hardly a clandestine tryst!'

'He said nothing to you that was out of the ordinary?' Jon asked.

'Nothing at all.' Cicely returned his look. 'Why? Was he not loyal to Henry when Francis Lovell and the Staffords raised their rebellion?'

Margaret laughed disparagingly. 'Too loyal by far. It was unnatural.'

Cicely was incensed. 'He cannot satisfy, can he? If he is disloyal, he is a vile traitor. If he is loyal, he is suspect and unnatural. What would you have him do, my lady? Swallow poison and remove the uncertainty?'

Margaret looked away.

Cicely turned to Jon. 'What is he suspected of doing? If, indeed, he is suspected of anything.'

Jon folded his arms. 'Margaret, you must say whatever it is you really came here to say. And Cicely remains in the room as you say it.'

'As you wish. There is word of an ... imposter ... coming to light in Burgundy. Some child, purporting to be Cicely's younger brother, Richard, Duke of York.'

Cicely gazed at her. *'Dickon?'*

'Yes, my lady, and now that it is known they set sail for Burgundy last year, it is obviously possible that this boy really is your younger brother. Equally, he may be a stranger, set up simply as a cipher, to foment unrest and rebellion. There is indeed a likeness to your younger brother, and the fellow is of the correct age. I know no more than this, but the king has certainly been informed.'

'And you think the Earl of Lincoln knows something of it?' Cicely asked.

'Certes, I do, Cicely. Lincoln is the most important Yorkist lord in the land, and if he decides to lend his support to this false boy, whatever his claimed identity, I do not doubt that disaffected Yorkists will flock to rebel.'

Jon paced a little. 'And you say the king knows?'

'Yes, and it has not exactly pleased him.'

Cicely could well imagine. *Had* this been what Jack would have told her?

Jon came to take his wife by the shoulders. 'Did Jack mention any of this to you?'

'No.' She could answer truthfully. 'Our conversation was entirely innocent, Jon. Truly, and I do not believe Jack will be guilty of treason.' Oh, the urge to cross her fingers behind her back.

Margaret looked at her. 'Then you will need to convince the king of that, my dear.'

'I will be able to face him in all innocence, Lady Margaret, as I am sure my cousin will as well.' Cicely looked at Jon. 'I do not know of anything, Jon. Please believe me.'

'I do, sweetheart. I do. Although whether I would trust your cousin as well is another matter.'

Something made her take his hand and hold it to her cheek. 'I have not done anything I should not, Jon. I have not lent my name to any Yorkist dealings.'

'And Jack?'

She looked at him. 'Jack is his own man, Jon, but I have no reason to believe he has broken his oath of fealty to the king.' Not yet, anyway. That Jack was about to, she did not doubt at all. But she would never say it, not even to Jon if she were alone with him.

Chapter Twenty-Eight

CICELY EXPECTED WORD of events in Burgundy to spread around the court like wildfire, but nothing was said. If it had not been for her being present when Margaret informed Jon, she would not have known anything at all about the boy who was apparently claiming to be Dickon. Who maybe even *was* Dickon. She decided to hold her tongue, even to Bess and her mother. If rumours spread and her name came to light, Henry would be certain to punish her. Not by hurting her, but by hurting the ones she had been seeking to protect.

But even so, there was a confrontation that brought out a violence in him she had not seen before. She was sitting with Bess and her mother. It was raining heavily outside, for which everyone was thankful because it cooled the air, and as a consequence, Bess was a little lighter in spirit and was seated by the window.

'Oh, I know there is nothing I can do about what lies ahead,' Bess said. 'I pray I have a healthy son, but if I do not, I will have to hope Henry accepts that I am not at fault.' She glanced away. 'In truth I do not know *what* to expect of him. Ever. One day he is sweetness itself, the next he is cold. How can I possibly know where I am with such a man?'

The Queen Dowager was at pains to reassure her. 'My dear, even if things are not as the king plans, there will be other babies. You *will* bear him a son.' She smiled. 'But if you do not, have you a name for a daughter?'

'I have not dared to think of one.'

'Then know it has to be Margaret. None other will do, I think.'

Bess looked at her in dismay. 'Oh, I suppose you are right.' She leaned her head back. 'I do not feel well again. I am suddenly hot.'

Elizabeth beckoned a nearby lady. 'A fan, if you please, and a cool drink for Her Grace.'

The lady curtseyed and hurried off, but as she reached the door it was flung open in her face and Henry strode in. Anger bristled from him, and it was no ordinary anger. His eyes were arctic, and as he halted, his rich clothes swung so much they all but lashed. 'Lady Cicely?'

Cicely was already out of her chair in a deep curtsey, but she looked up, unnerved by the way he addressed her. 'Your Majesty?'

'I will not have treachery so close to me, do you hear?'

'Treachery?' She was frightened of him.

Bess struggled to her feet. 'What is this, Your Majesty?' She shrank from addressing him informally when he was in this mood.

'This has nothing to do with you, madam.' He did not look away from Cicely. 'Well? Have you nothing to say for yourself?'

'I do not know what this is about, Your Majesty.'

'Oh, yes, you do!' Suddenly he stepped forward, seized her arm and dragged her to her feet.

Her mother was shocked. 'Your Majesty!'

'Silence! Before I reconsider *your* position as well!' Henry pinched his fingers tightly upon Cicely, and to everyone's amazement, hauled her from the room.

Cicely tried to free herself, but he was so caught up in his fury that he only tightened his hold. He bundled her along a passage and then into a vacant room, the door of which he slammed behind them, before almost flinging her away. She stumbled and lost her footing, but he made no move to prevent her from falling so heavily against the wall she was quite winded.

'You have lent your name to treason, madam! Treason!'

She stared at him, trying to draw deep breaths. 'But I have not! Please, Henry!'

'This is not the time for intimacy.'

She raised her chin. 'At least have the courtesy to tell me what I am supposed to have done.'

'Courtesy? *You* demand courtesy?'

'Yes.'

'You shall not have it. Explain yourself.'

She met his eyes. 'About what . . . Your Majesty?'

'Your precious brother, Richard, Duke of York.'

'What has happened?'

'Oh, I know you are aware of this imposter, for my mother has told you.'

'All I know is that someone in Burgundy is claiming to be my younger brother. That is all.'

'And on this small evidence you wrote to him? Wishing him well of overthrowing me?'

Her hand crept to her throat. 'I wrote no such letter,' she whispered, jerking her face aside, eyes tightly closed, face screwed up in readiness as he raised his hand and stepped forward threateningly.

He truly meant to strike her, but then he halted, lowering his arm again as he saw how she cowered from him. When she dared to look, he was gazing at her, a mixture of expressions vying on his face. 'Swear it, Cicely. Swear you did not write it.'

'I swear it, Your Majesty. I have not written anything to anyone. I certainly have not conspired against you.' She searched his eyes. 'What is really wrong? You are so bitterly angry with me, but not, I think, because of this conspiracy in Burgundy or any letter I supposedly wrote. There is no letter, is there? It is only something you fear I *will* write. What is it? What have I really done that hurts you so? I *have* hurt you, have I not? Although I do not know in what way. I have not done anything knowingly, Henry, I swear it upon all I hold dear.'

'Upon Richard's memory? Upon my uncle's life? Lincoln's life?'

'Yes, if that is what you wish me to say. I swear upon all those things.'

'Had you really made love to my uncle, when my mother found you both in that room? Had he taken you over a table? Had he?'

She stared at him, for whatever she had expected, it was not this. She had to be honest now, for anything less would be the height of foolishness. 'Lady Margaret is not discreet, it seems.'

'So he had?' He tossed his hat away and rubbed his hair with both hands. 'I cannot bear to think of it. You belong to me, Cicely, to *me*! The thought of anything else splits my heart.'

His anguish was almost painful to see, and its depth shocked her. She went to him. 'Henry, I do not belong to you. I am your subject, yes, but I do not *belong* to you. You would have to lock me up and be the only man with a key.'

'I have thought of it, you had best believe me.'

She continued, 'Nor should the secrets of my marriage belong to you, or the secrets I share with you belong to Jon Welles. I am two women, one a wife, the other a king's lover, and I cannot be truly, completely, absolutely faithful to either role. You know that to be so. I lie *with* you, Henry, not *to* you.' *But you do, Cicely, you do . . .*

'Dear God, Cicely, you always manage it, you *always* say

347

something that robs me of the upper hand.' He lowered his hands from his ruffled hair, and then bowed his head. For a moment she thought his shoulders shook.

Relief rushed through her, for the change in him was palpable. The rage had gone, and left him almost weak. 'Are you really this angry because I may have lain over a table with my husband?'

'Yes, damn you! *Yes!* I cannot bear it, Cicely. I am constantly reminded of how dear he is to you, and it devours me. Do you still not realize what you are to me?'

'Yes, I do realize.'

'I will have you tonight. I do not care how much lying and subterfuge you have to use upon my uncle, *I* will have you. He will be sent on some urgent business for him to attend to, somewhere miles away from here.'

'He is to be your Uriah the Hittite?'

'Yes, for as God is my witness, *I* am King David, and you are most certainly Bathsheba.'

'King David had Uriah murdered. If you do Jon Welles any mischief at all, I—'

'I will not, I swear it. I will not.' He turned to put his hand to her face. 'Sweet God, how I need you *Beth arall y gallaf ddweud,*' he breathed, sliding his fingers beneath her headdress at the nape of her neck, and sinking them sensuously into her hair.

'What does that mean?'

'It means "what more can I say?" I need you, Cicely. I need you beyond all endurance.' His voice was choked with emotion as he drew her towards him, and put his lips to hers.

He no longer seemed able to maintain his customary icy control, and she did not know what to do. He had burrowed his way into her affection. It should not be that way. It should *not!* He was responsible for Richard's death and John of Gloucester's madness, a fact that should never cloud her judgement, and yet here she was, wishing to *help* him!

He pulled back from the kiss, his fingers still toying with her hair. 'I am sorry, Cicely, sorry for what I have done today and on other days. You have become my obsession.'

'Then you must send me away.'

'No!'

'Yes, Henry. After the christening Jon intends to seek your permission for us to return to his lands in Lincolnshire, and I think it best if you allow it. For your own sake, as well as mine. You know I am right.'

'Put so many miles between us?'

She nodded.

'Is that what you really wish?'

'It does not matter whether I wish it or not, Henry. I must go, so that you may be yourself again.'

He sighed and moved away. 'I do not want you to go.'

'Please, Henry. Your child will soon be born, and God willing it will be the boy you pray for. If I am not here, you can turn to your queen. *She* is the one you should lie with, not me. She can provide you with more heirs, which is what you need if you are to found a dynasty. Is that not what you really wish for? The House of Tudor?'

'You *want* to go to Lincolnshire, do you not? You smooth butter all over me, to bring me to your view.'

She lowered her eyes. 'A little too much butter, evidently.'

'If it were indeed all over me, and you promised to lick it off, slowly, it would certainly not be too much.'

He said it so evenly and naturally that for a moment she did not know he teased her. Suddenly, yet again, the humour that never failed to make her like him. 'Henry Tudor, you should not say such things to a married woman.'

'The king can say whatever he wishes to whom he wishes.' He smiled suddenly. 'Cicely, if I let you go, you must promise that if I send for you, you will come immediately.'

'I cannot promise that, Henry. If I can come, I will. You know that.'

'But it will not be because you love me.'

'Please, Henry . . .'

He looked away for a moment. 'You will come to me tonight anyway. There is to be no argument. I need you and I will have you.'

'I will come to you tonight. I will say that Lady Margaret wishes me to be with her at Coldharbour. She will confirm the story should anyone ask. But for Jesu's sake, Henry, be more discreet from now on. You may have enjoyed Richard's discomfort when rumours spread about his so-called designs upon my sister, but will you exult so much if similar rumours abound about your *actual* designs upon your sister-in-law, who also happens to be your aunt? I think not, Henry. And do not tell me you do not care, because you *will*, believe me. I was with Richard, I *know* how much it grieved him to have to publicly deny the calumnies.'

'And you regard his embarrassment as being my fault?'

'Indirectly. I suspect it was mostly Lady Margaret's fault. There would not have been so many rumours and insinuations if she had not encouraged them.'

'Oh, probably. She is behind most things. And he *was* easy prey.'

'Please, do not speak of him like that.'

'I will have him out of your thoughts one day, Cicely, so help me I will.'

She did not comment, but looked at him. 'Are you yourself again now?'

'Only if I can kiss you.' He embraced her again, and

this time his kiss was so very tender and loving that it enveloped her heart. He was a man who never failed to astonish. Never failed to affect, one way or the other.

She found her arms moving around him as she began to return the kiss. It was impossible not to, for it made such sweet love to her that she could have wept for him. This kiss deserved to be received with all the love it offered, but she failed it. He had truly frightened her today, and she no longer knew quite what her feelings were, and so she held him, linked her arms around his neck, pressed to him, and *pretended* everything he needed.

And that was the awful moment when a second door into the room was opened, and Jon walked in with Margaret and Jasper Tudor.

Cicely closed her eyes and took her arms slowly away from Henry's neck, while Henry himself drew a long breath as he sought something to say. He and Cicely had been caught in an embrace and kiss that could never be mistaken for mere friendship. He released her and turned awkwardly towards Jon.

'You have me at a disadvantage, I think.'

Margaret was frozen to the spot. Knowing of her son and Cicely was one thing, seeing them together like this was quite another.

Jasper was outraged, but although he harangued Henry in Welsh, and she heard many heated utterances of Harri and Siasbar, the latter clearly regarded the fault to lie solely with Cicely, who did not need to speak Welsh to feel sure that when he gestured towards her and said words like *putain* and *ysguthen*, they were not complimentary. She was later discover that one meant "whore" and the other "bitch".

Jon gazed at Cicely, not at Henry, whom he did not even acknowledge. His silent reproach was so well placed that she had to lower her eyes to hide the hot tears that brimmed in them. Then without a word, he turned on his heel and strode out again.

She found her wits and ran after him. 'Please, Jon, let me explain!'

He walked on.

'*Please!*' she sobbed. 'Please, let me explain.' Her voice ended on a whisper, and she sank to her knees.

He turned then. 'If you wish to fuck my nephew, that is your business, Cicely, for as God is my witness, it is no longer mine!' He began to remove the turquoise ring, but then paused, still about to discard it. Their eyes met, for what seemed so many heartbeats, and then he strode away again, the ring remaining on his finger.

He passed the door of the room in which Bess was still seated with the Queen Dowager. The door was open. Of course it was, Cicely thought almost ferociously. How could it *not* be open at a time as momentous as this? Let everything go wrong! Let the *world* know her shame!

She knew her sister must have heard Jon's damning words, and to confirm it Bess emerged from the doorway, her hands clasped over her swollen belly. She gazed bitterly at Cicely. 'You cow! You *whore*! You had to have this king as well!' Then she gasped and clutched her belly more tightly as her pains began.

Henry sent for Cicely that night. She did not go to him.

Chapter Twenty-Nine

HENRY'S SON, HIS longed-for Prince Arthur, was born at just after midnight on the twentieth of September. It had been a long and difficult birth, and Bess was exhausted. The ague had returned during her travails, and her ladies strove to make her comfortable.

The baby was strong and healthy, and quite clearly *not* a month before his time. There was no hiding the fact that his parents had anticipated their vows. It would be regarded across the land as a sign that the royal marriage was a love match, but those in court circles knew differently. Whatever had brought the little prince into being, it had not been an act of love.

The birth of the heir to the throne was celebrated with bonfires in the streets and the singing of the *Te Deum* at Winchester Cathedral. Arrangements for the lavish christening had already been put in place, but now needed bringing forward a month.

Jon had left for Lincolnshire the same day he saw Cicely and Henry together. He neither sought the king's permission, nor took his wife with him. He refused to speak to Cicely and departed so suddenly that she had not even realized he had gone.

She found herself the subject of much whispering. As, of course, she deserved to be. She could not in all honesty defend herself. For how could she tell anyone that she had become the king's lover in order to shield the husband who now despised her, and the cousin who still made plain his affection and support for her? How could she confront the fact that she found so much pleasure in Henry Tudor's arms?

'Come, sweetheart, walk with me a while,' Jack said, coming to the apartment she had shared with Jon.

'I cannot, Jack. The one thing I dreaded has happened, and I have lost Jon.'

He sat beside her. 'You must find your Plantagenet spirit, Cicely. Hold your head up and to the eternal conflagration with them all, Henry included. Has he said anything to you? Offered anything at all?'

'Jack, he knows as little as me what to do in these circumstances.'

'He is the sovereign, he has done this to you and so he should protect you.'

'How can he? He is my sister's husband. She has just borne him the son he wanted, and she has first claim on him.'

Jack drew a long breath. 'If I could protect you, I would.'

'Your wife might have something to say about that. Besides, you help by coming to see me like this.' She managed a little smile. 'I am, quite literally, in a bed of my own making.'

'In a bed of Henry Tudor's making. Dear God, if Richard were here now—'

'Do not say it! Please, do not say it. Richard is the one who really matters to me. I still love him so much that I can hardly bear it. I love Jon, truly I do, but it is nothing compared to the feelings I have for Richard. It will never change.'

Jack put an arm around her shoulders. 'I would gladly have given my life for him. I can understand how you feel, Cicely.'

'I dream of him sometimes. I lie with him again and everything is so sweet and real that when I awaken, and he is not there after all, I cry. I cry so much.' She blinked back tears and smiled bravely. 'I should not tell you such things.'

'I can contain my excruciating jealousy.'

'Stop it,' she said, trying not to smile as she prodded him with her elbow.

Nothing was said for a moment, and then she looked at him. 'Am I still to hold the prince at his christening?'

'Yes.'

'But *why*? After what has happened, I am surely the very last person who should perform such an honour.'

'It is Henry's wish, and he will not be moved on it.'

'I sent a note to him, begging to be released from something that will deal my sister such an insult. He sent a message back. One word. "*No.*" How very Henry. I imagine he is enjoying it all. Certainly he will not be sad to have caused such a rift in my marriage.'

'You have captured him, Cicely, and I do not think he likes it.'

'I do not *want* to capture him, Jack, I want to be away in Lincolnshire with my husband. Now I do not think Henry will ever permit me to leave.' She looked away. 'Nor will Jon wish to see me again. Oh, Jack, what he saw looked so very loving and filled with desire, but it was not. Maybe it was on Henry's part, but not mine. He had just made a violent, totally unnecessary and unwarranted scene, publicly accusing me of treachery. He frightened me, and even though I am still greatly affected by almost everything about him, I could not respond to him as freely as I might have done shortly before. It was pretence.'

'Well, come the twenty-fourth, you have to perform

355

your task at the christening, Cicely. There is no choice. It would have been earlier, but the godfather, the Earl of Oxford, was still lolling in East Anglia when the birth was ... a month early, as we are supposed to believe. Oxford is coming with all haste, or so it is hoped. The twenty-fourth is the day of his reckoned arrival. Jon's abrupt departure has meant the Lady Margaret having to hastily find someone else to take his place alongside me at your side. I believe we are to have the pleasure of Thomas Grey, now Marquess of Dorset, no less.'

'My half-brother, Thomas the Tub.' Thomas was the Queen Dowager's favourite child, offspring of her first marriage, and he had been the one with whom she had plotted to prevent Richard, Duke of Gloucester, from becoming Lord Protector. It had been their conversation, in April 1483, that Cicely had overheard from that open window in Westminster Palace.

'Oh, but we still have dear Jasper with us on the day. No doubt his eyes will plunge daggers into your back every inch of the way.'

'He blames me for leading Henry astray, and so does Margaret.'

'Henry Tudor is a dangerous bastard who happens to be king.'

She smiled, but then became more serious. 'Jack, are you involved in this business in Burgundy? Because if you are, you should know that Henry is well aware of what stirs over there.'

'I have done nothing, Cicely.'

'Yet.'

He did not answer.

She put a hand over his. 'Please, Jack, as you loved Richard, do not fail him now by falling in a flimsy cause.'

'Are you so sure it is flimsy? Cicely, I am loyal to the true succession, and will never act out of self-interest.'

'Then God be with you, Jack.'

Cicely was alone in the bed that night. She could hear the festivities with which Winchester continued to celebrate the royal birth. Would they all have enough energy left to celebrate after the baptism? Did it matter? Did anything matter now?

Her fingers reached over to where Jon would have been lying, and fresh tears stung her already sore eyes. She felt as if her real self had slipped away to be with Jon at Wyberton. But her empty shell was still here in Winchester, wretched with distress and disbelief that for all her good intentions, she had come to this.

'Come to me now, Richard. I need your arms around me.' The unhappy little whisper seemed to fall upon empty air.

'My poor Cicely,' he said softly, and she turned her head to see him lying there, where Jon had lain.

'*Please* hold me,' she begged, reaching out to him.

He leaned over her to gather her close and she closed her eyes. 'I was too young and silly after all, Richard, and look at me now.'

'This is all Henry Tudor's fault, not yours. He has behaved without honour.' Richard kissed her forehead. 'As perhaps I did too. You steal the hearts of kings, sweetheart.'

'I only want one king.' She slipped her arms around him. How good it was to embrace him again, to feel him so close, to touch that body, so cherished and almost delicate. He had such an allure, such a spellbinding quality that she knew no other man would ever reach him. She saw no flaw, only the perfection of the uncle who had her total, everlasting devotion.

'I am not perfect,' he said.

'Do not keep reading my thoughts.'

'Your thoughts are mine,' he reminded her.

'Even now?'

'Even now.'

'I do still need you.'

'I know,' he answered softly.

'You will not leave me alone again? I can face them all if I know you are here.'

'I am always here. I will not go away, not until you are yourself again.'

'That may be never.'

He smiled. 'Such gloom and loss of all confidence? You are my sweet Cicely, and you are still precious to me. You will face them all at the christening, and be the princess you are. If there is one thing Henry Tudor has done well, it is to appreciate and love you. There is some hope for him.'

She gave him a little smile. 'I adore you, Richard Plantagenet.'

'And I you, Cicely Plantagenet.'

'If I were to make love to you now, what would you do?'

'Respond.'

'Truly?'

'Sweetheart, I am what you make of me, and this time, especially, I know how much you need me.'

'If only—'

'Enough, my sweetest Cicely. Make love to me, before I decide to start without you.'

'You cannot start without me, because you *are* me,' she said quickly, sitting up to look intently at him.

'So I am. I should not forget it, mm?'

She searched his eyes. 'You are *not* entirely my imagination, are you?' she whispered. 'Part of you really is here with me now.'

'Do not seek too many answers, Cicely.' He smiled, and pulled her down into his arms again. 'It is time to grant you your wish, and to give you so much pleasure you will be dizzy of it.'

'Is that a promise, Richard?' she breathed.

'You dare to doubt?'

Oh, imagination. *Such* imagination. . . . Was not it?

Cicely carried the new heir to the throne towards the great priory of St Swithin's. Little Prince Arthur Tudor wore a flowing mantle of crimson cloth-of-gold trimmed with ermine, and he made small snuffling sounds. Her own gown was the grey velvet, stitched with gold, that she had worn at Christmas and to her wedding; the one that echoed Richard's clothes of that other Christmas. And she had all her precious things in her purse. She carried herself proudly, as the daughter of Edward IV and beloved of Richard III should, and if there were whispers as she passed, she did not care.

Jack walked on one side of her, and her half-brother, Thomas the Tub, on the other. Behind her was Jasper Tudor, who occasionally stepped so close that he almost trod on her train. She ignored him, and hardly looked at Thomas, for whom she had never cared, but she glanced often at Jack, who winked. She knew he was pleased to see her so much better than when last he had seen her, and she wondered what he would think if he knew *why*.

Henry was not present, for it was the tradition that a royal baby would be taken to his or her parents *after* the baptism. When Cicely carried the baby from the private apartments, Bess had been lying on her vast number of pillows. She was still unwell, although better than she had been. Certainly she remembered what had happened, and would not look at her sister or speak to her. Nor would the Queen Dowager. Cicely was shunned by her own family.

Henry had been impassive. Or so it seemed, until

Cicely looked full at him. Although he met her eyes without flinching, she saw the feelings he had been unable to deny, and that had so devastating a result.

He was in love with her, she knew that, but she had now seen the brutality that lurked within him, and losing her husband as well had changed everything. Jon had rejected her, and there seemed no hope that he would ever want her back again. But he was still alive, and she would *never* stop protecting him with her body. Nor would she cease to shield Jack, her lovely Jack, who might never know how glad he made her.

And so she would go to Henry again, make love with him again, struggle not to like him again, and wish she found no pleasure with him. Henry would still threaten. He could not prevent himself. It was his deepest nature, and even if this scandal had not happened, he would still have used coercion. The struggle within him was a terrible burden, a slow excruciation from which he could do nothing to free himself.

She walked on into the great church, where the air was cool but filled with incense and shafts of light from the windows. It was crowded, with all the nobility of the land there to see the next King of England christened. The baby snuffled again and would have begun to cry had she not rocked him a little in her arms. Bess had been right; he may be Henry's child, but he was her sister's as well, and for that she would love him.

Then she saw Richard, leaning against a pillar, his arms folded, his body relaxed. His long hair was bright with colours from the sun-drenched stained glass, and his grey eyes were warm. She could feel his strength and support, his unquenchable love. Richard. Her king, her uncle, her lover. The father of her child. The true and only king.

He smiled, and so did she.

Holding her head up a little more, to show her pride and lineage to the world, she carried her nephew towards the font.

Author's Note

IN MY FIRST book about Cicely Plantagenet, CICELY'S KING RICHARD, I confessed to having no cause at all for creating a love affair between her and her uncle, King Richard III. In this present book, I therefore have no basis at all for there having been a son of their union. Nor can I claim any factual ground for further linking Cicely romantically with Richard's conqueror and successor, King Henry VII.

All these things are my imagination, together with an irresistible urge to always wonder . . . 'what if?' So, while both books feature real historical events and people, they're fiction, and should *not* be regarded in any other light. Fiction, set against true events.

With this in mind, I have also invented Henry Tudor's torture and mistreatment of Richard III's illegitimate son, John of Gloucester, who was imprisoned in the Tower and—it is believed—eventually beheaded at Henry's command. That John was Cicely's first young love is more roaming imagination.

John de la Pole, Earl of Lincoln, Jack, was not formally confirmed as Richard's heir, but there is sufficient evidence to believe Richard had indeed chosen him. What Lincoln actually looked like is not known, indeed he is quite hard to assess as a man. He was a proud young Yorkist lord, and appears to have been charismatic. Perhaps he had a dangerous charm. He certainly did not lack courage or direction, although I believe he was eventually to make one fatal error of judgement on his path to the Battle of Stoke Field in 1487. He also seems to have had a great talent for masking what he really thought or intended, and that when he was accepted at Henry's court, he had no intention of remaining loyal to the new king. He merely bided his time. To Lincoln, Henry was far more of a usurper than Richard had ever been accused of being. Jack de la Pole never, for a single moment, forgot his Yorkist birthright.

There is evidence now that Cicely was married first to Ralph Scrope, but the marriage was hastily annulled in order for her to become the wife of Sir John Welles, Jon. The whys and wherefores of this first union are not known, so the reasons I give in my story are what I think *could* have happened. I still apologize to Ralph for having denigrated his character. He certainly did not die on the marsh near Wyberton while involved in witchcraft, but lived on to inherit his family's title. He and Cicely could well have loved each other. It is simply not known.

That Cicely and Jon came to love each other cannot be confirmed or denied either. They were together until his death in 1498, which left Cicely in great distress. She did become very friendly with his half-sister, Henry Tudor's mother, Lady Margaret Beaufort. Of course, Jon cannot have married Cicely for the reason I give in this story, because there was no son of Cicely Plantagenet by Richard III. Maybe Henry simply sought to advance his maternal half-uncle's fortunes by giving him an important royal wife. Maybe it was love. We will never know.

Nor can it be said whether or not Henry VII and Elizabeth of York—Bess—were happily married. She is believed by many to have been in love with her uncle, Richard III, but there is no proof, and this belief about her affections might even be the result of the modern misunderstanding of medieval wording used in one of her letters, which has now been lost. The fact has to be conceded, though, that neither she nor Cicely ever spoke out against Richard. Nor, after his death, did their mother, Elizabeth Woodville.

Henry is recorded as being 'unuxorious', so I have to think his was a solely political marriage and never became anything more, although, like Richard III and his queen before them, he and Bess were distraught by the sudden death of their son, Prince Arthur. However, I have created Bess as she *might* have been, loathing Henry and submitting with great distaste to his obligatory marital attentions. That he was passionate and skilled between the sheets with Cicely, is, again, my 'what if?'

Henry's unreasonable moods and flashes of temper are also my view of how he *might* have been. Conjecture. He certainly became like that in later years, so who is to say it was not evident when he was still a young man? The coughing that I have begun to hint at is intended to be a very early indication of the tuberculosis that was eventually to be one of the health problems that killed him. He was not a robust man, and came close to death several times before he eventually succumbed.

Regarding his ruthlessness, he certainly set about ridding himself of potential enemies, and so did his even more fearsome son, Henry VIII. The Tudors were relentless. Richard III was not, and would have fared better if he had been. Henry was a deeply suspicious monarch, always beset by challengers, always afraid to trust anyone, always perceiving treachery in every shadow. And it was natural he should feel that way, considering his acquisition of the throne came solely as a result of Richard being betrayed. If lords have betrayed one king, they can most probably betray another. Henry had to live with that knowledge. He became old before his time, probably the result of all the stress, suspicions, fear and constant anxiety that dogged his life.

Towards the end of this story, the boy pretender claiming to be Richard, Duke of York, one of the 'Princes in the Tower', is, of course, the strangely named Lambert Simnel, who in 1487, after changing his identity to that of the young Earl of Warwick, was to pose Henry's first real test of kingship. But not his last.

Writing about Henry caused me, a staunch Ricardian, to feel unexpected sympathy for him. He certainly became a cruel king, but whether the cruelty was within him from the outset I cannot say. He won at Bosworth when he should not have done, and he clung to the throne he had stolen because he had *amazing* good luck. Fate always seemed to tip in his direction, but whether or not he ever felt truly happy is another matter. I believe he forfeited his real self. Perhaps he lost it in childhood. Maybe he sometimes wished he had never returned to England.

What the actual Henry was like can never be known, although there is a letter that he wrote to his mother in later years in which he confesses to having taken days to write it because his eyesight is so bad. It is the letter of a fond son to his mother. He was also said to have shot someone's cockerel by mistake while hunting, not realizing what it was because he could not see it properly. He was advised after that not to go hunting with a crossbow. I imagine that if he did, his companions were all careful to stand behind him.

Perhaps his true character surfaced when he allowed his young son to beat him at a game. In that, he was the loving, indulgent father. He also had a dry sense of humour that could not be imagined from his likenesses, although I swear it is there in his famous National Portrait Gallery portrait. He looks menacing and sly, with his hooded eyes, high cheekbones and hollow cheeks. But there is a glint in those eyes and a wry set to his mouth that suggests he finds something amusing . . . at someone else's expense, of course.

My overt support for Richard III is again evident in this story. I believe he has been cruelly misjudged over the centuries, and nothing short of his personal diary of abhorrent sins will convince me otherwise. Even then I'd have to see very definite proof it was his writing, not forged by one of his enemies! He showed quite breathtaking bravery at Bosworth, and died the rightful, anointed King of England. He also died a grief-stricken widower, and a father who had just lost his only legitimate son. Fate certainly did not tip in his direction. It should have, though, for he was a conspicuously just man who endeavoured to do what he considered to be the right thing. He thought of England and the wellbeing of his people, which Henry Tudor was certainly never to do. Henry thought only of Henry, and clinging to power regardless. In my opinion, had Richard lived he'd have been a great king. He was certainly a man ahead of his time.

His 'appearances' to Cicely are figments of her imagination, the result of her intense grief. He isn't a ghost, but through him she can talk of things that she already knows or thinks herself but does not understand or want to face. She also conjures him when she is particularly emotional. It is not witchcraft, sorcery, the Otherworld or any other venture into the paranormal, but simply her agony of loss and unwillingness to concede that the real Richard has gone forever.

But death *is* final, and Cicely has to live on without him. It's not easy, especially when faced with Henry Tudor, for whom she ought to feel nothing . . . but is forced by circumstance and her own nature to feel a great deal.

Sandra Heath Wilson
July 2014